THE PILLAR OF FIRE

Karl Stern

THE PILLAR OF FIRE

With an Introduction by Stanley L. Jaki

Urbi et Orbi/Remnant of Israel

This printing © Urbi et Orbi/Remnant of Israel
New Hope, Kentucky 40052
October, 2000

Introduction © Stanley L. Jaki

ISBN 1-884660-12-6

CITY OF PEACE

Studies in Catholic-Jewish Relations

The City of Peace series is a joint project of two publishing enterprises: Urbi et Orbi and Remnant of Israel. Of prime importance for this series of books is shedding light on the complex and fundamental connections and differences existing between the Jewish Faith and the Catholic Faith.

*　*　*

The publishers wish to express their gratitude to the children of Karl Stern for granting permission to reprint this book.

Introduction

IN *The Pillar of Fire*, Karl Stern (1906-1975), a prominent 20th century Jewish neuropsychiatrist, has given us a classic account of one man's struggle to reconcile his Jewish identity with the claims of the Christian faith.

Published in 1951, *The Pillar of Fire* narrates with great eloquence Karl Stern's difficult spiritual odyssey. It stretched from his boyhood in pre-World War I Germany through the Weimar and Nazi periods to his emigration to England and Canada and his conversion to Catholicism. The book is thus the moving account of a life-long effort to identify the ultimate form of the "land of promise" toward which a pillar of fire guided the Jews of old.

The story began when Karl Stern became a teenager, although this became clear to him only when he approached his thirties in the early 1930s. By then he was a neuropsychiatrist of promise in a land where Jews were beginning to be deprived of all the promises that normally go with life, including their very lives. This could but put an existential pressure on any Jew to rethink the purpose of life.

Many Jews in Germany around 1933 — Adolph Hitler came to power on January 30 of that year — did not perceive that the source of the pressure was primarily counter-religious, and racist only secondarily. This is why the Nazis much resented the label "neopagan" given them by Catholics.

It was precisely the radically anti-Christian nature of the challenge that made France, soon under the sway of the quasi-Communist Front Populaire, largely indifferent to the need of initiating a spiritual rearmament before speeding up weapon construction to discourage the Nazis' war preparations. England, already on its way to becoming the most de-Christianized nation in the West, applauded a Chamberlain who claimed to have brought from Hitler "peace in our time."

Equally incapable of seeing the true nature of the challenge was the political leadership of the New Deal in America. There people close to Roosevelt, and hardly without his knowledge, denied entry to ocean liners full of refugee Jews. Later, Roosevelt and Churchill, though both aware of the impending round-up of Jews in Rome, chose not to alert them. This newly disclosed piece of information may only be a tip of an iceberg still to emerge in its colossal proportion.

None of the leading politicians of the West could see anything significant in the declaration which Hitler's chief ideologue, Alfred Rosenberg, made in the April 1931 issue of the *Nationalsozialistische Monatshefte*. There he singled out the Catholic Centrum Party as the chief enemy and opposed to it the National Socialist German Workers' Party (Nazis for short) as the organ for which "once it had put on the brownshirt, there were no longer Catholics or Protestants but only Germans fighting for the survival and honor of their people." Ten years later, when Rosenberg unveiled the norms of the "German National Church" as void of crucifixes and Bibles, Martin Bormann, one of Hitler's closest associates, spelled out the Nazis' open secret: "National Socialism and Christianity are irreconcilable."

In Germany genuine Christians were the Nazis' first targets and such Christians were to oppose them first. As to the opposition, *The Pillar of Fire* contains a dramatic account of Karl Stern's attending in early December 1933 the first of Cardinal Faulhaber's Advent sermons in Munich's "Saint Michael's Hofkirche." This could only mean that he (and his younger brother Ludwig, only eighteen at that time) heard the sermon, which the Cardinal delivered in the Dom, as transmitted into a number of churches in Munich's central area, which has many churches indeed. They all were thronged by the faithful, sprinkled here and there with Nazi spies. These could readily obtain printed copies of the sermons that soon appeared also in a book form and, within a few months, came out also in English translation as *Judaism, Christianity and Germany*.

It was in the first sermon, delivered on December 3, that the Cardinal dealt with the relation of Christian religion to the Old Testament, and referred to new efforts to present Jesus as an Aryan from Galilee, efforts aimed at saving Jesus "from being Jewish" by providing Him "with a forged birth-certificate." The Cardinal stated nothing less than that through the Jewish maiden Mary all Christians were related to the Jews.

Such statements made an indelible impression on Karl Stern, who recalled that the Cardinal quoted from a sermon which Cardinal Manning had once delivered in a synagogue to Jews: "Gentlemen, where would we be without you?" This rendered well Manning's words: "I should not understand my own religion had I no reverence for yours."

Cardinal Faulhaber's sermons were, so to speak, a spitting on the racist flag, which Rosenberg thematically raised through his book *Der Mythus des 20. Jahrhunderts*, published in Munich in 1930. Karl Stern now could hear from a high ecclesiastical pedestal that Christians believed in the "God of Abraham, Isaac, and Jacob" before they believed in anything else. From that pedestal there came the voice of a Cardinal Archbishop who pointedly referred to his "having held the chair of Old Testament scripture in the University of Strasbourg."

It was now almost traumatic for Karl Stern to recognize the obvious, namely, that Christians had carried belief in Abraham's God to the four corners of the world and had done so in order to fulfill the vision of the prophets. All of a sudden God's election of the Jews appeared to Karl Stern as a small part of an incredibly larger and truly global or catholic religious landscape. It became also evident to him that the Nazis were logical in starting their anti-Semitic purge with the Christians.

That the Nazis did indeed begin with Christians is a fact that many, who should know better, prefer to forget. This was not the case of an

Israeli whom I happened to encounter by chance in Jerusalem on a sweltering early afternoon in September 1973. As I was trying to find my way in Jerusalem's old town I turned for help to someone who had just stepped out of a printing shop. I soon learned that he had grown up in a big apartment building in Berlin from which the Nazis first dragged away some Catholics before they turned their attention to some Jews. The nationwide rounding up of the Jews did not begin until the fall of 1938. Prior to that some Jews in Germany strained themselves to find hopeful clues in Hitler's various dicta. Ironically, as Karl Stern pointedly noted, their parents and grandparents had strongly opposed the admission into Germany of Jews, mostly orthodox, who tried to escape the Czarist pogroms of the 1880s.

The author of *The Pillar of Fire* was not to dissimulate facts. This was, of course, a still widely respected approach in 1951 when he published his book. A quarter of a century later plain references to certain facts were no longer tolerated in a press that increasingly blamed all the plight of the Jews on Christians, especially on the Catholic Church and in particular on Pius XII. There is indeed much more than meets the eye in the brief obituary which *The New York Times* granted to Karl Stern just after his death in Montreal on November 5, 1975. In those mere hundred or so words of five single-sentence paragraphs only one of Karl Stern's five books rated a comment, and a very terse one at that: "His book, *The Pillar of Fire*, published in 1951, detailed his conversion from Judaism to Catholicism."

One wonders whether today a mere reference to an enormous fact would not be accompanied by remarks indicative of some deep resentment and disapproval. A report in the same daily of what happened on April 27, 1995 in Jerusalem shows what a difference twenty years can make. Cardinal Lustiger of Paris, a Jew who converted at the age of fourteen, was in Jerusalem as an invited speaker at a Conference on "The Silence about the Holocaust" organized by the University of Tel Aviv. His having converted to Catholicism at that youthful age prompted many to protest his presence. The strongest protest, recounted in *The New York Times*, came from Yisrael Meir Lau, the Ashkenazi Chief Rabbi of Israel. According to him, though Aaron Lustiger was a boy when he became a Christian, he thereby "betrayed his people and his faith during the most difficult and darkest of periods." The curses formulated eighteen centuries ago against the "minims," curses still recited in some ultraorthodox synagogues, cast a long shadow indeed. And so does Christ, in spite of the official Jewish policy to treat him as a nonentity. The disappearance from Israeli bookstands of New Testaments printed in Hebrew speaks louder than words. And so does the attitude of some Catholics who cultivate the Jewish roots of Christianity but not the conversion of Jews.

Karl Stern would have been the first to protest. And through *The Pillar of Fire* his voice still speaks strong and clear. This is the reason the book should once more be available, for even after two thousand years it is not possible, or intellectually honest, to try to evade the challenge Christ posed to twelve Jews by asking them: "Who do you say the Son of Man is?" As Karl Stern repeatedly states in *The Pillar of Fire,* the question of whether the Son of Man is truly the Christ must be answered with a clear No or Yes. Intellectuals in particular can take no cover against the challenge of the question by simply treating it as one that has been settled around 80 A.D. by the gathering in Jamne of rabbis who tried to reconstruct Palestinian Jewry from the ruins epitomized by the destruction of the Second Temple. They did not consider that their chief mistake was to identify the Messiah with Jewish national aggrandizement. Their indictment is set forth in Josephus' *Jewish Wars.*

Half a century or so after that Synod of Jamne, Rabbi Akiba, one of the most prominent rabbis ever, took Bar Kochba, a firebrand, for the Messiah promised in the Hebrew Scriptures. Rabbi Akiba's mistake brought upon Palestinian Jewry the Emperor Hadrian's reprisals, far harsher than the ones meted out by Domitian after 70 A.D.

Two thousand years later most Jews who have not entirely renounced all Messianic belief, see its fulfillment in the State of Israel. Only some orthodox Jews disagree and with grave misgivings. Here too *The Pillar of Fire* contains details that are all the more instructive because they are now three quarters of a century old and because Karl Stern himself made two discoveries. One, that Orthodox Judaism was the only true form of Judaism, he discovered for himself long before Hitler came to power. Shortly after that he also came to perceive that the Catholic Church was a true unfolding of whatever there was positive in Jewish orthodoxy.

With all this enough has already been said to suggest something of the explosive significance of *The Pillar of Fire* in this age of Judeo-Christian dialogues that often turn Christ into a pale figure indeed if not into a nonentity. Yet, if anything, then *The Pillar of Fire* may make at least a dent in that dubious trend, well meaning as it may be in some cases. For the author of *The Pillar of Fire* had in his ancestry a long series of orthodox rabbis. No less importantly, he was born, on April 8, 1906, into a family where only some Jewish rituals were kept but not the belief that was supposed to go with them. Unlike two uncles of his, who openly scoffed at religious beliefs, Jewish or other, his father remained a "believing" Jew though not to the point of taking his religion seriously. The mother's mindset was more like that of a Quaker than of a Jewess. When Karl was sent, at the age of 12, to Munich to enter a Gymnasium there, his mother begged the wife of an orthodox rabbi with whom Karl was to board, not to expose him to orthodox religiosity. A vain request, because the home also served as an orthodox synagogue. As Karl Stern was to recall, "Frau Kohen had promised but she could not prevent the atmosphere of orthodox Jewry from reaching me." From a distance of almost forty years Karl Stern still could feel the mystical touch of a "white sea." It was the sight of the congregation on the Day of Atonement, all men wearing their prayer shawls and covered by the white shroud in which they were to be buried.

On returning home for the first long vacation, young Karl's father quickly saw that his son, only thirteen, had discovered orthodox Judaism. The young boy was soon addressed by the father as "rabbi," an appellation that hardly meant approval in this case. It was, of course, only later that Karl Stern perceived in the concreteness of orthodox Judaism the anticipation of Catholicism and that the two were, in their own ways, incarnational theologies. The belief in the Word made flesh was anticipated by the belief that man, the flesh and blood being, was made in the image of God. He also came to see that if a physical voice heard by Moses' ears was literally God's voice then it made little logic to frown on the claim that God himself became incarnate in a physical being, Jesus of Nazareth.

To be sure, young Karl's zeal of strict observance did not last longer than a year or two. Still he gained the life-long conviction that true Judaism could only be found among orthodox Jewry. He also soon perceived that without firm belief in the coming of a Messiah, Judaism made no sense whatsoever. In fact without that belief it was a form of racism, perhaps not tainted with inhumanity as was Nazi racism, but a racism nonetheless. Karl Stein would have been the least surprised on seeing that the contempt which some Israelis showed toward Palestinians prompted other Israelis to consider them as Judeo-Nazis.

The Messianism with which young Karl identified himself as he completed his teens was of a socialist type. Did not the prophets sound all too often as the heralds of an age of plenty and of universal peace on earth? And was this not precisely the socialist (communist) ideal which, not surprisingly, had a large number of Jews among its zealous promoters? In *The Pillar of Fire* Karl Stern three times recalls a story told by Martin Buber about a Hassidic rabbi in Jerusalem. On hearing some shouting, with the accompaniment of trumpets, that the Messiah was just arriving, the rabbi opened the window, looked right and left, and said: "I see no change." Certainly no Messianic changes.

Of course, Karl Stern, though only thirteen in 1919, was sensible enough to see through the fallacies of the brief Communist regime that took hold of Munich at that time. But for the rest of his life he nurtured a keen commitment to social justice and a profound concern for the poor and the weak. Politically he positioned himself very much to the Left, though only in the measure in which the Left stood for genuine concern for the underprivileged. By the time Karl Stern died he must have seen that the Left mainly stood for a resolve to undermine all ethical norms on the use of sex and the sanctity of life.

Karl Stern studied medicine during the mid-1920s at the Universities of Munich, Berlin, and Frankfurt where he received his M.D. in 1930. He began as an intern in the neurology department of Berlin's Moabit Hospital. After he had spent a year of residency in the University Clinic of Frankfurt, he obtained, in 1932, a Rockefeller Fellowship for the German Institute for Psychiatry in Munich. Those years meant for him a steady association with people of high cultural interests. All too often he withdrew from the harsh realities of life into comfortably theorizing about them. Even those who disliked Hilaire Belloc's dictum, "Europe is faith and faith is Europe," could not overlook the symptoms of the utterly harsh decadence shown by an Europe without faith. Then as now academics and even students well provided for could take daily flights into the world of music, excursions, and, last but not least, into intoxicating discussions with like-minded young "geniuses" over a mug of beer or a cup of coffee.

As a Rockefeller Fellow in Munich Karl Stern was member of a small informal group in which everyone thought of himself as a genius. As he recalls, one at least of the group, Hans Bethe, a future Nobel Laureate physicist, lived up to that billing. This group was not the only context within which Karl could take dreams for reality. Even more fascinating proved to Karl the Heidelberg home of Erich von Baeyer, a fellow medical student in Munich. The name von Baeyer was and still is synonymous with a clan famous for prominent scientists among them. The clan includes Johann von Baeyer, who received the Nobel Prize in chemistry for 1907. Erich's father (whom Karl does not mention by his first name) was Hans von Baeyer, a noted orthopedic surgeon and professor of medicine at the University of Heidelberg from 1919 on.

Karl found the von Baeyer home a sanctuary of art and music, and a place for an almost daily gathering of highly refined people. More importantly, there Karl met his future wife, Liselotte, Prof. von Baeyer's daughter. Most importantly perhaps, Karl saw that the mainstay of the von Baeyer home was a semi-illiterate maid, Kati Huber, a Catholic of plain peasant stock, who went to mass every morning at six. Liselotte, who grew up only with a vague semblance of Lutheran piety, gained from Kati's presence the unconscious conviction that if Christianity was true, it had to be Roman Catholicism.

From early on Karl Stern felt that music held the key to the highest form of truth and existence. His playing the piano served him socially no less than skill in tennis and golf serves one very well in today's America. His first, wholly unrehearsed encounter with Liselotte was their playing a piece for four hands. What Karl Stern says in this book of the *Missa sollemnis* of Beethoven and of Mozart is a key into his inner sanctum. No wonder that when around 1971 a stroke impaired the use of his hands he kept muttering to friends: "Ich kann nicht mehr das Piano spielen ... " English he spoke with a heavy accent.

About ten years after his first flirtation with orthodox Judaism, Karl Stern once more discovered it, though not to the point of becoming a strict observant. He rediscovered Jewish orthodoxy because the storm clouds, often embodied in Storm Troopers, began to hover over the Jews after Hitler's rise to power. Karl Stern began to attend the orthodox synagogue in Munich on High Holidays and other major festivals and found them an incomparable religious experience. The question of the Messiah began to press him again. In more than one sense.

The blows that began to hit Jews right and left found a ready target in the von Baeyers of Heidelberg. Professor von Baeyer, whose two grandparents were Jewish, was informed that he could no longer hold on to his chair. Prof. von Baeyer moved to the Rhineland where he did private practice before his death in Düsseldorf in 1941 at the age of sixty-six. By the time Prof. von Baeyer had been removed from his chair, Liselotte moved to London, never to return. She eked out a living in varied jobs, one of them being a tourist guide for Germans, finally winding up in the Warburg Institute as a skillful bookbinder.

In Germany Karl Stern was grappling with the problem of the suffering of Jews and of patently holy Jews in particular. It made him realize that unless the Messiah was personal and unless one's innocent suffering could be grafted on the Messiah's suffering, no suffering of Jews and of others made any sense whatsoever. In his words his belief in a personal Messiah was "as real as the paper on which he was writing."

No less firm became his belief that the Messiah had already come in Jesus. But, as he adds, it took him ten more years to accept Jesus' divinity. By then Karl Stern was in Canada.

He arrived there after spending about four years in London. It was in early 1935 that Karl Stern realized that even a Rockefeller fellowship would not protect him as member of the Neurophysiological Research Institute in Munich. On arriving at the pier in Harwich he was almost sent back to Germany. His medical talents soon obtained him a position in the National Hospital for Nervous Diseases in London, the leading British neurophysiological institute. On visiting Liselotte, he could not help noticing on the wall a huge peasant rosary, Kati Huber's parting gift to Liselotte. Karl and Liselotte soon married. Although Karl was eager to speak of religion, she was not. He was able to rescue his parents in early 1939. His brother Ludwig too joined him there briefly, after the Nazis released him from Buchenwald. Then he moved on to Palestine where he worked as a teacher in a kibbutz, until his death in 1980.

Watching from London the plight of his larger family and of many of his Jewish acquaintances in Germany, Karl Stern discovered the power of prayer and he began to practice it most earnestly. He did so every morning by stepping, as he went to work, into the Church of the Dominican Fathers in Hampstead. During that time, sometime in early 1939, Karl Stern came for the first time in contact with the thought of Thomas Aquinas, through a writing of Josef Pieper on hope. He now began to see hope no longer as a wish but as a virtue for which one had to work hard and honestly.

On June 24, 1939, Karl and Liselotte arrived in Montreal. But even there Liselotte was not to discuss matters religious, let alone conversion. So the matter was dropped until Karl, as if to justify his own reluctance to face up to Jesus' question, "Who do people say I am?" suddenly brought up to Liselotte his religious search. By then he had established contact with several priests in Montreal, one of them being the Dominican Père Couturier. Once more his wife merely replied that if she were to embrace Christianity, it would be Catholicism. Why then,

Karl called her bluff, would she not speak with a priest? As Karl was to realize before long, it was God who was calling his bluff.

Liselotte went to see Father Couturier and on Whitsunday 1941 she became a Catholic, bringing with her into the Church their two older children, Anthony and Katherine. (She may have been named in remembrance of Kati Huber as none of the parents' mothers bore that name. The Sterns' third child, Michael, was still to be born.) Meanwhile Karl Stern continued with his own search. Yet he did it on too high a level, without seeing how low it was in reference to the true spiritual heights of genuine Catholicism. He was bluntly reminded of this after he had expatiated to a nun on Saint Augustine, Pascal, Newman, and Maritain, and complained about his own darkness of the soul. The nun told him that unless he had perceived a foremost spiritual value in that darkness and similar interior suffering endured as partaking in the suffering of Christ, he might just as well lay aside all those books by all those great Christian minds.

Understandably, he was held back by the agonizing thought that by becoming a Catholic he would abandon his own people. This was the reason, it is well to recall, why Bergson did not take the step of formal conversion. But as long as one was a Jew imbued with religious Messianism, the question, "Who do people say I am?" became ever more pressing. It was a question spoken by a Jew to Jews above all.

On December 20, 1943 Karl Stern was received into the Catholic Church. Every convert has a more or less elaborate theology before making such a step. Or rather the theology, apart from being a plain acceptance of the Creed as preached authoritatively by the Church, is a collection of considerations that appear particularly compelling to a given convert. The theological considerations that appeared such for Karl Stern can be gathered from *The Pillar of Fire*, although one must read it carefully to disentangle them from a wealth of other very precious remarks on a number of other topics. Chapters 18-20 in Part III cannot be meditated upon long and hard enough by anyone seriously interested in the depths of the problems faced by a Jew in becoming a Christian, a Catholic. It contains nothing of the syrupy flavor of much present-day Jewish-Christian dialogues. On the contrary, it is always alive with the most dramatic personal involvement in profoundly existential truths.

The last part of *The Pillar of Fire* is its only part which is philosophical and theological in a somewhat systematic sense. It is a long letter addressed by Karl to Ludwig so that he may see the reason why his older brother followed belief in the Messiah to its logical conclusion. Of course, long before Karl could come to points of theology, he had to confront questions of philosophy, especially those stemming from scientism, an ideology attractive to Ludwig. This is perhaps the reason why some came to see *The Pillar of Fire* as a testimony in which a noted scientist shows that there is no conflict between religion and science. But to see this book in this light is a pathetic misunderstanding of it. The raving reviews of *The Pillar of Fire* quoted in the inside cover of its Doubleday paperback editions are, with one exception, so many classics of misconstruing its real thrust.

In writing that letter Karl could not help thinking of the words he addressed to his newly born baby brother: "You are my little brother. If later the big boys should ever threaten you, just call on me." By the time the baby brother became a little boy, Karl saw him only mostly during vacations. But the more he saw of his brother, the more he realized something which forms the opening note of that letter: "You and I are so much alike in our way of acting and thinking that people used to remark on it." Yet the younger brother was almost impermeable to religion. It was a huge chasm that the letter tried to bridge, or at least to explain what it was really about. As a whole *The Pillar of Fire* had the same aim. It was written, to quote Karl Stern, "not only to explain how I became a Christian but equally to help Christians understand their brothers the Jews."

The effort was to reach above a chasm, whose sight made him at one point (we are in 1934) feel that he was losing his mind. It was a year a good part of which Karl spent in a sanatorium in the Black Forest after he had been struck, a few months after he had attended the Cardinal's sermon, with a deadly combination of influenza and tuberculosis. The sermon made it clear to him that if Jesus was truly a Jew, then a Judaism without Jesus remained what it had been from the start, a form of racism, however justifiable on pre-Christian theological grounds. In perhaps the most dramatic paragraph in the entire book, Karl Stern four times begins his sentences with the words, "Do not be misled . . ." as he warns his readers about the fact that Judaism is racism, a form of religion riveted on racial togetherness, divinely ordained, but still racism which could appear especially ugly against the background of racism as glorified by the Nazis. If anything then this perception presented a dilemma testing the sanity of a perceptive Jew. Indeed Karl Stern says ten pages later that as he was in the grip of that dilemma he felt he was losing his mind. For everywhere around him he found people "who were wiser and better than I" and yet did not see the dilemma at all.

The dilemma's force as felt by Karl Stern appears most sharply when he recalls an observation of the German Lutheran writer Ricarda Huch and amplifies on it. According to Huch, Christ's demand that anyone who wants to identify with Him must first die to himself, demands from a Jew also that he die to his national identity. "This is one of the most profound remarks ever made on the so-called Jewish problem. It touches the very center of it," so goes the comment of Karl Stern who adds that "Jesus was rejected by His nation because He could not be their national leader and this in spite of the imminent danger from outside. . . The Jews maintained the idea of racial integrity when it had lost its transcendental meaning, for 'all was fulfilled' in Christ. . . . Only when the un-Christian national segregation is solved, will the 'Jewish problem' be solved too." Surely, these are unusually trenchant remarks especially when seen from the perspective of what has happened after he had jotted down these words.

What was then the factor that did not allow Karl to let go of the dilemma? Primarily, it was not a series of philosophical, theological, historical, sociological, and scientific considerations. The factor should have seemed indeed a most humiliating one from the viewpoint of the intellect, of reason. But it was the factor that put the supreme seal of genuineness on Karl Stern's plumbing into the depths of his finding the Messiah in Jesus. Those depths appeared to him with two aspects, about each of which Karl Stern could have rightly said that it was a laughing stock for the Gentiles and a scandal for the Jews. One aspect was the view of Christ's suffering as focal point in which all human agonies are anticipated and into which all of them are inserted and redeemed. Here Karl Stern refers to a sermon of Newman's on the Night of Gethsemane and assumes that his readers would be familiar with it. That sermon is to be rediscovered by Catholics living in the comfort zones of the globe.

But so is to be rediscovered what Karl Stern states about a fact, the standard practice of plain Catholics of doing the Way of the Cross or meditatively praying the Five Sorrowful Mysteries of the Rosary. On each occasion they formulate ever new aspects of the suffering Christ had endured. The profit they derive is a saintly life. It was exposure to that life in the daily lives of simple Christian maidservants that formed for Karl Stern the ultimate touchstone of religious truth. Or as he brings to a conclusion his Letter to his brother and of the book itself: "You remember that I remarked that I had a feeling of allegiance to the simple pious folk in Munich and that this feeling of loyalty prevailed over my Jewish loyalty." That feeling, prompted by the contemplation of plain facts, was even more powerful than the realization that by sticking with a non-Messianic Judaism he would side with the ideology of the torturers of Jews. Those facts proved to him that "these people lived, or attempted to live, a life of heightened mystic intensity, the only life which offers salvation to man." His finding of saintliness among ordinary people was, one may add, a seal of genuineness on his conversion, a seal paraphrased by Saint Paul as he warned the first Christians of Corinth that the gift of faith goes largely to the "lowborn and despised, those who count for nothing, to reduce to nothing those who are something" (1 Cor 1:28).

That Letter is a masterpiece of an argumentation aimed at a wholly agnostic Jew, his own brother. Karl Stern quickly brings up the essential, namely, the fact and power of Evil. He is not afraid to name it Original Sin as the factor that alone can explain the fearsome dynamics of human history. Then he turns to the intellectuals' inability to cope with sin, and indeed to their cowardly efforts to explain it away so that their self-centeredness and rank selfishness may not be exposed for what it is. Neither Heidegger nor Sartre escapes Karl Stern's stricture, nor a Goethe — all typical heroes of agnostics. Then he takes on science, the agnostics' ersatz god, which is nothing but scientism, the worship of science.

It is only then that Karl Stern brings up to his brother the question of a personal God, of Revelation, and of Christ. He presents Christ as the only answer to the reality Evil which so harshly hit the family into which he and his brother were born. He refers to their saintly grandmother. Why did she have to perish in a concentration camp, together with count-less other unspoken saints? Were not they all better than the two of them? Should one take despair and nihilism for answer? Or should one look for answer in a vengeful nationalist ideology, such as Zionism? Or should one resort for an answer to dialectical materialism? Or should one espouse a rationalist pragmatism, so fashionable in the modern world? To accept this fourth answer for solution would bring, and Karl Stern minces no words, not only "material destruction," it would "mean the end of Mankind."

The half a dozen pages which Karl Stern now offers on Christ and the Church do not allow a paraphrase, however brief. But they should be read against what Karl Stern writes twenty pages earlier in the same Letter, under the heading "Professor Heidegger and Babette Klebl." If there was a heading embodying a clash this was it. Who has not heard of the Professor? His greatest sin is seen nowadays, in some pseudo-Jewish circles, in his ability to turn Hanna Arendt, a Jewess only by race, into his lover. For Karl Stern, Heidegger was the paragon of those intellectuals who practiced so well the art of denial that in the end they could not assert the plain evidence.

But who has heard of Babette Klebl? She was one of countless maids of peasant stock serving in bourgeois Jewish families that hardly ever hired a poor Jewish girl for domestic. Babette was another Kati Huber, whom Karl Stern, as well as his brother, could see at close range as they visited the Hirsch family in Munich: "Obviously the Babettes and Katis have their own shortcomings and secret passions. But their approach toward life transcends ours. While we were engaged in a continuous flight from ultimate reality (our intellect lent itself so well for this purpose), there existed all the time among us people who lived unknown lives of humility and charity. And they did, believe me, with a mystical fervor." No less important, they gained prophetic insights which a great intellect like Heidegger failed to display even when he perorated on Saint Augustine until this was unsafe to do in Germany. It was from her genuine faith that Babette Klebl gained the insight which she promptly displayed when the blows began to fall on the Jews: "What do they want to do against the Jews? It will end badly with these fellows because our Lord Himself was Jew."

There are other places too in *The Pillar of Fire* where Karl Stern pays homage to the saintliness of plain common Catholics. If the reader fails to find those passages or finds them unimportant, he would miss the touchstone of truth of Karl Stern's unique story and the ultimate loadstone of his spiritual odyssey. The reader would miss something else as well. Those passages, amounting to a dozen pages in all, contain a theological depth compared with which the scores of volumes of *Theological Investigations* and the thick tomes of *Sacramentum mundi* should appear a meager fare indeed. *The Pillar of Fire* deserves to be seen as a story of conversion comparable only to Newman's *Apologia*.

The Pillar of Fire will forever overshadow the hardly negligible merit of Karl Stern's professional work and career. From 1940 to 1944 Karl Stern was lecturer in neuropathology at McGill University in Montreal and assistant professor of psychiatry 1944-1952. He served from 1952 on as professor of psychiatry at the University and, concurrently, from 1955 on as associate professor of psychiatry at the University of Montreal. From 1958 on he was psychiatrist-in-chief at St. Mary's Hospital in Montreal. For ten years, 1958-1968, he served as one of Canada's representatives at the UNESCO Institute for Education.

The engaging style Karl Stern displays in *The Pillar of Fire* may whet one's appetite to look up his novel *Through Dooms of Love* (1960) whose story plays out largely in a psychiatric ward and counseling rooms, all too well known to its author. But in that story of over 400 pages Karl

Stern once more lives up to his idea of psychiatric cure as coming only from surrendering to love, which cannot be full without embracing religion in its fullest, the Catholic faith. No wonder that various characters in that story remind us of persons we have already encountered in *The Pillar of Fire*.

Such a novel could only come from one profoundly convinced that Freudian psychology was, contrary to Freud's misconceptions about it, most germane to religion and to Catholicism in particular. The great outlines of that synthesis between the two is the theme of Karl Stern's *The Third Revolution: A Study of Psychiatry and Religion* (1954), which came out the following year in French translation. He is seen as a psychiatric publicist and a philosopher theologian in his collection of essays, *Love and Success*, which appeared in the year when he died. People with a great variety of interests have found much food for thought in Karl Stern's *The Flight from Woman* (1965), followed three years later by its French translation, *Le refus de la femme*. There the lives and reflections of such intellectual heroes of modern Western culture as Descartes, Schopenhauer, Sartre, Tolstoy, and Goethe provide grim material for case studies of psychology, or rather for the claim that some basic shortcomings of these great ones had much to do with their far from unselfish approaches to women. A full-fledged study of Karl Stern's more than 60 papers he contributed to professional journals (listed in volumes 1958, 1965, and 1973 of *The Index of Psychoanalytic Writings*) would well repay the effort. Contrary to Stern's obituary in *The New York Times* he did not write books under the titles, "The Hostile Mind" and "The Integration of Psychology and Religion."

In some professional circles it was held against Karl Stern that as a psychiatrist he brought in religion too often and emphatically. But if one recalls Jung's finding that in all the psychiatric cases he had studied a religious problem was at the root of the psychosis, the charge would appear false. Surely, Catholic psychiatrists, who try to ignore religion to conserve their professional "purity," could learn a great deal from Karl Stern. He will not, however, be remembered mainly as a psychiatrist, eminent though he was in the field. His fame for those, who want to remember him, will be that of a theologian. In *The Pillar of Fire* Karl Stern bequeathed above all a theological classic, vibrant with an existential force as theological truths should be, without compromising the status of Truth, a word which Karl Stern wrote on more than one occasion with a capital in *The Pillar of Fire*.

In *The Pillar of Fire* Truth is stated time and again with aphoristic force. First, some aphorisms of his that relate to the rapport of Judaism with Christianity and vice versa: "Heresies are based on denials. In this respect Christianity was no heresy from Judaism; it rejected nothing essential but made a new positive claim." Again, "The misdeeds of one member are more broadcast than the sanctity of a hundred of others." On the charge that Jews as a whole are responsible for Jesus' crucifixion, there is his reminder: "For centuries every Catholic man, woman and child prayed: 'I have crucified my loving savior Jesus Christ'," a reminder also appropriate about the steady reduction, in the "new" theology, of sin to a purely psychological wound administered by the self to the self.

Jews harping on the Church's shortcomings may ponder Karl Stern's reminder: "Do not forget a lesson which we know so well from the history of Judaism, that is the fact that Evil has more publicity than Good." Psychologists in particular should ponder such dicta of his: "Suffering cannot be quantified"; "Psychoanalysis gives us an embryology of love"; and "Either the psychological method is not valid to decide whether Christianity is true or not, or there are no truths which transcend the material plane of man's existence". Karl Stern portrays the protagonists of modern, secularized culture in grippingly graphic terms: "With Faith gone, they are in the same position as that shipwrecked man stranded on an island with crates full of canned food but with no can-opener." He unmasks the poor logic of those who ignore that some of the greatest scientists were also believers: "It is possible that they were Christians *besides* being scientists or *on account of* being scientists, but why should they have been Christians *in spite of* being scientists?" As to the deception of what can be seen from ivory towers he offers a great one-liner: "Philosophers and mathematicians feel at ease only in the abstract."

Such a sharp focusing on Truth has become devalued since the first decade following the publication of *The Pillar of Fire*. No wonder that from the early sixties on *The Pillar of Fire* went into a publishing eclipse. Reprinted practically every year during the 1950s, no new edition has appeared since 1962. Its French translation first appeared as *Le buisson ardent* in 1951 and reissued in 1953. A year later there appeared a German translation, *Die Feuerwolke*. The last year (1999) saw the publication of a Polish translation, *Slup ognia*. Of the easily well over fifty thousand copies printed of the English original one nowadays finds only on occasion a copy in second-hand bookshops. Is this a roundabout indication that the book's message has become antiquated in the welter of novelties that flooded over Catholics during the last forty or so years?

I first read *The Pillar of Fire* shortly after it was first published, or a year or so after my arrival in the United States. I did not see then its true value in full, perhaps because true values were still in honor at that time. When browsing in a crummy bookstore in late May of this year I spotted an almost pristine paperback copy, I did not suspect that I would spend much of the next night reading.

In writing this Introduction my sole purpose was to call attention to points in this book that will keep it a pillar of fire for those to whom Karl Stern intended it: for Jews to understand his conversion or rather to understand through it something supremely important to them; and for Catholics that they may see beneath fashionable platitudes of Judeo-Christian dialogues what truly makes Jews their brothers. To both groups may *The Pillar of Fire* become what it was to Bernard Nathanson: a move by "the hand of God."

June 2000   Stanley L. Jaki

Father Jaki, a Hungarian-born Benedictine priest, is the recipient of the 1987 Templeton Prize.

Contents

Foreword

A FEW years ago, at a psychiatric convention, I ran into a girl with whom I studied medicine and with whom I interned in the Neurological Department of one of the municipal hospitals in Berlin. We met in a big hotel in Chicago. It was a most fortunate meeting and we were both overjoyed. We had not met for fourteen years, and had heard little of each other. She had the same halting, absent-minded way of speaking, as if she were always thinking of two things at a time. She looked older and there were lines in her face which had not been there before. There was so much we had to tell each other. While she spoke of her didactic psychoanalysis in Zurich, her marriage, her child, her practice, about mutual friends who had perished in Europe, I was asking myself: "Shall I tell, or shall I not tell?"

If I were to say to her, "Since we last met, I have become a Catholic," it would be a statement entirely different from any other I could make. We both had many startling and unexpected things to tell; it could not be otherwise with two Jews who had parted in Germany in 1932 and met again in America in 1946. But the fact is that with that simple sentence, "I have become a Catholic," there arises a cloud of estrangement. No matter how much one attempts to break this estrangement down to the elements of social or political separation, of prejudices from childhood, and so on, there is something additional which cannot be explained so easily. What is it?

While the conversation was as far removed as possible from speculations of this kind, I told her of this decisive event in my life. She paused for a moment and then said simply and shortly: "Oh!" Her polite exclamation contained a cosmic abyss. It is about this "Oh!" that this book is being written.

When I meet a friend with whom I used to work in the Zionist Youth Movement or in a group of radical students, I realize the extraordinary fact that, when we come to the bottom of things, I have not really departed from their ideals. There is a core to their beliefs which I still share with them. It is contained in my belief. What must appear to them as a betrayal, is to me a fulfillment. I still understand everything they are talking about, but they cannot possibly understand me. This is what makes these scenes, as human encounters and as a meeting of friends, so agonizing. We talk about the Histatrut (the Labor Unions in Palestine), about the Poale Zion (Left Wing Zionism), the Kibbuz (the movement of cultivation of the land in Palestine, without private property), about my brother who lives as a teacher in one of those co-operative settlements, or of old friends who were killed as Trotskyites, as Social Democrats, or simply as Jews—and then it comes.

"What has happened to you?"

"I have become a Christian."

Some of my friends even pale and their pupils dilate. A common world falls asunder.

There are sometimes surprises, however. I remember the following unexpected exchange:

"What has become of Paul?"

"He was living in Brazil when I last heard of him."

"What has become of Rose?"

"She went to Russia, and I heard that she was killed in the Purge of '36."

"What has become of Yosha?"

"Yosha? Now this is something you would never guess. When we last heard of him, he was in England and had entered a monastery!" Laughter. ("Shall I say it now?")

To write the story of a conversion is a foolish undertaking, for the convert, the "turned-around," is a fool. He is a fool in the sense in which Saint Paul uses this word. All stories of conversion appear to have something subjective-arbitrary, some tragic secret. The communication contains something incommunicable. Even the story of Saint Augustine, told by a powerful spirit in the crystalline, translucent atmosphere of the Mediterranean, contains that foolish, devious something, the element of dark solitude.

All true love is subjective and unique, and at the same time creates communion. Here, as always, love of the sexes is an image of divine love. There is something about falling in love which cannot be re-experienced by the outsider; it is something lonely: the lovers leave everything behind them. Yet love is not true love when it is only unique and lonely; it must also create community. The Tristan and Isolde of Wagner are abandoned to death but the Tamino and Pamina of Mozart enter through the Gates of Life. What is true of those who love is also true of those who know. It is no coincidence that in Hebrew the word *Yadoa* is the word for knowing and for the physical consummation of love.

In spiritual love the two forces of solitude and community create power like the two poles of an electrical element. If the Christian religion were lived only in the cell of a Saint John of the Cross, it would become something lunatic and asocial. And if it were concerned only with the existence of the parish, it would soon resemble any business concern. In religion, if we must share the horrible cosmic solitude of the night of Gethsemani, neither must we refuse to belong to the multitude which is fed on bread and fishes.

Seen "from outside" a conversion is something adventurous and anarchic. We know from the story of poor Don Quixote how foolish it looks for someone to take ideas so seriously that he really rides away from home. However, the fact that the first voyage of Columbus appeared like a gigantic Quixoterie did not disprove the existence of the sought-for continent. If there are certainties, one must be able to find them.

That one simple question, whether Jesus of Nazareth was God incarnate, becomes increasingly decisive between people, as history moves forward. Dostoievsky once said that it is the one question on which everything in the world depends. The answer to this question cuts into human ties and seems to reflect even on the nature of inanimate things. What if all that is folly in the eyes of the Greeks, and scandal in the eyes of the Jews, is Truth?

I

BAVARIAN YOUTH

1. The Cattle Market

THE SMALL town in which I spent my childhood is one of the oldest in Bavaria. Not far from the Bohemian frontier, it lies on a hill over a vast river valley, and everywhere on the horizon are the delicate bluish mountain ranges of the Bavarian and Bohemian Forests. Part of the old wall and some of the medieval fortifications are still there and, in a nearby village, in the churchyard of a thirteenth-century Gothic church one can behold, through an iron grill, an "ossarium"—thousands of skulls and bones from bygone centuries stored in orderly piles.

All my ancestors, as far back as we can trace them, lived in Bavaria in parts of which there had been no Jewish immigration since the Middle Ages. At Floss, a peculiar town built on a tower-like hill, with columns of houses surging upward as if designed by El Greco, there was one of the oldest Jewish congregations in Bavaria. Several of my ancestors were Rabbis in that town. I went there only once, but I have a vivid memory of the narrow streets and the synagogue surrounded by a moat which could be reached only by crossing a little bridge.

In contrast to this somber town on a steep hill above the dark forests, our town was bright and gay, with its silvery river, the endless valley, and the mountains beckoning from afar. Since it held an intermediary position between the forests and the world outside, its business was very much concerned with timber. But the Jews had little to do with timber; they were not to be granted even the slightest activity associated with nature and the land. This was the more remarkable since there were a few Jewish families in nearly every small Bavarian town; they belonged to the picture as an integrated part, and were so regarded by the rural population. Josef Filser, a creation of the famous Bavarian humorist Ludwig Thoma, is a cunning but semi-illiterate peasant who represents his district in parliament, and in his *General Observations*, a treatise which deals with political and religious problems, Filser sums Judaism up in one sentence: "The Jews have a friendly religion and are mostly hop merchants."

In our area Jews were not even hop merchants. They had retail stores for such things as textiles, or wholesale stores which supplied the shoemakers in the villages with leather or tools. Thus they were middlemen between the big cities and the country. So there existed in our lives, when we were children, a peculiar discrepancy of which we became conscious only later. On the one hand we were rooted in the country; the valley, the river, the woods, the old little town, and the peasants in the villages had a determining influence on our development. (My brother, who after the Hitler revolution had a good deal to do with Jewish children from the industrial regions of Northern Germany, used to say that Man ought to originate in a small town in the Bavarian Forest.) On the other hand, we lacked active relation to the soil, to the stuff of which things are made, and to the making of things. One could argue that there are also intermediary occupations among non-Jewish people; of course, only a small portion of the retail shops in our town belonged to Jews. However, the non-Jewish store owners were single members of a chain which was otherwise composed of craftsmen and farmers. They stood, as it were, on the shoulders of the others. As far as we were concerned, no matter whether one looked back to our ancestry or around among our relatives, there was nothing of peasantry or craftsmanship visible. This discrepancy explains why, when the so-called "Jewish problem" had become so acute under Hitler, people like my brother regarded vocational re-orientation, settlement in the country, and craftsmanship as primary prerequisites for working towards a solution. I am sure that he was influenced by the experiences of our childhood, even if he was perhaps not aware of it. Of course, the purpose of the present story makes me emphasize differences, colors and depths of which we were hardly aware in those years. Actually, our Jewishness was woven imperceptibly into the background of things, much more imperceptibly than it might seem from the way I am writing now.

When I think of the house of my childhood it is as a limitless universe, inhabited chiefly by four people—my grandfather, my father, my mother and, for nearly ten years, by only one child, myself. First, there was the store. Its threshold was made of stone and contained indentations for the iron bolts with which we fastened the safety door at night. From this door one could see the Saint Florian fountain only three yards from the house. It was made entirely of granite, the stone of our mountains: the vast basin, the eighteenth-century statue of the saint, the two spouts flowing day and night, fed by what seemed an infinite source but was really an iron pipe which refed the same water. Across the street were the houses of the watchmaker and the plumber.

All this was linked by what struck my eyes as a continent of cobblestones, sidewalks, and gulleys in which the rain water collected. The intersection was called Rindermarkt (cattle market), and here on certain Saturdays the farmers brought their cattle to market. On those Saturdays I used to be awakened by mooing animals and sharp bursts of bargaining, haggling and chaffing. When I looked out of the window I saw a throng of men and beasts, heaving and milling in an endless stream. By afternoon one could hear the fountain again, but the store was full of customers. Many farmers converted their cash immediately into goods, corduroy and buckskin for the men, woolen and cotton clothes for the women, flannel for underwear, and bed linen.

To me the store, the street and the square represented Outer Space. It was vast, open, bright and contained no riddles. Behind the store was the office—the "comptoir" as it was called in those days—where Father and Grandfather worked. Behind this was the storeroom, where the bales had their ever so faint but characteristic differences of smell: various shades of a faintly sour mustiness, bales of thin prints, of herring-bone cloth, of chintz and of velvet. In the backroom these bales were anonymous; in the store and on the counter they received life. They were measured and tightly rolled again and lay there in Outer Space.

Upstairs was Inner Space. In my memory it is as unlimited as the entire outer world. There were the bedrooms, the kitchen, a large living-room, a small sewing-room and the drawing-room or "salon." On the third floor was the bedroom which I used during my teens and which later became the maid's room. Above this was the attic, under a slanted ceiling. There were changes in the rooms from time to time. Partitions were built or spaces enlarged, and all this seemed to correspond to chapters in our family history.

In the evening we often sat in the sewing-room around a small table. The lamps had green shades with curtains of pearl-strings; one could lower them by a pulley. When I think of our evenings I remember the family clustered in a ring of light.

The salon was hardly ever used. It contained a cupboard with books and thick easy chairs with useless tassels. Its only window, curiously enough, had been walled off and one had to turn on the electric light even during the day. Outside a fake window had been painted, a meaningless artificial eye facing the street. In the salon there were three huge albums called *The Nineteenth Century*, with pictures of Beethoven, Alexander

Graham Bell, Wagner, Verdi, Napoleon, Lincoln and Goethe. There was also Meyer's *Konversationslexikon* in which one could secretly study "Reproduction in Man," with color plates on the development of the embryo.

My grandfather was a man of medium height, broad-shouldered, with a potato nose and a walrus mustache. To us children he was a source of never-ending hilarity, and it seemed to us that his whole life was devoted to jokes. He was conscious of this belief on our part, and whenever we were around he "got going." When a farmer's wife came into the store he would walk up to her with the measuring rod and slap her gently with it; then he would immediately act as if he were smitten with feelings of guilt and regret. I was a grateful audience for this sort of thing. I remember no instance in which the customer reacted badly. On the contrary this increased Grandfather's popularity. He addressed every farmer who came to the store for the first time as "Sepp" (Joseph), and all peasant women "Kati" (Katherine), and since these were the most frequent Christian names in our area the customer was often overwhelmed by joyful surprise.

In our region, in which much beer was consumed, commercial custom required us to devote several evenings a week to drinking beer. Each innkeeper had a definite evening. My father and Grandfather hated this, and I often observed Grandfather looking around furtively for a place, usually a flower pot, to pour his beer. Obviously these barkeepers needed more blankets and buckskin than we did beer, or this extraordinary barter system would have made no sense.

A different kind of memory is also associated with beer. Instead of a synagogue the Jews in our small town had a prayer-hall which was rented from the brewery. In order to get there you had to walk through corridors piled with beer barrels. There seemed always to be pools of stagnant spilled beer, and the place had a special scent which I remember very well. Since smells seem to have a greater power of association than other sensory impressions, even today whenever I enter a brewery, it all comes back: a certain spiritual mood, melodies, liturgical texts, Friday evening with its atmosphere of peace, the Psalms (*Leho lerananu*), and the beautiful hymn *Leho dodi* of Yehuda Halevy.

While my grandfather could be incomparably funny to us children, he was at the same time a strict and authoritative man. In fact, we would not have enjoyed his clowning as much as we did, had he not been a man of such patriarchal authority. He came from Franconia where he had grown up as the youngest of twelve children of a poor family. As a young man he had begun to study to become a Rabbi but had given it up. Then he peddled china in his home country (we frequently called him "Porcelain Moses"), and even after we had the store, he would visit the country fairs in the neighborhood and put up a stand.

My grandfather was the only one in our congregation who had received Jewish instruction. He was, for instance, the only one besides the Cantor who knew the liturgy well enough to conduct part of the service during the holidays. For as long as I could remember, he had been the president of the congregation, which consisted of about twenty families including some from neighboring villages. Yet he was not at all orthodox, and assumed the somewhat lax attitude of compromise frequent with Western Jews. For example, he kept his store open on Saturdays, and took it for granted that his children did not keep the Mosaic dietary laws. On the other hand, he never missed a service except during sickness. He participated in three Sabbath services, those on Monday and Thursday mornings, many annual memorial services for the dead and, since there were such things as semi-holidays, it happened not infrequently that he went to the synagogue seven times a week. Whenever we thought he went to prayer-hall too often we called him "Frau Witzelsperger," after a neighbor who went to daily Mass and all other devotions.

In religious questions he had towards the younger generation

an attitude which is hard to describe. Whatever was a vital law
to him was not at all binding to those who came after him. His
own children lived in a world which consisted of a strange mixture of political liberalism, agnosticism, Lessing's religion of
tolerance, Goethean, and even Nietzschean ideas. He seemed to
regard it as a fundamental law of life that the generation of
"enlightenment" must follow the generation of "religious tolerance." This went so far that my grandfather did not seem to like
having his children emulate him. When I, his grandson, later
turned to Jewish Orthodoxy he was hostile and sarcastic. Was
he perhaps not convinced of the truth of his religious position?
I do not think so. I believe I understand him quite well now,
but I do not want to overburden this story with "psychology."

At any rate, this gave rise to some funny incidents. At one time
he was with his children, who were still young, in a station
restaurant; they had to wait for the next train, and there was
only one item on the menu: pork goulash. The children were
extremely hungry, and he ordered the meal. The children, who
apparently suspected something, insisted on knowing what they
were eating. In his plight he named the very first thing that came
into his mind—stewed pears. These "stewed pears" became proverbial in our family.

It is no coincidence that I have described my grandfather before saying anything about my parents. When I come to think
of it, I remember my parents only as my grandfather's children.
My father was my grandfather's oldest child and, according to
tradition, had continued my grandfather's business. However,
Grandfather actually never let go. In the office behind the store,
there was a huge oldfashioned writing-desk with two surfaces
sloping off on either side, in a roof-like manner. There Grandfather and Father sat opposite each other on high swivel stools,
whenever they were not occupied in the store.

Whenever I had done anything wrong my father would shake
his head and say: "You just wait until Grandfather hears about

this!" It never occurred to him to punish me himself. One day, for example, I decided to test my marksmanship by throwing one of the measuring rods at a clerk. The man quickly posted himself in front of a huge pane of glass which formed the back of the show-window. I gave him a firm order not to duck; he informed me that he would most certainly duck. Having just read the Song of the Nibelungen, I thrust the measuring rod at him as if it were a spear. The clerk ducked, and the glass pane broke with a tremendous crash. I ran into the office at the back. Father was sitting alone at the desk. He looked at me sadly and said: "You just wait until Grandfather hears about this. I would not like to be you." I ran quickly upstairs into the bedroom, threw myself on my knees and implored God to prevent Grandfather from hearing about the accident, or to perform some other miracle to spare me from punishment. I had barely time to finish my prayer when Grandfather came in, lifted me up by the back of my blouse, and carried me downstairs like a kitten. For some reason (he had never heard of Professor Pavlov), he always gave me my spanking in the same corner of the house.

Besides running the store we employed traveling salesmen who visited small retail stores in the villages of the Bavarian Forest. They also showed samples of merchandise to the farmers and returned at the end of a few weeks with their order-books. Father quite frequently traveled in a similar manner, and this may have increased my impression that he worked for Grandfather. The fact that he had the privilege of the first-born seemed to keep him always in subjection—that was the way I came to see it.

The second oldest son, Uncle Felix, had studied engineering and later law, and become an outstanding patent lawyer in the United States. The third son, Uncle Julius, became the co-owner of a lithographic institute. While my two uncles were like mythological figures, Father's life seemed to represent drab reality. Of Uncle Felix's existence I had at that time little more tangible proof than a popular edition of *War and Peace* whose margins he had illustrated with the most charming pen drawings in the style of the German painter Menzel.

Uncle Julius appeared, from time to time, on short visits and told us about experiences on business trips to India, North America, or France. It seemed somehow extraordinary that he, my father's brother, supplied Chinese merchants in Ceylon with perfume labels and that in his suitcase were literary reviews from Paris. He came traditionally almost every Easter. He made fun of Grandfather's paschal ceremonies. On Easter Sunday morning he recited the "Easter Walk" from *Faust*, and in the evening at some unexpected moment he would quote the words of the Night Hymn from *Zarathustra*. He recited softly, with the peculiar restraint characteristic of the most progressive actors of his youth. He was a bachelor, probably the only man from our little town who spoke French and English fluently. He was Grandfather's favorite. It was taken for granted that his life was not guided by the same rules as life at home. Grandfather suspected him and Friedrich Nietzsche of something which he called "social democracy," and it would be impossible to enumerate all the things which were summed up under that heading.

My father was the opposite of all this. He was a man of natural humility and simplicity. He was probably the most guileless person I have ever seen; this was the more striking since in his rôle of submission to that sadly inverted right of the first-born, there would have been, under the best of circumstances, hundreds of possibilities of resentment, envy and jealousy. If he had been merely simple he would undoubtedly have become entangled in all this. I later encountered other people who appeared to have chosen a small corner of life. It was as if there had occurred a simple willful act of choice quite early, at the very dawn of a person's history. His rôle of my grandfather's son, and the contrast between this rôle and the dazzling world of his brothers, were embarrassing to me.

The only thing which seemed to link him with the faraway fantastic world of my uncles was his beautiful stamp collection. I still see him bent, with magnifying glass, over those colorful little pictures from the Transvaal, Peru, or the Dutch East Indies. Instead of bringing home, like Uncle Julius, dressing-gowns from Japan or illustrated magazines from London, Father brought me, every week, a bar of chocolate which he had purchased in the station restaurant in Miltach near Straubing.

2. *Feast Days and Rudolf*

THE PEOPLE of my parents' generation were almost entirely cut off from Jewish tradition. They hardly understood Hebrew, and therefore were unable to follow the liturgy. The time between 1870 and 1914 was a secure period which produced in most people a feeling of material happiness. Although everybody adopted an "attitude" on ultimate matters, nobody bothered about formulating it. If someone had compelled my mother to define her view of life with words, the result would have been an amiable mixture of political liberalism, Goethe's "Noble be man, helpful and good," and Lessing's conciliatory Deism. Had she lived in a big American city instead of a Bavarian country town, she might have joined one of the Ethical Societies. I must conclude, however, from some of her remarks, that at times she was interested in Quakerism.

I know that my mother was deeply familiar with the pathos of solitude, of suffering and of self-denial, but she was too restrained with herself and with us ever to use such words. Perhaps she never reflected upon these things and only lived them. It was part of her tolerant eclecticism that she helped with the preparations for all the beautiful religious ceremonies in the house. She enjoyed getting ready a Friday Evening or a Seder table but she liked equally decorating the Christmas tree for the maids and the children. Christmas was always celebrated because Mother was afraid lest it cause me anguish if all my friends in the neighborhood enjoyed a feast full of joy and light while we were sitting in a dark weekday room. To be "different" and "outside" has a permanent sad influence on children; if one is sure of one's cause, then one cannot spare one's children this injury. But was the generation of our parents sure of its Judaism?

At times it happened that Christmas and Chanukkah coincided. Chanukkah is the Jewish feast which commemorates the conquest of the temple after it had been defiled by the Greeks under Antioch Epiphanes. This re-inauguration of the temple is commemorated by a feast of one week beginning on the twenty-fifth day of the Hebrew month Kislev. In every Jewish house the lamp of eight candles was lit—one additional candle each night. After returning from the synagogue we would walk into the living-room. Grandfather sang the prayers of benediction and lit the Chanukkah candle. Quite often he let me sing the benediction and light the candles. I am sure I did not understand very much of what I sang, and what it was all about, but I can still hear the melody in which I thanked God for having "protected our fathers in those days and in that time." This was followed by the old Hebrew hymn whose verses and melody are so full of familiar sentiment to every Jewish child.

In the meantime Mother had prepared the Christmas tree and the presents in the adjoining salon which she kept locked. I returned to my room and, after another hour or so, I heard the fine tinkling of a bell. This was the sign. I remember that, before leaving my room to go to the salon, I used to look through the window into the dark winter street. It would be completely abandoned, though one could see the lights of Christmas trees in windows. Somehow I did believe that the Christ child had silently passed from house to house.

The salon had thousands of smells. Besides its usual mustiness, arising from bric-a-brac, velvet and books, there was the smell of pine, of burning wax, of fresh pastry. After I had received my presents it was the employees' turn. They used to stand around awkwardly. Since we had a textile store they had their free choice, and each knew beforehand what he was going to have. The fact that there was no thrill of surprise in their gifts disappointed me. Then Mother intoned *Silent Night* and we all joined in.

I was never aware of any conflict or discrepancy in all this. Since most Christians as well as Jews had forgotten about the spiritual meaning of their feasts, it did not matter much anyhow, and the two celebrations fused for the child into one mood of winter poetry, kindness and friendship. Of course the story of Christmas seemed more concrete and understandable. Often I went with my friends from the neighborhood into the churches to see the crib with the Christ child, the Blessed Virgin, Saint Joseph, the shepherds, the angels and the animals. Little did I realize that on the eve of Chanukkah I had prayed in ancient Hebrew with David: "To Thee, O God, I have called, and Thou hast prepared my salvation." Not long before Mother's death I found out that each year on Christmas Eve she used to go, secretly, to the poor of our town with meat and other things. Not even Grandfather or Father knew about this. In her later years she made me help her, because she was ill, and probably in order to set me an example. I remember the meat particularly because we had to pick it up at the butcher's shop before making the rounds.

Christmas was the feast of the Christ child. Saint Nicholas came on the evening of the fifth of December, the eve of his feast. He appeared to go from house to house, often accompanied by his servant Ruprecht. Saint Nicholas had a long beard and carried birch rods, heavy iron chains, and a big bag full of gifts. I had to wait in the sewing-room until I heard the clanking of chains

in the street and the noise of heavy boots slowly coming upstairs. Finally the door opened, and he was there. He always
displayed an amazing knowledge of one's behavior during the
year, and it was a question of either birch rods or gifts. Finally
he left his gifts, a shower of apples, nuts, figs, dates, candies.
From the noises going on in the streets it seemed that there were
several Saint Nicholases. We had a heavy black felt blanket,
the sort of thing one used on horse-drawn coaches. Saint Nicholas
was draped in that very blanket and he wore Grandfather's boots.
I believe I was almost eight before this struck me as an extraordinary coincidence.

I received my first schooling in the kindergarten which in our
little town was conducted by nuns. Here, too, my mother broke
with tradition. Up to that time no Jewish child had ever been
sent to the Catholic kindergarten. Thus my first formal religious
education was Catholic. We had no catechism but we were entertained with stories from the Bible, particularly from the New
Testament, which were illustrated with colored pictures on the
wall. There was also a little prayer now and then. I must have
been impressed by the pious atmosphere; I have only vague recol-
lections of the stories, the pictures, the May devotions, and our
Christmas play in which I had a rôle. Soon I moved on to public
school.

Here, as in the kindergarten, there was the important fact that
children of all social classes were together. Since the poor are
everywhere in the majority, they gave everything a characteristic
pattern. As a whole you can say that in the small towns and
villages of a rural country many problems of formal education
are solved in a natural way, questions about which ponderous
theses are now being written. At present everybody is interested
in the "problems" of education; I have heard very clever people
make speeches about it. Even with all we now know about the

matter of education, I still think our country schools were quite good.

For instance, it now appears a very important fact that we were taught to love beauty. This was done in an informal, not at all planned way. The things most deeply rooted in my memory were obviously not contained in the curriculum but derived from the teacher's own inclinations. Whenever we had been particularly good boys, Herr Gradl, the *oberlehrer*, read to us. This was our reward. We were then allowed to bake our apples in the huge tiled stove in the classroom and the old teacher with a crown of white hair read "Rock Crystal," a short story by Stifter. In this story there are two children who get lost in the snow, spend the night on a mountain and are found next morning. Stifter is little known in Anglo-Saxon countries; he was a poet of deeply hidden powers whose real greatness was recognized only by Nietzsche. Stifter had lived not far from us in the Forest area. Although his great art is more than just "idyllic" and "full of local color," I still associate his name with teacher Gradl, the smell of apples baking in the stove, and a snowy winter in the Bavarian Forest.

Teacher Gradl was in private life an enthusiastic botanist. During the summer he used to take a group of pupils with him on some of his excursions in the vast meadows of the Regen Valley. There we would collect plants and identify them. He liked to be visited in his house during vacation. Then he would read from Schiller's poems and dramas, or poems of medieval romanticists of the late nineteenth century. At that time all German philology professors had broken out in an acute attack of drama, epic and lyrics; it was as if millions of Wilhelminian sofa cushions had to be covered with a crochet of knights, pages, monks and ladies. Oberlehrer Gradl's cheeks would flush when he read the epos "Thirteen Linden Trees." I have a dim recollection that he read poems of his own to me; at any rate I am sure that he wrote poetry.

Another teacher, in fact my very first one, was Kaspar Russ. He was a giant out of a fairy tale; everything about him seemed much too big—his skull, his mane, his hands, which looked like an unwieldy arrangement of ham and sausages, his feet, his snuff box, his handkerchief with colorful flower patterns, and especially his nose, which resembled a huge silo filled with snuff. He was deeply religious, musical, and there was something clumsy and giantesque about his goodness; his benevolence seemed inexhaustible. He was organist in the parish church and choirmaster of the St. Cecilia Verein. He came originally from another town not far away, and one of his friends there had been another schoolteacher, the father of the composer Max Reger. He had an intimate love for the theory of harmony, and he coached his people zealously in the boring church music of Rheinberger, sparingly interspersed with Mozart and Haydn. Traditionally he performed Haydn's *Seven Last Words* every Good Friday at church. He was proud of this, and I was always invited.

Like many people of unwieldy build, he was shy. He was clumsy but it was not difficult to find camouflaged behind a cloud of snuff a heart full of charity. He had a particular love for the Jewish children. This went as far as a display of favoritism.

I have said that everything personal, spontaneous and improvised in our schooling stuck much better in my memory than those things which correspond to the official curriculum. It was always like this, even later at high school and at the university. Just as the stories by Stifter and the botanic excursions with Gradl had a decisive influence on us, I found later that those teachers influenced us most who showed a good deal of improvisation outside of, or instead of, the curriculum; these were teachers who gave one something personal by means of a personal approach. One of the greatest dangers of present-day education is the impersonal dishing-out of the "teaching material" by an official. It is apparent that growing industrialization has produced a depersonalized type of education. Here, as in many other things, decentralization is perhaps the solution, though of course, one cannot reconstruct small Bavarian country towns of 1912 and equip them with synthetic Kaspar Russes.

Many of the problems of education which are now taken so seriously lost much of their ponderous significance in our school. For example, there was corporal punishment, but I do not believe that it did me any harm. As a whole the punishments were standardized. The teacher had a cane (a so-called "Spanish cane"), and we received slaps on the palm of the hand, a definite number for a particular type of misdemeanor. When the entire class had misbehaved, we all had to file past Russ and put our hands out. Teacher Schmaus had a ring with an ivory seal which he used for boxing our heads. Behind the school were the railway tracks, and whenever I turned around to follow a gorgeous freight train the ivory seal dropped down on me.

The beautiful days of the child in a small town: the smoke of burning potato leaves in the fires of autumn, rising over the cool misty meadows; the smell of washed laundry drying on the lawn in the summer sun; the cool moldiness underneath the town walls; the smell of the old wooden beams beneath the roof; the sensation of hot slate roof under hands and feet; or the eternal lure of pale blue mountains far away. Then there are the dark experiences, the days when we approach for the first time the frontiers of life: sex, lunacy, crime and death. One morning the boy who had been sitting in front of me at school did not come in; he had been drowned the day before. I still see the empty place with photographic accuracy, the pattern in the wooden plank of his bench. The first sensation of death, the awareness of it, moves into the center of the child's retina like a gray spot.

One day all along the river there were groups of people chatting excitedly, because over in the dark forest a poor old man had hanged himself from a tree. I had known the man. The forest was suddenly tinged with strange significance. I also remember the girl in the neighbor's house who was so deeply entangled in

sin that she painted her face. Nobody seemed surprised that she
was soon stricken with consumption and died. Then there was
the old peasant woman with a discharge running from her eyes
who came screaming into our store, telling us of her visions; she
had seen Hell. The world of twilight and darkness always at-
tracts children much more than the bright and orderly world of
the drawing-room.

Rudolf, my best friend in the neighborhood, was the son of a
little shoemaker who was always drunk. Their house was overcrowded with children, and it stank indescribably. I was impressed by the fact that one of Rudolf's brothers, incidentally the
most industrious and decent one, was a true hunchback. I was
equally impressed by the fact that Rudolf stole and lied. He did
not seem to be subject to the regular laws of life, and I admired
and revered him. Even the fact that my most beautiful toys disappeared did not matter. Rudolf was our leader when we played
soldiers; when he ordered it we remained lying on our stomachs
in the mud. He told us about large gymnastic halls in his house,
with many bars and climbing ropes which were installed exclusively for him and his brothers, and although we never saw
those halls we believed in their existence. Father and Grandfather called him "the devil"—nobody except myself ever used
his real name. All except Mother looked with misgivings upon a
friendship which could bring nothing but perdition. Mother, for
some reason or other, maintained that one should not interfere
with a child's friendships; she left me entirely to Rudolf whenever
I wanted to be with him. Later, when we had grown up, he did
land in jail.

That autumn I urged my grandfather, whenever we were on
our way to the synagogue, to tell me when the candle feast
would be (Simchath Torah, the feast of law-giving). This is a
feast during which children make a procession through the
synagogue, holding candles and singing hymns. He kept putting

me off until the actual date of the feast would arrive. One evening
I came home late from the fields with glowing cheeks, broke
into the room, fell on my mother's neck, and shouted with pride
and joy—Rudolf had promoted me to the position of captain.
Everyone looked at me in a cold and strange way; I had missed
the feast, the procession and the candles. Grandfather looked
stern and sad; obviously there was nothing one could do against
the devil.

Since I had entered school, things concerning religion had
changed. At school the Jewish children stayed away during the
hours of religious instruction, and had their own religious class
on a free afternoon. There were only a few Jewish children and
the class was therefore composed of several age groups, the be-
ginners and the advanced pupils. There was no Rabbi in the
town, only a Cantor. Our Cantors at that particular time were
far removed from the ideal of a pastor of souls. I remember the
first one very well, a short young man whom we disliked for
some reason which I cannot remember. When the First World
War broke out he was drafted into the army. We children used
to stage plays in which one of us acted as sergeant major and
bullied the Cantor in a most miserable way; only then were we
satisfied.

In religious things children separate the human and personal
aspect from the spiritual in a much more natural way than adults
do. The hateful Cantor was the first teacher since the nuns to
convey "religion" to me. And yet this circumstance had no influence on my religious development. The external features
seemed as repulsive as possible; there was the miserable Cantor,
and the bare prayer-hall inside the old brewery. Nevertheless, I
was again attracted to this spiritual sphere, and it was precisely
in this environment that my religious growth was nurtured.
Finally, after an interlude of several other Jewish schoolmasters,
a Cantor arrived who was to stay in our small town for almost
twenty years, until the Hitler revolution.

Cantor Mohrmann was more awe-inspiring than the previous ones, he seemed to sing with more beauty and fervor and, while the others had been bachelors, he brought a Biblical household with him—at least it looked like this because there were three generations. My grandfather was his only friend; apart from this he was rejected by the entire congregation. Mohrmann was a "personality." He introduced a children's choir and enlivened the service with beautiful songs. He aroused in us glowing enthusiasm for the beauties of liturgy; the "Hear Israel," the Psalms, the Eighteen Prayers. We learned to translate from the Hebrew, word for word, entirely without grammar.

This translating was like some sort of unwrapping. I remember very well that during certain parts of the Morning Prayer I felt as though I was taking jewels out of a box, unwrapping them and letting them shine in all their color and golden beauty. I had the experience of unfathomed mystery whenever he took a few of us aside and showed us a Talmud volume or a Scroll of the Torah, with unpunctuated Hebrew words. Whenever he read all this fluently he seemed to us like one initiated in some esoteric cult. Everyone, even among those who know nothing about it, is esthetically impressed by a Talmud print. There are the beautiful characters, the noble spatial arrangement of columns printed in varying magnitude, representing the text, the commentary, and the commentary of the commentary—the style of an early aristocratic humanism.

Certainly Mohrmann was not initiated in an esoteric cult. Any true Hebrew lay-scholar could have easily shown him up. However, he did not claim to be a scholar, and it was not his fault that he impressed the children as if he were one. Anything mysterious and full of implications is spiritual food for children. I remember well how deeply impressed I was when he told us that the Old Testament had prophesied wireless telegraphy. There is some text, I believe in the Psalms, which says that the Word goes around the earth with the speed of air.

We were not at all disturbed by the fact that Mohrmann at
the same time was like a man of vices, full of pride and vanity.
He played expensive card-games throughout the night, with a
dark passionate addiction. Perhaps he had some peculiar attitude
towards money. Father and Mother were very much disturbed
by all this; they did not want to accept the word of God from
a man like that. To us children this did not make any difference,
since children are much less inhibited than adults by the personal
element in their religious experiences. There is another thing
which I saw again later in other children—the natural way in
which children associate the ascetic ideal with the spiritual. Our
parents had brought us up without teaching us the laws of diet,
and had observed just enough of them so as not to hurt other
people's feelings. The moment we learned about these laws in our
religious lessons we began to impose them voluntarily upon
ourselves. We did as much of it as we could. The discipline of
supernatural obedience to which one has to submit in the choice
of food and in the life of Sabbath—all this was to us children
quite naturally tied up with the more poetical values of religion.
I am inclined to take this child-like tendency as a sign that
there is a true and an organic inner relationship between praying and fasting. These tendencies of children seem in a peculiar
way linked with the true nature of concepts. Psychoanalysis has
shown how the child, during the years preceding adolescence,
counters sexual impulses by imposing on himself rules of discipline. As far as the natural plane of things goes, this is a profound observation. But this natural history of asceticism does not
tell us anything about the true value and meaning of ascesis.

It was probably also an ascetic feature that made us feel
that the bare and poor prayer-hall in the brewery was better than
the parish church with its interior of golden baroque. On
Corpus Christi there was always a procession through town,
with several open-air altars, one of which was invariably set up
opposite our house. It was a grand feast when the various asso-

ciations of young men and young maidens passed by with colorful banners. The priest came dressed in white and golden vest-
ments, walking underneath a canopy carried by four men, and
stopping at the altar opposite our house. Unlike our neighbors
we kept the windows closed, but watched from behind the curtains. I am sure we never gave these matters much thought, and
of course they take up more space in this narrative than they did
in reality. Nevertheless, if someone had examined us closely at
the time he would have found that we considered all these colorful ceremonies as pagan and that we considered ourselves closer
to truth with our poor and undecorative forms of worship.

On the morning of the fifth of December, 1915, the eve of
Saint Nicholas, Father woke me up and said: "Come over to
Mother's bedroom." I said I would but went on sleeping. He
came again and made it more urgent; it was half-past five in
the morning. When I entered the room, Mother had a peculiar
smile and said: "You've got a little brother." I dropped on the
floor and looked underneath the bed. I had some dim idea that
babies were "thrown" (the German expression used for the birth
of animals). However, he was in the bed lying right next to her,
a bundle of fresh-smelling linen. Through a small round hole I
saw a tiny area of pink skin. I probably thought a serious word
was expected from me at this moment, and presently I addressed
pink-skin in the following way: "You are my little brother. If
later the big boys should ever threaten you, just call on me!"
Later in life the big boys threatened him quite a bit, but he
never called me.

On this day, contrary to tradition, no Saint Nicholas came to
us. One big event a day was apparently enough. In the evening
I heard the clanking of chains in the streets. Saint Nicholas
was going into the houses. The new little brother was such a
thrill that I was torn with conflict. I ran quickly to the neighbors,
couldn't wait for Saint Nicholas, and rushed back home to be
present when baby brother got his bath. They first called him

Wilhelm after the Kaiser, but mitigated it, at the last minute, and named him Ludwig after the King of Bavaria.

3. *Munich: Music and Civil War*

IN OUR little town there was no high school. Therefore, all those who did not want to take over their father's business or trade had to be sent to a bigger town for "studying." Some went to big boarding schools. Most of them were taken in as boarders by families, either alone or with one or two more boys. The schoolboy as boarder is a rather typical Southern German institution. The little paying guest even plays a rôle in literature; he occurs in the books of Ludwig Thoma and Hermann Hesse, and in books less known. Curiously enough, he is always a tragic figure. Even in Ludwig Thoma's humorous stories there is a faintly tragic undertone whenever he is dealing with the little boarder, an undertone distinctly discerned by any boy who ever lived "abroad" (the expression commonly used). These boarders usually lived with families of subaltern officials who in this way supplemented their meager monthly salaries; or with widows, or teachers who were on the staff of the school to which the boarder belonged.

I went "abroad" at the age of ten. Ebenburg is a drab industrial town in the east of Bavaria, not far from the places of origin of the composers Gluck and Reger. It is really drab and sad, not only in my memory; I was able to convince myself of that much later when I revisited it.

We were boarders at the Jewish teacher's home. The high school was just across the road. Our teacher was a brother of our Jewish teacher at home, but the brothers were on bad terms. This astonished me; I had been wont to believe that it belongs to the very definition of family to be on good terms. It is difficult to imagine anything more oppressive than the life of such a *Kultusbeamte* (cult official). He had hardly any religious education, and there was not very much of the living fire of the Torah. I can still see him, a man of medium height, a little rotund, with a tiny goatee. This was during the First World War and he was in uniform. The tie of such Cantors with Jewish tradition was only external and historical, their function purely social.

This mediocrity and apparent lack of inner content in people who are professionally concerned with religion makes a revolting impression, particularly on agnostics and atheists. Those who don't believe in God make high demands on those who believe in Him; particularly on those who "make a living out of it." Our poor teacher would have presented an ideal victim for the wrath of the godless. There was hardly anything left of the world of Isaiah—just a little establishment for circumcisions, for funerals, and for the singing of prayers on certain days. We lived on the second floor of a dismal building which contained the synagogue, and the prayer-hall was right below my bedroom. All we had to do to attend a service was to climb a staircase.

We were three boys—Leo, sixteen; Alec, eleven; and I, ten. We lived together in one room and came from the same town. Mother had warned me that life in Ebenburg was to be quite different from things as I had known them at home. She left on the evening of the day of our arrival, but Alec's mother stayed for a few days.

On that evening I was alone with Leo, while Alec spent some time with his mother. Leo took me to a window and pointed at the building across the street. "See the lighted window in the basement? That is the janitor's apartment, where Grete lives, right in that very room." He told me that Grete was sixteen and his girl friend. We looked intently across the street towards the lighted window. After a while I began putting my things into drawers, but Leo kept looking. Without even turning, he asked me if I knew that it was scientifically proved that hair kept growing on corpses' heads after they were buried. This, he said, had been established beyond doubt in people who had been exhumed. I asked what "exhumed" was, and he explained it to me. I said that Alec was lucky that his mother was staying on for a few days. Leo replied that Alec was a sissy and that I seemed to be a sissy too.

Suddenly he exclaimed: "Look, quickly!" I rushed to the window. A girl had emerged into the street, apparently from the house. She walked slowly away and Leo, panting with excitement, said: "See how she looks up to me?" I pressed my face against the window pane but could only see her walking away. I wondered what made Leo certain that she looked up to our window. This was repeated every evening like a ritual. Leo made us believe that there was an adventurous link between him and the janitor's daughter. But this link remained mysterious. What Mother had told me was true: everything here was different from the world at home.

The Cantor would suddenly appear in the morning in our room, pacing up and down with his hands folded over his back; this happened whenever his wife had thrown him out. At least this was the explanation given us by Leo. There was the Cantor's wife who had appeared so fashionable to me when she met my mother in the drawing-room, and yet everything seemed to be in disorder after my mother left. There were so many mice that they even ate the bread which I kept in a bag suspended near my pillow. There was a maid to whom Leo used to talk in obscure and meaningful allusions. He was able to say things which we could not understand and which roused peals of laughter from the Cantor's wife and the maid; we admired him for that.

Everything seemed alien, bad and terrifying, and I believed that it was so utterly different that I could not possibly make it understandable to Father and Mother. Gradually I developed the idea that "abroad" had to be something altogether different from "at home"; it was another cosmos which one forgot completely the first minute of the holidays. Thousands of other boys had to go through this—like soldiers who, while on active combat, do not meditate on the philosophy of war.

Vacations had developed into something which you might call furlough in heaven. From my window on the top floor of our house, just underneath the attic, I was able to see, beyond the neighbor's house, the distant mountains. I had only to run down two stairs, and I found myself in the homely sphere of Father, Mother, Grandfather and little brother. There were only a few steps to my friends' homes. We spent our days swimming or with a book, or we visited the old schoolteacher, or we hiked in the woods. The dark world was hundreds of miles away; but the more the golden days advanced, the more that darkness approached.

After one year I was sent to Munich. I was again a little boarder, this time with people of quite a different kind. I lived with an orthodox Jewish family, a widow with three children. Frau Kohen was the widow of a banker. All members of the family were midget-like, so much so that whenever I visited other people I felt for a moment as though I were among giants. The entire Kohen family exhibited a really bee-like industriousness; everyone contributed to the household. Even the son, only two years older than myself, made some money by giving lessons. Herr Kohen had died a sudden death and had left the family in a helpless condition. Moreover, one of the daughters, a private teacher, suffered from epilepsy. In spite of all these hard blows of fate, there was an atmosphere of security in this home which is often found among pious folk.

Munich, in spite of the war's shadow, in spite of *ersatz* goods, dried vegetables and lack of fuel, had lost nothing of its incomparable charm. I had been there once before with my father, at the age of eight, when he took me to see the puppet play of

Doctor Faust. A magic world was now opened before me; all the things of which I had read a lot were at hand—the museums, the operas, theaters, concert halls, churches, parks, the Isar valley, the mountains and lakes. That Munich does not exist any more. But cities, even if we disregard our nostalgic sentiments, have something like immortal souls. Munich meant some sort of harmonious synthesis of North and South, of East and West, of Art and Nature, of rural and urban civilization, a vanguard of serene Latinism in the gloomy North, a Gothic sentry in front of the porch of Italy. With the exception of Paris there has never been a town which had so much individual expression, so little of the artifact and so much of natural growth.

At this time an influence came into my life which has remained a most powerful and decisive one—Music. Since this book is intended to describe the journey of a spiritual discovery, I must talk about music. From the beginning to the end it has been for me the most immediate expression of spiritual realities. "To talk about music" is a miserable paradox, and contains in four words an admission of incongruity. I remember the embarrassed feeling I had when I read Kierkegaard's somber theological speculations on Mozart and *Don Giovanni*. Is *Don Giovanni* not just a "charming" opera which has a place on the repertoire somewhere with *Carmen* and *The Barber of Seville?* Or is it something entirely different, opening up the fathomless abyss of human existence? There is a hierarchy of values, the validity of which cannot be proved by what one calls ordinary means. In this respect, as in others, the Good and the Beautiful are intimately related. To me Mozart's quartets and Bach's *Well-tempered Clavichord* are in essence much more closely akin to Saint Thomas' *Summa* than to Wagner's *Götterdämmerung,* although the latter is music and the *Summa* is not.

I had started with music in our hometown. Kaspar Russ as a rule gave no lessons but for some reason he made an exception for me. In vain did he try to convey to me his enthusiasm for the theory of harmony. He tried to do this simultaneously with the elementary teaching of piano. Even today, when I hear something about a diminished seventh or about enharmonic transformations, the smell of snuff and the sensation of his huge hands comes back to me. Counterpoint played no rôle at all. Nevertheless, he came to the lesson one day with a sad face: "Yesterday the greatest contemporary musician died." I said: "Wagner?" He shook his head sadly and said: "Reger." I understood nothing about his theory of harmony, and all I was interested in was how to play the piano. I loved sonatinas by Dussek, and the play of bells from *The Magic Flute,* and I harmonized *Lorelei* with the most luscious chords long before we had ever reached diminished sevenths. At the Cantor's in Ebenburg there was no musical stimulus outside a melodramatic song, "The Seaman's Fate," which seemed to fit in with the dust-catching furniture and the oil prints in the drawing-room.

Munich seemed like a second birth. There was the Hoftheater in which opera was played every night. I saw it perhaps twice a year. We had to begin queueing at five in the morning, and at ten the box-office was opened. Then we went home, and there was a whole day of beatific expectation. This reached its climax during the last half-hour when we were sitting in the top gallery, waiting for the various curtains to rise—the second one (with Guido Reni's "Aurora" which seemed to indicate what was going to happen later) and finally the last one which separated the audience from the stage and which was to rise after the Overture. The tuning of the instruments, the gradual dimming, the appearance of the conductor and the last seconds of silence; all these were phases full of significance, meaningful like those of an esoteric cult of antiquity. I was equally impressed by everything, no matter whether *Lohengrin, The Barber of Seville,* or *The Magic Flute.* However, Wagner dimmed more and more and my love for Mozart deepened as the years went by. This love became a decisive factor in my life, going far beyond the realm of music

With concerts it was rather similar. Every year at All Souls' there was the *Missa Solemnis,* and during Holy Week *St. Matthew's Passion.* Here, too, the thrill was heightened by queueing in the early morning. I remember the annual performances of the *Missa* in every detail. I know now that they exerted a powerful influence upon me which was reinforced much later in a somewhat different direction. The late Beethoven, he who wrote the *Missa* and the last string quartets, is an awe-inspiring phenomenon, not only musically but in the history of mankind. Is it not extraordinary that this Promethean, whose life crosses the epoch of the French Revolution and Napoleon, should arrive at the end in some space of mystic loneliness? Nobody who has heard the last quartets and the "Benedictus" can deny that the composer entered into a sphere which has found its verbal expression in Saint John of the Cross. It is a platitude to say that Beethoven in his last quartets was far ahead of his time; actually he was there ahead of Time altogether. What an astronomic span in one man's life! What if those were right who say that geniuses anticipate the course of history?

At that time I was far removed from such speculations. I possessed a small reading score which still contained as a printed heading Beethoven's original motto: *"Von Herzen, möge es zu Herzen gehen—*May heart speak to heart." These words touched me in a very special way. Beethoven had called the *Missa* his greatest work. In this connection this dedication is particularly moving, as if he had been concerned with the act of communication, of correspondence with the hearer. This was precisely how I felt. From the first majestic D-major chord which introduces a longing Kyrie to the "Prayer for Internal and External Peace" of the Agnus Dei with its naive operatic intermezzo of the Miserere and the final bars of supernatural happiness, there is nothing like it in the history of art. It is as if you beheld European man, a late estranged European man, already half cut-off from his moorings, just once more stirred in the depth of his heart by an experience of infinite importance. I knew from books that Beethoven had the text of the Mass translated to him word by word, and that he attempted to interpret its content verbally; thus I followed the text as closely as possible. The experience was overwhelming every year. I remember well that for a few hours after leaving the Odeon Hall the world seemed altogether changed. People in the street, even the tramway cars, everything seemed in a state of transfiguration, everybody appeared to be reconciled and full of peace. Later, after the religious world of Bach and Mozart had opened itself to me, I maintained that particular personal relation to Beethoven's *Missa*, in the way one may feel towards some person who has played an important part in one's destiny. By chance my wife and I, just before our departure for Canada in 1939, heard the *Missa Solemnis* in London under Toscanini. This was our farewell to Europe.

During my first few years in Munich, I was under the influence of two currents which have nothing to do with each other. At Kohen's I came for the first time in contact with the world of Jewish orthodoxy; on the other hand in Munich during the armistice and the post-war years I found myself on the stage of the social revolution. In Munich everything was to occur which had happened on a large scale before in Russia, and which was later to happen on a large scale in Germany.

The Kohen family belonged to the orthodox congregation of Munich which had its center in a small, inconspicuous synagogue at the Herzog Rudolf Street (the "canal" synagogue). The liberal congregation was by far the bigger one. It had a big "reformed" synagogue in the center of the city. This synagogue resembled a big, fashionable Protestant church, and contained an organ. The canal synagogue, however, was a gray house, hardly distinguishable from the poor houses of the neighborhood. Contrary to the liberal synagogue it was always full to capacity, and had unbelievably bad ventilation. Jewish orthodoxy, like all orthodox religions in the world, does not keep pace with modern hygiene. There were assembly rooms, and schoolrooms for children and adults in a side wing, and you could be sure that something was always going on. Moreover, the orthodox families chose their dwellings near the synagogue (if only not to be forced to use vehicles on Sabbath day) so that the synagogue became a living center, the heart of the congregation.

What attracted me as a child was not any particular detail of the doctrine but the entire atmosphere. It is quite true that in exploring religious truth you have to exclude all emotional influences. Nevertheless, all religions have a way in which they are lived by people rather than thought, they have their gestures and elements which cannot be formulated; all this has an overwhelming, penetrating power which no child's heart can resist.

Take, for instance, the Sabbath. From the late afternoon on Friday to the first stars on Saturday evening, it was as if time and space had become a spiritual enclave. From the time when good tiny Frau Kohen put out the white linen, with the solemn cutlery of silver, and the candles, until Saturday night, when the Week was welcomed with a special ritual, there was an atmosphere of peace and enchantment. Life seemed to continue within a strange outer space in which it was subjected to laws different from those of the world. There were hundreds of little, seemingly senseless Talmudic precepts. You were not allowed to go on a vehicle, to write, to switch on any electric light (this was done by the maid!), you were not supposed to carry anything in your pocket, not even the key. Erwin, the son, even had his handkerchief pinned to the lining of his coat so that it would be part of his clothing, and not "carried." This was the famous "fence around the Torah" which the Wise had erected so that not even a shadow was possibly darkening the Law of Sabbath. This entire time-enclave was used for service, for private devotions, for the study of the Torah and the rabbinical Fathers.

All these activities were interrupted only by gay meals, Hebrew round-songs, and occasional short walks.

It is remarkable that even the poorest orthodox families celebrated the Sabbath in this manner. For in many cases this meant a great financial sacrifice. Many stores had to remain closed on Sunday so that the merchants lost the income of another weekday. This was one of the reasons why many Jews said that for practical reasons one had to conform with the times, and that orthodoxy was impossible in a "modern world."

Service in the orthodox synagogue was, of course, entirely different from anything I had seen until then. Even the outward appearance differed, because here the men wore their prayer-shawls over the whole body. In liberal synagogues the men wear their prayer-shawls folded up around the collar like mufflers. This is done in a sort of diffident way to conform with the times. Many prayed for themselves without paying attention to their neighbors, often without reference to what the Cantor was doing. Many closed their eyes in devotion and made characteristic rhythmic movements forward and backward. This diminished the danger of distraction. Everybody seemed to know the liturgy by heart and followed the reading of Torah and Prophet with the most amazing knowledge of detail. Anyone from the congregation might be called upon to read from the Prophets. Although you never knew beforehand whose turn it would be, everyone was apparently able to recite any Prophetic text with perfectly accurate intonation. This is an art in itself practiced from early youth. The synagogue was an organic continuation of religious life in the family; whoever had finished the Eighteen Prayers earlier than the Cantor did some religious reading or talked to his neighbors.

The Munich orthodox congregation was at that time under the leadership of old Rabbi Ehrentreu. Doctor Ehrentreu was an extraordinary man, of a type I have never encountered again in life. He looked as if Rembrandt had known him, a stooped, thin old man with a long silver beard. I still see him leading the Sabbath procession of the Torah, wrapped in his prayer-shawl, so that only his face was visible. There was something non-physical about him; whoever remembers him remembers a conspicuously high and broad forehead and huge gazeless eyes which seemed to behold something which was not visible. He preached rarely and, contrary to the liberal and reformed synagogue, the sermon played a very unimportant rôle with him. Whenever he spoke at all he gathered the men and discussed some very technical Talmudic problem. Although he confined himself to dry special questions, everybody felt the undercurrent of wisdom and goodness.

I thought of that much later when I read what Franz Rosenzweig said of Jewish orthodoxy, of its rough, almost indigestible shell which contains such a rich and sweet nucleus. Somewhere underneath this seemingly impenetrable crust of formalism the essence is buried; there you find, says Rosenzweig, words such as "Love Thy Neighbor as Thyself," words which are seldom expressed, as if out of some pious diffidence. Here he makes a strange comparison with Christianity which, as he says, exhibits its sweetness on the surface. The interesting thing is that in Christian orthodoxy, too, the onlooker often sees nothing but empty formalism behind which one cannot see the "Christian ideas" any more. Here, too, the Catholic Church represents the most direct development from Jewish orthodox tradition. Doctor Ehrentreu was a typical son of those Eastern Yeshivoth–Jewish centers of teaching which had an atmosphere of extraordinary spiritual intensity. Some Russian Christian philosopher once said that the Yeshivah is an incarnation of the Hegelian Absolute. You must have seen Yeshivah disciples to be able to understand this remark. I am not speaking of unequaled virtuosity of memory and knowledge. There were men who knew the Bible visually so well that when you pierced the book with a pin they were able to tell you through which word on each page the pin was stuck. I am rather speaking of an absolute and perfectly natural way in which everything material became secondary, a pure means for a purpose; how these people are, into their innermost biological strata, possessed in the literal sense of the word. There is a famous short story by Perez of a Rabbi and his disciple who, while slowly starving to death, discuss Talmudic problems, with red eyes and glowing cheeks; these types really exist, I have seen them. With all this the Western orthodox congregations were only a shallow reproduction of what existed in the East.

It is quite natural that I was then much more attracted by the aura of religion without. understanding much of the details. In all religion the unexpressed and the inexpressible are as important as all those things which are verbalized in prayer-books and treatises. Within the whole structure the air-filled spaces are as significant as the pillars. This must be one of the main difficulties for the people who study "comparative religion" with "scientific methods." All they get are marble slabs, pillars and blocks but no interspaces. The interspace is an emotional element organically interwoven with the rational structure. There is nothing purely rational which is strong enough to bind the heart of man.

I had not started early enough to study scripture. All children around me read Hebrew without effort, with or without punctuation. At that time I knew hardly anything of the true liturgical content of the Day of Atonement, nothing of the Sacrifice of the Scapegoat, nothing of the incomparably beautiful Isaiah chapters, hardly anything of the Book of Jonah; I just knew barely enough of the prayers of contrition which are mechanically repeated all day long while the entire congregation, men, women and children pound their chests. But what I grasped entirely was the gesture of the day, and this penetrated my limbs as it does every child's. The ten days of preparation, and then the solemn eve of the Day of Atonement!

The entire congregation resembled a white sea because the married men wore not only their prayer-shawls but also the shrouds in which they would one day be buried. No one was to enter the house of God with shoes on his feet. When the ceremonies began with the solemn Kol Nidrë, twice repeated, there was a faint rustling going through the crowd. Would the next twenty-four hours bring a remission of sins? None of the grown-up men left the synagogue from morning till night. Some supplemented the twenty-four hours' fast by some special penance, for instance, standing during the whole day. In the evening we children were so hungry that from this alone we concluded that our sins must be forgiven.

When we came home, Frau Kohen had prepared the food. I felt good, and I thought that life was beginning anew on a spotlessly clean new page.

Similarly profound was the experience of Passover. Here, too, the preparation was important. Frau Kohen and the maid needed days to purify the house according to the precepts of Passah. Finally the first Seder evening arrived. The Seder plate was prepared, the horse-radish (the bitterness of Egyptian slavery), applesauce (the clay of Egypt), the lamb, and other symbolic objects. I knew the Seder from Grandfather. The Hagadah was recited by Erwin, the son; I, the youngest, had to put the famous question: *"Mah nishtanah haleilah haseh micol haleiloth?—*What is the difference between this night and all other nights?" Everybody ate and drank a lot, and as the evening advanced Erwin, who interrupted the Hagadah with considerations from Midrash, seemed more and more admirable to me. With all this we got clear chicken broth with balls of unleavened bread in it, and many other delicious things. Whenever the ritual of the Hagadah prescribed the drinking of wine, we children drank too; we dipped our fingers ten times into the wine, corresponding to the ten plagues of Egypt. Towards the end I had too much wine, and the final round-songs seemed outrageously hilarious to me; the lamb that was eaten by the cat, the cat by the dog, and so forth, until the Angel of Death appeared to slay the butcher who had slain the ox. From then on for one week there was only unleavened bread, for the commemoration of the Exodus. Everything had to be eaten from dishes which were not used otherwise during the year.

Thus, life was arranged according to some high order; there was the rhythm of weeks and Sabbaths, of seasons and of feasts, and there was the profound symbolic separation of "pure" and "impure" which reached down into every profane activity.

Simultaneously with the aura of piety something else penetrated my life, of an altogether different nature—my contact with the social revolution. Although I was only twelve at the end of the war, I remember very well the scene of the post-war revolutionary period in Munich.

It all started with a book. Uncle Julius, on furlough from the front line, made a casual remark of praise about Barbusse's *Le Feu,* a war book which then was being widely read in all belligerent countries. I read it, and it was as if scales had dropped from my eyes. A new world was opened up, a world of new insights and feelings. I was at the age during which children develop the spiritual organs of emphatic perception; i.e., at the age when for the first time the strange neighbor in the street car becomes a feeling human being, a person who has the same eyes, the same sense of smell, the same brain, the same sensations as I myself. It is the age during which the range of sympathy suddenly extends far beyond those nearest to us, in fact it runs for some time the danger of cosmic dilution.

Until then war had been something distant, something that happened "out there"; it had been a matter of geography, of little colored flags pinned on maps. Now for the first time I saw what it really was: the dirt of trenches, the rain, the snow, floods, rats and corpses, the death of so many single human beings whom I might have known personally, and it was a fact that innocent human beings killed one another. The fact that all

these people could just as well have been personally acquainted
with one another, and could have been friends, was the most
stunning insight. It seemed due to an immoral clique of murderous capitalists and industrialists that these workmen, artisans,
clerks and peasants were sitting in mudholes for four years,
waiting to kill one another. Barbusse described with terribly
penetrating power, because he was devoured by a deep sense
of justice. At the end of his book he exhorted the soldiers with
the wrath of a prophet to make an end of a world of filthy op-
pression of which all the bourgeoisie, the society of bankers, professors, lawyers, priests, were guilty. The taximan of Berlin and
the factory-worker of Paris would have been good friends, had
they been living in the same street. Now they sneaked up on
each other until one could find an opportunity to shoot a bullet
into the other's head. I understood that this senseless deviltry
was somehow deeply associated with the faults of our society
and with the position of money in the world.

It was Karl Liebknecht who on August 1, 1914, had cried
"Down with War" in the streets of Berlin. It was Jaurès who had
been assassinated around the same time for his internationalism.
I read the letters of Rosa Luxemburg from prison. I read the
pre-war Reichstag speeches of Karl Liebknecht, in which he
compared infantile mortality in the rich and in the poor quarters
of Berlin. Liebknecht was shot from behind; Luxemburg's head
was bashed in with a rifle butt and her body was thrown into
the Landwehrkanal. All this was to me quite obviously connected
with the Berlin taximan and the Paris factory-worker; even the
most brutal crimes had to be committed to prevent their becoming friends, because this was dangerous for those who had accumulated much money.

I myself lived in the sheltering atmosphere of the middle-class,
the world to which my parents belonged. I experienced little of
the misery of the masses during the post-war years except for
what I saw in the industrial quarters of Munich and in the trains

during my home journeys. But misery, hopelessness and injustice were like a cold fog which creeps through tiniest fissures and through your very clothes.

Henri Barbusse had opened a door. In later years I wanted to get to the bottom of all this, and I began to study Karl Marx, and even the fundamentals of Hegelian philosophy. It seems strange that those two worlds, the world of Piety and the world of Revolution, were then not at all irreconcilable. I met many people with whom it was very much the same. Karl Marx has strongly Old Testament features of which we are not usually aware because of the disguise of nineteenth-century frills, Feuerbach's materialism and all that. If one were able to study him as a human being, one would probably find that his "opium for the people" is nothing but fury over those who use religion as opium for the people. His anger at industrial slavery, his apocalyptic concept of history are fed from the eternal well of truly prophetic anger. He had a glowing sense of justice, but he lacked metaphysical sense altogether. A justice which is of this world, a justice not at all transcendental, is something very dangerous. This I did not see at the time. Therefore, Karl Marx and the religion of the Old Testament represented two reconcilable ideas; in fact, their compatibility was not even questionable. Later I asked myself how it came about that I saw no contradiction between the world of Rabbi Ehrentreu and that of Karl Liebknecht. When, much later, I read what Berdyaev had to say about the prophetic-Messianic character of Marxism, I appreciated more fully my sentiments of that time.

The great religious philosopher, Martin Buber, must have been thinking of something similar when he called Gustav Landauer a "Jewish Prophet." I remember Landauer from a workers' parade, a haggard man with a long beard. He belonged to those who were brought in contact with politics after the war, during those years of misery. They were driven into politics, or at least into something they thought was politics. Before that he had written a monograph of two volumes on Shakespeare. Later he became the fiery representative of an non-Marxian socialism, the Utopian ideal of Proudhon and Fourrier; he foresaw that a Marxist revolution would, in the end, give birth to a monster which would far outdo Capitalism in lack of humanity and outright cruelty.

Around Easter, 1919, there existed in Munich a short-lived Soviet Republic. The Communists had become impatient because the World Revolution had stopped too long (two years) at the frontiers of Russia. Wanting to speed things up a bit, they chose two more or less rural lands, Hungary and Bavaria—one of those poor jokes of the demon of history.

I was then thirteen, and I just caught one of the last trains to leave Munich before the beleaguered city was in the midst of a civil war. I was eagerly awaited at home. Although it was usually a journey of half a day, it took us almost two days to reach our destination. Journeys like these brought us bourgeois children in contact with a life which seemed to be outside the pale of protection. I had to sleep on the floor of a railway station between workers with tin cans and peasant women with bundles.

On this particular occasion people asked me where I belonged, and without further explanation took me to a small town in Lower Bavaria, where they sheltered me for the night in their house. I saw that they were butchers with a small inn beside the shop, as used to be the custom in Southern Germany. I was taken through dark and musty corridors into a room without windows in which there was a high bed with an oil print of the Blessed Virgin above it, and a small lamp. The next morning an old cook woke me up at five, gave me breakfast and showed me the way to the station. When I arrived home I realized that I did not even know the name of my hosts, nor could I have found their house again.

My arrival was expected eagerly because this was to be my Bar Mitzvah (feast of confirmation). This solemn feast is cele-

brated when a boy is thirteen and approaches for the first time
the scroll of the Torah to pronounce the formulas of benediction.
In houses with religious tradition the boy recites from the Torah
and from the Prophets himself. This is done after he has been
coached carefully in the proper intonation. My grandfather had
given me the necessary instructions during the preceding vacations, and there were several rehearsals with the scroll which is
written in Hebrew without punctuation.

Another boy happened to have his confirmation on the same
Saturday. He had a peculiar lisp. The Cantor said to me: "Whatever you do, don't laugh. You are peculiar—even while you are
serious you look as if you were laughing."

Finally the appointed day came. We put on dark blue suits,
white shirts with collars and ties. At home the women busily
prepared a gorgeous meal. There were many guests from abroad.
The boy with the lisp said only the formulas of benediction.
Nobody understood Hebrew or knew anything about the meaning of the texts, but this was a solemn moment; I suddenly heard
myself sing with a loud voice, while the entire synagogue seemed
strangely silent. It was in March, and the prophetic text of that
Saturday was from Ezekiel:

The hand of the Lord was upon me, and brought me forth in the
spirit of the Lord: and set me down in the midst of a plain that was
full of bones. And he led me about through them on every side: now
they were very many upon the face of the plain, and they were exceeding dry. And he said to me: Son of Man, dost thou think that
these bones shall live? And I answered: O Lord God, thou knowest.
And he said to me: Prophesy concerning these bones: Ye dry bones,
hear the word of the Lord. Thus saith the Lord God to these bones:
Behold, I will send spirit into you and you shall live. And I will lay
sinews upon you, and will cause flesh to grow over you, and will
cover you with skin: and I will give you spirit and you shall live,
and you shall know that I am the Lord. And I prophesied as he had
commanded me: and as I prophesied there was a noise, and behold
a commotion, and the bones came together, each one to its joint.
And I saw, and behold the sinews, and the flesh came up upon them:

and the skin was stretched out over them, but there was no spirit
in them.

And he said to me: Prophesy to the spirit, prophesy, O Son of Man,
and say to the spirit: Thus saith the Lord God: Come, spirit, from
the four winds, and blow upon the slain, and let them live again.
And I prophesied as he had commanded me: and the spirit came
into them and they lived: and they stood up upon their feet, an
exceeding great army. And he said to me: Son of Man: all these
bones are the house of Israel: they say, our bones are dried up, our
hope is lost and we are cut off. Therefore, prophesy and say to them:
Thus says the Lord God: Behold I will open your graves and will
bring you out of your sepulchres, oh my people, and will bring you
into the land of Israel. And you shall know that I am the Lord, when
I shall have opened your sepulchres, and shall have brought you out
of your graves, oh my people. And shall have put my spirit into you,
and you shall live and I shall make you rest upon your own land:
and you shall know that I the Lord have spoken, and done it, saith
the Lord God.

When I came home, Aunt Clara said it had been beautiful,
she had almost cried. This was an attempt to be sarcastic. There
was a gift table with the collected works of Schiller, Kleist,
Uhland and Eichendorff, and numerous works on Polar expedi-
tions and on Tibet. The dining table was drawn out to double
its length. I said the thanksgiving for dinner. After that one of
my cousins played Wagner's "Magic Fire" from *Valkyrie* on the
piano.

By the time I got back to Munich the Soviet Republic had
collapsed. Wagons full of soldiers were racing through the streets;
the soldiers had white badges to show that they fought Communism, some had swastikas. The Communists, incidentally, had
persuaded Gustav Landauer to join their government. After much
hesitation he agreed. He must have known that the things he
had to do were mostly the opposite of what he was thinking and
saying. When the counter-revolutionary troops entered Munich,
Landauer was killed. He was kicked with soldiers' boots and
hit with rifle butts until he was dead.

4. Youth on the Move

THESE were the years of the German Youth Movement. On all country roads during the summer you saw groups of young people with long blouses made of some sort of dyed burlap, similar to Russian peasant shirts, tied with laces over the chest and reaching down to the knees. These *wandervögel* wore leather belts, rucksacks and heavy boots; some carried mandolins, guitars or flutes. They spent the nights in youth hostels and barns, or in the houses of peasants whom they helped with the harvest. During the winter they met in cheaply rented houses in the big cities, in converted garages or stables; they wore their strange costumes only during the summer when they began to migrate. While they gathered around fires in the forests or in the fields they practiced eurythmia, played ball games, or they "read." There was always something heavy, problematic and solemn about that reading. They read Plato and Ibsen, Dostoievsky's "Great Inquisitor" and Nietzsche's *Zarathustra*. There were Ultra-Nationalists (they undoubtedly formed the nucleus for the Hitler Youth to come), Catholics, Communists, Zionists and many others—and just plain *wandervögel* who did not bother with any "ism."

All of them had one thing in common: a rebellious attitude against their parents' generation, or at least against the mode of living of that generation. There was a sort of ascetic protest against everything "bourgeois"—no drinking, no smoking, no smart clothes. One boy denounced another as "bourgeois" because he ate chocolate candies filled with liqueur.

In the summer, incidentally, they did not migrate aimlessly; there was one central aim, the bundestag. It was the climax of a year; boys and girls of one bund from all over the country congregated, and there were speeches, resolutions, dancing, plays, singing, games and "reading" until late in the night around the fire.

Looking back at it now, we see what profound spiritual restlessness had seized the heart of Europe. For some unknown reason, the relationship between generations, particularly that between father and son, seems much more problematic in Germany than in Anglo-Saxon countries. Generalizations like this are usually questionable but here there is something quite characteristic, if one could only put one's finger on it. A teacher who was loved by his pupils was a great exception. As a whole, the relationship between teacher and pupil was quite different. In German funny magazines, in short stories, in Wilhelm Busch's poems, and on the stage, the teacher was always a victim of aggression and hostility. He was attacked by means of glue on the chair, stink bombs in the stove, noises of mysterious origin. It was not always funny. In reality, to some teachers life was hell on earth, they were ill-treated until they became sick. One has only to look at Wilhelm Busch's *Max and Moritz*, a children's book which has the same importance in Germany as *Alice* has in Anglo-Saxon countries. There the two boys play pranks, some of them murderous, on adults, and only adults, never on other children. Gunpowder is put into the teacher's pipe so that he literally explodes after lighting it and only his charred body remains. The lunch of an old widow is being lifted through the chimney by means of line and hooks.

Incidentally, that extraordinary significance of the struggle of generations, that most peculiar biological revolt is nothing new in German history. It existed as "Sturm und Drang" in the eighteenth century, it is immanent in the story of the Reformation, in other words, in the entire history of that German "protest" of which Dostoievsky spoke. There is no doubt that the anti-Christian attitude of the great and tragic Nietzsche was rooted in that sphere of personal experience. It was, more than anything else, something resembling a neurosis, a revolt against the father's house, with its delicate, bourgeois, somewhat emasculated Christianity of the nineteenth century. Other ministers' sons of the nineteenth century became evolutionists, vitalists or materialists; Nietzsche, however, made fun of God and tried to decapitate Him, acting just like Max and Moritz.

In the German Youth Movement which began before the First World War with the foundation of the *wandervögel*, youth par excellence—the Platonic idea of youth, so to speak—found expression and a specific form. Youth aspired to be more than a stage of development or a miniature edition of adulthood; it was something *per se*.

You could see that even in the Jewish Youth Movement in Germany. In Poland and in Russia there were Zionist youth associations the main function of which was to spread Zionist ideas and to prepare young Jews for life in Palestine. There was an immediate connection between the group in Poland and the settlements in Palestine. When it came to "Blau-Weiss," that Jewish *wandervögel* organization which was originally the strongest of its kind in Germany, the whole thing was quite different. More than anything else "Blau-Weiss" was reaction against middle-class culture, against a parent-generation, against a colorless form of liberalism and assimilation, against the "German citizen of Jewish denomination." There were, to be sure, individual cases of emigration to Palestine, but those who had emigrated abandoned the Youth Movement as their moral and cultural basis. By the time youth ended, movement came to an end too.

However, it was not always like this, as we shall see presently. The "Jung-Jüdischer Wanderbund" (Young Jewish Wanderers) to which I belonged was similar to "Blau-Weiss." In the beginning it claimed to be neutral in its political tendencies; you could be Zionist or anything. This changed as time went on, perhaps under the influence of growing anti-semitism. When I belonged to it, one might have called the whole thing pluralistic. Some of our older leaders were strong personalities. They were not chosen on account of any particular allegiance, either German or Zionist or Socialist, but merely because they happened to be good at softball or literature. Due to this fact, the bund had something loose, free and mobile, something really youthful. Almost every one of us had a leader whom he followed. They were usually university students whom one could ask for advice.

Our "home" was in the Thierschstrasse, next to Hitler's original headquarters, above an old garage. Here we had our evenings and our courses. I gave a course on *Macbeth* for girls. In summer came migration and the bundestag which was usually held in Franconia or in Thuringia, preferably in a castle. Off we walked into the mountains or along the Main and Rhine valleys. In retrospect I must say that the dances, the softball, the tour, and the nights in the barns were the most beautiful parts of it all. But that is not the reason why I dwell on such details. I do so because, with all that playfulness, there was a general mood which seemed to point at events which later came to pass. Latent in the situation were sorrows, questions and doubts pointing towards the great Jewish catastrophe—or rather the great European catastrophe with which the fate of the Jews was interwoven in so mysterious a fashion. Let me take as examples the stories of three of us, which are fairly representative.

There was, for instance, Erna, a girl of fifteen from Munich. She came from a typical Jewish middle-class environment; her father was a lawyer. She was a slim, tall girl with blue eyes and brown hair, which she wore in long braids. When it came to walking, cooking, washing or softball she seemed to have inexhaustible energy. She was a source of freshness, health and cleanliness to all around her. In the woods she would heat a kettle of gruel over the open fire, and at our "home" she was an untiring scrubber. One day she began to occupy herself, all of a sudden, with the social question. This seemed to happen under the influence of one of the leaders, but soon we noticed that she worked more and more in the slums, and after a few years she joined the Communist Party. I lost contact with her until one day when her name appeared in newspapers all over the world. Single-handed, she had liberated her husband, a young Communist worker, from a prison in Berlin. It was an incredible Wild West story; somehow she got into the Moabit jail and threatened an unarmed guard with an unloaded revolver. A successful hold-up carried out by a girl in a jail in the middle of Berlin! The police never found them, though much later I heard that during the Hitler era she was deported by some South American government back to Germany. According to another version, she was killed in Russia during a purge.

The second story is that of Friedel Fränkel. Friedel Fränkel was a short, broad-shouldered boy with ugly, coarse features, wiry hair, a low forehead and a long upper lip. He looked like a bull calf of the Aberdeen Angus breed. He looked bluish-black even when he had just shaved. He was an employee in one of the best Munich stores. Friedel showed very early contempt for all that was called Capitalism, which was quite a lot. The more he read Dostoievsky, Tolstoy and the writings of the early Halutzim (Zionist pioneers who established co-operatives; they were, incidentally, influenced by Tolstoy), the less he found their ideas compatible with his career. Curiously enough, and this is the reason why I write about him, his attitude towards Marxist socialism was just as bitter. It was mainly his study of the great Russians and his simple and peasant-like way of reasoning which brought him to that conclusion. He was stubborn. He wanted to have nothing to do with the socialists who, he thought, were intellectuals whose main function it was to chat in cafés and studios while the workers had to fight on the barricades. As to Dostoievsky, to him Western capitalism and Marxist socialism were practically the same thing and towards the socialists among us he was rather sarcastic. He was not intelligent, in fact he was a little stupid, but he was original and followed a straight line. There was no one else among us whose ideas were exactly like his. With stubborn self-restriction he did what he thought was right; he gave up his promising position in the store and became an apprentice to a cobbler in a suburb. His relatives had hoped for a rocket-like career, as a retail merchant-king; they were bewildered and offended. The moment he made his first pair of shoes all by himself, he sailed for Palestine, settled in a village, and founded a family. His was the story of a successful *narodnik* (as those Russian intellectuals who "took to the people" used to be called). When he is an old man and succeeds in getting through all the political earthquakes while his colleagues in the retail business are killed or dispersed over the globe, somebody ought to write his history. It could be done in the style of Tolstoy's folk stories, under the title "The Cobbler from Munich."

Rudi Herz was a boy of the same generation. He was a child of an environment which is unique and can never be quite described, the "better" Jewish middle-class. I believe his father had to do with the textile industry. There has never been a Sinclair Lewis to describe the peculiar void, the lack of purpose, the absence of anything which would give roots or blossoms to this environment—the colorless "goodness," the efficiency without inner goal, the peculiar anemia deprived of the red blood of Jewish tradition, and transfused with the saline of a political liberalism. Rudi Herz began—also, it seemed, suddenly—to delve into Hebrew, Scripture and Talmud, and to associate himself with an Orthodox community. His parents found him with *tephillin* in the morning, wrapped in a prayer-shawl. He kept all ascetic exercises, and very soon no longer partook of his parents' meals and began to eat from his own plates. He changed from a business clerk into a strict ascetic who sat in the evenings stooped over huge volumes of Talmud. This, however, was not enough. He, like Friedel, found his occupation in discrepancy with what he studied in his books. He quit the career which his parents had chosen for him, and became a farmer. He was one of the first leaders of the farming schools for Misrahi, the Zionist movement of Orthodox Jews. He is now one of the leaders of the *misrahi chalutziuth,* those Orthodox Zionists whose central theme is a movement back to the land and to handicraft and life in co-operatives. Incidentally, he had a genuine inner relationship to art, particularly the Primitives and Renaissance painting. He always had reproductions of medieval altar pictures and of Giotto on his walls. All this belonged to him in a way I cannot define—a Jewish-Orthodox farmer with a Madonna of the early Rhenish School!

Three young people illustrate the doubts which were shaking the young generation, and the various roads which we took. They show the mood of bewilderment and restlessness which had seized a great part of Jewish youth ten years before the catastrophe. They are examples of brave ones who acted as they thought right. For the majority, to which I belonged, the Youth Movement was half play; we followed the line of least resistance. The leader who had converted Erna to Communism became a well-paid business executive in the United States. Today, when I think of the invisible Church, I see those three young people who, during the first grumblings of a cataclysm, followed their pure hearts and remained steadfast. I particularly see Rudi Herz with his ascetic features and his black skullcap, and behind him reproductions of Giotto and Michelangelo.

I was the only other one who had turned to religion. My experience was quite different from that of Rudi Herz, whose parents admired him for his conversion. I too began to live the life of an Orthodox Jew. I got up one hour before school time and, after having said the appropriate form of benediction, I wrapped myself in the prayer-shawl. Then, again with the prayers of benediction, I put on the *tephillin.* These are leather straps to which a capsule is attached. This capsule contains on a small parchment the famous Biblical passage: "Hear Israel the Lord thy God is one. Thou shalt love thy God with all thy heart, all thy soul and all thy power. . . ." It also says, "Take my words well to your heart . . . as a sign tie them to your hand and as a band between your eyes . . . write them onto your doorposts and onto your doors. . . ." Consequently pious Jews the world over, during Morning Prayer, tie these words written on parchment onto their left wrist close to where one feels the pulse; a second capsule is tied to the forehead; another capsule is permanently nailed to the door.

After the *tephillin* have been put on, the Morning Prayer begins with the words: "How beautiful are thy tents, O Jacob, and thy dwellings, O Israel. . . ." The Morning Prayer is a long and tedious affair to anyone who does not read Hebrew fluently. If one attempted to dwell on every word, it would take hours. Actually it has a harmonious liturgical structure, with the Psalms, the repetitive formulas (comparable to Litanies), the "Hear Israel" and the Eighteen Prayers. The latter are a liturgical text which is contained in each one of the three prayers of the day— the Morning Prayer, the Afternoon Prayer and the Evening Prayer. Pious Jews make these three devotions every day. They often do this with astounding rapidity, but not at all irreverently; they get into the spirit of the liturgy without having to dwell on the meaning of each word.

When I first came home on vacation, my parents and Grandfather exchanged glances of bewilderment. I used to get up long before breakfast and, in my room underneath the gable of the house, in solitude I began to put on the prayer-shawl and the *tephillin*. It takes a long time of repeated performances to tie the *tephillin* around one's left arm and one's forehead quickly, in routine fashion. Then the entire Morning Prayer faced me like a huge body of water. The trouble was that I could read Hebrew only with considerable effort:

As long as this soul is in me I thank you, Lord, my God and God of my fathers. Master of all creatures, Lord of all souls. Blessed art thou, O Lord, who returnest the souls to the dead. . . .

Thou who makest the blind see, who clothest the naked, who freest the prisoners, who comfortest those who mourn, who hast made the earth so that it renders all that is necessary to man and also to myself. . . .

Lord of all the worlds, not on the grounds of any virtue of ours but relying on thy infinite mercy. . . .

But we, thy people, the fellows of thy covenant, the children of Abraham, to whom thou hast assured thy love on the mountain of Moria, we, the descendants of Isaak, his only son who was offered to thee on the altar, the community of Jacob, my firstborn son whom thou, out of love, has named Israel and Yeshurun. . . .

Thus it went on, through many Psalms of David to the Hymn of the Celestial Host, to "thy servants of many kinds" who

chosen in love, carry out the will of their creator, they open their mouths in purity and holiness in order to sing hymns and praise the holy name of God, blessed be He. They all take up the yoke of the heavenly kingdom and sing with their creator the holy song of praise. With a joyful mind, in pure tongues and in holy devotion they humbly say: "Holy holy holy is the Lord Sabbaoth, all the earth is full of his glory."

From this it went on to the "Hear Israel." By the time I had finally reached the Eighteen Prayers the end was in sight. To those of my friends who had grown up in the orthodox religion all this was pleasant and they said everything by heart. I had always that dragging sensation. In many places I did not understand the words, and towards the end I was glad to get through. When I came downstairs, nobody was left at the breakfast table.

I kept strict dietary laws, as much as I could in a household as impious as that of my parents. I kept even my own set of china and cutlery, and soon I was surrounded by a cloud of ascetic detachment like a yogi. At dinner after having eaten I would remain at the table and, with a black skullcap, say the long benediction which follows every main meal. They all tried to get up before that, or to look away. They behaved very much like a family of which one member has gone insane. Father tried to see it all in a humorous light and teased me goodheartedly. He addressed me as "Rabbi." Grandfather was annoyed, and Mother was deeply distressed. When she first sent me to the Kohen family, she had asked Frau Kohen not to influence me in the direction of Jewish orthodoxy. Frau Kohen had promised, but she could not prevent the atmosphere of orthodox Jewry from reaching me. And now this! It was as if I had turned on some dark machine of superstition upstairs in my room every morning. That entire world of Spinoza, Goethe, Voltaire, Heine, Uncle Julius, political liberalism, and the Age of Reason seemed to be denied by an act of lunacy. For some obscure and repellent reason I had turned my back on progress. I am sure Mother was afraid I was going crazy.

A family council was called. Uncle Julius made a special trip and the family delegated him to talk to me. He came into my bedroom and told me that all this was perfectly idiotic and impossible. He told me about his trips around the world; there were hundreds of millions of people who believed one thing with absolute conviction, and hundreds of millions who believed another with the same degree of conviction. He told me particularly about his experiences with Hindus and Mohammedans. The gist of it was that religion was a purely relative cultural phenomenon. Anyone who, as a Western educated person, found absolute truth in one religion, must be either insane or imbecile.

I found his argument about the many religions very strong and said that I did not know anything about Hindus, Buddhists and Mohammedans but that we Jews had a special mission in the world. He said: "That's what all the others say, too." The thing that annoyed me was that he did not acknowledge me as an even partner in the discussion, and kept insisting on his age and his greater experience. I was fifteen, and he was forty-one, and therefore he believed I had to listen to him without argument.

It seems extraordinary that, within the Young Jewish Movement, Rudi Herz and I were quite isolated. Those who had become Zionist spoke of the rejuvenation of Jewry, of the reestablishment of a Jewish homeland, of the soil of Palestine, and of the revival of the Hebrew language, as if it were something like the rebirth of Yugoslavia, or Ireland or Czechoslovakia. The specific element of the Jewish religious tradition was missing. Many were enthusiastic Socialists. The Bible, that is to say the Old Testament, came in only as cultural tapestry, very much as if a Scandinavian country were to revive a study of the Edda. Socialism, on the other hand, was embraced with religious fervor, and it represented for most a realm of justice and charity far transcending its actual political meaning.

Equally peculiar was the fact that we were all very much under the influence of Christian writers like Friedrich Wilhelm Foerster and the Russians. Friedrich Wilhelm Foerster is a German pedagogian, very close to the teaching of the Catholic Church. He was a radical Pacifist; so much so, that after the First World War he denounced to the Allied Commissions anything which in the remotest way resembled rearmament, either technically or ideologically. In his pedagogic writings he exhorted young people to a life of heroic virtue, a life of self-denial and sacrifice. On account of his radical pacifism he was extremely endangered by German rightist groups, and it may have been for the purpose of protecting him that the radical socialist Government of Bavaria made him Bavarian minister in Switzerland. Although he was not a Catholic he was in the habit of quoting such writers as Saint Catherine of Siena and Saint Teresa of Avila.

We were even more influenced by the religious writings of Tolstoy, his legends and his folk-stories, and by the great Christian figures of Dostoievsky—Prince Myshkin and Alyosha Karamasov. Friedrich Wilhelm Foerster's heroic asceticism, for example in his *Guide for Youth,* exerted considerable influence on many young members of the Misrahi, the Jewish Orthodox Youth Movement.

As far as my stab at Orthodoxy was concerned, I very soon yielded to the pressure brought upon me by my family. I have a strong suspicion that I used it as an excuse to discontinue Morning Prayer, Afternoon Prayer, Evening Prayer, and the sacrifices involved in the dietary and the Sabbath laws. I had an alibi: it created too much friction and unrest in the family. My faith cannot have been as strong as that of Rudi Herz and that of my Misrahi friends; or I would not have given way. There were many conflicting influences, and I was ready for compromise. After all, not even Friedel Fränkel understood why religious forms and the liturgical life were necessary. Perhaps even my Marxist friends were right; or Mother and Uncle Julius, Voltaire, Heine, the *Berliner Tageblatt,* and Progress.

If I thought that Mother was more accessible to the national ideas of the Jewish movement, divested from their religious context, I was very much mistaken. I argued with her. I said that it was very fine for Romain Rolland or Bernard Shaw to condemn national or racial ideas but that the people in the street and my classmates regarded us as an alien people. It was un-realistic to listen to a handful of European intellectuals, instead of accepting the fact that we were not regarded as Germans in Germany or Frenchmen in France. She would have to admit that Einstein was also very learned, and he was a Zionist. When-ever he was asked for his nationality, he proudly stated he was a Jew. She said she did not care how great a physicist Einstein was; nationalist philosophy in any form, whether Jewish or Japanese, was detestable to her.

I was torn by conflicting motives. On one hand I admired the noble super-racial, truly European spirit of such people as Ro-main Rolland and Friedrich Wilhelm Foerster, which was shared by my mother. On the other hand I thought it ignoble and cowardly not to identify oneself openly and emphatically with a despised minority. There seemed to be nothing very noble about the fact that so many Jews had a blind spot for their Jewishness.

This was in the early Twenties, and in the Ukraine around that time occurred one of the worst pogroms of the pre-Hitlerian era. It was carried out during the course of the civil war in Russia, under General Petljura, one of the leaders of the White Army. Thousands of Jews were killed, among them old people, women and children. We, the members of the Jewish Youth Movement, canvassed the Jewish families in Munich in a campaign to raise money for the victims of the pogrom. In the light of what occurred to us later, I remember my experiences as a canvasser very well. The Ukraine must have seemed very far away; the horrible fate of the Jews struck quite a few of their brethren in Munich as something remote and foreign. Even those who gave me money reacted as if I were begging for victims of a mining accident in South America. German apartment doors have a small window just big enough to allow one eye to look through, and a safety chain. A single eye would gaze at me, and the door would open slightly with the safety chain on. I made my little speech about the Ukrainian pogroms. Quite often, I am embarrassed to say, the door closed again without the safety chain being taken off; one heard a shuffling of steps, and there was no further response. Little did we realize what was to happen ten years later.

5. Franz Burger

THOSE post-war years in Europe were times when the soil of history seemed to be plowed and receptive for any kind of grain. Germany was more than ever a world of contrasts and obscure tension. In the Ludwigstrasse in Munich one saw old generals martially decorated, like stuffed horses on wheels, while nearby in a Schwabing bookshop an etching was exhibited: the Crucified, nailed to the Cross by scoffing soldiers of the Reichs-wehr—"To the Memory of Karl Liebknecht." The teachers were already stuffing us with Nibelungengeist and political sauerkraut.

They all did it, except Franz Burger. He came from the Inn valley near Wasserburg, a region which had always received a stream of immigrants from the south, originally Romans, and much later artisans from Italy. He had been a Catholic to begin with, and I believe he had studied for the priesthood. When I knew him he was estranged from the Church but he was one of those creative, serene-tragic Mediterranean humanists who sow the seed of culture wherever Fate puts them.

He was our teacher in German and Latin. Under his guidance the *Annals* of Tacitus became documents of vital interest. Ovid and Virgil came alive. During the German lessons he read with us the poems of Rilke and Werfel. He even told us about Freud, Adler and Jung, as far as we eighteen-year-old boys were able to take it in. I remember Goethe's *Tasso* with which we did part-reading like actors on the stage, single poems by Goethe, André Gide's *Prodigal Son*, Horace, and especially Virgil.

One day, when he spoke during the history lesson of indus-trialization during the last century and of Karl Marx, an elderly pedagogic official appeared for inspection. Our teacher carried on quietly as if nobody were there for inspection. After that we were sure something was going to "happen," but nothing did. He was admired by everybody, including his enemies.

We knew that there was something sad and painful in his life. His wife was insane, and he kept her at home. Often I visited him at his home, especially later after I had left school, and I shall never forget that weird picture: Franz Burger, the human-ist, in his library, a large room with huge bookshelves all around the walls, a room which exuded an atmosphere of spiritual shelter; and somewhere hidden in a room behind there was a pale, delicate Ophelia who appeared suddenly, when one least expected it. The daughters, Marcella and Melitta, were beautiful, proud and downcast at the same time. Thus, the world of this man who was to make such a lasting impression on all our lives was a strange mixture of Goethean detachment and Dostoievskian demonism—a symbolic image of those post-war years in which we grew up.

During the last years of his life he was seized by some horrible disease, the nature of which was never quite known. He developed a severe spastic condition of his legs combined with cerebellar symptoms. He became very thin. His beautiful head became more transparent and ghost-like, and his deep-seated eyes shone like huge dark lakes. In the few years that were left to him he could neither stand nor walk. But he did not want to rest. His pupils fetched him, on their own accord, every morning in a wheel chair, and after school they took him home.

Thus it went on until his last few weeks. When I saw him then he was bedridden. It was spring, 1933. The Hitler Government consisted then of a coalition which was called conservative, and which impressed most people as an embarrassing episode. Burger gave me then, a week before his death, a peculiarly lucid forecast of all that actually came to happen.

When I think of Burger today a flood of seemingly disconnected impressions and sensations comes back to me. First there was the big handsome man with such a fascinating head that people in the Leopoldstrasse would turn round to look at him. Then there was the man fatally ill, lying on the pillows. On one side there was the German Gymnasium [high school] with its cloud of cultural mist and sweat; on the other was this man who came out of the cloud like a strange, mythical messenger. He instilled in us the religious sense of justice present in those socialists of the early industrial period—Marx, Engels, and

Lasalle; and he used to warn us not to mistake the philosophical materialism of the writer Karl Marx with the moral conduct of the person. "A man who lives in a London attic and saves money for a theater ticket is not a materialist in the sense in which the bourgeoisie uses this word." It is true that most people who understand the inherent evil of the philosophy of historical materialism have never experienced the transcendental dynamism which characterized all early socialists. It was Engels who once said that people think a materialist is a man to whom eating and drinking are the only important things in life.

Burger had one weakness: a secret love for Bismarck. He shared this paradox with many German liberals of his time. Perhaps it was due to the fact that Bismarck was the first man to oppose Kaiser Wilhelm the Second. Alas, those charming Bismarck lessons! Living today in a world of partisanship, forced on us by current events, it is perhaps difficult to imagine the logic immanent in that phase of humanism.

Once Burger asked me who my favorite poet was. I answered: "Liliencron." He was really disappointed, because Liliencron was a Prussian Junker who wrote "healthy" poetry, a sort of provincial Kipling, whose work was pervaded by the smell of horses and leather. Burger would so much have liked me to share his love for the *Duino Elegies* of Rilke, or for Franz Werfel. Like many adolescents, however, I was shy of everything that was twilight-like. If poetry had to be, then I preferred the horses and stables of Liliencron.

It was 1924, one year after the failure of Hitler's and Ludendorff's beer cellar *putsch*. Germany was already in the throes of an infectious disease to which it would finally succumb. Around this time Rilke's room in a boarding-house near our school was ransacked by the Bavarian police. He swore never to return to Germany and I believe he never wrote another German line until his death.

Just as the generals were displaying their medals, our classmates wore daggers, revolvers and arm-ribbons. It is incomprehensible to me that, in spite of their admiration for Burger and their scorn for the Nibelung professors, not one among them adopted Burger's social and cosmopolitan pathos. I gave such fellow-students Romain Rolland's *Jean Christophe* and Henri Barbusse to read; I spoke to them of Gandhi. However, Rolland and Gandhi were "aesthetes" who represented Judaism and weakness to them. Judaism and weakness were expressions of one single thing which they could not define. They appreciated Barbusse, but only as a naturalist painter of battles and of soldierly life. This made it possible to forgive him his social and political conclusions.

It often appears that everything revolutionary has somewhere at its roots an impulse of justice, no matter what degree of brutality it reaches in the end. To be sure there were perhaps a few fellows who were sincere in their protest against the Versailles "dictate of shame." Apart from those few, however, I saw examples of rebellion without aim, of a cynical liking for revolution, and a love of protest and force for their own sake.

Even today, when I think of those eighteen-year-olds, I have the feeling one has while facing a man with some uncanny mental disturbance. The writings of Nietzsche or Dostoievsky or Rauschning about the German "Protest for the sake of protest," and the "Revolution of nihilism" may seem like historical speculations. But I can say that I really saw it operating among the youngsters in Munich during the post-war years.

At that time, ten years before Hitler, there were social rules and regulations about the Jews similar to what one saw ten years later all over the country. Jewish children learned, as a matter of course, to take a position comparable to that of the Negro below the Mason-Dixon line. A friend told me that he and another boy, the only two Jews in the class, always stood apart during recess because nobody ever spoke to them. During a

school trip to one of the lakes there were only two rowboats on
hand; they had a boat to themselves.

It was not quite so bad in our school. It became still better
when Franz Burger became our class professor. One day he asked
me to give a lecture on the Jewish problem. He asked the leader
of the Nazis to prepare himself for opening the discussion. This
leader was a giant of a boy who made a cult out of "thunder of
steel," "Front experience," and dying and yet there was something sultry and expansive about his emotional life; with all his
war philosophy he would read poems about his mother with
tears in his eyes, and faint during vaccination.

I was not looking forward to my speech. My adversary prepared himself with the usual "data" about the "Protocols of Zion"
and such things. One could never know beforehand what "scientific material" he might bring up. It so happened, however, that
the day chosen for our discussion was one of the high Jewish
holidays. Burger refused to change the date and decided to give
the lecture himself while the Jewish boys were absent. Thus, on
the Jewish New Year in the autumn of 1924, while we were praying in the synagogue, our teacher made a brilliant speech in
favor of us during our absence. From then on, our position among
our classmates was even more improved.

In our class at that time there were four Jewish pupils. Three
of these, including myself, were more or less Zionist and one
belonged to the *Kameraden,* the German-Jewish group who devoted themselves to "German culture." It is interesting that the
Nazis were friendlier to the three of us who were "consciously
Jewish" than to the poor lad who gave his annual class lecture
about some German war poet. They identified Zionism with
racial segregation of the Jews, and they were right in doing so.
Therefore, they thought they recognized in all this a part of their
own national ideology and developed a benevolent attitude
towards us.

6. Mother

I NEVER understood why Mother was never radical on any one of these issues. She was not outspoken enough for my taste, at any rate. All her sympathies were with the Independent Socialists and Pacifists. I remember the following example.

We all were deeply moved when the first premier of the new Bavarian Republic, Kurt Eisner, was assassinated by a Monarchist, Count Arco. Eisner, incidentally, was the one who had sent Professor Foerster as Bavarian Minister to Switzerland. He was one of those revolutionaries who are quite out of place in the game of practical politics: I always remember that he wrote an essay on the Ninth Symphony. He was one of those idealistic Marxists with a thin "materialistic" veneer that could be found all over Europe in the early post-war years. He was certainly an incongruous figure in a Bavaria which was rural and petit bourgeois with not much industrial proletariat. However, to Mother and me he was an embodiment of the ideas we stood for. One day, while on his way from his office to the Parliament buildings, he was ambushed by Count Arco and killed instantly. I learned of it accidentally, overhearing a conversation in a street car, and I reacted with the violence of youth in the face of injustice and brutality. I could not understand why the entire world did not feel and think like Liebknecht, Jaurès, Eisner, Barbusse, the radical socialists and the radical pacifists. I was stunned and bewildered to see violence destroying these people; it was like being overwhelmed by the mystery of iniquity. Is it perhaps this utter incomprehensibility which leads young people to accept the Marxian dialectics of history, because by this cold scientific system the disquieting mystery of Evil seems to be explained away? On hearing the news that day, I rushed to the place of assassination. There was a spot of fresh blood on the sidewalk and in front of it a poster: "Proletarians, take your hat off before the blood of Kurt Eisner!" Most people passed by. A few stopped and stood there sheepishly. No one took his hat off. Soon meetings were being held by students of the University of Munich demanding mitigation of the punishment of Count Arco. He was celebrated as a hero and as a liberator from tyranny. Mother felt that they should be as mild towards him as possible. This I simply could not understand; things had to be black or white.

Similarly, although she condemned Zionism on principle, she admired many of my Zionist friends. This, too, seemed illogical to me. There was Reha Freier, for instance. Reha (short for Rebekka) was, when I first knew her, quite young. She was married to a Rabbi. She was beautiful, of a simple Biblical beauty, someone right out of the Old Testament. She represented a type which occurs in every political or religious movement, the sort of person who causes others to despair. She seemed utterly disorganized and full of unbelievably impractical ideas. Although she was a mother of five I am not sure whether she could have fried an egg or made tea. If she did it she might have kept her hat on, even her overcoat—and it would most likely be a man's coat. She was an extraordinary linguist, and she was able to keep an audience spellbound. Her Hebrew was beautiful. When she had, in an emergency, to travel to some Balkan country, she was able to learn, on the train, enough of the language to make a speech. Since she thought and lived on a plane of practical impossibilities, she actually carried things out which no practical person could have achieved. She was the first one to have the idea (long before anyone knew what Nazis were) of getting Jewish children out of Europe and settling them on farms in Palestine. She had this idea before the great American Jewess Henrietta Szold conceived it, or at least quite independent of her. When there was a pogrom in a Rumanian town, it was not impossible for her to travel there and appear before the mayor, demanding that they organize a transport of Jewish children, a special train and everything. It was her strong point to appear before the most unlikely people, wide-eyed and with flowing robes, speaking not in terms of committee meetings and majority resolutions but in the language which King David used in his Psalms. With this embarrassingly naive and direct method she occasionally had stunning success. My mother was fascinated by this woman who presented in every respect the opposite of her own disciplined and spartan attitude.

As a young married woman Mother had suffered a bad attack of rheumatic fever. After Ludwig's birth she showed increasing signs of heart disease. Like so many fragile and sensitive people, she was intolerant towards anything that smacked of self-pity, and much of her ascetic philosophy seems to have been an attempt to overcome her tenderness. This, at any rate, is the way the psychologists would put it. As we see so often in people who have this streak, she drew no line between hypochondriasis and common medical prudence. Thus, when she was expecting Ludwig, she knew of her heart condition but made a point of disregarding it. I remember so well that even on the eve of his birth she worked in the store, lifting bales of cloth. During the early years of Ludwig's life she became short of breath but practiced numerous tricks to conceal it. She would go with us on hiking trips in the surrounding country, or to village church feasts, and would find some pretext to pause and catch her breath. These pauses increased in length. The women of the neighborhood told her to look after herself, but she laughed about it.

One evening in 1923 she asked me to play the piano to her while she rested in the adjoining bedroom. While I was playing, I suddenly heard a peculiar moaning sound from her direction. When Father and I got there she looked at us in a strange questioning way and muttered some incoherent syllables.

Her left side, arm and leg did not move. The doctor told us that it was a case of embolism. Her speech was restored within a few hours, but her left side remained paralyzed. Her left arm remained completely out of action, her left leg shuffled with the typical gait of the half-paralyzed.

The next two years entailed much agony. She laughed and cried more easily than before, and laughing or crying looked like a cramp of the face. She lost nearly all her hair. I had a suspicion that Father and Grandfather were embarrassed about her appearance, and that she felt it. Again she worked in the store. She even made business trips to visit wholesale firms in Munich. She refused to give in, and people had to pretend that there was nothing wrong with her. She had no illusions about the future. Father appeared irritated when she urged him to remarry in case anything should happen to her.

It was during these two years that she drew very close to me. Ludwig was only seven, and she was worried about what would become of him. It was probably then that I got my first glimpse into the meaning of anonymity and simplicity in the face of suffering. In January, 1925, just two months before my matriculation, she and Father visited me in Munich. I told her that the class, probably under the influence of Burger, had elected me to give the valedictory address at the final celebrations. However, I was in competition with another fellow, one of the "parallel class" (there were usually two or even three classes matriculating simultaneously in one school). In the event that I was the final choice, I had what I thought to be a very clever idea. I wanted to go up to the platform and speak to the teachers, parents and guests about the fact that we who matriculated were a chosen lot, chosen only by virtue of the economic or social strata into which we were born. Every pupil should know that, on the same day on which he was born, a boy was born in the slums. This boy might be in possession of the same mental and physical talents, but what would his life have been up to this moment? I intended to continue to describe not the course of our lives up to the solemn hour of matriculation, but that of one of those unknowns who grew up in our shadow. Finally, I would allude to the possible moral and political responsibilities arising from all this. I was very much impressed by this idea. It was quite unconventional, and I thought I was smart. When I considered all the stuffed-shirt professors and parents who would be in the audience, I was frightened by my boldness but the more I was frightened the more it appeared an unavoidable duty. I liked to see myself as a courageous rebel.

My parents were in Munich only for two days. As usual they wanted to go to plays and concerts. The first night we went to hear *Parsifal.* I still see my paralyzed mother there, looking and listening. In the Prinzregententheater the orchestra pit is invisible, especially designed by Wagner himself. On the stage there moved some high-bosomed women and obese men, enacting some sort of unreal slow-motion tragedy. From the bowels of the theater came the wailing sounds of a music whose humid sensuousness and subjectivism is intended to indicate "religion," or something which the artist believed to be religion. It was a strenuous and embarrassing experience. The only bright spot was the interval with sandwich rolls and beer. The next evening we went to see a comedy *The Dead Aunt,* an extremely hilarious play, which dealt with the reactions of people to the death of a relative. Mother identified herself with the dead aunt, and as the evening progressed she recuperated from *Parsifal.* Even on the platform, while saying good-bye, she remembered the dead aunt and began to laugh her distorted spastic laughter. Speaking of the dead aunt, she asked me not to stay one day after matriculation, and to hurry home as soon as I could. She thought my great speech was not so important.

On March tenth, on the last day of the matriculation exams, I received a telegram; Mother was seriously ill and I should come home immediately. I took the next train. Two stations before our home-town I discovered one of our neighbors in the same carriage. He came over to me with swaying gait and his breath smelled of beer. "My most cordial condolence," he said. This is the German stereotype formula of courtesy. It meant that Mother had died.

In small Jewish communities there exists no such person as a professional undertaker. Even liberal communities, which otherwise are lax in formal religious tradition, adhere to the old custom of the "Holy Brotherhood," that is a group of men and women who voluntarily attend to the dead. This is regarded as an important act of charity. In case of the death of a man there exists a group of men, in case of a woman there is a group of women. Their business is to wash and clothe the dead man and keep a nightwatch at his bed during the night he remains at home. In all religions, when it comes to matters of death, even the most liberal groups and individuals tend to retain traditional customs.

The Catholic cemetery was close to the center of the town. The Jews had a small plot of land which was situated on a hill, in the middle of fields, quite far from our town. Everything Jewish was a matter of curiosity and weird fascination to the non-Jewish people. Hence it often happened that boys would climb over the walls of the Jewish cemetery. In order to prevent this the top of the wall was spiked with glass fragments. There was neither chapel nor morgue, it was just a bare plot of land without buildings. The Catholic morgue had a little sideroom for the Jewish dead. As is well known, Jewish custom forbids anything decorative associated with funerals. The dead must be buried in unadorned boxes. Not even flowers are allowed. This serves to stress the fact that in death there is no class distinction, and symbolizes the equality of men before God. Thus, when I saw Mother, she was resting in some sort of unpainted oblong crate. I still see the bare sideroom with an unlit pipestove in the middle, the cement floor, the crate, Mother's face with the mouth a little open, the eyes closed, and yet not sleep-like, with an expression of remoteness, as if looking away from all of us. The funeral was a huge affair. It looked as if half the town had turned out. I do not know how much this was due to curiosity, and how much to the popularity of the dead person.

The cortege gathered near the precincts of the Catholic cemetery, then we walked behind a horse-drawn hearse for about two miles along the highway, then along a dirt road up to the hill. The entire Jewish cemetery seemed full of people; boys managed to cling to the wall, notwithstanding the glass fragments. Somewhere in the middle we were standing, a group of men with our hats on. Grandfather, as usual, was quite pedantic about the details of the ritual. He seemed to conduct everything. The Cantor made a speech which was obviously taken from some book of speeches, and had no personal relation whatsoever to the deceased. Father and I said the Kadish, "Glorified and sanctified be thy great name. . . ." Ludwig was only nine, he was not supposed to say anything. He just stood beside me with his hat on. Then we threw the first clumps into the pit. My grief at the time seems to have been surprisingly short. I had just finished high school, and I had to make a decision about the future. It was a time of transition and of many excitements. When a girl friend in Munich met me for the first time after my mother's death, she approached me with a deadly serious face and stretched her hand out. I had to stop and think for a moment to realize what it was about.

During the following year Grandfather, Father and Ludwig lived in that house like three sailors marooned on an island. When I was at home, it became even stranger. Since I was then nineteen and Ludwig only nine, there was the impression of four generations of men. It was a house of four males who appeared to walk around with an air of aimlessness. When I later read in the medical literature of the behavior of men in high altitudes, the "first stage" always reminded me somehow of us four in that house. In a sense, the atmosphere really had lost a certain amount of oxygen; all this in spite of the fact that we still had Therese, our faithful old maidservant, and Mother, after all, had been quite out of action the last year of her life.

Grandfather and Father seemed to watch one another more than usual. Father told me that he intended to remarry, mainly on account of Ludwig; Mother had asked him to do it. I even knew of some of the candidates. It seemed peculiar that Father discussed all this with me. The fact that his remarriage was something planned for the welfare of the entire house, appeared to make it a business item, something subject to hazards and accidents, and this again reflected on Mother. My parents' marriage had always been one of the fixed points of my childhood cosmos. Now, retroactively, it was made a product of chance.

Finally, after a little more than a year, my stepmother appeared on the scene. She was just about my mother's age. She was a roundish jovial person with a great treasure of affection. Grandfather erected a wall, but she pretended not to see it. I tried to address her as "Mama," which in our neighborhood was a rather formal and stiff way of talking to one's mother. She brought a second piano into the house (she was a piano-teacher), and very soon after her arrival we played the Bach D-minor Concerto and some duos. Whenever during the music anything went wrong, I got impatient and pounced on her; she laughed. But the "Mama" hurt her deeply, I soon found out. Ludwig never called her anything but "Mother," and he meant "Mother." It was quite wonderful to see him so quickly transformed. It was as if patience had returned to this house, patience and kindness and warmth. After a short time that cold element of the fortuitous and accidental disappeared. In fact, at times I had a vague feeling that Mother, our real mother, had been instrumental in sending "Mama" along. Soon I stopped calling her "Mama" and called her "Mother."

II

MEDICINE

7. *Medicine*

When I look back today at my years as a student of medicine in Munich, Berlin and Frankfurt, I see that the true influence did not come from the curriculum of learning but from something outside. Karl Jaspers has pointed out that all academic learning presents one of three elements. First, the pure transmission of knowledge, of factual material. Secondly, the teaching of the Master. This means that the personality of the teacher is truly formative, much more so than a mere acquisition of facts would be. This element is still quite obvious in such subjects as painting and music and sculpture, but it used to be present everywhere. When a medieval student went all the way from Ireland to Paris to study with one of the theological doctors, it was not only because he was unable at that time to obtain it in a printed correspondence course. When Freud traveled to Charcot, he got more out of it than neurology. When Harvey Cushing went to study under Kocher, he experienced more than a course in surgery. There is something, even apart from technical tricks, which you cannot take down in notes. It is a formative principle which disappears with the death of the professor, though one can still discern it in a diluted form in those who belonged to his school. Thirdly, there is the Socratic method, a lively exchange between professor and students; the results obtained are the outcome of that method.

Medical science, at least the preclinical parts of it, could easily be handed out in an impersonal way. In fact, it is being handed out in such a fashion in many schools. However, Medicine is an art as much as a science. It is, apart from factual knowledge, based on attitudes, on intuition and on wisdom.

In spite of the false scientism which followed in the tracks of science the medical schools and the universities in general still had a strong humanist hangover, particularly on the European continent. Therefore it rarely happened that one student did all his studying at one school. There was the ancient tradition of migration. If Medicine were nothing but a compilation of factual material, it would not be necessary for the undergraduate to attend a different school ever so often. Moreover, there was no fixed curriculum. If you wanted to take Special Surgery before you had had General Pathology (although this is an extreme example, and you would be foolish to do so), you could do it. You could learn certain subjects at home from books, and during the time allotted for lectures in that subject you could have listened to lectures on the history of art, or on philosophy. There were hardly any written exams. Therefore it was much harder to "cram" for an exam according to some point system. It was up to the professor to see how much true understanding of the subject you had. Perhaps this was a remnant of an aristocratic way of teaching and learning—aristocratic not in a political, but in a humanist sense. The University was not yet a technical school but a *universitas.* All this had, of course, its discrepancies too; it made for snobbery, and for that false intellectual feudalism which became so sadly apparent when the Nazis were in power. Moreover, since there was no control on attendance you could go and drink beer instead of listening to a lecture. If your father had money, you regarded it as a matter of honor to live like this for a whole semester or two.

However, in addition to all the technical knowledge, the "extra" element of humanity and art made the medical schools lively and exciting, paradoxical and stimulating. In Frankfurt we had as a teacher in anatomy a Swiss with a long, flowing beard who in his free time wrote books on pacifism and on Gandhi. On the other hand, the famous professor who taught us this subject in Munich was particularly interested in anatomy for artists. He produced about two thousand lantern slides of nudes to teach us what he called living anatomy. His taste in art was somewhat strange and seemed to include everything academic and cheap. When he described the relief of the hand, he began to speak of "mothers' hands" and started crying. This happened about once a year. He would strain our imaginative power by as- suming that the amphitheater was the womb, and that we were to "follow him on a walk around." Presently he conjured up some fairyland which would have been, in addition to its didactic significance, an ideal hunting-ground for Bachofen or for Freud. With all that, these experts in their fields transmitted, with a wealth of detailed morphology, a profound sense for *morphe* itself.

In Frankfurt our teacher in physiology was the celebrated neurophysiologist, Albrecht Bethe. On hot summer days he took the entire class to the swimming-pool, and in between swims he demonstrated muscle physiology in the living. There was always a certain amount of improvisation and freedom which elevated the matter of teaching into something creative.

Of all the basic sciences, the most exciting ones were those associated with biochemistry. I was extremely fortunate to re- ceive my chemical grounding from Richard Willstätter, famed Nobel prize winner for his work on the green pigment of plants; my biochemical training from Embden, one of the pioneers in the chemistry of muscle contraction; and my pharmacology from Straub. All these men seemed to be in the possession of dazzling magic when it came to the matter of teaching. When I look back at every one of those lectures, I feel like some old opera addict when he ruminates over his evenings at the Metropolitan. For years I thought that my work would have to be in that particular line of science.

However, I received the strongest and most permanent impression of my undergraduate years through Volhard, the internist in Frankfurt. Volhard combined in an ideal form the three elements of academic teaching which I have mentioned. He had the personality of an exuberant and expansive artist of the Renaissance. He had originally intended to study for the Lutheran ministry, then for a naval career, and finally decided on medicine. He did everything in some strangely large and strong style. He was a perfect illustration for Thomas Mann's type of man in whom health is the force of creation. He had that same intensity of sensory perception, of smell and of touch which Thomas Mann ascribes to his earthbound creative geniuses. He raised a family of ten children (something so rare among the educated that he became famous for this alone), and seemed to be eternally fascinated by women. He tried to remember all the students personally, and those whom he favored he addressed by their first names and with the familiar "thou." He had preserved many of the artistic-intuitive and shrewdly computating methods of the great clinicians of the nineteenth century, and he claimed to be able to diagnose any, even the most complicated type of valvular lesion of the heart, without even touching the patient.

This was no idle boast. He trained us systematically to observe. He never gave any formal didactic lectures (you can learn all this from books) but confronted us with a patient at the beginning of the hour. It was amazing how much one could *see* without examining the patient or without knowing anything about the history. The entire diagnosis and the decisions as to therapy were evolved by some sort of parliamentary method. He planted his questions so shrewdly that in the end we actually thought that we had produced results. He would come in with an air of distress, as if he felt lost about some clinical problem and needed our help. To make it more attractive he used this method particularly whenever he had been called in to consult over the sickness of some "person of high standing" abroad. As a result, no student ever forgot any of his lectures.

Like all great personalities he seemed to be full of contradictions. He is known all over the world for his work on cardio-renal diseases. He wrote the largest monograph ever written on this subject, a truly Teutonic affair of two thousand printed pages. After he had written it all in longhand during his "free time," the publishers lost the manuscript and he had to write it over. He had a profound attachment to the basic sciences associated with clinical medicine, particularly to physiology. Once he made a speech in which he claimed that modern medicine has so wonderfully progressed that one could make diagnoses from laboratory reports, without ever seeing the patient. This from him who was a true artist when it came to clinical diagnosis! Those who did not know him, and deplored the mechanistic trend in modern medicine, were infuriated. He seemed to love everything that could be tabulated or presented in mathematical formulas. Yet he was the only German internist who gave ancient homoeopathic methods a try-out. Even then he was interested in that complex no-man's-land which is now called "psychosomatic medicine," and he wanted me to work in this field later in his hospital.

He was a good violinist, and on hot days he would sit with three of his sons, all in bathing trunks, and play string quartets in his garden. After having incurred his wrath over something or other, we placated him by playing chamber music in his house. He was a staunch conservative, and we used to hate what seemed a reactionary outlook. Yet when the Nazis were in power he was more decent in his attitude towards his Jewish co-workers than several of the professors who had previously excelled by their political liberalism. When censorship was tightest he sent me his portrait with a personal inscription to London—an unwarranted gesture. Needless to say, he was finally removed from office. After the war he was reinstated by the Allies.

When I think of such teachers as Volhard, I seem to know the answer to the problems of academic education. It is solved only by personality in the Goethean sense, by that element of soul added to the lifeless body of mechanical transmission.

After graduation I worked as an interne in Berlin in the neurological department of the Moabit Hospital. Kurt Goldstein, the director of that department, is well known for his brilliant attempts to overcome an atomistic and mechanistic approach in the field of organic nervous diseases. In no medical subject did the mechanistic trend of the machine age have greater and more genuine triumphs than in neurology. If you wanted to think of the "human body as a machine," here you had your legitimate chance, with electro-potentials manifesting themselves in an intricate network of neurons which "fire," inhibit, and release one another. The diagnostic procedure is indeed the same as that by which a garage mechanic finds out where the motor is failing. The greatest achievements in modern neurology are based on a body of observations which underlie this ingenious concept.

However, Goldstein was one of the first to point out that the disturbances of cognitive and expressive functions which follow circumscribed injuries of the brain cannot be explained on this basis. He and the psychologist Gelb had followed single cases of brain-injured soldiers for years after the First World War. They tried to replace the mosaic-pattern of brain function by a different approach; that means that they looked at these disturbances in an entirely new way. The injured man was not a machine with one link broken in a certain place. There were basic modes in the functioning of the mind which were affected no matter what the anatomical localization of the injury might be. The whole thing was extremely involved, and since the atomistic theory of a neuron mosaic had proved so exceedingly useful regarding the "lower functions," such as locomotion and sensation, the main problem consisted in finding a new working concept. Consequently the chief of the department spent hours in discussing rather abstract problems while he was confronted with a patient.

The Moabit Hospital was one of the large municipal hospitals of Berlin, situated in the middle of one of the slum districts. It consisted of a main building with various additional ones, and numerous one-story huts. All this was sprawled over a huge terrain. At times it was quite comfortable to be able to go by ambulance to one of the more remote buildings. The interne quarters were located in the main building facing the street, just one story above the Admitting Office. It was the rule that the internes themselves had to carry out the routine examinations of urine and blood. Thus, every morning at ten o'clock after ward rounds, we appeared in the main laboratory, and under the supervision of an old laboratory technician we did the various routine procedures of boiling, precipitating, staining and microscopy. We envied the senior resident staff who were not obliged to do this. At meals there was a strict order according to which we were seated. At the head of the table there was one of those Chief Assistants who were not married and therefore "lived in." I beheld him only from afar. Then there followed a hierarchic scale, all the way down to us.

The sick people had their contacts in an order which was exactly reversed to this hierarchy. They had the nurses all the time, the Internes frequently, and the remaining staff less frequently—up to the Chief of Staff of a department who would exchange only an occasional word with any single patient. However, the Chief appeared god-like at the ward rounds, encircled by post-graduate workers many of whom had writing-pads on which they marked his sayings. Nearly everybody admired and envied the Chief, and aspired to be a Chief himself sometime. There were also some who just wanted to be ordinary general practitioners. They also took notes but only to learn how to do a good piece of work. In retrospect I realize that I must have regarded these people as "poor fish." To be a Professor was the thing that counted. Among the senior resident staff there were some who possessed a stunning quantity of knowledge about their specialty, book knowledge as well as personal experience. Yet, for some technical or personal reason, they had never attained an academic appointment. Some of them were in the odor of Superior Knowledge; they knew more than the famous Professors. Whatever may have prevented their academic advancement they failed to achieve the Title, nor did they care to go out into practice. They stayed on in the hospital, middle-aged gentlemen, always carrying with them a nearly imperceptible nimbus of resignation and ever so faint embitterment. We regarded them with a mixture of admiration and pity. To linger as a poor relative outside the gates during the Academic Banquet, this seemed to be the prototype of tragic failure, a living reproach against the injustice of society.

All this and our whole life were singularly dissociated from the life of the community around us. The Moabit Hospital was surrounded by endless rows of tenement houses, with overcrowded flats and small, cave-like stores. Wherever you looked there were endless flights of streets with that combination of old brick, advertising signpost, fire-escape and washing-line which, all over the world, is the face of the City of the Poor. There lived the people whose lives spilled over into the hospital. We received them when they were sick or injured or delirious or dying, or when they were bearing children.

When we were not on call we went paddling on the Wannsee, or dancing in one of the open-air restaurants in the fashionable parts of Berlin. When we were on call we invited girl friends, or had parties, at times in the room of one of the senior staff. We talked about science and politics. Experimental Medicine appeared to be only one aspect of Dialectic Materialism. When we did not talk about Science and Politics we discussed one an-

other. This we did incessantly and with apparently infinite patience. Everybody analyzed everybody else. In the world of my
childhood nobody had cared to discuss anybody else's motives.
To be sure there had been such a thing as gossip, quite a lot
of it; but this was quite different. We sat around, for hours and
hours, and dissected with a seemingly detached scientific air
one another's weaknesses, loves, hatreds, aspirations and despairs.

There is a lot of this going on today wherever young "intellectuals" meet. Present-day psychology with its particular idiom
lends itself extraordinarily to this sport. In Burger's time I had
shied away from all modern forms of psychological analysis.
Now we all were inebriated by some miasma emanting from a
mixture of Freud, the Russian novelists, Mann, Gide, Joyce and
others. We were smart boys and girls. Although there remained
nothing mysterious about any given individual, there was actually never an end to our talks. This is the most extraordinary
feature about it. We talked until the small hours of the morning
and began to talk again next evening. We talked and talked.
Whenever we were on duty, and had no work in the wards, or
no girl-friend engagements—we talked.

When I was a small boy and someone in our town stammered
or had a peculiar twitch, I felt compassionate or, more often,
secretly made fun of him. Now when someone stammered or had
a twitch, we felt neither compassion nor mockery. We *knew why*
he stammered or had a twitch. We had him all down. We took
him apart, looked inside, and instantly knew what made him
stammer. Then we left him there and took up the next. One case
led to another, like eating peanuts.

At times, our discussions would be rudely interrupted by a
rap at the door: "Doctor Stern, one apo!" *Apo* was one of the
abbreviated catch-words which made up the intricate jargon of
orderlies and internes. What the orderly wanted to indicate by
"one apo" was that a sick man with apoplexy, brain stroke, had
arrived by ambulance. With a sigh I would grab stethoscope,

reflex hammer and flash-light, and descend to the ambulance. Inside the ambulance the air was sticky, with a mixture of the smell of leather, human sweat and gasoline. An old man was there, covered by a red woolen blanket and tied down with leather straps. When the beam of the flash-light touched his face he turned his head and moaned. I "went over him," as we called it, quickly and with a few movements, to test his reflexes and take his blood pressure. Then I would phone orders in advance to the ward, to have everything prepared. I drove on with the ambulance, fulfilled my duty, and went back to the interne quarters to go on talking.

When we spoke of our patients at all, it was in terms which must sound strange to an ordinary man: "There is a fellow Braun over in building E who has the most peculiar blood sugar curve." "How is Schmitthammer?" "His albumen-globulin ratio is going down all the time." Such answers were often determined by the sort of "research" an interne was doing. The life and death of the people in the slums around us was alien to us and reached us only in small fragments of abstraction. It was rather symbolic that the last thing we saw of a man were little glass slides with colored bits of tissue and a number (his post-mortem number) written on it.

Needless to say that there were some among us who did heroic work, particularly in situations of emergency. But this had nothing to do with the process of de-humanization and mechanization in the medical curriculum which has, if anything, advanced since those days.

The man who made the most lasting impression on me while I was working in Moabit was Ernst Haase, the chief assistant of the Neurological Department. His interest extended far beyond the technical aspect of medicine. Ernst Haase was a rather tall, gaunt, cadaverous man with dark eyes. He had his office right in the slums of Moabit, though he was a highly specialized neuro-psychiatrist. He was a man with a profound social consciousness and that peculiar air of sheer human kindness and wholesomeness which was so characteristic of many of these people. At the same time he possessed what one used to call, in cheap novels, "hypnotic" qualities. In fact he could have been a very fashionable ladies' psychiatrist if he had so desired. I have never seen anyone so much liked by the poor people. When the Nazi revolution came I was certain that he, a Jew with his social consciousness, would be one of the first to land in a concentration camp. When I met him and his family again much later in 1939 in London, I learned to my amazement that he had never been in hiding for a day, not even during the general round-up of Jews in that fateful autumn of 1938. He was never molested; God only knows what protected him.

Twice a week Haase ran a municipal clinic for drug addicts and alcoholics. There I worked as his assistant. The hours were from six to eight but frequently we worked until well after midnight. There I found myself in a strange and extraordinary world, entirely different from anything I have ever seen before. We saw a continuous stream of clients. There were mothers with children who had just left a home destroyed by an alcoholic. There were drunkards, morphine and cocaine addicts, the hopeless, the destitute, those who had cynically and rebelliously isolated themselves, bound to a life of increasing solitude and destruction, and those who had succumbed to the deficiency of a loveless world. This was a cross-section through the darkest layer of the city. It was that fringe of life where human existence is ultimately atomized and surrounds itself with a void, a space of negation. It would take a whole book to describe all this so that the reader would be able to re-experience it. In the middle of this Haase would sit, seemingly unperturbed. He combined the physician and the superb social worker in one person. Sometimes drunkards would suddenly appear on the scene with loaded revolvers. In this sort of situation Haase was at his best.

Haase, in spite of his excellent training, seemed to believe in the scientific aspect of Medicine only in a relative way. He was a keen diagnostician, but apparently he did not believe in the absolute separation of the doctor's profession from that of the social worker. Once he had diagnosed and localized a neurological lesion he wanted to know where the patient's children obtained their supper. At the conferences he looked unashamedly bored. There was a very large area of "research" which he almost seemed to despise. But in that endless stream of misery which flooded the Center for Alcoholics and Drug Addicts, he was like a rock of salvation. In every case, no matter whether it was that of a "better class" alcoholic who now slept under bridges, or an East Prussian village girl who had ended with prostitution and cocaine, he penetrated right into the core of the psychological and social situation. When it came to find the rational solution, he seemed to have unlimited resources of imagination and "know-how." He drew an appallingly small salary for all this but I often noticed, when he believed himself to be unobserved, that he slipped money into the hands of some alcoholic's wife.

I never quite recovered from these experiences. That means that I never recovered the undergraduate's boundless admiration for science and for the absolute sacredness of research. When I returned to Volhard, one year after, I was changed. The graphs, tables and formulas had lost their absolute value. I had discovered the other side of medical practice. Although I had more scientific training later, I never forgot those experiences in Moabit. They seemed to have put the abstract scientific aspect of Medicine into its proper place. It is just one side of a profound and complex development that with many of us science and art in Medicine are no longer integrated. As science in general, medical science has gained in extensiveness what it has lost in intensity. You can perceive the twilight of a humanist medicine if you listen to those conversations of internes about their patients. When "Smith" is described as "Bloodsugar 100.2,

NPN 73, BP 210 over 115 . . ." we get not just a practical ab-
breviation of the clinical chart, but something much more significant. Smith, the patient, has been conveniently reduced to a
formula.

If you had asked me during my student years what my philosophy was, I probably would have answered you without hesitation. I was convinced of the truth of dialectic materialism. I used
to belong to radical student groups, and we were all interested
in such things as collecting money for the famous British general
strike in 1926. There was nothing in the social or cultural sphere
which did not readily fall into the pattern of either Marx or
Freud. There was no disturbance that could not be diagnosed
that way. Theoretically, at least, it could all be remedied. I must
have had a blind spot for most of the deficiencies inherent in
these systems. With reference to the Marxist attitude toward
religion, however, I remember to have entertained certain doubts.
I wondered about that vast area of individual misfortune which
was not determined socially and economically, all that which
modern existentialists call the "marginal situations," injury, sickness, death. There seemed to be a gap somewhere, and there
were situations in which you were left in the lurch. I used to
bring this up from time to time in discussions, but it did not
worry me more than that; it was just a little blotch in the picture.

8. *Kati Huber and Others*

WHICH memories are important for this story; which ones
can I leave out? Let me put together, in any event, those images
which give an impression of happy and carefree years, a time in
which it appears in retrospect as if politics and the social ills of
our time, philosophy and religion were all remote forms of ab-

stractness. Life then was something like the blue lakes, the gay meadows, the bright blue sky of Bavaria.

At the Café Gassner in Munich a number of us met regularly at a certain table for lunch. There was Peter Kohnstamm, son of the famous neuroanatomist and psychotherapist; Walter Seitz, now Professor of Medicine in Munich; Hans Bethe, now Professor of Mathematical Physics at Cornell University and world famous for his theory of solar energy production (later he was chief mathematical physicist at Los Alamos); Erich von Baeyer, cellist, painter and medical student; a few others, and I. A lot of our conversation, in those days, struck us as sparkling wit. I have a dark suspicion that we thought of ourselves as geniuses, or at least somehow set apart from the rest of the student body. It is now consoling to think that in the case of Bethe this was true.

I remember Hans Bethe, Peter Kohnstamm, and myself going on a Sunday trip to the Benedictine Monastery in Andechs for the scenery and the beer, both of which were famous. It was a bright June morning. In the train Bethe began to recite comic poetry and then, by heart, the railway schedule of the Deutsche Reichsbahn which to him was a meaningful symphony of figures. Peter and I were preoccupied by the girls in the compartment. Bethe said: "I wonder how one could come to a quick and abbreviated form of arithmetic with the duodecimal system of the Assyrians and Babylonians." We arrived at Andechs, climbed the hill of the Monastery, sat on the lawn under the old chestnut trees and drank cool beer. The place was crowded with farmers, men, women and children who, in their best Sunday clothes, flocked towards the white church. There was also a stand in the open air at which the faithful bought rosaries, candles, little statues, and pencils with glass beads at one end which showed a picture of Saint Benedict when one held them against the light. By this time Bethe had worked out an arithmetic system by which one can multiply and divide numbers in groups of sixes and dozens as quickly as we commonly do it in groups of tens. He used a round beer-mat made of cardboard to write out the explanation. I felt hopelessly behind Peter's quick puns and repartee and Bethe's duodecimal arithmetic. On the way down we played a guessing game, and Bethe had to guess the word "anachronism."

Many memories of this period have to do with "house music." Chamber music, the music of small ensembles of string and wind instruments or of these instruments in association with piano, has been written by the great masters primarily to be played, rather than listened to. The fact that people listen to it is a complication which has to be reckoned with. In many corners of the world there still exists the tradition of chamber music which is several hundred years old. The initiates speak a common language, they recognize one another by certain mannerisms. After years of experience one can, from their physique and demeanor, distinguish cellists from violists, and oboists from string-players. Cellists always start right from the beginning in their shirt-sleeves, pianists take their coats off after having played a full piece in three movements. As experience grows one knows exactly where and when difficulties and mistakes come in. In a famous quartet by Mozart for piano and three string instruments I know exactly where the violist will come in, one bar too early; I sense it about ten bars beforehand and brace myself for it. I also know to which violist this will happen, and which will remain free from sin; it shows in their faces. A few years ago I said to Mr. Rudolf Serkin: "I want to ask you about a certain technical problem in Beethoven's trio Op. 97 . . ." Before I could name the difficulty, he interrupted and said: "That mordent in the first movement; you play it best as five equal notes."
We often took trips in collapsible boats on the Alpine rivers—the Isar, the Salzach and the Inn. We were usually mixed groups of boys and girls. Once on a canoe trip from Salzburg to Passau

we spent the night in the sleepy town of Braunau. In Salzburg
we visited the Mozart house, and I remember my feeling when
I touched that famous little spinet, just to play a chord on it.
When we arrived in Braunau in the evening there was a man
with formidable whiskers near the landing-place who told us
that we were in the birthplace of Adolf Hitler. This was, of
course, years before the Nazi revolution.

The Brahms B-major trio, Beethoven's B-flat major trio ("the
big one"), the two Mozart piano quartets, the two Schubert trios,
the warm summer nights on the bank of the Isar, the lilac of the
Englische Garten to be stolen towards the small hours of the
morning—all this blends in memory into a poem of happiness.
The stars seemed to stand still, and Brahms' syncopations and
plant-like asymmetries said aloud what the ancient walnut trees
outside the window were saying silently. I had been an anti-
Brahmsian because of my adolescent devotion to Romain Rolland's *Jean Christophe* until the cellist of our chamber music
ensemble, Erich von Baeyer, persuaded me to play Brahms.

Erich was heavy-set, of bear-like muscular build, with a thick
thatch of smooth straw-like hair and enamel-blue eyes. His hands
were characterized by baroque muscular bulges. Apart from his
cello playing, he was an exceptionally gifted painter and an
expert draftsman. When I met him for the first time, he made
a rude remark about the shape of my ears and proceeded to draw
me on a paper serviette. Usually he said very little and, apart
from his good scholastic record as a medical student, there was
no indication that he ever reflected. He once silently climbed a
difficult rock in the Dolomites with pick-ax and rope, and then,
dangling his partner over the abyss, finally said: "Now I have
your life in my hands." This was considered a good-hearted joke,
and it really was. His humor was that of a big dog.

Erich would perch his massive frame on a small chair, and

after having repaired a broken bow with the help of his teeth and a little carving-knife he would begin, sweating and gasping, to play the cello. Presently the chords and melodic sequences of Bach's solo suites would roll through the night. The landlady's room, furniture, knick-knacks and all, were transformed into a huge vibrating organ. In this music there was the sureness, power, lassitude and beauty of nature itself. If Erich had taken up the cello as his profession he would, I am certain, have ranked among the first. Even so he was better than many professionals. He did everything with the keen sensory organic receptivity of an artist; abstraction was alien to him, sometimes interesting and at other times repulsive. He was one of the first students who grasped intuitively the true nature of National Socialism. He did it with his eyes. He went to National Socialist meetings, and came back with a collection of drawings: drooping bellies, fish eyes, and thin-lipped faces.

We became friends from the moment of our first meeting. He reflected too little, I reflected too much; it was, actually, only through art that we understood one another. He was baffled by my conscious Jewishness and at times, I think, he felt it was something similar to what the Nazis had, only on a more intellectual plane. However, he sensed that there was some danger to the values of Europe. At that time there were gatherings of German and French pacifist students in the German-French border zone. Unfortunately these affairs were isolated gestures by comparatively small groups of high-minded people who tried to perpetuate the spirit of Briand and Stresemann. Erich went to these gatherings on his motorcycle, with cello, pencils and carving-knife. He was a favorable representative of German youth because the Gothic beauty emanating from that cello belied the ferociousness of his appearance. However, all he brought back with him were greetings of good-will and a caricature of André Gide.

This was rather characteristic of the numerous attempts to

save Europe which we witnessed around that time. The men of Locarno, particularly Briand and Stresemann, were genuine in their efforts to stem the tide of rising nationalist passion. There were exchanges of lecturers and artists and elite groups of students between France and Germany. However, no matter whether Thomas Mann lectured in Paris or Georges Duhamel spoke in Berlin, or Erich played his cello in a Lorraine village— the seed never sank into the ground. There was a peculiar esthetic remoteness about all these attempts, they lacked resonance among the masses of the people. Just as Cézanne and Matisse were appreciated by a small number of intellectuals while the people in general adorned the walls of their rooms with atrocities from the department store, European consciousness had lost its roots in the urban masses and had become something like an esoteric luxury. In fact, it looks as if this remoteness of true art and the disappearance of a true cosmopolitanism had a common origin. There was that peculiar symptom of double vision, of dual attitudes and ambivalence which is so characteristic of our time. It is a commonplace to state that nationalism is incompatible with Christianity, and that there is nothing more appalling than nationalist Christians. However, we usually overlook the fact that an anti-Christian internationalist, such as Nietzsche, is just as atrocious as a nationalist Christian. Only his atrociousness is much more subtle and sophisticated, and it takes much more to point out the incongruity and paradox of his position. The great Christian mystic Dostoievsky who was at the same time a vulgar pan-Slav politician, and the noble cosmopolitan Nietzsche who at the same time "finished" Christianity in pamphlets which overflow with a unique form of tawdry arrogance, were twin brothers of the nineteenth century.

Some of the leading artists and intellectuals of Germany and France shared Nietzsche's duality. They rediscovered Europe and hated petty nationalism, but their Europe lacked content, it was a vague concept of some sort of esthetic harmony. How could this sort of thing ever have taken root in the people?

However, there was no plural consciousness, none of that complicated intellectual bookkeeping about Erich, who soon invited me to stay as a guest of his family in Heidelberg.

They were most extraordinary people in a most extraordinary setting. His father was a Professor at the University there, a well-known orthopedic surgeon. Among his ancestry there was the most varied collection of names one could find in encyclopedias and *Who's Who*. Their house was situated just above the river Neckar close to the Old Bridge. It was a rather old house, probably the most perfectly decorated private house I have ever seen. Its beauty was obviously due to a slow growth over generations. One of the celebrated ancestors had been Tischbein, the painter friend of Goethe. Furniture, paintings, sketches, musical instruments and books looked as though they were strewn about by a careless spirit, without obvious planning, without the air of the museum, yet perfectly harmonious. All this was the work of Frau Professor. There was a large glass veranda and a sloping garden behind the house. In this garden the students of the University put on open-air performances of Shakespeare.

I usually came for chamber music. If I were unfamiliar with a piece, I was given the score and put in a room on the top floor where there was an upright piano, out of hearing. After being given a certain amount of time to look at the score, I was allowed to come down to the music room. Erich used to have an excellent string ensemble. I remember particularly one violinist, the wild-looking wife of a Russian painter, whom he used to fetch on the spur of the moment from her husband's studio, transporting her back and forth on a motorcycle.

There seemed to be a gesture of careless improvisation about everything. There were always friends at dinner, or "aunts" who were not really aunts. It was impossible to know who really belonged to the family in the strictly biological sense, and it did not seem to make any difference. At times there was an impression of snobbery, for there seemed something planned in the way in which Thomas Mann or Adolf Busch "dropped in," but one was quickly reassured because everybody dropped in. A physics student from a village in Hessen appeared one morning at breakfast, and it turned out that he had spent the night in one of the small rooms on the top floor. I was astonished, but nobody seemed to give any thought to it; the Professor, who hardly ever spoke, asked him with a slight twinkle whether he was satisfied with the bed.

One day when our viola player was unable to play, Erich's youngest brother came from one of the upper floors to substitute. He handled the instrument rather adeptly but vanished after completing his task. When I inquired next day, I was told that he had gone skiing in the Alps. He was a handsome young chap, the child prodigy of the family. He was a nuclear physicist.

In contrast, the oldest brother was the picture of a German professor out of *Punch*—stiff brush hair, metal-rimmed glasses and all. He was a psychiatrist. It was a long time before I heard him say anything. I know that he was a follower of a German philosophy which had its roots in Kierkegaard's existentialism. He worked in a mental hospital and had Spartan habits. The apparent dissociation between the members of the family was remarkable. They all stressed this a little, it seemed to me, as if in willful parody.

One day I had to pass through a room in which a tall young girl was sitting. She was surrounded by big drawing-boards, raw leather, the implements of lettering, and leather tools. She was bent over a huge piece of parchment, doing some lettering in raised gold. I noticed that she was strikingly handsome. She was working without looking up, and in the corner of the room sat a man who silently watched her. Erich said: "This is my sister."

He looked at me and laughed as if he expected me to be bewildered. Later when I walked through the room and nobody was there, I saw that it was beautiful work. The lettering was of strong classical simplicity. The accuracy, the special setting, the craftsmanship showed beauty and strength of creation.

Next morning I saw the girl again. She appeared while I was playing the piano (I thought she had come through the wall), and watched me. I introduced myself in a provincial manner. Her name was Liselotte. To cope with the situation, I asked her to play a duet with me. She said that she got clammy hands at the thought of a duet and that she could not play, but she did play. It was a short and simple piece, the second movement of the fourth Brandenburg Concerto, in Reger's arrangement. When she disappeared again, Erich came into the room and said: "I presume you love my sister."

The Professor was a huge and hulking man, always slightly stooped, with beetle brows which overshadowed his blue eyes like awnings. He came out of his library for short meals and watched his family silently as one looks at an aquarium. In order to appear interested in orthopedic surgery, I once asked him at lunch to explain Perthes' phenomenon of the hip-joint. (I had read only the day before that such a name existed for some very special symptom.) At first he did not answer, which made me feel embarrassed and I looked down at my plate. Presently he took a match box, three matches and a fork, and constructed before my eyes a model of a pelvis with a diseased thigh-bone. He made it move, first in one way, then in another, without uttering a word. I guessed that the first movement was normal, and the second one abnormal—Perthes' phenomenon.

After lunch he took me into his study and showed me a model demonstrating the mechanics of joints. It was the puppet of a Hitlerian storm-trooper who marched and gave the Fascist salute. At that time storm-troopers were still funny. Later I observed that the Professor sat for hours in his study in front of a desk without any book. All of a sudden he would pull out a carving-knife and a few wooden blocks and strings and make a little man. I was told that these little men were models which demonstrated an entirely new and ingenious theory of muscular mechanics. When he was invited to make an official speech at the International Orthopedic Congress he arrived with a large suitcase from which he pulled a number of wooden men, mammals and arthropoda. He made them stand, walk, bend and roll, and he made them do the most astounding things with any given joint.

There prevailed in those years in Heidelberg a rather highbrow attitude of esthetic aloofness. There was a conglomerate of philosophers, historians, and sociologists who seemed to regard the social disease of Europe as one would sit in front of an over-heated bowl of soup. Quite a few people of this intellectual *jeunesse dorée* came to Erich's house. They laughed about Hitler but they talked in a precious and ambiguous way about Hegel, and the "idea of the state." They made round mouths and drew their shoulders up when they spoke. The Professor, like all people of his type, was fascinated by the abstract which was strange to him; nevertheless he had a keen perception of smugness and insincerity. On such occasions he remained silent for some time without moving his huge frame, and it was not even certain whether he had heard anything. Then he would remark that, in his opinion, Germany as a political unit ought to be destroyed. After something like this he usually withdrew to his study.

The dissociation in the lives of the various members of the family seemed to be largely counteracted by the presence of Kati. Technically, Kati Huber was a domestic servant; in actuality, she provided something like a collective conscience for the family. Nobody appeared to know where anybody was at any given time, except Kati. She had the omniscience which hotel desk-porters pretend to have. She was able to tell you that Herr Professor was having a nap, Frau Professor was at the linen cupboards, Fräulein Lisi was doing bookbinding in Schlierbach, Herr Walter was visiting a hospital.

Kati Huber was a semi-illiterate peasant girl from a village near my home. She had come into the family more than thirty years before as the children's "nanny" and she had brought them all up with the same methods of care, reward and punishment which she knew from her own childhood. She had no idea what all these Professors and Doctors were up to, but that did not give her any feelings of inadequacy. Her religious upbringing gave her the conviction, never formulated, that everybody has his appropriate place in life. The so-called "inferiority complex" and true humility are two opposites. She treated fellow-domestics and visiting Nobel laureates to her crude little jokes with naive equality. Her warnings and criticisms were usually given in the form of proverbial "sayings"; many of these aphorisms contained dark and incomprehensible metaphors, and it was never certain how much of this was ancient folklore and how much freely improvised variations by Kati Huber. She lived a life of piety and went to Mass every morning at six o'clock. By the time I knew Kati her strength was already reduced, but she was still an important institution. She was respected and liked by the children, probably most by Liselotte. I felt that Liselotte's anti-intellectual rebellion was in some way intimately associated with her affection for Kati.

Liselotte had left school at the age of fifteen and secretly entered the services of a small bookbinder in the town. Her job was to open the shop in the morning, tidy it up, and to get beer for the master at lunchtime from the nearby inn. She kept this up for some time until her father discovered it, and sent her to a famous bookbinder's school in Weimar. There she was the only girl among craftsmen. Moreover, her colleagues came from craftsmen's families or from the working-class. They were mainly Communists. She learned to look at her own class from down below upward, but in a way different from that of Kati Huber. They became proud of her, and asked her to their meetings. She was taught to discuss the problem of social justice, to drink beer and to sing round-songs. While she learned the craft of bookbinding and lettering from the masters, she also pursued her one favorite study, that of Giotto, Cimabue and Fra Angelico. She went to Italy one spring to study all the paintings on the spot, and returned to Heidelberg and opened a studio for bookbinding and lettering.

One bright morning in 1932, a Whitsunday, Erich and I were sitting at the breakfast-table in the house in Heidelberg. He looked at the cloudless blue sky outside and said: "Let's go to Paris."

We packed a few things and mounted his motorcycle. The roads were white, dusty and hot. In two hours we were past the French border. When we stopped in a village for lunch, we found entire families of three generations in the restaurant sitting around big tables with white table-cloths. The children had starched white collars, neatly parted hair, long pressed pants, and looked like miniature grownups. Everybody had claret with his food.

A buxom woman, the innkeeper's wife, served us. She said in French: "There is not a single French boy of your age who would have a motorcycle like you. We French are economic and careful people. You Germans come over in the most flashy cars and motorcycles, and then you claim you cannot pay us any reparations." We laughed an embarrassed laughter.

At tea-time we arrived in Verdun. I had not put any hat on in the morning and had not felt the sun because of the air which kept whizzing past. Now I had a terrible headache and looked like a lobster; it was a minor case of sunstroke. Because of our experience with the French innkeeper's wife, we tried to conceal the fact that we were German. First we went into a teashop. Then we bought a dictionary in order to find out the French word for aspirin. The dictionary said *"aspirine, f."* However, in spite of *aspirine,* I began to feel every small pebble on the highway. In Meaux I let Erich continue alone and took the train. In the evening we met again in Paris. We visited a Frenchman who had at one time been Professor at the University of Heidelberg. His wife was in the garden behind the house. She was tall and beautiful, with an old wide-rimmed straw hat and a rather old-fashioned costume. I still see her standing there, playing with her children; there was something archaic and at the same time foreboding about her appearance, as in certain paintings of Picasso.

On our way home, after a few days' stay, we stopped in Fontainebleau. We saw an old-fashioned hotel with a plaque outside which said that Napoleon III had dined there. We entered and found ourselves in a big dining-room in the style of the Second Empire. There were many small tables most of which were occupied by old ladies of a peculiar sort we had never encountered before. From their conversation with the waiters we thought they spoke English. Their hair seemed blue, and many of them were sitting alone, accompanied only by lap dogs. We were thunderstruck to discover that the cheapest menu cost what would correspond to eight dollars. I wanted to leave but we decided to stay and eat only soup. The waiter told us that one had to have the entire menu. After a while he beckoned us to follow him, and took us past various *salles* into a small room next to the kitchen. Here there were many men in dark blue uniforms eating. The waiter explained that they were the chauffeurs of the people in the big dining-room in front, only here the same menu cost two dollars. The chauffeurs welcomed us with noisy cheer and explained to us that the people in the dining-room were Americans. They took it for granted that we

were chauffeurs too and asked us whom we drove. I pointed at
my friend and said: "He drives me." This statement was greeted
with great applause, and we were offered wine. The chauffeurs
told us in rapid French a lot of things about the Americans. The
waitress came along and said to us: "I suppose that your masters
in the front room are going to pay for you."

That haphazard decision at the breakfast-table to go to Paris;
the goddess in the garden that evening; the beauty of the house
above the Neckar; the nuclear physicist and the Existentialist;
Liselotte with her bookbinders, Giotto and Fra Angelico; the
Shakespeare plays; the giant Professor with his ingenious toys;
Kati Huber—all this blends together for me now as the last eve-
ning-glow of Europe. One is almost inclined to think that this
could not have gone on; it was tinged with that trace of death
which is said to be immanent in beauty as long as we live on
this earth.

9. *Medicine Again*

FROM 1931 to 1932 I was Resident Physician in the Medical
University Clinic in Frankfurt under Professor Volhard. For
some reason, which even today I cannot understand, the professor had called me back from Berlin and I became Lecture
Assistant. This was a distinction among the Residents. It was
the duty of the lecture assistant to prepare the daily lecture in
Internal Medicine. He had to select the patients according to the
diseases which were to be discussed, or those patients who prevented a clinical symptomatology of striking didactic value. The
lecture assistant was placed like an acolyte next to the professor
in the center of the amphitheater, and he remained there during

the entire lecture. In many universities it was he who recited the patient's clinical history before the professor began to discuss it.

In Anglo-Saxon countries one distinguishes between clinical and didactic lectures—that is, between lectures in which patients are demonstrated and their histories discussed, and lectures in which, after the fashion of textbooks, clinical medicine is taught in an abstract form. This distinction does not exist in German-speaking countries. The two elements are combined. No clinical condition is ever discussed without being illustrated by the demonstration of a patient and a discussion of his history. Therefore the clinical teachers depended a great deal on the sort of illnesses of which cases were available on the wards. This increased the element of flexibility in the academic teaching of medicine, and made the schedule less rigorous.

Every morning at eight I appeared in the Chief's private office and presented a list of patients for teaching purposes. Strictly speaking, it was a list of illnesses. Like a chef who proposes the menu of the day, I would say: "We have today a mitral stenosis, a cirrhosis of the liver with ascites, a cancer of the colon, a chronic pericardial adhesion, and a spastic hemiplegia," and he would reply: "Always the same stuff. Can't you get something different once in a while, not ever?" At nine o'clock the lecture began. The history was read and then the bed was wheeled into the amphitheater.

Volhard had an unorthodox method of teaching, quite unique even compared with other German universities. Frequently the patient was brought in without any preliminary introduction. The professor raised his hand in an imploring manner, glanced all over the audience, and then looked long and pensively at the patient. Presently there was a hush over the big room, and one could have heard a pin drop. The only thing one heard was the patient's breath. This silence went on for several minutes which seemed like half an hour. The master looked as if he was oblivious to the world. Suddenly, as if collecting himself, he addressed the students who had been called down to the floor of the amphitheater: "What do you see?" This was the first sentence spoken and it presented the first words of an involved ritual. There was again silence because usually nobody answered right away. Until the very end of the procedure all technical helps such as X-rays, laboratory findings, charts were banned. We were supposed to be physicians, true physicians in a Hippocratic sense, devoid of all the props of modern technology, and the first act was the act of seeing.

Presently, a voice would rise from the middle of the amphitheater: "There is dyspnea. The respiration is thirty-five per minute." The professor remained pensive and immobile as if he had not heard. Someone else said: "Pallor around the area of the mouth," and again someone remarked: "Club-shaped fingers." Things became more involved when a student in the first row discussed the appearance of the veins of the neck. After the students had observed the most minute details, including the pulse of the carotid and the appearance of the nail-bed and duly described what they had seen, they were allowed to feel the radial pulse. After they had seen asymmetries in the expansion of the chest, they were permitted to feel the circumference of the ribs during the rhythmic movement of breathing. Usually students were allowed to touch only after everything that was to be seen had been seen. It was quite extraordinary to experience the varieties of tactile sensation. There was, quite aside from the world of sight, an entire world of touch which we had never perceived before. In feeling differences of radial pulse you could train yourself to feel dozens of different waves with their characteristic peaks, blunt and sharp, steep and slanting, and the corresponding valleys. There were so many ways in which the margin of the liver came up towards your palpating finger. There were extraordinary varieties of smell. There

was not just pallor but there seemed to be hundreds of hues of
yellow and of gray.

After looking for five minutes, and after sniffing, feeling, listening, the students began to compute the data. This was the great
tradition of classical medicine of the nineteenth century, a sort
of craftsmanship of the senses. Now the diagnostic picture began to arise. The signs became meaningful in their context and
in association with what we had learned about, let us say, the
physiology of circulation or the biochemistry of sugar metabo-
lism. Only when the students, at the end of the parliamentary
discussion, had come to a definite conclusion were they finally
presented with X-rays, graphs and figures.

All this was conducted by the professor, and accompanied by
the most extraordinary histrionics. Other German professors in
clinical medicine, particularly those who had attained international fame, had in their teaching an impersonal, God-like manner, and conducted themselves with pompous solemnity. When
a Geheimrat wanted to show lantern slides, he bellowed "Dark,
please!" and you saw a visible trembling go through the row of
assistants. These assistants were seated on a bench at the
Geheimrat's right hand, in hierarchic order, from the associate professor down to the voluntary assistant physician. At the
command "Dark, please" it was as if the Captain had shouted:
"All hands on deck!" Everyone went into action, at the projector,
at the window blinds, and so on. Then they all fell, in the manner
of marionettes, back in their seats waiting to be re-mobilized at
a word. This atmosphere prevailed in most German teaching
centers.

With Volhard it was quite different. The to and fro of dis-
cursive teaching was accompanied by volleys of cajoling, sarcasm,
flattery, ridicule and praise. At some stupid reply he would wince
as if from physical pain. Yet he retained an amazing degree of
natural authority. This was due to his overpowering physical
presence and his amazing, universal knowledge of detail in

which he was always far ahead of the most widely read among his co-workers.

Curiously enough the patients enjoyed these teaching sessions. Perhaps they were welcome interruptions of the hospital routine. At any rate, there is no doubt that Volhard succeeded. He instilled in us something which one might call clinical sense. Furthermore, by his colorful and highly personal way of representation, he fixed clinical pictures in our memory with extraordinary lucidity. Pneumonia, typhoid fever, various types of cardiac lesions or of nephritis represented not just textbook categories but acquired the vividness of drama. Pathology, "the science of suffering," knows some mysterious and fascinating laws of development, some sort of weird negative counterpart of the laws which underlie growth and creation.

Every day at eleven o'clock there was the clinical conference. The Chief and, all in all, perhaps thirty people were seated at a long green table. The large number of clinical workers was due to the fact that there were always quite a few voluntary assistants, foreign guest workers and visitors present. The professor officiated at the head of the table. Administrative, clinical and scientific problems were discussed in an informal, random manner. All cases of death had to be reported by the resident physicians, and were discussed at length. "Literature" was distributed by the Chief. These were innumerable reprints of scientific papers which had to be reviewed at certain gatherings once in a while in an evening at the professor's house.

I have already said that he loved the extreme. While he had been professor in Halle and already world-famous he refused to have an automobile and did all his consulting practice on a bicycle. However, he insisted on being the only citizen of Halle to ride his bicycle on the sidewalks. For this prerogative he had to pay so many fines to the police that the money accumulated to a substantial sum. Finally, the Prussian police gave in, and he remained the privileged bicyclist. When he came to

Frankfurt he obtained a Maybach, the German equivalent of a Rolls-Royce, with chauffeur and all. Transitions like this, from bicycle to Maybach, were quite characteristic, and in retropsect I must say that they symbolized the atmosphere in which we lived, while working under him, an atmosphere of the expansive and the contradictory.

There was a large amount of laboratory research going on. Volhard had conceived, rather early in the Twenties, the hypothesis that chronic high blood pressure could be caused by a substance which originated in damaged kidney tissue; that the high blood pressure, in turn, damaged the kidney more, thus establishing a vicious circle. This hypothesis was proved not in his clinic but, much later, by the ingenious work of Goldblatt. Nevertheless, the fact that the professor tried to prove a very definite though hypothetical point and that all his experimental co-workers were trying to ferret out a certain chemical principle gave the research department the intensive air of sleuths-and-hounds. At least this was the way he wanted to see it. I, too, by a peculiar combination of circumstances was given a bio-chemical problem for my Doctor's thesis. The specific problem itself, incidentally, was absurd and uninteresting but, even apart from this, I maintained by main interest in Neurology and Psychiatry. All the large medical university clinics had in those days a sub-department devoted to the neurological and psychiatric borderline problems of internal medicine. Usually one man was especially trained for this type of work.

In the Twenties there had begun the interest in what is now called psychosomatic medicine. The Heidelberg neurologist von Weizsäcker was one of the first to emphasize, in a grandly conceived and daring theory, that the dualism of "organic (i.e., anatomically visible) versus psychogenic" in medicine no longer holds, and that in all organic illnesses there are deeply hidden psychological mechanisms at work. When in the Twenties Thomas Mann's *The Magic Mountain* appeared, with its astounding insight into the mental roots of an illness as "anatomical" as pulmonary tuberculosis, there were many medical people who began to focus on this huge uncharted field. Even surgeons, usually the most mechanistic in the profession, congratulated the novelist on his work, and confessed that their outlook on illness had been changed. Of course, all this was strongly affected by psychoanalysis which had for quite some time begun to influence medicine as well as the arts.

Volhard wanted a trained neurologist on his staff but entertained at the same time some vague idea of what one now would call psychosomatic work within the Department of Internal Medicine. For these two things he had me singled out. He called psychoanalysis a *schweinerei* because of its preoccupation with sex, but he did not mean by this to imply a judgment of value. Thus, while he was distributing medical reprints for review and he came across, let us say, a psychoanalytic study on bed-wetting he would say: "Here comes something dirty—Stern, this is for you!"

The evenings would approach on which the papers had to be reviewed. This was done in the professor's residence, and was associated with beer, sausages and potato salad, and with a great amount of leg-pulling and general rambunctiousness. It went on like this interminably, from bone-marrow reactions caused by bacillus abortus to the influence of hypnosis on water-metabolism. The only one who could endure this fare without the slightest sign of fatigue and with what seemed to be mounting attention was the Old Man himself. He followed it all, criticized, dissected, conducted, argued and commandeered—a scientific Jupiter, with an air of omniscience. In spite of this, there was no hint of pompousness, and when we chaffed him, or pointed out some stupidity he had committed in the course of an argument, he roared with laughter until tears rolled down his cheeks. In the small hours of the morning he packed a large number of us into the Maybach, got hold of the chauffeur and took us to a hotel bar in Wiesbaden where he treated us to Rhine wine.

During this time I must have forgotten the social and human approach to medicine of which I had first become aware under Haase's guidance in Berlin. Vólhard himself showed a fervent passion for knowledge combined with a cool detachment when it came to the social aspects of a case. It was the same sort of childlike pagan detachment, almost with a faint note of cruelty, of which Goethe and Leonardo were capable while looking at Nature. When looking at these people it seems as if the laws of truth and the laws of charity lived side by side in mutual independence.

Besides being the lecture assistant, which was certainly no full-time occupation, I worked in a cardiological ward and in the laboratory. The head nurse in the cardiological ward was a blonde middle-aged woman, an ardent Catholic from Westphalia. She devoted herself with extraordinary fervor to the welfare of each patient, and I remember that I had an awkward feeling in her presence. I know for certain that I felt her silent disapproval of our jovial "scientific" detachment. She was, although not really related, more or less like a member of the household of Professor Friedrich Dessauer, the famous leader of German Catholicism. There was another person, a senior physician, Doctor Hildebrand, incidentally also a Catholic, who showed a very human approach in his work in the ward. Although there was perhaps nothing heroic or extraordinary about all this, and it was less impressive than what I had experienced in the Center of Alcoholics in Moabit, yet it all is prominent in my memory because the general atmosphere, to which I myself contributed, was "scientific" in a "superior" manner.

Professor Dessauer was one of those incredible figures who arose in Germany during the sunset of German history, just before the present night fell. He was chairman of a "Department for Physics Applied to Medicine"; today we would call it a department of biophysics. In those days his establishment was unique in Germany, perhaps in the world. It occupied itself with all those aspects of research which lie on the borderline between physics and medicine. He had been one of the early pioneers in the field of X-rays and radium. However, he was one of those encyclopedic German types and could, without any difficulty, in fact with equal facility, have been chairman of a department of Physics or of Medical Therapeutics or of History or of Political Science or of Economics. He was a member of parliament in the Catholic Centrum and belonged to the parliamentary nucleus of that party. He was deeply religious, a mystic and ascetic. He was a thin and fragile man with a huge dome-like forehead. Like all the earliest pioneers in the field of very hard electromagnetic waves, he had acquired cancer of the exposed parts of the skin. Thus his hands and face were withered, and when one first saw his tremendously high wax-colored cranium, surrounded by a wreath of brown curls, the hollow face resembling that of a pale starved child, with deeply set intense eyes, and his thin, tapering, truly cadaverous hands, one had the experience of something almost purely cerebral with a trace of physical appendage. In contrast to this he had a strong, warm, mellow voice, and hearing him speak on ultraviolet rays or on Christian socialism, one could not get rid of the feeling of a friendly apparition.

He had a truly overwhelming power of oratory. While Volhard was at his best in a small circle of students whom he seemed to mold by sheer physical action, an artist and creative improviser, Dessauer made his greatest impression in formal lectures to a large audience in a big auditorium. Even people who had never been interested in physics or in political science or in history sat on the edges of their chairs and forgot to sneeze or cough. I shall never forget a lecture on cosmic rays. He had built some contraption in which gamma rays of cosmic origin could be registered by a Geiger counter. The click of the counter was amplified by a loudspeaker. I still see the eerie apparition (the "Professor" out of a story by E. T. A. Hoffmann) from whom emanated the oratorical flow of a scientific Bossuet. He interrupted his speech; the audience sat motionless in absolute silence; and every minute or so a click was heard over the loudspeaker, a friendly little tap from outer space.

This was less than one year before Hitler came into power. Professor Dessauer, one of the leaders of a democratic Catholicism, was then very much exposed, and his complete and utter fearlessness in all his public political appearances was in striking contrast to his physique. He was not only a profoundly religious Catholic but also, I believe, the descendant of a Jewish family which had been converted a few generations before. Any storm-trooper could have annihilated him with one hand and, later, they nearly did.

In spite of such vivid impressions in my immediate surroundings, I was not in the least influenced by them. On the contrary, I maintained what I now think was a very foolish and unrealistic philosophical attitude. I remember particularly a conversation with one of my friends who was engaged to the daughter of one of the refugee Menshevik Russian leaders. While I again held forth on the principles of dialectic materialism, he told me a few very concrete things which happened to his fiancée's family under the Bolsheviks. I shrugged my shoulders with a "That's too bad" attitude, and pointed out to him that there is "no surgical operation during which there must not flow a certain amount of blood." To think that I, who had never made the slightest material sacrifice for any one of my numerous convictions, said that. However, I was soon to get a first-hand experience of the inner dialectics of modern revolutions, at the receiving end.

In those days I was greatly disturbed by the lukewarm attitude of the leaders of liberal thought in Germany. Perhaps I felt that National Socialism could be counteracted by a radicalism of equal violence. While recovering from an attack of influenza early in 1932, I collected my wits and wrote a letter to Thomas

Mann. I remember its contents very well; I must have felt a great deal of disquietude at that time. I started out by praising his lucid rationalism. This was the more remarkable, I said, since he had apparently been sorely tempted by the magic of German romanticism and irrationalism (which was quite clear from the things he had written on Wagner). I indicated that he had succeeded in coming back to rationalism but not to the rationalism of the French thinkers of the eighteenth century. His rationalism was tried in the fire of German irrationalism of Wagner and Schopenhauer and purified in all those currents which had contributed to the rise of Nationalism. His was a return to rationalism on a higher level, a phenomenon which showed the spiral movement of history. In retrospect this part of my letter sounds to me like sophisticated apple-polishing, but I am sure it was meant sincerely at the moment. However, I then proceeded to take the famous man to task for his ambiguous attitude in all questions pertaining to the social revolution. I wanted him to commit himself. I pointed out that there was a parallel between the cultural skepticism of Freud and that of Karl Marx. Since Mann had recognized the great purgative element in the former, it would be only fair to recognize it also in the latter. I told him how distressed I (one of his admirers) was to see that in the *The Magic Mountain* he lumped Marxism together with Catholicism by presenting them in one and the same person, Naphta, an unsympathetic person at that. How could he! And he presented his own political philosophy in the pleasant, humane and humanistic person of Settembrini whose European liberal attitude was as far removed from Marxism as from Catholicism. This, I thought, was highly unfair to Marxism, and it was this sort of thinking which had contributed much to the misery in which Germany found herself at the moment.

It was not long before I received a lengthy reply. Although Mann wrote most of his letters in longhand, this one was typewritten; he explained this by saying that he was recovering from an attack of influenza and had dictated the letter. Since I have forgotten most of the contents of his letter, it is even more interesting to note what I remember. First, I remember that the famous man called my letter very intelligent, and he hoped he would meet me sometime personally. It is not difficult to see why this should have impressed me. Second, he remarked that people got erroneous ideas of his position on certain questions because he also changed his standpoint as time went on. He quoted, somewhat cryptically, Goethe who once said that "when people think I am still in Jena I am already in Erfurt." Third, he indicated, though I do not remember the context, that "the Catholic Brüning might still save Germany."

It was around this time that Professor Volhard decided finally that I should go away for post-graduate studies in Psychiatry and Neurology. Thus, in the summer of 1932 I went to Munich to work as a Rockefeller Fellow at the German Research Institute for Psychiatry.

10. *The Psychiatric Institute*

THE German Research Institute for Psychiatry was a tall building, modern after a fashion, situated in the outskirts of Munich. Its grounds adjoined those of a general hospital. Its wards were actually located within that hospital, and the building of the institute proper was entirely devoted to research. It was a so-called Kaiser Wilhelm Institute. The Kaiser Wilhelm Society was the largest German association for the support of research, comparable in many ways to the Rockefeller Foundation. It supported research in fields as far apart as plant physiology, eugenics, nuclear physics, and psychiatry. This particular institute was the first institute for psychiatric research, I believe, anywhere in the world. It had been founded by Kraepelin, the patriarch of classical descriptive or "school" psychiatry. Very early Kraepelin had conceived the idea of combining under one roof all those branches of science which he regarded as ancillary to psychiatry. Consequently the Deutsche Forschungsanstalt für Psychiatrie mirrored in its very organization the scientific approach of the turn of the century towards psychiatry. On the ground floor there were the offices of the clinical department and those of the department of genetics, the science of heredity. On the second floor there was a department of Serology and a department of Spirochete Research. The entire third floor was occupied by the department of Neuropathology, devoted to the microscopic study of the abnormal human brain. On the fourth floor there was a department of Biochemistry. There was something cosmopolitan about the place, interwoven with a quaint Teutonic element. The cosmopolitan atmosphere was due to the fact that the institute, particularly its neuropathological department, enjoyed an international reputation and attracted research fellows from many countries.. At one time we had guests from the United States, Canada, Brazil, Scotland, Poland, Czechoslovakia, Switzerland, Turkey, Estonia, Spain and Sweden. Although a part of the Kaiser Wilhelm Society, the institute had received its financial foundation from James Loeb, the American banker of German-Jewish extraction, and from the Rockefeller Foundation. In addition to this, the head of the department of biochemistry was an American scientist who conducted its proceedings by proxy, and appeared only on visits. All this gave to the place the air of an enclave of pure science, free of national and political boundaries. On the other hand, in marked contrast to it were certain German elements, particularly in the department of genetics and in the clinical department. Ever since the end of the last century, all those people who had been attracted to human genetics had some affinity, conscious or unconscious, with a biological, racist outlook on human affairs. Racism presupposes that a man's way of living is largely determined by some innate qualities which he receives from his ancestors; hence there exists in this world noble and mean persons, not by their free choice but on the basis of the chemical structure of their chromosomes. Marxism, on the other hand, postulates that a man's conduct is determined largely by the social and economic qualities of the environment into which he is born. In either case man's freedom is denied, in the first by some intrinsic principle, in the second by something outside ourselves. Consequently there were, even before Hitler, in the genetics department some scientists with a geneticist bias which had originated in the racist, anti-semitic literature of the Nineties, just as there had been in Russia, even before the Bolshevik revolution, geneticists with an environmental or Lamarckian bias. In either case the persons had not become racist or Marxist as a result of their scientific findings, but had gone in for human genetics because of a preconceived political idea.

The clinical professor was a thin short man with dark piercing eyes and a sharp profile which somehow conveyed the tension of a half-opened pocket knife about to snap. There was something Spartan-soldierly about him which covered a delicate sensitive core. He was known to have in his possession a collection of German romantic poetry in neat flexible Moroccan volumes. He belonged to the so-called phenomenological school of psychiatry which is derived from modern German philosophy. Its central idea had something to do with the question of how much one can understand a patient's actual, conscious mental symptoms by re-experiencing them, by putting oneself into the sick person's mind, so to speak. It emphasizes a sharp distinction between this method, and the method of interpretation of symptoms. Therefore, it set up a marked contrast to psychoanalysis. Although this school was theoretically interesting and more important than it would seem today, it remained completely sterile from the point of view of the treatment of patients.

The professor of genetics was a square heavy-set individual, with a chunky head, white brush cut and white goatee. He had done some interesting work way back in 1910 on the heredity of insanity. Ever since then he had apparently lived on his reputation. However, many years before anyone knew anything about Hitler he had begun to advocate the sterilization of the mentally afflicted. Curiously enough, this seemed originally not altogether incompatible with his Swiss Protestant background. It is quite possible that he had conceived it not only as scientific (which it was not) but also as humanitarian and philanthropic.

On the staff of the genetics department was Doctor Leo Mager. He was slim, blond and blue-eyed. We knew that he belonged to the Nazi Party and had a "low number," i.e., a party card number which indicated that he had been one of the early Nazis. It was rumored that in the event of Hitler's seizure of power he was slated for a very high position, probably Minister of Health of Bavaria. His blue eyes had a peculiar staring gaze, he walked with a stiff staccato gait, looked Nordic, and behaved in general like a ham actor impersonating a Nazi. He refused to sit at a table with me or any other Jewish doctor, and when I entered he left the room. He had, incidentally, developed a mysterious theory on the origin of certain diseases, and had been given a considerable research grant to prove it. He claimed that the distribution of these diseases was related to geological properties of the land. His research grant included large traveling expenses, and he drove all over Germany, sampled soil, and drew complicated maps in which he indicated graphically the incidence of sicknesses in the population, on one hand, and certain properties of the soil on the other. The relationship seemed to become more complex as his research progressed, the figures and maps were hard to understand, at least to me, and even to this day, whether his theory is valid or not, in my mind it remains associated with his theories on the influence of the Jews, or the Freemasons, or the Catholics on world history.

There was another man in the genetics department who fascinated me in the beginning, merely by his appearance. Doctor Schulz was short and round, with a huge pumpkin-like head, and enormous cheeks which were furrowed by parallel saber scars, tokens from his student years. He had jug-handle ears, and the way in which his jowls protruded in the direction of the shoulders gave the impression that he had no neck. I often watched him saunter through the corridors, with his feet turned outward in a Chaplinesque manner, and I used to watch the foreign doctors' reaction to this apparation, the caricature of German Academic Man. In the doctors' dining-room he always sat beside Doctor Mager, and therefore I began to associate the two in my mind. Doctor Schulz was quite aware of his appearance; he claimed that he owed his life to it. During the First World War, he told us, his company was smoked out from a dug-out by a group of French soldiers, and every German emerging from the entrance was bayoneted. However, when Schulz appeared, the French said: "Voilà, un cochon!" and let him live.

The chief of the department of research on spirochetes, Professor Brosam, was the example of a true specialist. Spirochetes are delicate silvery microorganisms of corkscrew shape, and one variety of them is the infectious agent of syphilis. It was said that the professor knew by heart five thousand references in the literature on spirochetes and from talks with him I am quite prepared to believe it. But he did not seem to think or talk about much else. His appearance was the opposite of the delicate structure to which he had devoted all his life and energy. He was huge, with a bald round head, a face that looked as if compressed by a blast, and an accidental vegetation of mustache. His limbs were enormous, and his long arms seemed to dangle uselessly when he was not making microscopic slides. He had huge animal colonies and spent night after night working in the animal house, infecting little beasts with syphilis; I never found out exactly for what purpose. He once had invented a stain for spirochetes in the brain which subsequently had become world-famous. As happens so often, his name became identified with the field in which he had gained his reputation, so that in the end the matter of creativeness became completely irrelevant. In his case there was something bizarre and uncanny about it.

On one occasion, one of our clinicians discovered a little ferret in his basement. Not knowing what to do with it he gave it as a present to Professor Brosam. This seemed reasonable enough because Brosam was the only one with large-scale facilities for animals. Half a year later Brosam read a paper at one of the medical meetings which began with the remarkable statement: "About six months ago one of my colleagues had the great kindness to hand me a ferret which he had found in the basement of his house. There I was, confronted with the problem of how to make the best and most extensive use of this animal. After deliberating for two days, the idea occurred to me that I could infect it with syphilis." It had taken him two days.

I had my own headquarters in the department which was devoted to the microscopic study of the sick human brain. This was the part of the institute in which I was supposed to begin my career. I was made assistant to the head of that department, Professor Spielmeyer, on the terms of the Rockefeller grant. Apart from having to do research on "Idiocy" and "Circulatory Disturbances," my main duty was to instruct the research fellows. There was a spacious bright laboratory with comfortable glass-topped working tables. There were a certain number of guest workers from various countries, and each was allotted a certain amount of space, a microscope and other facilities necessary for this kind of work. After an introductory period of training, I had, for a large part of the day, to wander from microscope to microscope in order to instruct the guests. Frequently there were not two from the same country.

Doctor Adam Opalski, now professor of neurology at the University of Warsaw, had his working place next to mine.

Opalski was a short, squat, muscular man, and most people might have spotted him as Slav but would have mistaken him for a cavalry officer. He made an extensive study of the abnormal anatomy of the ependyma (the inner lining of the brain), and for this purpose studied microscopic sections from two thousand cases. Except for certain areas of the cortex, i.e., the surface of the brain, which resemble one another too closely, Opalski was able to identify any area of the brain under the microscope. To him this was something like a sport, and at times he did it on the basis of bets. Soon he taught me to do the same; in fact, most of what I know about the normal microscopy of the brain I owe to him. Later, he and I staged competitions of this kind for the benefit of the guest workers. He would glance into the microscope, at a medium or high-power magnification, slap the bench, and say: "This is the small-celled part of the anterior nucleus of the thalamus" (a certain area in the interior of the brain). He was one of those people gifted with an almost mysterious sense of morphe, the structure of created things. His brother was professor of astronomy, also in Warsaw, and he himself was able to translate in his mind all these plain microscopic sections into three-dimensional concepts with a functional meaning.

The brain, like any other organ, consists of microscopically small particles, the cells. Unlike other organs, for example the liver, the appearance and function of these cells is not the same in any two different spots. There are about two billion nerve cells in the superficial layer of the brain alone. Each one of these cells looks approximately like an octopus. It has a body with a nucleus, and processes which resemble tentacles. Frequently one of these processes is much longer than the remaining ones. In this case, it is usual that the short tentacles conduct nerve impulses *towards* the cell body, and the long tentacle conducts them *away from* the cell body. In other words, each single cell can be compared to a sort of telephone center. The short processes receive incoming calls, the long process sends a call along to another cell.

If a person does something simple, for example, if he moves his little finger, a large set of these cells in the brain is required. If one tried to describe the wire connections which correspond to such a thought and its transmission to the muscles of the hand, one would have to write an entire book. Such a motor impulse going out from the brain *towards* the muscles of one's little finger is continuously accompanied by reports from these muscles coming into the brain. This means that, while the little finger is moving, reports are being received by the brain about the position of the finger joints, the tension of the muscles, and so on, at any given moment of the action. In fact, the brain cells are able to send proper orders out into the executive organs (in this case the muscles of the little finger) only if they receive continuous incoming calls about how the orders are being carried out. From this little example alone it can be seen that the wiring must be of infinite and wondrous complexity. In fact, even people who have never worked in this field will readily understand why so many research workers in the medical sciences throw themselves into their work with a selfless fervor which resembles religious devotion. In the department of neuropathology there were not only psychiatric and neurological guest workers but also pathologists, that is, people who devote their work to the study of morbid anatomy. The normal and abnormal anatomy of the brain is so complicated, and particularly the methods of investigation are so involved that most anatomists refrain from dealing with it to any extent unless they have been trained specially for this task.

When I walked from one microscope to another, I traversed immeasurable distances as far as the people with whom I had to deal were concerned. There was, for example, a Japanese animal pathologist from Mukden who studied a peculiar form of brain disease occurring in silver foxes. I shall have to talk more about him later. Next to the Japanese was a Nazi psychiatrist from Northern Germany. Once a week we assembled with the clinicians in an amphitheater, microscopic slides were projected onto a screen, and I had to discuss them.

The chief of our department, Professor Spielmeyer, and the chief of the serological department, Professor Plaut, formed the counter-balance to all the Teutonic elements. Both were scientists in the better sense of the word, open and cosmopolitan. This had not always been so, at least not in Spielmeyer's case. Shortly after the First World War he had made a remark in the foreword to a textbook which had been generally interpreted as bitterly nationalist. But since then he had broadened more and more so that he actually arrived at detesting any form of narrow provincialism. Professor Spielmeyer, a tall, lean man with fair hair and blue eyes, came originally from Northern Germany. Plaut was from an old Southern German Jewish family. It was Plaut who had been closest to the great Kraepelin and had accompanied the latter on a famous world tour which led them to visit almost all psychiatric centers, including lunatic asylums on tropical islands. Spielmeyer had been on lecture tours in North and South America. It was due to all this that Spielmeyer and Plaut, the two friends, had succeeded in creating that undefinable atmosphere which goes with the catholicity of science.

One of the Rockefeller fellows in the biochemical department was Lydia Pasternak, daughter of the Russian impressionist painter, who had been one of the intimate friends of Tolstoy. He was the first to illustrate *War and Peace* and *Resurrection*, in close collaboration with Tolstoy himself. The walls of the doctors' dining-room were decorated with several lithographs by Leonid Pasternak, signed by the painter himself. One of these lithographs was Tolstoy's portrait.

It must be obvious that the doctors' dining-room was an unusual place. When I come to think of it, it seems quite remarkable now that nobody ever talked shop. But I learned the most varied things there. Doctor Essen-Möller, an unbelievably tall and bald-headed Swedish clinician and geneticist, now professor of psychiatry in Lund, introduced me to the after-dinner sport of lifting a raw egg up from the floor with the aid of a dessert spoon. He and Lydia Pasternak, neither of whom spoke German as their mother tongue, composed ingenious poems in the style of Christian Morgenstern, a profound German mystic, who has written poetry of a bizarre childlike humor, somewhat like Lewis Carroll. Some of the clinicians used to sit over their coffee in what, to me now, seem like endless huddles about Kierkegaard and existentialism. I can still see American doctors from the Mid-West, a doctor from Brussels, and a Chinese psychiatrist from Peking sitting in on this with an expression of open curiosity, but I found out that in spite of the heavy Teutonic terminology they actually understood what it was all about.

The most extraordinary phenomenon (I had occasion to recall it later in all its details) was a couple of Nazi doctors from the Rhineland who held forth on the so-called "Theory of Permanent Revolution" of Trotsky. This theory was familiar to me from the "political" activities of my student-days but that it should be expounded by these people was something entirely new and quite astonishing. After listening to their discussions a few times I said: "Gentlemen, I understand that you draw a good deal of your theory on political strategy from Trotsky. Does it not strike you as extraordinary that you—Nazis—quote Trotsky, a Bolshevik and a Jew, as if he were your evangelist?" They turned to one another, laughed, and looked at me as one would look at a political yokel (which I was). That their reply should have been such a revelation indicates our political naiveness at the time. To begin with, they belonged to a then quite powerful wing in the Nazi party, which was in favor of an alliance of Communist Russia and Nazi Germany against what they called Western Capitalism. They claimed that very few of the Nazi leaders were really anti-semitic, and that anti-semitism was quite consciously used merely as a political tool to obtain the support of the petite bourgeoisie. It was quite possible, they said, that Hitler took his anti-semitism seriously but most Nazi leaders were not even interested in the Jewish question and employed it only in the way indicated. As to Bolshevism, it was the same. The anti-Bolshevist campaign was initiated only in order to obtain support from big industry, particularly in France and England. From this they proceeded to develop their own dialectics, which were, in an eerie and weird fashion, similar to, and yet slightly different from, those of Marxism.

I cannot quite understand today why this overwhelmed me. I had already dimly perceived a change in the image of Communism. It was as if the original passion for justice, that religious sense of identification with the poor which had been so apparent in figures such as Henri Barbusse and Vera Figner, had given way to something new and altogether opposite. Another generation seemed to have arisen, scientifically-trained engineers of destruction. The means had become the end. Ernst Haase had already told me, from his experience of close contact with Russians, that a new social machine was no longer related to the thirst for justice which had, at least in part, underlain the social revolution. We did have a vague idea of things which, a few years later, first came into the open in André Gide's book *Retour de l' U.S.S.R.* But only here, in the doctors' dining-room, and in conversation with Nazis, did all this crystallize into a simple insight. It was extraordinary to listen to these cold, thoughtful lectures. All that remained was the most cynical Machiavellism; when one was not listening very carefully, one was never quite sure whether they were talking Nazism or Bolshevism, and in the end it did not matter much. This experience was startling and has remained with me until today. I was not at all surprised at the Non-Aggression Pact in 1939, and I was extremely surprised when the German-Russian war was interpreted in the American press in 1941 as an ideological war.

It also seems in retrospect so obvious that a cold intellectual approach to matters which are actually of the spirit is one of the deadly sins of our time. There we were sitting, talking away, on Kierkegaard, on Existentialism, on Dialectic Materialism, but without the moral decisiveness, the *raison du cœur* which all these questions demand. Most of us lived the same life, a life of libertinism and *laissez-faire,* and therefore any subject on which we touched in our intellectual pursuits became equivocal, amorphous and meaningless. One can see precisely the same thing now among many intellectuals in North America. Many of the people in that dining-room were later forced by fate to make a moral decision, to live a heroic life and (in some cases) to die a heroic death. But it took much time and agony.

Not at all sophisticated or Machiavellian was the Communism of Herr Eisinger. Eisinger was the chauffeur of the institute. He had a tower skull (an abnormality not infrequent among the Alpine races) which gave him, falsely, a feeble-minded appearance. His task was to drive the chiefs in a limousine, and to run errands between the institute and various hospitals and firms of supply. He growled like a bear whenever he was given an order. He was quite open with me, and whenever we drove into town together he was more talkative than usual. Eisinger gave me a clear and precise forecast of the political future of Europe. While we were transporting jars with brains through the magnificent Arch of Victory and Leopoldstrasse towards the Institute he explained to me that it was a good thing that England and France rearmed. If they did not, and Hitler came to power, there would be war. He spoke a broad Bavarian idiom. He told me that quite a few of the professors at the Institute were *rindvieher* (cattle) and implored me not to believe them. He also told me that he and the Herr Cooperator (assistant parish priest) of Sendling were on the Nazi blacklist. It seemed that the S.A. District

Leader of Sendling, a Munich suburb, had informed Eisinger that he and the assistant parish priest would be shot on the first day of the seizure of power.

11. *Herr Eisinger*

I MUST have done something to my back at the time, I have forgotten what. At any rate I was lying on my stomach with a couple of electrodes for diathermy over my back when another patient in the physiotherapy department of the Schwabinger Krankenhaus said: "Hitler has become Reichschancellor." This seemed to be a statement of utmost importance, and my first reaction was to get up from the table, go home and pack, or at least do something about it. But since nobody in the room seemed to get as excited about the news as he should have, I remained quiet.

I had a feeling of tingling warmth in my lumbar area, and I pretended to go on dozing. The physiotherapist, an old man with a round peasant face, made a few dark hints to me. At first I did not understand, but during subsequent diathermy treatments he indicated that the Bavarian youth in the Alps were prepared and ready to get going. They were secretly organized and armed to defend Bavaria, and put "our king" back on his throne. They just waited for their password to be given and Hitler did not stand a chance. The more often he spoke about it, the more detailed did his account become; and gradually I also began to see the boys with rakish green hats adorned with woodcock feathers secretly gathering near the mountain lakes by moonlight. Incidentally, he did have something there. In March, 1933, it was a question of a few hours and the Crown Prince Rupprecht would have been proclaimed king by a *coup d'état*.

Bavaria would have become a Catholic monarchy separated from a Hitlerian Reich. However, all monarchists seem to be as thoughtful, slow and methodical as my friend in the physio-therapy department, their techniques are not as up-to-date as those of their adversaries, and the final outcome is well known.

Gradually, the Institute began to show changes. At the first scientific meeting Brosam gave a lecture. The topic was syphilis, and the professor said it was historically certain from the Old Testament that Moses simply killed off all patients with venereal diseases. A more humanitarian attitude towards the sick came with the ascent of the Aryan peoples. At the mention of Moses everybody glanced furtively at Professor Plaut whose appearance, incidentally, was in no way suggestive of prophetic Israel. It so happened that Brosam had always been a personal adversary of Plaut. One might have expected the transition to be more subtle, but it was not.

It seems that the professor of genetics had, for a long time, drafted a legislation for the sterilization of the unfit. This was, as I said, quite independent of party politics. In fact, similar legislations had been drafted in other non-Fascist countries. However, in 1933, Professor Rüdin, probably to his own surprise, saw himself suddenly dragged out of scientific semi-obscurity into the limelight of the German opera. Presently he was made Reichsführer of all German psychiatrists, and he saw the sterilization law passed in its most radical form. I still feel that he was acting in good faith, at least at that time, and he did what almost any other professor would have done if his life's idea, no matter how bizarre, were suddenly carried out by a government, no matter how constituted. All schizophrenic, manic-depressive, feeble-minded patients, and I believe almost all psychiatric patients had to be sterilized by surgical operation.

Because of the extermination plants, the concentration camps and the killing of the mentally afflicted during the war, this earliest of the Nazi atrocities has received much too little attention in history books. Every case with a psychiatric diagnosis had to be reported to the authorities, under threat of heavy penalties, very much as in other countries in the case of certain contagious diseases. Sterilization Courts were set up, with a hierarchic structure of higher and higher courts, up to a Supreme Sterilization Court. There was an incredible amount of red tape involved in all this. The important thing to realize is that, more than any other Nazi undertaking, it had the semblance of scientific objectivity, and here for once the "Aryan" and the "non-Aryan" were treated with complete impartiality. The premise, namely, that all these illnesses were determined by an inherent factor, was utterly false. But granted that the premise was true it could be mathematically computed by what time the German people would be free of mental illness. I mention all this because there are many people in the Western countries in favor of sterilization, even if not to this extent, and particularly because this gave me the first inkling of a society managed on so-called scientific principles.

There were some extreme instances. I remember the case of a housemaid, a devoutly Catholic spinster in her early forties who had broken down with a severe attack of melancholia. She was immediately slated for sterilization. A gynecologist, Doctor Albrecht, objected to the operation. He reasoned that the combination "melancholy, devoutly Catholic spinster of over forty" abolished all chances of offspring anyway, and that, on the other hand, such an operation, because of its profound meaning to the patient, would considerably diminish all possibilities of recovery. The case passed various levels in the pyramid of Sterilization Courts, but in the end she was sterilized. There were often heart-rending scenes on the part of patients and their relatives.

We are appalled at the wholesale killing of the mentally-afflicted in Nazi countries, at the experiments carried out in mental hospitals, but it happened not infrequently to me later, in a different cultural environment, that I heard similar desires expressed by people who believed whole-heartedly in Democracy and even fought for it. In mental hospitals you pass rows and rows, hundreds and hundreds of chronically demented men and women, drooling, staring into empty space, crouched motionless or rocking incessantly. In many cases their condition goes on for decades before they die a spontaneous death. Suddenly someone next to you is heard muttering out of the corner of his mouth: "At times I often ask myself, why don't we really let them die a peaceful death, at least the hopeless ones, would it not be so much more humane?" It really does not make much difference whether the thought is spoken out loud by someone else, or passes as a faint shadow in the depths of one's own heart, or appears as a fact reported from a faraway country. From a strictly pragmatic point of view, lacking a metaphysical concept of Man, there is no reason at all against such a step. We, in a non-dictatorial environment, are clinging to many patterns because of a Christian heritage, of which we are no longer conscious and not because we actually believe in the Christian doctrine of vicarious suffering, or the Hindu teaching of karma, or simply in man's immortal soul. In fact, most of us do not believe in any of these things. Thus, we cling with one hand to modern pragmatism, and with the other to the Hebrew-Christian philosophy. But the gap is widening all the time, and there will be a moment when one hand will have to let go.

Death, the Greek philosophers used to say, is the origin of philosophy. They should have added Insanity. And the chronically insane and the idiots, challenge our morality and gauge the inner dynamic tension of Christianity. There was a famous Lutheran pastor, Bodelschwingh, who built up a huge colony of feeble-minded, idiots and epileptics in Bethel in Western Germany. During the war, when the Nazis carried out the slaughter of all mental patients, Pastor Bodelschwingh insisted that he would be killed together with his inmates. It was only on the basis of his international fame that the politicians let him get away with it, and let him and the inmates of his colony live. This was a kind of last-ditch stand of Christianity.

The clinical director began to show statistics (I still see him write figures on the blackboard in a quiet and systematic way) which proved that since the introduction of Labor Camps, the number of psychoneurotic individuals encountered in the hospitals had considerably diminished. It was meant to indicate that the new era had brought a boom as far as the mental welfare of the population was concerned. Here, too, the State had sanctioned something which presents, poorly expressed, a widespread popular idea, namely, that milder psychiatric cases should be brought to their knees by a more disciplinarian attitude. It was quite extraordinary to watch this thin, sensitive man become enthusiastic (so at least it seemed) about his figures which symbolized the triumph of a soldierly Spartan life over the intricacies and agonies of the human soul. It occurred to me that he must be weak.

Incidentally, speaking of the clinical conferences, I am reminded of one amazing scene. A man was brought in who had been picked up as a psychiatric case in one of the medical wards. He had been admitted there on account of a stomach ailment. A psychiatric consultant had been called in for the following reason. There had been, as it is often seen in public medical wards, a rather close contact between the patients. Our man had used this contact to spread his ideas, those of a conscientious objector. He had "preached" (so the clinical report said) to his fellow patients, and to the nurses and internes he appeared to be a crank. The assistant read this history and presently the patient was brought into the conference room. He was a rather tall, thin, soft-spoken man with a sallow complexion. The fact that he was in his pajamas, dressing-gown and slippers, and we were all dressed, some of us in white doctors' coats, seemed somehow to put him at a disadvantage during the ensuing conversation. However, he did not seem to think in these terms. On the contrary, he was most affable and pleasant. As usual he gave his history very much as it had been reported. He told of the First World War and of his experiences in the trenches. There, in combat, he had suddenly come to the insight that killing people meant killing people, regardless of the circumstances, and that it was against the law of the Gospel. He said that he had resolved right there and then to tell everybody about this, his belief, and that since returning from the front he had attempted to devote his life to prayer and good works. He felt it was his moral duty to spread this idea. It was only natural, he said, that we as psychiatrists would look at all this from a different point of view. He understood that most of us were bound to think that he was crazy. He would never hold it against us, regardless as to what conclusions we came about his case, and what practical steps we might take. While the professor "explored" him, he maintained this most natural friendliness. After he had left the room, the professor summed the case up and came to the diagnosis of schizophrenia. I was startled. This meant not only insanity, but it implied, automatically, sterilization. There was never any discussion. During the entire scene I had a most painful sensation of familiarity, some sort of *déjà vu*. I could not remember, for the life of me, where I had seen this before. At this moment something strange happened. I was walking back from the hospital wing to the institute in the company of Doctor Bruno Schulz, the man with pumpkin head and the saber scars. It was dark, a dismal oppressive winter evening, and nobody spoke. All of a sudden I remembered. There is in Tolstoy's drama, "The Living Corpse," a scene in which the hero, a religious conscientious objector, is being examined by a panel of psychiatrists and declared insane. That very moment Schulz turned to me and broke the silence:

"Do you know what this reminded me of? Tolstoy's 'The Living Corpse.' There you'll find a completely analogous scene."

During the subsequent conversation, I got my first glimpse of

one of the noblest and most beautiful souls I have ever encountered. Schulz came originally from Braunschweig. His background
was Northern German. He had been the German beer-drinking
and saber-fighting student. It seems, however, that the front experiences during the First World War had a shaking impact on
him, perhaps not exactly in the same manner as in our poor patient, but somewhat similarly. Like many people of a Northern
German Protestant background, he had been decisively influenced by the Russian religious thinkers. As far as I know he was
not religious in any formal sense, but he simply lived a life of
charity. It emanated from him. There are several Jewish physicians on this continent who owe their lives to him. The word "underground" activities had not yet been coined in those days, but
this is what Schulz was engaged in all the time. His appearance
was Germanic in a ludicrous manner. No German professional
man has ever appeared in a political cartoon looking as bizarre
as Bruno looked in reality He was generally considered a funny
man. He had his hats specially made for him in Braunschweig
and, like Mark Twain, he did all his writing in bed. Like many
geneticists he was a good mathematician and he entertained
something like a mystic relationship to numbers. He believed
firmly in the theory of serial clustering of chance occurrences, a
statistical theory which comes close to a science of superstition.
He carried on a scientific correspondence with the famous statistical mathematician Weinberg, who has contributed much to
the mathematical theory of genetics. This correspondence was
written entirely on postcards. As some people play chess by
mail, Schulz and Weinberg exchanged series of postcards which
were covered with formulas on some technical aspect of the
theory of probability. Looking at his superficial appearance one
could see that nature had equipped Schulz with the most perfect
smokescreen for almost any sort of secret activity. Later, he
often discussed with me the possibility of emigrating. But his appearance and his lack of gift for languages must have inhibited

him. Looking back, it was better that he stayed. Not only do I know of many Jews whom he helped, he also applied a brake to the psychiatric Reichsführer. Moreover, he often had to examine patients clinically for the question of sterilization, and he committed extraordinary distortions to save them from the knife. I know now that he had numerous close escapes but he was the psychiatric Reichsführer's assistant and, more than that, he had a unique camouflage.

It was in connection with Doctor Schulz that it first dawned on me that the Great Dividing Line in Europe, in fact in the entire world, is not the line between Right and Left. All of us who grew up in the intellectual atmosphere of the Twenties were sincerely convinced that people who were politically to the left of the middle acted under a moral incentive. Indeed, as I have said, in most radicals there had been during the early post-war period, underneath it all, a love of justice and a compassion for the multitude. Conversely, it was held that people were conservative out of material motives for conservation, no matter how much some of them were able to deceive themselves. In this respect the Nazi years taught us a lesson. It happened not infrequently that you met a friend whom you had known for years as a "staunch liberal," and he turned out to be eagerly ready for any compromise to save his skin. On the other hand, we saw people whom we had disdained as "reactionaries" go to concentration camps and to the gallows. In the beginning it seemed confusing. But gradually the issue became clearer, and it was obvious that the only thing that counts in this world is the strength of moral convictions.

How dangerous and misleading it is to think in purely political categories! Political terms achieve the same power which certain words hold in the archaic-magic world of the primitive. There are some people who use the word democratic for a society which upholds the moral traditions of Europe; other people speak of democratic but mean technocratic. To them a society which is stripped of all transcendental values is truly democratic and the traditions of a Christian society are out-dated and "reactionary." It is interesting that I do not know to this day about Schulz' political convictions. He might have been a social democrat ("left wing liberal"!) or a German-Nationalist ("reactionary"!)

Doctor Leo Mager also turned out to be a surprise, although this came about in a different way. Doctor Mager belonged to a small group of Nazis who really believed not only in "National" but also in "Socialist," although the latter in an obscure petit bourgeois meaning. This group felt itself betrayed from the beginning. At any rate, it was strange to observe that very soon after the seizure of power, just when his great chance would have come, Mager returned his party membership card. First openly and later secretly, he worked very much like Schulz against the new masters. He often berated me because "Jewish World Power" (this concept was still a remnant from his Nazi days) did not act more vigorously against Germany. Jewish World Power and I were shamefully embarrassed. In his case I also know that he helped numerous people under most dangerous circumstances. During one of the purges in the course of the war he escaped to Switzerland.

At the very beginning of the Nazi era there was still an element of cops-and-robbers about it all. On the very day after Hitler's seizure of power, on the first of February, 1933, Herr Eisinger went to see the S.A. leader of Sendling. He kept his fist in his right coat pocket in an ominous manner and said: "You threatened to kill the Herr Curate of Sendling and me on the first day of the new regime. Here I am, kill me." According to Herr Eisinger's version, the leader receded a step and merely said: "You know I didn't mean it." As Herr Eisinger repeated the story a few times, the leader's reaction became more panicky:

"He grew as pale as a sheet, walked slowly back toward the wall, never taking his eyes off my pocket, and he said, 'You know perfectly well, mein lieber Herr Eisinger, that I never meant that seriously.' "

Right after that ominous first of April, 1933, the day of the anti-Jewish boycott, all my Jewish friends, all those who had graduated with me, in fact all Jewish professional people "except for world war veterans" lost their jobs. The clause ". . . except for world war veterans" was intended to give the impression of a just and humane decision, and one could see that this was the psychological effect it had on our professors, technicians, dish-washers, janitors and charwomen, all except for Herr Eisinger and a few other people. A few months later the Jewish veterans lost their jobs too, but without anyone ever hearing about it. It was right at the beginning, in April, that Professor Spielmeyer called me into his office and said:

"Don't think of leaving. I want you to stay on. After all, you are paid by the Rockefeller Foundation, and if they dare to touch you, I'll see to it that no more American money will come into this place, and believe me, they know that very well."

This gave me the feeling of becoming a hostage, a pawn for bargaining, and I did not like it. Moreover, the fact that all my Jewish friends lost their jobs one by one gave me a feeling of isolation. I was not elated at all; on the contrary, I felt like being left behind in the enemy camp. I told Spielmeyer so but he gave me an involved theory the gist of which was that "this Government could not possibly last more than a year." He had interesting details to tell about Downing Street and the Polish Government and the Quai d'Orsay and Economics, but even then I had a faint but accurate premonition. History has its own immanent apocalyptic laws of progress, laws which seem to be surprisingly independent from what we read in the daily newspapers. I was then dimly aware of something of that sort, although I might not have been able to express it in so many words. However, I resolved to stay on for the time being, and I began to look around abroad.

The Forschungsanstalt was a funny place. Except for the Reichsführer for Psychiatry and Sterilization, the professor for spirochete research and a few of the clinicians, one could just as well have been working in Geneva or in some small University in New England. The fact that the Reichsführer was surrounded by Schulz and Mager and Spielmeyer and Herr Eisinger seemed to neutralize him.

Herr Eisinger's exploits seem in retrospect extremely bold, and it is hard to understand how he got away with them. It was already required by law that during any public speech of Hitler the loudspeakers in all institutions and factories had to be turned on, even during working hours, for the employees to listen. Herr Eisinger accompanied every speech with a running comment for the benefit of the listeners, the janitor, the glass-washers and the charwomen. I can still hear him interpolating unequivocal remarks such as " 'stretching his hand out to France for lasting friendship,' *heilige Maria, Mutter Gottes*, listen to *der Depp der damische* [that crazy fool], nobody believes him."

12. *Home*

Most people think that the anti-semitism which we encountered under Hitler, is the same anti-semitism as one encounters anywhere else—in drawing-room conversations, in universities, in clubs, in railway compartments and in church groups, in the unwritten laws pertaining to the allotment and hierarchy of jobs— only exaggerated to an utmost degree of injustice and cruelty. This is a serious error. Quantum physics teaches us that energy, in its transformations, does not increase in a continuum but by "jumps." There is something similar about Evil.

In Bavaria, during the Wittelsbach monarchy, there had been

a little of what we later called the "good old pre-war anti-semitism." Jews labored under handicaps similar to those under which numerous racial and religious minorities labor in other parts of the world. They were barred from certain public offices, if not constitutionally, at least by an unwritten law. There was the element of the "Christ-killer" and all that in some of the children. But as a whole most of the Catholic people (and they constituted the majority) shared the views of Herr Josef Filser quoted in the first chapter. The old king liked the venerable chief Rabbi of Munich, Doctor Werner, who was not infrequently seen at court. Herr Fränkel, an extremely Orthodox Jew from one of the oldest Munich families, was made Royal Councillor for Transport and Trade. Catholic children earned a little pocket money by switching the electric light on and off on Friday nights in the households of Orthodox Jews. The Regensburg cookbook in which pious Frau Maria Schandry included numerous recipes for Lent and Christmas, also gave with complete impartiality, and not without fondness, the recipes for certain bakeries and dishes which the "Israelites" consume on Friday night and on Passover.

All this had changed after the First World War. With a wave of chauvinism a new brand of anti-semitism appeared which I mentioned in connection with my school days. The Jewish Youth Movements and the Zionism of the young people were a reaction to this. During this time my parents received a large amount of literature, mainly periodicals, which seemed to emphasize that German Jews were Germans. The Jewish Community in our town resolved to build a synagogue, a real building, something like a Protestant church, which was to replace the old embarrassing prayer-hall inside the brewery. There was at least one community meeting every year concerned with the plan of that synagogue. It struck me that those who were interested in the building, including Grandfather, did not seem to care for it so much from a religious point of view (one could serve God equally well in the old prayer-hall) as from a desire for something like collective prestige. There would be a solemn opening, the mayor of the town, the official representatives of other religious congregations and the representatives of various *vereine* would appear; there would be a brass band; there would be speeches; and there would be, last but not least, a detachment of Jewish war veterans. (This last point seemed to have an importance which was quite disproportionate. The question of how many people have fought in a war, and how many have been killed, seems to be one of the most important in the social struggle of minorities. When, before the Second World War, a British submarine remained submerged and its entire crew was lost, I read in one of the Catholic London papers a statement as to how many of the sailors on board were Catholics. This may have arisen out of the same sentiment; at any rate I do not understand why anyone would care for such statistics.)

The building of that synagogue never came about. But at those community meetings Grandfather and Herr Kommerzienrat Gross used to speak of the plans of the new synagogue with eagerness which had nothing to do with the Zeal of Thy House. It rather implied that it was about time to display something; what exactly, nobody knew. This was precisely what we in the youth movement meant when we spoke of "spineless, undignified, cringing assimilation." In the face of increasing anti-semitism the older generation seemed to repeat anxiously and with increased frequency: "But look, we are exactly like you," while we said: "Yes, we are different from you, we are Jews, and if you want to know, we are proud of it!"

Now things in our little town were different. When I left Munich and the Institute to visit my home-town for the first time, during the Nazi era, Father received me at the railway station. It was evening. The station platform was dimly lit. There was the usual cluster of people behind the ticket barrier, and looking from the car window, I spotted Father among them. He was slightly stooped, his hands in his greatcoat pockets, and he peered searchingly towards the train. I had seen him like this hundreds of times before. Yet, without any physical detachment, he was detached from the crowd. Or did I perceive something which was not there? There was his sudden smile of recognition. After I had passed the barrier and he embraced me we seemed to be, by this simple gesture, more isolated from the people around us.

Herr Weigl, the bicycle dealer, said: "Guten Abend, Herr Stern," perhaps louder and more forcefully than had been the custom. Presently I smelled again the old familiar smell of the railway station, a stale smell of soot, human beings, sandwich parcels, glue, paper and apples. Father said: "Nun, wie geht's? Tell me something!" There had been times, in my teens, when I might perhaps have said to myself: "Why does he not, once in a while, use a new phrase, just one new one?" This time I felt like moving up more closely to him while we crossed the hall and walked towards the town. The people around us, Herr Weigl's loud greeting, and the smell of the station conveyed a new strangeness. Father said: "He is decent," referring to Herr Weigl, and I felt incredibly embarrassed.

On the Bahnhofsplatz was an enormous sign in enamel: "In this town Jews are undesired." I had known of the existence of these signs in all German towns, on all places in front of railway stations; but the moment I saw it I realized that, somewhere deep down, I had entertained a dim, ill-defined belief, bizarre and illogical, that our town might be an exception. We passed the lumber yards which adjoined the Station Avenue. In the shadow, just outside the pale of the big arc lamps, one could see the quadrangular piles of wood. Their silhouettes looked like rows of fortresses. This is what they had been to us when we were children, little forts in which we hid for hours, waiting for the enemy gang which was camped in other lumber fortresses up on the height of the Taubenberg. We went along the main street, the Ludwigstrasse, past the huge elaborate monastery of the Redemptorist Fathers. (When I was small Mother used to tell me that it had cost a million marks to build it.)

In the light of a street lamp, Judge Deigendesch passed us and took his hat off. Father took his hat off, perhaps a trifle more eagerly than usual, and bowed, perhaps just a little more deeply than usual, or did it only appear to me like this? "He is also decent—one of the decent ones," Father remarked, and I felt again the same embarrassment. As we neared the railway bridge there was a streamer across the street: "The Jews are our misfortune." I tapped the wide stone railing over which I used to run barefoot as a boy, the glistening steel lines deep below. One had to do this with one's eyes fixed on the sidewalk of the bridge, and the purpose had invariably been to achieve a mild and agreeable throbbing of fear. This evening it was too dark for the rails down below to be seen but I looked at the signal lamps getting lost in the distance, and they seemed to be at one with some world through which Father and I had never walked before.

We passed a few more people, some of whom said, "Guten Abend, Herr Stern," and the ceremonial repeated itself. We passed all the familiar places. There was a bierkeller with a bowling alley. There we used to sit on summer evenings at tables with our sandwiches, drinking beer and eating big white radishes. On a square not far from it was a big showcase, brightly lit, and above it a sign: "The Jews are our misfortune." I knew those showcases. They displayed a weekly paper which was entirely devoted to enlightening the population on the Jewish question. There were detailed stories of, let us say, a Jewish lawyer of Magdeburg who assaulted his non-Jewish secretary; or an Orthodox congregation who kept German girls in the cellar of their synagogue for the purpose of commercial prosti-tution; statistics of the part played by the Jews in the Russian revolution and in the organization of "Wall Street." Of course, Father and I did not stop to read it. Perhaps in passing it we walked just a little more quickly. We knew the kind of information which was displayed. We glanced furtively out of the corner of our eyes and remarked simultaneously that nobody was standing there reading it at the moment. "I never see anyone stopping there," Father said.

We passed another square, in the middle of which was a fountain with a bronze gilded Saint Sebastian, tied to a bronze gilded column and pierced by bronze gilded arrows. At this square Herr Steiniger, one of the competitors of our firm, had his store. "You would be surprised—he is not decent at all, he does not greet any more." Presently we passed Frey's, another competitor's textile store. "He still greets, good sort."

When we finally arrived at home Mother was standing in the corridor behind the store, at the landing of the stairs. She had her kitchen apron on, which meant that she had prepared something special for me, otherwise she would have left that to Therese.

"Where did you stay so long?" she asked.

"We've made something special for you," Therese said, emerging from the kitchen.

"Pot roast and maccaroni," Mother added quickly.

The table was set with shining linen. Ludwig was sitting in the living-room reading a book by B. Traven.

"Well, well, at last," Father said after we had entered the dining-room, and he gave me a hug and a kiss as if I had returned after ten years in Central Africa.

"Wow, sauerbraten and maccaroni," Ludwig remarked.

"That's for you," Therese beamed.

Those were the rituals of homecoming, unvaried and precious since I had first gone into the Big City Far Away as a boy of ten, to return only on vacations. During the supper Father said that one of the apprentices in the store had joined the Storm-troopers, that Herr Ruhland had assaulted Herr Neuberger and the police had looked the other way, that Herr Gruber would not work for us any more, and that the butcher Vogl was decent.

"In the street they greet you as before"—meaning the Vogl family. It was obvious that the mankind which surrounded Father was simply divided into two breeds, those who "greeted" and those who had stopped greeting.

Doctor Marlinger was decent, Doctor Lagally did not greet any more, one Gebhardt family was friendly, the others had stopped greeting. The parish priest who had never "greeted" before began to "greet" now ostentatiously. "Awfully decent of him, that's something you've got to admit." Father, ever since I remembered him, seemed to be vaguely conscious of his naiveness; he tried to defy us and at the same time looked for approval. The human cosmos of the small town had become to him a dualist system, made up of those who kept on exchanging ordinary courtesies with him, and those who had stopped doing so. This was more involved than it sounds. "Herr Drexel stopped right on the Market Place to talk to me the other day, so, incidentally, did Doctor Marlinger." This was one step more advanced than "greeting."

"Listen to what *he* did," Mother said, referring to Father. "The Storm-troopers went around to every Jewish store and put the official labels to the show windows: 'Do not buy from the Jew!' He just went out in open daylight, in front of all the people and tore those labels off. The only Jew in town to do such a thing. They could have hanged you for that, and nobody could have done anything about it!"

"Ah, nonsense, hanging! Do you know"—he turned to me—"who the chairman and the vice-chairman of the party are?" He named two young men, both of whom happened to be sons of unmarried women from the lower class. "Take *that* as food for thought," he said.

I did not know what he wanted me to think but it occurred to me that illegitimate children in small towns are exposed to extreme and bizarre forms of humiliation, and that here the Revolution was displayed with simple crudity, with its raw flesh so-to-speak. It seemed all too primitive for History, the faraway Goddess.

"Think of those two chaps sitting up there in an office, in upholstered easy chairs, and with secretaries," he said.

Before we all retired Ludwig went downstairs into a niche near the cellar door and pulled a switch. Mother explained that he had installed a gadget by which he could interrupt the current of the doorbell during the night. There were people in the neighborhood who stuck matches or putty into the bell button at any hour in the morning between one and seven, and we were no longer in any position to ask for the protection of the police.

I lay awake for some time listening to the sound of the running water in Saint Florian's fountain. I had a sense of foreboding. The feeling I had that night seems now much more natural and less strange than it actually was, because of the many things that came about since then. In reality, nothing very much had happened at that time. That there were some people in town who stopped to say hello; that there was a showcase with pornographic leaflets, or that there were some big posters on display; that there were hooligans ringing doorbells—all this was of the order of nuisance and bother, with just a touch of the vulgar and unsavory. It seems trivial in the light of intervening memories. Yet that night—I cannot explain why—I suddenly sensed that all this would end only with our complete and utter destruction.

I looked through the window. Nothing could be seen. It was the same sleepy quaint little town, under a night sky. And yet it was as if we were huddling on the barque of our childhood, and around us there was an evil force which seemed to be in tune with infinity.

13. Exit Leo Nikolaievitch

THE FEW Nazi guest workers in the Institute behaved as if they found themselves in enemy territory. Even those who did talk Nazism, somehow seemed to fail to fit into a recognized pattern. I remember a biochemist, a blond and somewhat anemic youth with an open candid look, who at the dinner table expounded to me the neo-pagan Germanic Religion.

"I used to be terribly anti-semitic, you know, until I came to study the writings of Doctor Hauer. Then I found out that what we hate in the Jews is not the Jews. It is Christ and the Christian religion. This religion is something so utterly alien to the very spirit of the European peoples that they revolt with their entire being against it. But although they feel a revulsion they are not aware of its true origin. Hence that irrational hatred of the Jews, because people vaguely feel that it is actually a Jewish way of feeling, thinking, acting, a Jewish norm of living that has been stuffed down their throat for the past two thousand years. Once you have found out that it is actually Christianity which is the painful foreign body in our flesh, something curious happens, you stop hating the Jews. You regard them with the same kind of sympathy or antipathy as you might regard any other foreign nation."

I asked him in what way the Christian, or rather Hebrew-Christian, way of thinking was so alien and indigestible for the Northern European nations. He replied that the moral teaching of the Bible imbued the people with a disastrous sense of anxiety and guilt. "The New Testament claims to have done away with fear, but it builds up a sense of fear even more dramatically than the Old Testament. It's only a continuation of the same thing."

He claimed that the Indo-Germanic peoples had a much higher idea of the ultimate destiny of man. You had only to read the description which Tacitus gives of the German people of the pre-Christian era to realize that. "There has been one revolt against the shackles of an alien thought—that was Luther. But with Luther it was still unconscious—Luther did not realize himself that what he was actually fighting was not Rome; it was an element that had arisen long before the Catholic Church and far away from Rome, some kind of desert mentality which was grafted upon the mind of the Aryan peoples and had thwarted and dwarfed it. Thus Luther made the mistake of reviving instead of abolishing that spirit, although the unconscious root of the Lutheran rebellion lay actually in the depth of the Aryan mind." Hitler was even worse, he said, for Hitler deflected the anti-Christian forces into vulgar Jew-baiting, and by doing so removed, perhaps forever, the chance of the revival of a truly Indo-Germanic spirit in Europe.

I asked him, since he had such an Aryan chip on his shoulder against the Ten Commandments, how he would prevent children from lying and stealing and murdering. He told me something, which I have forgotten, about the Indo-Germanic mentality, and that he would certainly do anything to prevent his children from getting acquainted with a desert deity who appears under thunder and smoke on a mountain. The reader must realize that this was a clean-looking, sympathetic young man, and no Nazi ogre. On the contrary, he was the sort of young idealist who might easily have landed in an actively anti-Nazi camp, and perished there. I have lost track of him, in fact I have forgotten his name. The point is that he expressed something, under the quaint make-up of a Teutonic *weltanschauung*, which, under varying disguises, many people say today in many places of the world. Moreover, he expressed quite clearly what I believe now to be the true background of the entire Nazi revolution.

Gradually the Psychiatric Institute became suspect. Professor Spielmeyer, scientist of world renown, descendant of a Northern German family of pastors, struck up a peculiar kind of alliance with Herr Eisinger, the chauffeur. Leo Mager saw to it that not a single portrait of The Leader was hung up in any one of the offices, although this was now the rule in all public institutions. One never heard "Heil Hitler." Doctor Margarete Bülow, the chairman of the doctors' dining-room committee intended, at all costs, to maintain the dining-room as a clean, aseptic enclave. There had existed for a long time, slowly and gradually accumulated by the doctors' efforts, a record collection. This collection was unique of its kind at that time and in that sort of dining-room; it contained everything from Bach partitas to Brahms concertos. Doctor Adele Juda began to act as if that collection had assumed an extraordinary importance and meaning.

From the windows, just beyond the trees of the Englische Garten, we could see the factory chimneys of the Maffei Works and the Bayrische Motoren Works smoking again, day and night; far away in the fields, in the direction of Schleissheim, one could perceive an even rhythmic crawling movement, tanks, armored vehicles and mounted guns. The charwomen, glass-washers and animal keepers stopped working, and watched intently. It was as if a supernatural power communicated with their little lives and showed in their faces. There were wonderment, tension without aim, and paralyzed fascination. Gradually more and more began to say "yes" to all this, as if their "yes" were outside the laws which underlay logical assent.

Herr Eisinger could still be seen talking to small groups of two or three, but he stopped his running comments on radio speeches. His face, with tower skull, Hitler mustache and all, showed faint traces of pessimism. "They are all *rindvieher,*" he told me but it appeared to come out of the mouth of a sad clown. The janitor began to say "Heil Hitler," an outward sign showing that Herr Eisinger's authority was broken.

It was around that time that the Nazis began a campaign against vivisection and cruelty to animals. The air of make-believe, of a diabolical yes-and-no, of whirling and whizzing ambiguities, was increasing, and soon the stokers, professors and storekeepers were surrounded by an optical wall which separated them from reality. Herr Eisinger began to collect material to report Brosam to the authorities for "cruelty to animals."

One day Professor Spielmeyer, Herr Eisinger and I were riding in the car which belonged to the Institute. I had balancing on my knees a jar with a human brain floating in formalin. Eisinger spoke to us as to two intimate friends. "Listen to what happened to me the other day. I had lent my camera to a friend who wanted to take a picture of his kids. Know what happened? Without ever telling me about it he had a secret Communist printing set-up in his basement." He did not give Doctor Spielmeyer or me any time to think about this last statement, and continued quickly. "The police came on a *razzia,* arrested him and his associates, and took all his implements away, including my camera which I had lent him in good faith." There was again an increase in tempo. "Hoppla, I said to myself, Eisinger, you won't let these fellows get away with it. You know what I did? I went straight into the Polizeipraesidium in the Ett-strasse, and did I tell those fellows off! To take away the camera of an innocent working-class man . . ." Here he paused. "Only because I am good-hearted enough to lend it to a fellow who makes me believe he wants to take pictures of his family. No, sir. You know what they did? They apologized! 'Herr Eisinger, it was an oversight; you understand the circumstances.' I got my camera back."

Herr Eisinger's stories no longer sounded funny. Although their veracity was undoubted, the world of cops-and-robbers no longer existed. It was a kind of pretense. There was something similar about the dining-room. The egg-from-the-floor act still evoked laughter. Lydia Pasternak and I became increasingly popular, because we were Jews. We became sensitive to our rôle as mascots. Keeping us preciously no longer prevented that enclave from being dissolved. One could still sit at night and listen to the partitas. But all that which went on within a circumference of a hundred feet seemed to pervert even Music herself.

The führer for psychiatry and sterilization felt endangered and compromised by the reputation of the place as a "hornets' nest of reaction." Around this time the murder of Dollfuss occurred. Numerous Nazi doctors fled Austria and sought refuge in Germany. All the psychiatrists among them were allocated to the Institute, and a new era began. The spell of the dining-room was finally broken. Forceful young men appeared, dark and brooding, and handsome in a sensuous fashion. One of them remained after dinner, sitting at the piano, playing free improvisations which sounded ominously like *Das Rheingold.* Soon there were two camps, the Nazis (whom the staff members called "Austrians") and the old guard. Doctor Margarete Bülow appeared sad. The cell had succumbed to osmotic pressure. After-dinner conversations were suddenly broken off when someone opened the door. We began to talk shop, on cerebral changes in epilepsy, and on the chemical structure of cerebrosides.

One day one of the "Austrians" took all the Pasternak pictures off the wall, and replaced them with one photograph, The Leader's portrait. Doctor Margarete Bülow ran to Doctor Schulz. They drafted a note of formal protest, not because The Leader's portrait was hung up (that was too dangerous a thing to do and would have meant the concentration camp) but because changes had been made in the dining-room without consulting with the fräulein chairman. But the deed was done and Tolstoy lay, face down, on a laboratory bench. A secret meeting was called, and Doctor Schulz read us the drafted protest. Everybody present wanted to sign. It was strange to see how these people who apparently had suppressed a sense of shame over their enforced passivity got incensed, and suddenly risked their jobs and their future over an issue which lacked all practical significance. "Lydia and you must not sign on any account," Schultz said to me, "because you are considered biased, and moreover you would certainly be arrested and put into a concentration camp if your names were found here." There was a long and proud list of signatures which, for obvious reasons, I shall never forget. From a practical point of view it was foolhardy and senseless; all that came of it was that the Gestapo received a little dossier for future reference. There was a general exodus from the doctors' dining-room. Everyone, except for the "Austrians," ate in a nearby restaurant. Then the führer for psychiatry and sterilization made a move; he apologized on his part for the incorrect demeanor of the "Austrians." Several people, including Doctors Schulz and Mager, never entered the dining-room again. The little incident was heavily laden with symbolic significance. Exit Leo Nikolaievitch. Enter Adolf. A new era had begun in all our lives, not only in my life as a Jew, but in the lives of Doctor Spielmeyer, and the janitor and Herr Eisinger, the people around us, and the nations of the earth.

III

THROUGH THE INTERIOR

14. *An Unusual Barter*

THE Psychiatric Institute gave us the best that classical psychiatry could offer. In these institutions of research, the sting was taken out of all this, the animal was tamed. In the department of genetics, in thousands of files, stored on shelves, in cupboards and in crates was the disease of generations. It could be reduced to mathematical formulas, to graphs of predictability, and it seemed to lose all the passion and the fortuitous chance of suffering which had been experienced in each single "case." In the Department of Clinical Research we observed human experience and behavior. We created precious categories. In the Department of Neuropathology there were hundreds of museum jars with brains, and thousands of microscopic sections, in colorful stains, mounted on glass. Most of us got out of this some sense of assurance and power. Sickness, insanity, begetting and dying—all seemed to be objectivated and made to conform with the cleanliness and brightness of our laboratories.

During all this time one of the great mass psychoses of history was taking its course, right in front of our windows, and the destructive force erupting from the depth of life was something to which our very frame of reference was not applicable. In spite of the fact that I enjoyed my work I was, nevertheless, aware of the void. In order to know Man I had to study myself.

It was around this time that I was introduced to one of

our foremost analytical therapists. Doctor Rudolf Laudenheimer was like some sort of anticosmos as compared with the Psychiatric Institute. He had originally come from the school of classical psychiatry, like all therapists of the analytical school at that time. As a young man he had been lecturer in the department of psychiatry in Leipzig, under Flechsig, a famed brain anatomist. He had been working in areas in which Internal Medicine, Human Physiology and Psychiatry overlapped. However, at the dawn of the century he broke with traditional psychiatry of the academic school. He had, since his student days, been associated with a group of writers and poets who later rose to fame. He had been in contact with Freud at an early stage, later with Jung. At any rate, in the middle of a promising academic career he broke off in a way which was baffling to those who knew him. He and his wife took a loan and rented a small farmhouse. For some time they had to live there with one patient. This, their historical first case, was a rapidly deteriorating General Paretic—a man afflicted with a syphilitic disease of the brain which at that time was still incurable. Frau Laudenheimer described vividly how they lived with their patient in the semi-wilderness, how they bathed him, fed him, cleansed him and how they waited through his endless attacks of restlessness and yelling.

Soon after the paretic, a few more patients had arrived, this time persons who were in need of psychological therapy. After a few years a small sanatorium was begun, and after a few more years more buildings had to be added until the enterprise had grown into one of the best known private sanatoriums in Germany. Ten years before I first met him, the Doctor had retired, at the height of his fame, into private practice in Munich.

Frau Laudenheimer had been a girl from the East Prussian countryside; she must have been strikingly beautiful in her young days, and even now one could see her beauty under the mask of age. The apartment was furnished with very good taste. There were warmth and nobility of style.

Doctor Laudenheimer looked like a Jewish nobleman. His silvery hair and beard, and his penetrating, melancholy eyes, made many people who first met him think of Freud. His wife was tall and strong, there was something fierce in her beauty, and her gray mop of hair seemed to radiate like a forbidding crown whenever she let her temper go. He was rather reticent when not in intimate company, she spoke incessantly as if she wanted to crowd out silence. This somehow appeared to be associated with the fact that she had no children. There is a peculiar tragedy about childlessness, a dim, just faintly perceptible form of sadness which is never quite expressed. Such people, deprived of a certain form of creativeness, seem to be, in another way, more in harmony with the sadness of creation.

In the evening Frau Laudenheimer told Sanatorium stories. She paced up and down the floor and spoke in the words and with the gestures of a famous Prussian General, whose wife had just been admitted in a state of depression during pregnancy. Or she was transformed into an obsessive-compulsive novelist who is helped by the nurses to unpack his suitcase. Or she propped herself up in front of the grand piano and began to sing Brahms, as a celebrated singer would when, as a patient, she was about to entertain fellow patients. Her eyes, her heaving breast and her wild hair looked more and more Wagnerian as she struggled along with Brahms. Her voice was cracked and tinny but she pronounced each syllable formidably as one used to in the theatrical classes of the nineties. This Great Sanatorium, a strange combination of opera, Wild West drama, and Magic Mountain, was an inexhaustible source of entertainment. It was something utterly different from what her husband had actually been doing all these years, different from the agony of each single patient. However, she knew that perfectly well. Whenever her eyes began to gleam threateningly and it looked as if she had identified herself perfectly with her rôle, she suddenly began to laugh, shook her gray hair and the spook vanished completely. The Doctor looked at all this silently and with good-humored tolerance. There was no maliciousness in it, nor any of the resentment of past glory. Here in Munich, the house was still a center for artists, musicians, writers, scientists, and the practice was still flourishing.

Laudenheimer's main interest, outside Medicine, had been the History of Art; so much so that even during the middle years of his life he had still been toying with the idea of changing his occupation altogether. It was fascinating to observe how he spoke, in connection with what seemed to be "specific psychiatric problems," of Goethe or Manzoni, of James Joyce or Chinese Art. I realized for the first time something of which I had perhaps been conscious dimly and in a shadowy form; that the "problem of human behavior" cannot be tackled in the artificial isolation of laboratory and clinic, or by all those scientific methods which reduce the infinity of life to sterile quantification. This was not a matter of sour grapes with him, because he had earned his original fame with strictly scientific investigation. Nor was it anything like sophistication; he had the humility of all genuine people. It was rather a natural transcendence; he had his roots in the soil of the nineteenth century but he spread his branches towards something which seemed to be beyond the twentieth. He rejected almost instinctively all determinism, whether of Freudian or Marxian or any other coloring. I remember him saying: "If I did not believe in the Freedom of the Will, I'd give up being a physician." Although he was a Jew by heritage, he had been brought up as a Christian since childhood: he, too, had that elevated Protestant humanism which I have seen in others of his generation, enlivened and warmed, as it were, by a Jewish sensitiveness. Although his clinical approach had been molded decisively by Freud, he belonged to the circle around C. G. Jung. However, like all humanists, he was pluralistic almost by nature, and he made one forget everything about "isms." Just as Haase and the experiences in the Moabit slums had sown the ferment of social consciousness into my medicine, he added the ferment of what I would now call a personalist attitude.

There prevailed at that time among the young Germans a peculiar brand of irrationalism. This was a reaction against a rationalist pragmatism which had been handed down to them. *Bios*, Life, was extolled as something that had a primacy over *logos*, the Spirit. Even those who were avowedly anti-Nazi used to sit over their after-dinner coffee in the Psychiatric Institute and talk about D. H. Lawrence and Ludwig Klages, the German philosopher of the *bios*.

I think that with D. H. Lawrence it had been a vigorous rebellion against an emasculated bourgeoisie, rather similar to that of Nietzsche. With Klages it had become a form of shadiness, one of those specifically Teutonic forms of the European illness. Thomas Mann was one of the first to recognize the danger in all this (perhaps after having first discovered it inside himself) and he spent half his life combating it. For many people there seemed to be a dark fascination in this magic brew. Something similar could be seen in some of the followers of Jung. It was a strange form of mysticism, a mysticism which opposed itself to Reason.

Although Laudenheimer belonged to the circle around Jung, he escaped this danger, perhaps because of his profound affinity to the classical, perhaps because of his strong though ill-defined Christian belief, perhaps because of his Jewishness. It seems almost as if a Jew cannot be an irrationalist; Bergson's apparent irrationalism was actually the deep personal struggle of a man of the nineteenth century for the Metaphysical, and found its solution in Christianity.

During one of my first conversations with Laudenheimer, he said to me: "When you go home today, bring a copy book and begin to collect all your dreams." This advice was given with the air of a routine procedure, as a dentist tells his patient to buy poultices and apply them three times daily. When I returned, he said: "Lie down on the couch over there, relax and close your eyes." He made a further proposal: "As a form of payment, I ask you to play Beethoven sonatas to me four times a week."

During the subsequent two and a half years I spent a considerable time lying on that couch, relaxed and with my eyes closed. There were not enough Beethoven sonatas I was able to reproduce half adequately. A good deal of Mozart had to be added, and Schubert. I think he loved Schubert more than anything else, and since Schubert sonatas are very beautiful and very long, and since one of them does for a whole evening, and can often be repeated, I was delighted. He said: "I am like old King Saul. I don't want your money, I want music."

Thus started the strange procedure of an analysis, on the basis of an unusual barter. A good analyst is everything—father, recording machine, Mephistopheles, Virgil and Beatrice, all in one. I was slowly and painfully taken through quagmires and seraphic regions. Among the numerous things which changed in my life during this time was an extraordinary fact: when I first lay down on the couch I was a convinced dialectic materialist; when I arose from the couch for the last time I was absolutely convinced of the primacy of the Spirit.

15. Bones to Philosophy

THE National Socialist Revolution had, not only materially, a devastating impact upon German and European Jewry. It acted like earthquake and flood because the masses of Jews were, in spite of years of gathering clouds, psychologically and ideologically utterly unprepared. Most people think of us as cunning, foxy, with a great amount of practical foresight. The years after 1933 proved us to be as sentimental in our attachments, as emotional and stupid in our practical decisions, as much given to wishful thinking and self-deception as any other people.

It was a great paradox that one of the vilest and most cruel racial persecutions in history hit a people which was amazingly well integrated into the cultural life of its "host." For the German Jews, as is well known, were the most assimilated and most deeply rooted Jews in Europe, perhaps with the exception of the Italian ones. This natural fact was unfortunately used by certain political groups. When Eastern Jewry had to migrate due to the horrible pogroms of fifty years ago, certain groups of German Jews locked their doors to them. No wonder that this caused much bitterness and misunderstanding on the part of the Russian and Polish Jews; they came to look upon the assimilation and cultural deep-rootedness of the German Jew as some sort of treacherous camouflage which it certainly was not. Out of their bitter experience, prejudice and resentment were carried over to a second generation and to this continent; even those of us who never dreamed of any discrimination among ethnic groups have come up against this sort of thing. A few Eastern Jews felt something like the glee of just retribution when the German persecutions started; it never occurred to them that the forest fire would spread to Eastern Europe. In the end all were united in an apocalyptic flame, in a terrible communion of death.

In the beginning, however, one could still discern groups and different psychological reactions. The large number of middle-class families, most of whom owned retail stores, began to sit back, listen to the Swiss and Austrian radio and to every little scrap of story or anecdote that resembled a small-scale Nazi defeat. Much calculation was going on, on the basis of some form of classical out-of-date economy, as to how long "they" could carry on. Since the new government did not have "solid business foundations" it was believed to be doomed to bankruptcy in the good time-honored style of the bourgeois world. Most of those who deceived themselves in this way had in the end to emigrate without any material goods whatsoever; they were swallowed up in such centers as Shanghai. The more fortunate ones were able to reach the big cities of North or South America, or go to Palestine. Others, particularly those who had no relatives, or childless couples who did not have anyone to break the path for them, underwent the fate of concentration camps, sealed cattle-wagons and extermination plants.

A large number of the young people belonging to these families became Zionists. The Zionist Youth Movement for the first time in Germany was no longer led by a somewhat isolated, detached group with a *weltanschauung;* all of a sudden it became a powerful means of solving an urgent practical problem. They established a well-organized *hach-sharah,* training camps for farming and craftsmanship, so that youths would not arrive in Palestine altogether unprepared and again be swallowed up by some city civilization such as is represented by Tel Aviv.

Skilled academic workers, physicians, scientists and artists found employment abroad. They seemed to be least affected by the deluge. Of all the Jews they seemed to have experienced ideologically and materially the least impact. There was no **sign** of reorientation. They seemed to think, feel and work very much in the same way in hospitals, institutes and factories as they had been wont. However, there was a current of restlessness and a shift of values underneath the surface. Although they were taken in by countries in which freedom had persisted, the more sensitive among them retained a profound feeling of uprootedness and insecurity just as one has the sensation of rocking and vibration after a stormy sea voyage. They felt that the peculiar nineteenth-century brand of liberalism and unrestricted individualism which was characteristic of the social strata to which they belonged was a hollow structure. On the other hand, they recognized the immorality behind that new irrationalism of Klages and Spengler. Most of them had no roots whatsoever in Jewry. Its positive values, its great traditions, its spirit were entirely unknown to these people. A senseless and cruel stigma was all that Jewry had become to them.

There was a particularly small group of those who had identified themselves so much with German culture, not only the Germany of Goethe but the Germany of Bismarck, that their forcible exclusion struck them as an explosion strikes a child. They groped blindly around in some sort of no-man's-land. Among these were the first cases of suicide of which we heard.

Socialists emigrated to the Western countries and resumed their activities; but most of those whom I happened to know did it in a rather abstract, literary sort of way. It seems almost that in order to be creative and useful in the labor movement one has to grow up in the country in which one works. Although the problems and worries of the working-class seem the most uniform and international phenomenon in today's world, in order to help effectively New York garment-workers, or Yorkshire miners, or Norwegian lumberjacks, you have to have been among them almost from childhood.

In all this uproar, bewilderment and confusion, the most realistic and positive way seemed to be that of the Zionist Youth. These people felt that they were born into a new life. The German turmoil was an almost welcome pretext for them to shed the clothes of Western Jewish bourgeoisie, the position of economic intermediators which it held in a capitalistic world, its pale abstract existence in the foam of a drying-out current of civilization. Maybe they had got too big a dose of Teutonic pessimism with reference to Western civilization in general, and this played an unconscious part in it. That does not matter now. It is amazing with what eagerness all these children of a long purely commercial and intellectual tradition took to manual work on the soil and in workshops. Ludwig played a leading part in this movement. I believe he got his first stimulus from me. For his plans were not laid yet, the Nazi Revolution coincided with his matriculation from high school and it just needed the hint of a suggestion to make him choose his life work; it was profoundly different from anything he would have done if life had gone on in a conservative undisturbed way.

This was a healthy, optimistic and wholesome crowd of youngsters; they were, with the exception of certain purely religious groups, the only happy and well-adjusted people I encountered at that time in Germany. They all seemed happier than they would have been if, under normal circumstances, they had taken the unavoidable career of traveling salesmen or of textile merchants. Some of them seemed, with cynical humor, to regard the advent of Hitlerism as a boon. Incidentally, the training farms were favored or at least not molested by the Nazis during the first five years, as was everything which in any way contributed to the emigration of the Jews. It sounds paradoxical, but it is true that this group of young Jews was the only group with a genuine, wholesome enthusiasm at that time in Germany, at least among the people I saw. Among the Nazis there was too much compulsion, over-organization, and among those who were eagerly "in it" there seemed to be that faintly perceptible but constant sultry background of psychosexual maladjustment which has been described by many observers.

By a most extraordinary coincidence, I was the only Jewish physician of my age in a non-Jewish institution in all Germany who was not affected by the "Aryan" laws. This was due to the fact that at the time of the Big Change I was holding a position under the Rockefeller Foundation. Thus I stayed, but since I could not change my profession I took part in the activities of the Zionist groups. We arranged courses on history, on Hebrew culture, or anything we were able to do with the children.

Nevertheless, even then, as it had been the case ten years

before, pure Zionism with the somewhat noncommittal appendix of "Jewish culture" left me dissatisfied and with the definite sense of a void. Don't mistake me. I am, of course, not speaking of the practical achievements at the time. I know that my brother and all my friends have done more for suffering and endangered people than I shall ever be able to do in all my life, and that was all that mattered then. There was Reha Freier, of whom I have spoken before. I want to mention her particularly because it was she who founded the German Youth Alijah; nobody thinks of her today, and all the credit and fame for getting European Jewish children into Palestine goes to others. How shall I ever be able to do what these people have done?

No, it is not that. It is not the question of the immediate practical necessities. Perhaps even then I felt at the bottom of my heart that a mere withdrawal into a national culture was not a solution for the Jews, and what we needed in the end was a universal solution, a solution which was equally applicable and equally binding on those poor devils around us who persecuted us. Moreover, there was the question of the Jews themselves, that big majority for which there would never be any space in Palestine. What about them? Should they be cast off as the injured parts of the bodies of certain animals are cast off? To bridge this gap in Zionist ideology Ahad-ha-Am had put forward his idea of Cultural Zionism. Palestine was to be a cultural center for those who were unable to live there. The Jews in the diaspora should receive their creative impulse from Jerusalem. However, was this not a religious concept under disguise, and if not, was the concept of cultural communication rather shallow and abstract? Whatever my actual reasoning process may have been at the time I saw once more that a national solution of the Jewish problem was no solution at all if it was not at the same time a religious one. Here was the perfectly unique case of a people which was unable to solve its difficulties (what a euphemism!) in a purely "realistic" way.

Something essential was missing. The fate of the Jews was inextricably interlaced with the fate, in history, of their God. This much I knew.

Thus I went back to the Orthodox Synagogue. I argued that if anyone was in the possession of the crystal of truth, no matter how deeply buried in accidental superstructures, it must be these people who had been huddling around something for several thousand years and through all weathers. I was distrustful of Jewish Liberalism and the so-called reformed Synagogue because of all the possible distortion and dilutions of the Word which must have occurred during an assimilation of Jewry to a benign, somewhat colorless and noncommittal Deism of our Western society.

There had been similar tendencies before and my case was by no means unique. I have spoken of Rudi Herz who ten years before had abandoned the liberalism of our general environment and been converted to the strict Orthodox position. The most famous case was that of Franz Rosenzweig, a highly spiritual personality who had adopted Orthodox Jewry as a young man. He exerted considerable influence on German Jews towards Orthodoxy. His most famous work is a peculiar word-for-word translation (with many extraordinary neologisms!) of the Old Testament which he edited in collaboration with Martin Buber. There is also Ernst Simon, who, I believe, has worked a good deal towards reconciliation with the Arabs in Palestine on a religious basis.

Then I was not at all concerned with these examples, in fact, I believe I knew little about them. Since I had left the Synagogue ten years before I had gone through a philosophical Odyssey but not, as it seems now, with the burning urgency which characterizes the seeking of truth. After having been caught, like almost everybody else, by the magic fascination of Schopenhauer's world, I had abandoned myself to Kant's triumphant rationalism and afterwards to Hegel's dialectic and its particular offspring, the dialectic materialism of Karl Marx. There had not been any "problem" for some time.

Perhaps we should not deny the merits of Hegelian dialectics if we remain aware of the fact that they are limited and that they will yield correct results if applied within limits—to the surface layer, so to speak. They work very well with the partial aspects of a given problem, aspects which are artifically isolated. But they never work with the whole of a phenomenon. Under no circumstances can we ever "explain" such a phenomenon as the fate of the European Jews during these last twelve years on the basis of economics, or social psychology, or psychoanalysis or any other science.

It is either meaningless, or, if it has any meaning at all, this must be of a transcendental nature. This was then and still is my firm conviction. It would be easy to prove that once you have experienced this truth everything else follows logically. We shall see what I mean by "everything else."

Here I should like to remark parenthetically that the great fault of our time is not so much woolly thinking in itself but that artificial isolation of partial aspects of wholes, when truth can be attained only by contemplating a whole. This is where at a later stage present-day philosophy helped me a good deal, particularly what little smattering I had of modern German phenomenology and of Whitehead.

16. *Milk to Faith*

IN THE Orthodox Synagogue I was received by my old friends as if I had never been away. It seemed strange, and it was at the same time consoling to me, that all through those ten years these men had been going on praying their regular three times a day and "learning" in their free time. I do not deny that the emotional frills of religion, the icing on the cake, were quite important. To re-experience the atmosphere, to hear the familiar tunes, to relive again the rhythm of the week and of the year, to be again imbedded in the stream of the liturgy gave me a feeling of security and shelter in those days.

On Sabbath afternoons there was a study course of the Prophets conducted by a young man of my age. We took the original text in Hebrew and accompanied it by the traditional exegetic literature such as Rashi and certain texts of the Midrash, Besides this we also studied some medieval Spanish-Jewish mystical literature, eschatological writings of tremendous grandeur and beauty. This, however, was more in the way of recreation besides the "work." Those were wonderful days. I lapped it up, to use an idiomatic expression. I was like a man who has been living for a long time on canned food who suddenly gets home-made bread and vegetables freshly picked in the garden. If there was, in the midst of this mad and tumbling world, Life and Truth—this was it. I knew that with all the fibers of my heart.

Incidentally, most of my friends of the *halutziuth,* including my brother, had a strongly anti-Orthodox bias, and most of them saw no necessity at all for religious tradition in any form. Their prejudice was associated with the fact that most Orthodox rabbis held rather conservative and reactionary views with regard to all Jewish questions. The attitude of these boys towards the religious tradition can be best illustrated by a little conversation which my brother had with a stupid overseer of a synagogue. (I happened to overhear this dialogue.) The man asked my brother whether he was fasting (it was Tisha b'Av, the day of the destruction of the Second Temple). My brother replied that he was not.

The man said: "And these are the people who want to build up Palestine!"

"Palestine won't be built up by fasting," replied my brother.

This was the general attitude. Quite a few of those who had been studying in Yeshivoth stayed, by way of demonstration, at home on the Day of Atonement and took their meals.

Professor Büchler, the head of the Jewish college in London, told me in this connection that he once acted as guide to a group of parsons of various Christian denominations through the co-operatives (*kvutzoth*) in Palestine. After having been through a few of these, the ministers of religion asked him: "But tell us, Dr. Büchler, where are the houses of prayer?" And he had to admit that there were not any. "Jews in the Holy Land—and without synagogues!" They just couldn't understand it.

Those boys and girls who in their lives showed extraordinary examples of self-sacrifice and of a profound sense of justice and charity did not realize that they themselves were actually living on the immense treasure of Orthodoxy. The attempts, in the Western world, to live on pure Ethics deprived of all form are barely a hundred years old. They have not yet been tried in the fire of time. This much we can say: Orthodox Jewry has preserved Judaism unadulterated in its purest and richest form over thousands of years. Pure Ethics is an artifact isolated by a purely rationalist, "modern" process from the huge organism of tradition. Even if we do not see anything wrong with this fact in itself we must admit that, historically speaking, the burden of proof lies with those who are the enemies of Orthodoxy.

To go back to the study group. I have said that the drama in history which I have witnessed myself, the fate of European Jewry, was either meaningless, or else its meaning was transcendental. There is no other alternative. Now if you believe in the existence of God the first possibility is excluded, and that agony of horror which we have witnessed in our time must have a meaning which transcends all materialist dialectics. Since I believed in the existence of God, the answer was obvious.

From this the next steps in my development followed quite

clearly. If all that was going on around us had any hidden meaning, where was I to look for it? If I had not been studying the Prophets at that time, I would still be looking around in helpless confusion. There were men of the remote past, separated from us by two and a half millenniums, who spoke of the drama of history in dark and at the same time colorful, in meek and at the same time overpowering words. These words had withstood the test of corroding time, and they were obviously spoken to you and me. The element of grandeur and power was the only thing I found which matched the grandeur and power of the catastrophe going on around me and, what is more, it was obviously meant to match it. Anyone who has lived through those years when man's face was distorted either in senseless hatred or in a cry of agony can make a simple test. First read a clever and scholarly article on "The Jewish Question," and then read any chapter of Isaiah or Amos, and you will know what I am talking about.

It was around that time that I became convinced of the absolute truth of Revelation, and this conviction too has remained unshakable. Some people among those who read these lines will be disappointed. Because, although I said that I am deeply convinced of the transcendental meaning which is immanent in the historical fate of Jewry, I did not know that meaning. I believe I am closer to it than I was at that time.

I must admit that in the beginning I, like many of us, had a somewhat childlike and simple idea about it. I thought that these catastrophes in Jewish history happen as a punishment, and that the terrible persecution had befallen us because most of us had forgotten that we were Jews and had abandoned the ways of God laid down in the law. This is a rather simplified and anthropomorphic version of the prophetic concept of history. Its absurdity becomes obvious when you consider events in the light of individual cases. My own grandmother, Mother's mother, who lived an exceptionally saintly life, died at the age of eighty-six in a concentration camp. What was she "punished" for? No, if the suffering of our people had a meaning transcending common historical and social concepts, it could not be expressed in that simple formula.

Simultaneously with my conviction of the absolute divinity of prophetic Revelation, I became convinced of the profound significance and central position of the Messianic idea in Jewry. I began to believe in the truth of a personal Messiah as I am convinced of the reality of the paper on which this is being written. In the light of what I have said on Revelation this statement sounds rather superfluous. And yet, it is not quite so. For, in many phases and currents of post-Christian Judaism, the Messianic idea has curiously lost its central position. It has moved over to the periphery and has become pale and ill-defined.

With regard to the Messiah, various views are held by faithful Jews. The most widely held view is associated with the glowing picture of the Messianic Age which is given by the Prophets, a picture of peace and complete fulfillment. "Without the Messiah, no Peace on Earth" means to them at the same time "Without Peace on Earth, no Messiah." The Messiah is signified here, in this world, by the lion lying with the lamb.

Characteristic of the Jewish attitude is the remark which a friend of mine, a Yeshivah student, made to me in Munich during the Abyssinian war: "They say that their Messiah has come nineteen hundred years ago, and just now they are slaughtering one another with the most advanced and cruel weapons."

Very characteristic also is the Hassidic story related by Martin Buber. A Rabbi who happened to be in Jerusalem heard the great trumpets blow, and there was a rumor that the Messiah had come. The Rabbi opened the window, looked around and said only: "I see no change."

I held the same opinion quite firmly. In an ill-defined and yet quite certain way that mysterious meaning of our collective suffering and the Messianic idea were closely connected with one another. I remember that when I was in London the Rabbis used to preach that the Jews were persecuted as the bearers of the Messianic idea, and they left it at that.

17. *Frau Flamm and the Yamagiwas*

IN SPEAKING of the Forschungsanstalt, I have not spoken of friends who came into my life at that time, and who were to play a very decisive rôle. They were Frau Flamm and the Yamagiwas. The latter were a Japanese couple, a doctor and his wife. He was a veterinary pathologist, head of an Institute for Animal Pathology at Mukden, and the son of the world-famous pathologist Yamagiwa, the discoverer of experimental tar cancer. His wife helped him here and there with odd things in the laboratory. Since one of my regular duties was the instruction of our guest workers in neuropathology and neuroanatomy, I came in close contact with this remarkable couple. I soon noticed that they were regarded with feelings varying from distrust to hatred by all the other Japanese. This, I found out, was due to the fact that they were ardent Christian converts and pacifists. The other Japanese were more or less fanatical Nationalists. Mrs. Yamagiwa must have struck them as a particularly distasteful specimen because her father had been a well-known artillery general in the Russo-Japanese war. One of the other Japanese fellows, an ultra-Nationalist, had found a simple explanation for it. He took me aside and told me quite confidentially that in Japan a woman like Mrs. Yamagiwa would generally be regarded as hysterical. She was, he said, utterly un-Japanese, to a degree which to us must be quite inconceivable. It sounded familiar to me; this Japanese was an ideal object for Nazi propaganda. Once when I told him that I was going to visit my grandmother, who was then still free, he asked me whether she was living in Palestine. At first I did not understand. Then it occurred to me that propaganda had succeeded in making these people see in us Jews some sort of second-generation Germans.

To the Yamagiwas I was from the beginning a definite object of curiosity, and it did not take me long to find out why. Except for a pastry cook in Mukden, I was the first Jew they had ever met. They had heard a good deal about it in their Lutheran Bible class in Tokyo. Whenever Saburo Yamagiwa and I were not entirely occupied by neurotropic virus diseases in animals he cornered me about the Jews. I must admit that during those years neuropathology was not always in the center of our interest; we were much too much distracted by all the strange things going on around us. Thus, Yamagiwa succeeded in persuading me to get a Hebrew edition of the Old Testament into the lab and to translate to him straight from the Hebrew whatever little I knew. Thus whenever we were tired of the cyto-architecture of the human midbrain we put in ten minutes of discussion on Isaiah. Strange happenings in a research laboratory, but then I must say everything was in a stage of mild derangement in those days.

Frau Bertha Flamm was one of our technical assistants. For a long time I knew her only for her extraordinary technical skill in making silver impregnations of nerve cells or microphotographs. She occupied, on account of her talents, a special laboratory of her own and we rarely saw her. When we met her at all she was rather silent and seemed inaudible in her movements. She was quite natural, without any aloofness or pose, in spite of her obvious detachment. In fact there was an air of goodness and warmth about her, and although she was isolated and remote she seemed to be the confidante of all the lab girls. She had, for instance, tea by herself in her room but you could usually see one of the girls keeping her company and whispering something to her. She was the type of Alyosha Karamasov, the person who does not belong to the gang, and yet is liked by every single one for his own special reason; that was exactly her position. Here, too, I soon found out that it was not all neuropathology.

Associated with her remoteness there was some strange fascination. Everybody knew a little bit about her, and when you pieced the bits together you had at least the outline of a picture. She was thirty-six, and had a daughter of eighteen. She herself had been a moderately well-known actress as a young girl. She lived apart from her husband in one of the poor districts of the town, in an apartment of one of the dense and narrow dwellings that huddled around old St. Peter's. This was in the center of the old city of Munich. As if to make it a bit more romantic, there lived with her an eighty-year-old washerwoman, Frau Weiss, who, it was said, had adopted her when she was a little child. Frau Flamm went to early morning Mass every day on her way to work, and in the evenings she did household work for mother and daughter. She was extremely meticulous and patiently pedantic in her histological and photographic work, and usually worked overtime. Curiously none of the other lab girls regarded this as unfair competition because nobody ever doubted her motives. She lived a life of heroism in small things. Maybe stories of heroic goodness without glamor tend to sound sentimental and tawdry, and that is why people don't like to read stories about saints.

There are several reasons why I speak of Frau Flamm and the Yamagiwas in one breath. First of all they were both primarily interested in religion, and their tender hearts soon met in a profound friendship. Secondly, Frau Flamm, too, seemed to regard my scanty and recently acquired knowledge of the Old Testament as a source of information vital and burning. Thirdly, all three of them were quite naturally, without the glimmer of a doubt, convinced of something which it had taken me a long and involved struggle to see—the hidden significance of the Jewish tragedy which we were experiencing. They did not seem to know exactly what it meant, but that it reached in its significance beyond the natural plane was obvious to them. I thought I had made a startling discovery but they knew it all the time; it appeared to be linked with something they had learned at school.

I was glad that they did not try to convert me. And yet, it seems now that there was something in the situation which prepared a profound evolution in the depth of my soul. For a long time there was nothing extraordinary in it. Here we were sitting, a Protestant couple, a Catholic and a Jew, and whenever we were not looking at microscopic slides or discussing world politics, we talked about religion. These people were an island because they had preserved human decency. This in itself was a consolation. And yet, in my state of spiritual restlessness, the situation contained at the same time an obscure challenge for me. Here were people of the Japanese and the German race who thought the same thoughts as I, and felt the same feelings as I— entirely different from the pagans around us but also different from those of my Jewish brethren who were agnostic or irreligious. Here I was, in the midst of an ocean of treachery, vileness, cunning and cruelty, separated by two thousand miles from the Land of Canaan, and by two thousand years from the Second Temple—and found people of strange nations who had the words of David and Isaiah engraved in their hearts. This was a miracle. I felt it to my innermost depth but I refused, somehow, to admit it in its fullness and in all its implications.

Two things happened during that time which proved to be very important. One was a chance remark made by the young man who conducted our Sabbath afternoon Bible class. I think it was at the time when we discussed those particularly "Messianic" chapters of Isaiah. He said: "You know, occasionally, when you contemplate these two thousand years of Galuth [dispersion] without even any remote hope of return, you are almost inclined to wonder whether Jesus was not the Messiah after all."

For "Jesus" he used a dark word which orthodox Jews occasionally use, perhaps out of some superstition. Of course, he discarded the thought, it actually had occurred to him as something silly but, as it happens with chance remarks, it stuck with me. My immediate reaction, perhaps already on the basis of my experiences, was: "How do you know he wasn't?"

One evening in December, 1933, I was walking through the streets of Munich, my heart full of the disquietude which accompanies spiritual journeys, and even more by the disquietude caused by the mounting persecution, when my eyes fell on a leaflet pinned on the notice board of a church. It announced Advent sermons to be preached by the Cardinal on "Jewry and Christianity." It had never been my habit to look at notice boards of churches; in fact, it was the first time in my life I looked at one. Since I had just been pondering that very moment about the question of "Jewry and Christianity," I first had the feeling you have when you are deceived by what psychologists call an affective illusion. However, I believed what I saw, and the following Sunday evening my brother and I went to St. Michael's Hofkirche. There was an enormous crowd of people. We were pushed and carried to some place not far from the pulpit. I believe that most people came because they gathered from the title of the sermon that something was going on against the Nazis. This was a rare occasion, probably the first one of its kind.

At that time the Nazis had not only started their onslaught against the Catholic Church and the confessional Protestants, but they had also made big strides in integrating Christian tradition into their system. This was not easy. The Old Testament had to be discarded as alien to the Nordic spirit, and Christ declared an Aryan and anti-semitic, in order to be acceptable to good society. It is difficult now to believe the extent to which these currents had penetrated into the minds of the intelligentsia and the middle-class city dwellers.

Cardinal Faulhaber's sermon was actually very simple and un-sophisticated. All he did was to clarify the birth certificate of Jesus of Nazareth who was a Jew in the flesh, and to reassert the oneness, the complete organic unity of the God of the Church and the God of the Patriarchs and Kings of Israel. He made only a few brief hints as to the preservation of the Jews after the Resurrection. He referred to Saint Paul's ideas on the subject as revealed in those famous chapters of the *Epistle to the Romans.* He also quoted some other Cardinal (I believe it was Manning) who, while preaching to Jews in a synagogue, said: "Gentlemen, where would we be without you?"

The sermon came as if it had been specially timed and written for my personal consumption. It had a profound, irrevocable influence on me. I remember well that, with the few meager hints he gave of the Paulinian idea with regard to post-Christian Judaism, he opened up an entirely new vista. I felt like a child who had known its own house from inside and from the garden, and who is now, for the first time, shown it from far away as part of the landscape.

Every Jewish child is taught that his religion is the mother religion of all monotheist religions, and that this mother has given birth to two daughters—Christianity and Islam. The mother is older, and usually wiser and more venerable than the daughter, and it is somehow or other implied that the Christian sect is Judaism in a modified and somewhat diluted form. Here, in the church and during the sermon, in the midst of this extraordinary setting of Munich in 1933, I suddenly realized for the first time in my life that things were not as static as all that. Did not the Prophets imply that through the Messiah the Word was to be carried to the "farthest islands"?

There was no use denying that this had happened. Contemplate for a moment the fact that there had once been a tiny people at the periphery of the Roman Empire, submerged within an ocean of a thousand creeds, which jealously guarded the precious treasure of Revelation within the walls of its City—and here I was standing two millenniums later and listening to those who did not belong to Israel in the flesh but defended the God of Abraham, Isaac and Jacob, of Moses, Isaiah and Job as if their own lives were at stake.

My first claim, my proud assertion, all that which had been an anchor in the storm of persecution, namely that the election was "ours"—seemed suddenly to be taken away from me. I must admit that I was caught up in a great inner turmoil and confusion. My first reaction, during my conversations with the Yamagiwas and Frau Flamm, had been pride. This pride was not very well defined but it was approximately the idea: "What would you be without us?" Most Jews conscious of their Jewry have this vague sentiment at one time or another—the pride of the first-born, the pride at the discovery that Christianity has emerged from Jewry, as if we allowed them generously, so to speak, to live on our heritage. All this is felt in a vague and ill-defined way.

Now I was shaken out of my inner sureness by the following fundamental and indisputable facts. Firstly, there were two parties who unanimously and in perfect agreement maintained the racial wall around the God of Sinai—these were the Nazis and the Jews. Let there be no mistake. Jewish religion up to this day is based on the axiom that Revelation is a national affair and that the Messiah to the Nations has not been here yet. Do not be misled by the fact that Jews in their personal ethics are anything but exclusive and racist. Do not be misled by certain noble Talmudic principles such as "The just of all nations have a share in the world to come." This latter idea has no bearing on the question discussed here; it deals with what to Jewish antiquity was the "invisible church." Do not be misled by fine cosmopolitan sentiments and actions of reformed Judaism which are often prompted by noble hearts but at the same time by much vague thinking and by a luke-warm dilution of the most profound and world-shaking elements of the Judaic treasure. No, there is no getting away from it. Revelation was still contained within the precious vessel of the Nation; I only had to look at our liturgy to see that this was so. Jewish religion was racial exclusiveness. Mind you, it was racial exclusiveness in its noblest, most elevated form—in its metaphysical form, so to speak. It was a racism exactly opposed to that of the Nazis, but it was racism just the same. It was racism with the highest, divine justification—as long as its one basic premise was correct, namely that the Anointed One was still to be expected.

Secondly, Jesus had come not as the "founder of Christianity," of the "daughter religion"—no, he had come first and foremost to us Jews with the claim of being the Messiah, the Son of the living God. The question then whether he was what he claimed to be had still to be answered with a clear Yes or No.

Thus I found myself suddenly in what seemed to be very dangerous waters. Having grown up in a materialist world, having worked for years in scientific laboratories, a type of work in which an agnostic and materialist position was more or less implied, I had proudly re-stated, at least before myself, the absolute reality of the things of the spirit. The bold and defiant cry of the seventeenth-century mathematician, Pascal, that God is "not the God of Philosophers but the God of Abraham, Isaak and Jacob" had become my own.

And now, not long after the beginning of my journey, I was facing the eternal question: "And who do you say that I am?" What was even worse was the vague feeling in the back of my mind that this question had to be answered fully, and without any possibility of evasion or compromise. There is a common German proverb, "Whoever says A must also say B." I had said A, and all of a sudden there seemed to be a B to it, and I had the dim notion that I might have to say it.

Actually the B was very remote just then—much more so than

would perhaps appear from the way this story is related here. In fact, the more I felt irked and later haunted by question B the more I seemed to cling to the stark overwhelming reality, to the call of the Jewish communion which had become the tragic communion of Fate. I intensified my study of Hebrew as far as I could besides the work at the laboratory. I took part more frequently in study courses and in the services at the synagogue. My intention to go to Palestine became more serious. I wanted to do something constructive in spite of the fact that, contrary to my brother's case, an occupational re-orientation was out of the question.

During that time I was frequently in the house of one of the leaders of the orthodox congregation in Munich, Eugen Fränkel. He was a true example of Jewish piety, and his house breathed the very spirit of Jewish tradition. This man was overwhelmed not only by the sorrow of the persecution but by the personal sorrow of chronic suffering (there was a young daughter bed-ridden for years with some hopeless progressive disease). But he had the translucent spirituality which I have often witnessed in the Orthodox and which seems to be so utterly unknown to most people who discuss the "Jewish problem." In his demeanor, in his actions, thoughts and feelings, he seemed to personify the spirit of the Torah. God dominated and permeated his entire life, from the Washing of the Hands to the stirrings in the innermost depth of his heart. His daughter's agony was double agony to him, yet I have never seen Job's "The Lord has given, the Lord has taken" *lived* as much as in his life. It was his natural gesture, so to speak, and not a strenuously acquired and debatable philosophy. There is an ancient Midrashic tradition that the author of the Book of Job was none other than Moses himself. This legend has always had a deep and touching significance to me. Does it not mean that the writer of the Law which seems to imply that suffering is nothing but wrath and just punishment knew all the time that suffering has also an altogether different aspect?

I had at one time looked after the daughter while she was in the hospital. Thus I was invited to spend the Friday evenings in Dr. Fränkel's house, and this I did almost regularly. I also saw the daughter quite frequently on Saturday afternoons. The Friday evening ceremonies, the round-songs after the table prayer, particularly the Psalms, and Dr. Fränkel's informal chats on a few lines of medieval exegetic literature—all this provided part of my background at that time. I am still convinced that this is the only form of Jewish life worthy the name. Dr. Fränkel had a son who was a well-known biologist, a "pure" Zionist without much religious allegiance. I was unable to understand his position, and particularly why he had doubted what seemed and still seems to me today the very nucleus of the Jewish life. Incidentally, the father had originally maintained the strictly orthodox view with regard to Zionism. Basically the orthodox had been anti-Zionist, because it was generally held that the Jews should not return to Zion unless the Messiah had come to lead them there. Later, however, a compromise was found. Settlement in Palestine and the cultural re-orientation connected with it was no longer regarded as incompatible with orthodoxy. Those orthodox who held this view were called Misrahi. I remember that it had been quite an event when old Fränkel was converted to Misrahism by his children. This had happened many years before the time of this story. In the winter of 1935 Dr. Fränkel proposed my name as that of a possible leader of the Young Misrahi group. At that time, however, I had experienced a little the sensation of Dr. Jekyll and Mr. Hyde. However, I regarded it as a hopeless undertaking to acquaint Dr. Fränkel with the ideas that went through my head. He was so deeply rooted in tradition that he would not have understood me, and I would only have hurt him. I am sure he would have been disturbed and bewildered if he had known about my evenings at Frau Flamm's house. Perhaps he might even have doubted my honesty, although he was too charitable to do this.

Frau Flamm lived in that section of the town in which the poor and faithful had been living for centuries. I believe that there is something similar in all big Catholic cities in the world. In countries like Bavaria the basic layer in the structure of the Church besides the farmers are the little tradesmen and their families, the cooks, washerwomen and maids. There may be much smallness, rigidity and resistance to progress but, at the same time, there is perhaps the greatest treasure of anonymous sanctity. These people always seem to be concentrated in certain areas where the apartments are narrow, dark and overcrowded. There is always enough of mustiness and the smell of poverty in the air to make everything appear just pleasantly unhygienic. [A self-confident man from Hammersmith once said to me: "They say that Roman Catholic countries are dirty."]

In one of those houses, on the third floor, in a dark and somewhat hidden flat lived Frau Weiss, the old washerwoman, and Frau Flamm with her daughter, Ruth-Maria. In Frau Flamm's room we had many evening sessions. It so happened that when I got to know her she was studying Soloviev. Among German Catholics during that time there was a strong interest in the Eastern Church and a trend towards union. I remember that the only decoration in Frau Flamm's room besides a reproduction of El Greco's Madonna was a portrait of Dostoievsky. I do not know exactly what I learned then about Soloviev. The only book I remember I borrowed from her was his famous essay on Plato.

During those evenings with Frau Flamm and her daughter, or with the Flamms and the Yamagiwas, there was a harmony of spirit which equaled that of the Friday evenings with the Fränkels. There was no doubt, it was the same atmosphere of peace and understanding. You will say, "Well, that sort of thing is always present whenever you meet decent people—no matter of what philosophy or religion." No, that was not it, there was something else. It was really the spirit of Judaism I rediscovered in this strange setting, enriched by remote peoples, and cleansed of its purely ethnic elements.

It was not quite the situation of Dr. Jekyll and Mr. Hyde. In fact, I remember very well that Frau Flamm and the Yamagiwas loved and understood the world of Dr. Fränkel, and encouraged me in my endeavors to embrace Orthodoxy. What a strange phenomenon! Yet Dr. Fränkel would not have been able to understand their world. Thus, I made another important discovery. Christianity confirmed and believed everything which Jewry believed but added one fundamental assertion which Jewry rejected. Heresies are based on denials. In this sense Christianity was no heresy from Judaism; it rejected nothing essential but made a new positive claim.

It was about that time that I went to see Martin Buber about my increasing spiritual difficulties. I told him that I had been studying the Epistles of Saint John, and that I found there the spirit of Judaism expressed with such purity and in such overwhelming intensity that I could not understand why we did not accept the New Testament. I reminded him that he himself had once called Christianity the "first Hassidic movement" among the Jews. To this he replied that it was true that the Epistles of Saint John were Judaism at its highest, and that he could well understand my enthusiasm. "However," he said, "if you want to accept Christ and the New Testament, the maxims of the Epistles are not enough. You must also believe in the Virgin Birth and in the Resurrection of Christ from the dead." These things are hard to believe, he said. He began to talk of the giving of the law on Mount Sinai, and whether God really pronounced the ten commandments Himself in His own voice. He wanted to indicate that this, too, was hard to believe. He became quite pensive and said something to the effect that we do not know how to take this description of the miracle of Sinai, and whether the people actually *heard* God. "Perhaps there was only one word said." To me it did not make any difference with regard to the nature of the miracle whether one word or a thousand words were said. Buber's answer disturbed me greatly. I realized that my newly acquired interest in the New Testament which had developed into a profound attachment was actually a rather emotional and romantic sentiment. Buber had put it very clearly. In questions like these, vagueness and compromise were excluded. To me as to every Jew the very concept of the divinity of Christ was something utterly alien and incomprehensible. It was incompatible with the spirit of the Old Testament, and a blasphemy. "Nobody sees God and lives." ". . . Because that thou, being a man, makest thyself God."

In retrospect it is interesting that I could not at all understand why the Voice of Sinai as a true physical phenomenon, something which was actually heard, presented a problem to Buber. He was much more logical than I. Because if that Voice was possible, then the Incarnation was possible too; both phenomena were on the same level. His doubt, on the other hand, had something to do with a general paling and lack of fresh immediate concreteness in matters of faith which is so characteristic of modern non-orthodox Western Jewry. This is due to the assimilation of Jewry, on a cultural plane, as the carriers of agnostic humanism. It seemed to me that Buber, whose original merit had been to open up the treasures of Hassidic piety for the western world, had become a victim of the same process. He was not aware of this. I remember that once, during a conference, he told us: "Several of the young Jews in the Youth Movement came to me and said: 'When we take up a prayer-book we have difficulty in saying *ata* [thou]. It is impossible for us to address God directly just like that!'" If I understood his subsequent remarks correctly, he meant to say that this was a wonderful sign of religious awakening, the experience of immense distance

and awe. In reality, however, Jews who find difficulty in address-
ing their Father in Heaven directly in the second person singular present a very sad picture indeed.

I must state here in anticipation it took me very long, nearly
ten years, to accept the divinity of Christ. The more I came to
believe in Him as a Messiah the more He remained at the same
time the historical person, the prophet who exceeded and fulfilled
all prophecy. One calls this sort of thing Arianism. Had He not
Himself warned us: "Call me not Master . . ."? For a long time
I believed that old Tolstoy was right; he wanted to strip the
Gospel of the supernatural altogether. I agreed with him that the
Church which upheld and defended this supernatural element
of the Gospel misused this very element in order to keep the poor
ignorant, dependent and oppressed; those sects, however, which
preserved nothing but the ethical nucleus of Scripture seemed
to stand for true charity and justice.

I suppose everybody who comes to accept Christ reaches this
goal in his own particular way. It looks as if this uniqueness
were associated with the ultimate secret of the personality.
Somewhere in the back of my mind I knew all the time that there
was something wrong with Tolstoy's position, and that is why I
was not satisfied with it. If the divinity of Christ was an error
or a lie, certain formative forces which radiated from this very
idea and fertilized the depth of the soul were impossible to explain. In a certain inverted and paradoxical sense Tolstoy was
right. For without the divinity of the Messiah the simple piety
and heroic sanctity of some of our peasant maids were somehow
unthinkable, but so were Chartres and Grünewald, and Bach and
Mozart.

This experience of the "historical argument" was very intense
and, it seemed, quite personal. I discovered much later that
Pascal wanted to make it the foundation stone of a great and
lofty form of Christian apologetics. It is obvious from the *Pensées*
that he intended to build on this indisputable fact the scientific

evidence of Christianity. One of my great teachers in Medicine used to say that in order to be a scientist you have to have only one talent—to be astonished at the proper time. The scientist Pascal was astonished at an obvious and simple fact. Just as the Prophets had predicted it, the fruit of Israel had burst at a definite historical moment, the seeds had been flung to the far corners of the earth and had brought forth plants a thousandfold. It seems that Pascal planned a gigantic apologetic work because he, a mathematician and physicist of the Cartesian epoch, was aware of the dangers of modern positivism. He may, in nights of mystic fever, have sensed the wave which was to flood and drown the Western world.

However, we do not know. History is acted in Time, its very matter is Time, and being tinged with Time it is tinged with not-being, with Death. With this our present-day existential philosophers are only varying what Plato and Saint Paul have expressed before. They have rediscovered it under the fear and dread which pervade modern man. If history's very essence were time it would be a formless and structureless matter unrolling itself like permanent finality, a horrible antagonist of eternity. Indeed materialist dialectics, if it were brought to its logical conclusion, would come precisely to this image of history. The only phenomenon which invades history with an element of timelessness is Prophecy. The prophetic view elevates history and enlightens it with Eternity. Eastern Christian thinkers, with their Platonic tradition, such as Soloviev and Berdyaev saw this very clearly. The great Eastern religions leave history aside as a chaotic structure. Only in Judaeo-Christianity do Time and Eternity meet in History.

This is the miracle which overwhelmed Pascal in the seventeenth century. Perhaps with him it was only a "thought." However, for men living in times of seemingly chaotic transition it is an immediate experience, something affecting them in their very being. We have an extraordinary example of this in Saint

Augustine. He was shaken by the transcendental forces immanent in history. When one reads certain parts of the *Civitas Dei* one almost feels as if this had been the very nucleus of his conversion.

However, at the time which I am discussing here I knew nothing about either Pascal or Saint Augustine, at least nothing about the way in which the "historical argument" or the immediate experience of history had overwhelmed them. I emerged from the Synagogue, from our study course on the Prophets, and I met non-Jews who thought my thoughts and felt my feelings, who seemed to glow under the radiation of *shehinah*, the very seat of the Word. Somewhere deep down I felt that all of us Jews who reacted to nationalism around us with national vigor were closer to the Nazis than these people who believed in the God of Abraham, Isaak and Jacob.

There was no getting away from it. If this German woman and that Japanese couple were right, then I was wrong. For if the Messiah had come nineteen hundred years ago then Revelation was no longer enclosed in the precious vessel of the *am ha' amim*, the people of peoples. Then the true bond between the four of us was beyond the blood of the nation; it must have been provided by Him.

If they were wrong, then the Nazis were right. If they had falsely accepted the word of some obscure Jewish preacher of nineteen hundred years ago as the word of God then they were, as many of our Nazis believed, the victims of some monstrous fraud.

Here you have a neat problem. Just try and let one of our scientists, our historians, sociologists, solve it. It is one of those formidable "either-or" problems of Kierkegaard, one of those stinging questions which go on paining you in the depth of your existence until you have given a clear answer.

There were times when I doubted my sanity. Everywhere around me I saw people who were wiser and better than I, and who did not see what seemed to me the essential alternative. Here I was, one of my people in the middle of the most dreadful persecution we had ever suffered and, like a faint shadow, the possibility arose of leaving this community of destiny. This seemed madness. It seemed madness the more since it was my natural urge to stay with those with whom I was born to suffer. Was the swastika not a modification of the Crucifix under whose sign we had been tortured before? This is what it seemed to be if one took history on the natural plane. Perhaps all this was a "build-up," carefully framed by my subconscious to camouflage an escape from Jewry.

I was easily able to dismiss this thought because I saw that during persecution it was only the "race" that counted. Christian Jews did not fare better than their brethren. On the contrary, they often fared worse because socially and politically they frequently belonged nowhere.

Modern man can no longer take spiritual realities at their face value. His is the tragedy of Hamlet. He does not only experience; he reflects. And once he tries on himself all those up-to-date tricks of psychological investigation, he is lost. He lacks naiveness and is distrustful towards himself; soon he sees himself hopelessly entangled in an inextricable network of purely psychological references. Then comes the great turnabout; the only thing which is real, ultimate Reality, appears as something relative, as a pure mirror-phenomenon; and the network of references appears as something very real. At that moment the great negation is completed. This is one of the spiritual pitfalls of our time. I suppose each cultural epoch has its own specific form of negation, and the process I have just described is rather specific for us who are alive right now.

18. *Anguish of Regeneration*

No MATTER in what dangerous straits my people were I knew that, as far as ultimate truth was concerned, I could not make *ressentiment* the basis of my future life. I know that many of my Jewish fellowmen make this mistake. They say: "I am not a Jew in a religious sense but we have been despised and persecuted so much that a decent man could not possibly . . ." This is what Nietzsche called *ressentiment*. It is one of Nietzsche's indisputable merits to have shown the uncreative and destructive qualities of *ressentiment* in history. Mind you, this motive is very understandable and may be justified under certain circumstances but it contains a nucleus of pure negation.

Intermingled with *ressentiment* there is a good deal of pride, not only of wounded pride but of pride pure and simple, of a feeling of national superiority. I do not say it is present with those people whom I have just quoted but I know it was very much so with me.

The great German Lutheran writer, Ricarda Huch, once remarked that for the Jews to become converted to Christ means an extraordinary sacrifice. Not only, says she, must the individual die with Him in order to live; it is the whole people that must die with Him. By some mysterious twist of fate the Jews are the only people which cannot remain a people and be Christian at the same time. Christ extolled a double sacrifice from His people; not only the individual Adam has to die to be dissolved in Him—the group too has to be dissolved.

This is one of the most profound remarks ever made on the so-called Jewish problem. It touches the very center of it. The Jewish contemporaries of Christ who rejected Him knew that by accepting Him they would sacrifice the nation. The one and only condition under which they would have accepted Him, He had to refuse. He could not be their "national leader," and this in spite of the imminent danger from outside. This was a super-human demand. It seems a natural right of every nation to defend itself in times of danger. In the case of the Jews the word of the "seed that falleth into the ground . . ." referred not only to the individual but to the group.

The Jews maintained the idea of racial integrity at a time when it had lost its transcendental meaning; for "all was fulfilled" in Christ. If death, as Berdyaev expresses it, "gives meaning to life," here the ultimate death of a nation will give meaning to its life. But before that happens our people is condemned to live on as some sort of a ghost representing the idea of racism. It seems that in modern times the fate of the Jews becomes more and more intimately associated with the fate of the racist idea. Only when the problem of the un-Christian national segregation is solved, will the "Jewish problem" be solved too.

It is interesting to see how Christians (I do not mean non-Jews but those who profess to believe in Christ and follow His gospel) react when facing the Jewish problem. It is those who are still tortured by nationalism who are anti-semitic. This is what psychologists call projection. They hate their own demon in something they see outside themselves. Read carefully Dostoievsky's anti-semitic pamphlet. There is, page after page, a tone of irrationality and of passion which cannot be explained on the basis of the subject he is dealing with; that is his attitude towards Jewish nationalism. Like all great hatred, this is self-hatred. All the motives he projects into the Jews are, deep down, his own. Just replace the word "Judaism" by "Panslavism," and you know what I mean. Dostoievsky was one of the deepest Christian thinkers of the nineteenth century but there was one way in which he succumbed, like so many other men of that century, to *chthonic* or "earthly" forces—in nationalism. That was his impurity. That is where his own world is incompatible with that of Alyosha and of Myshkin. And what does he do? He bursts forth in an epileptoid fury against Jewish nationalism.

This touches closely upon the secret of why Jewish shortcomings, Jewish vices, Jewish impurities are hated more than those of other people. Because the physical existence of the Jewish people is, from the point of view of the metaphysics of history, an incongruity. The Jews are here, they are living, whereas the ultimate meaning of their existence as a people is that it should transcend itself. This is perhaps the reason why not infrequently Jews who approach Christ struggle more against His final embrace than anyone else. In all those Jews whom I saw approaching the Church and remaining with one foot on the threshold there is, besides a thousand natural obstacles, besides the fear of cowardly betrayal, besides the anxiety of isolation, something else; there is a seemingly invincible horror, something which reaches deep down beneath the social and biological strata of the personality, something that seems to arrest the pulse and make the blood curdle in the veins, there is a cosmic fear, a panic of death and dissolution. It is as if the agony of a people were compressed into the space of an individual existence, as if the agony of all peoples were contained in the night of Gethsemani. This is where being and becoming reach those timeless spheres which are contained in History.

According to the biogenetic law of Haeckel, the embryo's development is a condensed and rapid version of the development of the species. In a similar manner every Jew who is conscious of his Judaism and is converted to Christ goes, in his lifetime, through the spiritual destiny of his race. Hence this particular intensity and agony of development, hence this profound anxiety which is nothing but primeval fear of death and of birth. I think it is ultimately on the basis of this fear that we can explain some of the paradoxical attitudes, the writhing movements which we witness in people like Franz Werfel. Read this passage written not long before his death: ". . . [the] Jew who goes to the baptismal font deserts Christ Himself, since he arbitrarily interrupts his historical suffering—the penance for rejecting the Messiah—and in hasty manner not foreseen in the drama of salvation, steps to the side of the Redeemer, where he probably does not at all belong, according to the Redeemer's holy will; at any rate, *not yet*, and not here and now." This is what the panic of total eradication will do to our thoughts. We all go through these and similar mental contortions before we have torn up all our earthly roots and let ourselves fall into space and into the great embrace.

If I speak of the ultimate significance of the dissolution of the Jews, I mean it in the Paulinian sense. I do not speak of "assimilation as the only rational solution" of the Jewish problem. This idea is a typical product of nineteenth-century liberalism. It is the very counterfeit of the conversion of Israel. A religious Jew who chose to be burned at the stake by the Inquisitor rather than let himself be baptized is obviously closer to God than a modern Jew who is baptized to solve the problem of anti-semitism for his children.

Jacques Maritain once said that the Nazis adopted certain elements of the Old Testament and applied them in distorted form (racism) and the Communists did the same with certain elements of the New Testament (the brotherhood of men). In the light of this thought, it is interesting to see how these two movements approached the Jewish problem. The Nazis, in denying the historical significance of the coming of Christ, tried to re-establish a pre-Christian status, and produced a diabolical caricature of the segregation of the people of Israel. The Bolshevists, during of political pantomime of a Messianic fulfillment, attempted some peculiar state of assimilation of the Jews. At least originally (things have developed differently during the Stalinist period) the Bolshevists gave our poor Christians of the West a lesson in racial tolerance, not only of the Jews but of all minorities. However, this solution presupposes a purely naturalist concept of Man. It is logical only if we believe in nothing but the materialist dialectics of history, it is one of the practical shortcuts so characteristic of modern materialism and nominalism. It may have, like communism in general, begun in individual impulses of a longing for justice but it ends up in that form of equality which is a feature of machinery, of a world of machinery in which human life loses its creative significance.

Thus, the orthodox Jew who rejects Christ vigorously is much closer to the Christian than enlightened intellectuals who keep the "sayings" of the "great social reformer" Jesus on their bookshelves next to anthologies of Confucius. Because, by their vigorous denial, the Orthodox constantly re-state the potentiality of a true Messiah and of His divinity. Whereas the others, no matter how good their intentions may be, rob the God of History and the God of the thornbush of His devouring fire. If one believes in a concept of history which is not materialist, then one must admit that the dynamics of spiritual development is constantly fed and upheld by the dialectic antithesis which exists between Synagogue and Church. Forces of evil have separated the two. How much would be won, even today, if Christians could have a glimpse of orthodox piety. That monstrous phenomenon, religious anti-semitism, could never appear again. If a Hassidic mystic and a follower of Saint John of the Cross could know one another, not separated by a barbed wire of social and political prejudice but in a spirit of charity, they would be amazed how akin they are in their striving. However, for some strange reason that does not seem to be possible. Nevertheless, it is, as we have said, just that dialectic tension which is of creative significance. This is, undoubtedly, one of the meanings implied in Chapter IX of the *Epistle to the Romans*.

It was a perturbing experience for me, just when I had rediscovered Judaism, just when I had become immensely proud of my spiritual heritage in the middle of the most plebeian stupidity, just when I had found something absolutely certain while others around me were choking in the fear created by a world of shifting uncertainties, to see that I might have to abandon what I had found. Today I know that there was actually nothing I had to give up. On a spiritual plane Christianity is Jewry. It is Jewry led to its fulfillment. There is no essential truth of the Old Testament which the Christian denies.

At that time I was, like most of us, so enmeshed in social and political concepts that I did not see this simple fact, and I did not want to see it. I had an almost triumphant feeling about the stupidity of our persecutors. Since the word "Christian" today is synonymous with "non-Jew," I made great use of the confused issue and said, like many of my fellowmen: "See . . . the Christians . . . how they behave?" As to those poor real Christians around us such as Frau Flamm, the Yamagiwas, our good and noble Dr. Schulz—it was just too bad for them. Whenever Frau Flamm spoke to me of Christianity, I felt as if I had to look through the window, like the Rabbi in the Hassidic story, saying: "I can see no change." As violently as I had been hit by the experience of what I called the "historical argument," I seized upon the historical counter-argument. Perhaps the Messiah had been realized in that small group of people around me, but what about mankind in general? Where was the lamb feeding with the lion? I had only to look through the window to see every bestiality, every horror, every stupidity ever committed by Babylonians and Egyptians. The peoples were still the *goyim.*

It was only gradually, in the course of years, that I began to realize that Freedom of the Will, the greatest gift bestowed on man by God, was not abolished by the appearance of the Messiah. If that central historical event nineteen hundred years ago had changed the fundamental ontological structure of man, then there could never have been any idea of man, nothing—as I would put it today—corresponding to the second person of the hypostatic union. If Christ by his very appearance had created a complete social change on earth then the Messianic idea would be a *contradictio in adjecto*. [Incidentally, the post-Christian development of the Messianic idea among Jews is by no means uniform. I believe that there is, for instance, an interesting Midrashic tradition of the Messiah sitting unknown to everybody at the Gate of the City and dressing his wounds.] To transform the world mechanically by an extraneous event would distort the *te' munah*, the *image* which man represents. Therefore those of us are utterly wrong who, like the Hassidic Rabbi, look through the window and say: "With towns and villages of innocent people bombed, with millions of innocents thrown into machines of annihilation, it simply cannot be that there was a Messiah here on earth."

The more I became convinced of this, the more I felt that reasserting the Jewish position meant agreeing with the Nazis against the Christians. My remote feeling of triumph was nothing but a dangerous form of pride. I believe that the position of post-Christian Jewry is somewhat the same as that of the Prophet Jonah. After his message is delivered to the *goyim* he remains outside the walls, grudging with God. To be a Prophet and in his function of a Prophet not to be associated with the idea of the nation is so horrible that he would rather drown than fulfill his mission. It is the enemies of his people whose conversion is at stake, and to sacrifice his national pride for the conversion of others is more than his human nature can take. There seems to be profound symbolic significance in the fact that the Book of Jonah is the reading on the afternoon of the Day of Atonement.

I saw then that the fate of my people was intimately associated with the fate of Christ in the world, that there were people around me who held in their hearts the God of Israel, although they were not Jews; and in the intensity and profundity of their lives I saw the Messianic prophecy of Isaiah fulfilled. This was the beginning of a new outlook on life. Something old had burst, though I did not want this fact to be true. Something new had sprung up. I did not know where I was being led. But I felt that insight meant obligation. I knew that there would come a time when I would have to make the big jump into the unknown.

Under the indescribable dread of persecution, I began to see the meaning of the mystery of Israel. However, no matter how intense this experience was, it only initiated a change in my life. Christ is not only the Messiah to Israel. If He means anything then His meaning transcends all national destiny, it would affect you as a person even if you were alone on this planet. Experience may stir you up in your depths and make you receptive. But if you were left like this you would be nothing but a hollow recipient. Marx said about Hegelian dialectics something to the effect that philosophers have thus far interpreted the world but it is for us to change it. In the same manner we can say that after having interpreted our destiny we have to change ourselves.

At the end of January, 1934, just two months after the Cardinal's sermon, I was seized by a severe influenza. When I tried to get up I could not. My limbs felt like lead, and I was unable to walk for a distance of fifty yards. The doctors told me that the hilum of my lungs showed a peculiar knotty swelling and that my sedimentation rate was way up, one hundred and thirty. The fever, they said, was negligible. I was told to take it easy, and I remained in my room in an attic in Schwabing. I felt so sick that I was unable to move. After three weeks I went to the Students' Health Service. They fluoroscoped me and told me that I had to go immediately to a students' tuberculosis sanatorium in Agra, Switzerland. When I got there I found out that the place was, although in Switzerland, a German Nazi enclave. Back I went to Munich.

I presented myself to Professor Lydtin, a well-known chest specialist. He said: "My dear boy, what you have got is miliary tuberculosis." I had learned that miliary tuberculosis is one of the few hundred per cent fatal illnesses. He looked at me and quickly added: "Don't be afraid. If this had been able to kill you, you would already be dead." Then he gave me a long lecture about extremely rare types of miliary dissemination over the lungs in which there was some peculiar allergic tissue reaction which enabled the body to vanquish the illness. "Of this form only two dozen have been described in the medical literature— and to think that you are one of them." He took me in front of the X-ray showbox, and there, radiating in a milky light, was the picture. A huge hilum-like cumulus cloud, and all over the lungs as far as you could see, snowflakes. "Now I understand why you feel so rotten, the worst feeling you must have had was before the tissue reaction appeared." I did not believe any of the things he told me except "miliary tuberculosis" and I was certain that it would kill me. Even if it would not kill me—a German Jew, in the academic profession in 1934, afflicted with illness—I found myself suddenly at the margin of existence. It was a death sentence with a peculiar type of execution. I looked back at my life and found it singularly meaningless. I looked ahead and was seized with fear.

They sent me to a private sanatorium in the Black Forest. For months I lay in bed and saw nobody except the nurses and doctors. Then I lay outside on the gallery for several hours, twice a day. I spent about ten months on my back, thinking all the time. On the mattress to my right was a young man of a Prussian noble family. He was a philosophy student, and had studied under Heidegger. His entire life history, since childhood, had been interspersed with episodes of tuberculosis. He was very stoic about it. He belonged to the Confessional (anti-Nazi) Protestant Church and was a good Christian.

On my left was a sociology Professor from Louvain. He was one of those Catholics who sympathized with the Nazi movement, out of a romantic idea about the Holy Roman Empire or something like that. I pointed out to him how incompatible his position was with Christianity and told him about the struggle of the Catholics in Munich. He became quite attached to me and his attitude seemed to change entirely. However, a few years ago I heard that he was a collaborator with the Nazis in Belgium during the war, and was condemned to death after the liberation of Belgium.

Von Lössl, the young Prussian, always had a volume of Aristotle in the Greek original with him. I used to read the Old Testament in Hebrew with the aid of a Hebrew dictionary. We exchanged bits of Bible and Aristotle. Von Lössl gave me lectures on "being," of which I understood nothing. He tried to be more explicit by using the Greek terms from the original. With this method I understood even less. He told me that he intended to study Saint Thomas under Gilson or Maritain in Paris. Nevertheless, when Lemans, the Belgian, was not present he told me that the Jesuits had secret trap-doors in the Vatican into which they lured their adversaries; underneath the trap-doors were cellars full of skeletons.

In July, 1934, the snowstorm picture of my lungs had become denser, and the Doctor stopped showing me my X-rays. However, in September they began to clear up. By that time I had had much opportunity to think and to study something about *being* in spite of the fact that Lössl's Aristotle was somewhat obscure. At the end of 1934 my lungs were clear and I was able to return to Munich, even though it was winter.

19. *The Wrong Schmid*

FOR MANY years life moves forward as something fortuitous and inconclusive. It is as if destiny had withdrawn itself into a far corner. Then there come months when everything seems to be tinged with the infinite. Lives are extricated from the haphazard stream and symbolize what is beyond the accidental. Thus it was in Munich, as it had been in Heidelberg and in Paris. There was a peculiar, almost painful, intensification, as if everybody had been forced to present all that was in him, in a condensed meaningful way, before we were finally called by destiny.

I had come to Munich with several introductions. There was a circle of musicians, with which Frau Masser made me acquainted. Herr Masser was a banker, attached to the Dresdner Bank. When the Dresdner Bank dismissed all its Jews, including those in prominent positions, Herr Masser came home with the news that he was pensioned. He thought that this was fair, and that business people had a better chance than those of us who were in the professions. This pension was some hint of Justice, a remnant of fairness. It saved the music-room with the Bechstein grand piano, an island of beauty and friendship to be preserved until the flood would have subsided. There was one child, a boy of eight who could not go to school any more because he was Jewish. What should become of him?

Shortly after the news of the pension arrived we had some chamber music in the large music-room. Late in the evening Frau Masser played one of the Bach solo suites for violin. Her sad eyes, her handsome face, the Bach with its virile romanesque beauty, all this seemed to leave the Dresdner Bank and the pension behind. It was as if she owned a magic carpet by which she could save her little boy instantly, on the spot. But, beyond, Herr Masser knew, there were the strange cities of Australia in which a man of fifty-three would be ground into the milling stream. "Out there" it looked like certain perdition. There was no doubt. Herr Masser was enough of an economist to know that the Nazis could not last long. He showed it to me in figures. The debts of Germany were appallingly high, even without full-fledged re-armament. Frau Masser said that she would rather take her fiddle, and no money at all, and go to Australia. Incidentally, it was often the women who sensed the greatness of the impending catastrophe and who wanted to take chances.

The Massers acted as if their disagreement were accidental. Herr Masser did not like Bach. He said it was dry stuff, and he whistled Offenbach operettas to tease his wife. As a matter of revenge, on Herr Masser's birthday, she sneaked up to the bedroom door while he was still asleep and began to play a Bach solo suite. On our music evenings Herr Masser got the stands ready, unpacked the instruments and saw to it that the musicians were well regaled. He was proud of his wife, and said that he would be content to be an usher and live on his pension. There was a strange game of mutual half-humorous, half-tragic deceit going on. Thus, the pension developed into something unlimited by human whim, like Time itself. Wolfgang, the little boy, stayed at home; the Massers kept on waiting and making music.

In our ensemble was an excellent viola player, an elderly high school teacher, short, with a round protruding stomach. He came from one of the oldest Munich families of generations of schoolteachers. He appeared silently, took his appointed place, played beautifully, said little, wrapped his viola in a silk scarf, packed it in the case and vanished silently. His name was Käsbohrer. Like every true musician he was strict and forbidding when it came to exactitude of performance. In the middle of a passage he sighed or threw a hand up like a disgruntled station-master (this precisely was his appearance). Presently he pulled an old reading-score out of the pocket of his luster jacket and pointed at a combination of legato bows and staccato dots. Either it was because he was the only non-Jew and therefore accentuated the element of isolation, or because we were too sophisticated and nervous by comparison, or because he was so silent and matter-of-fact; there was something unreal about Käsbohrer. He took his place in our midst like a ghost. After a few weeks, however, I found out. Someone told me that Käsbohrer was a staunch Catholic. When the Nazi persecution of the Jews began he made a vow to make music from then on only with Jews. This was his form of protest.

Frau Masser said to me: "You must meet Julia Menz and Willi Schmid." Julia Menz, the famed harpsichordist, and Willi Schmid, music historian and critic, were both Bach experts. Julia Menz gave concerts abroad and when Frau Masser spoke of Julia flying from India to Java, I realized that Julia was Frau Masser's other self, her ego by desire. In this way Frau Masser must have been flying in her dreams, from India to Java, from Australia to New Zealand. There was still some world in which Bach's sequences sounded as if in a pure atmosphere, far away from Hitler and the Dresdner Bank and pensions. Frau Masser and Herr Käsbohrer kept insisting that I must meet Willi Schmid and Julia Menz. They meant to arrange for it at the next possible occasion. I never met either of them.

In the case of Willi Schmid the reason was quite extraordinary. On June 30, 1934, during the famous purge, he was taken away from his house and shot. No reasons were given. On the same day it was discovered that he had been the victim of a mistake. The SS guards, in their great zeal, had mixed up two people of the same name. A storm-trooper by the name of Willi Schmid, apparently one of the traitors of the party, had been on the black-list. The mistake was barely discovered when it was corrected. The true Willi Schmid was also shot the same day. In those days for every person who perished and for every person who was saved there seemed to be an element of the seemingly fortuitous, that puzzling element of chance, of hit and miss. There is no reason why I should not have been killed in a gas-chamber and the Massers should not be alive in Canada. But Willi Schmid's case, the story of the two names, seemed so blatant that it kept haunting me for years.

Perhaps it was the bizarreness of his story, perhaps it was the obvious symbolism implied in his common name; at any rate, whatever it may have been, I began to feel about Willi Schmid precisely as the Friar in Thornton Wilder's *The Bridge of San Luis Rey* felt about the victims of the collapsed bridge. I began to become interested in any data about his life which might give a possible meaning to such a murderous coincidence. A few years later Willi Schmid's friends published a collection of his essays, letters and poems, and a biographical obituary by Father Peter Doerfler, Bavarian priest and writer. This book was published in 1937 in Germany; it contains little that would compromise Schmid politically—anything of that sort would, of course, have prevented its publication. Yet there were a few sentences which could be interpreted in such a compromising way. On the other hand there were remarks which can, if one tries, be read as if Schmid belonged to those intellectuals who strained themselves to find a bridge toward Nazism. In other words Schmid was perhaps an example of those "non-political" Germans who represented a puzzling and disquieting phenomenon in a world in which political and moral issues are too closely intertwined for the comfort of one's immortal soul.

The story of his childhood sounded rather like the romantic biography of a Southern German poet and musician. His spiritual food was Goethe, Stifter, Moericke and Latin and Greek poetry. There were people who later remembered him as a schoolboy sitting in a Munich streetcar with a volume of Virgil or Catullus. It was the custom that the boy who led his class should give a speech at the commencement exercises. He was chosen to do this but, instead, performed a cello sonata by Richard Strauss.

He began his university years by studying philosophy and romantic philology at Munich, later the history of art in Rome. When the First World War broke out, he enlisted as a volunteer. The war left him stranded, like so many others, barely alive. Typhoid fever in Serbia, an abdominal gunshot wound at the battle of the Somme; both left him an invalid for years to come.

During those years he studied pedagogy, art history and music, and in 1923 received his doctorate with a thesis on Don Bosco.

In 1924 he first began to edit old choral works and Mozart's church music in Pustet's *Musica Sacra*. At the same time he found employment as music critic on one of the Munich papers. During the following ten years he was most productive, unearthing ancient pre-Bachian music. His journeys of research took him to Berlin, Prague, Paris, Milan, Turin. He made some most delightful discoveries. Even the month preceding his death yielded valuable findings in monasteries at Ravenna, Cividale and Padua. However, deciphering those scores alone did not satisfy him. He studied the old instruments, especially ancient types of viola, like the viola da gamba, and soon he was able to perform the music. This he did together with other violists and with Julia Menz. Moreover, it was he who supported and stimulated Wolfgang Graeser during the reconstruction of the *Art of the Fugue*, Bach's gigantic musical testament which, up to that time, had consisted of seemingly unconnected fragments like a rubble of stones that has to be rebuilt into a celestial temple.

When I tried to look at him against the background of the weird, ghost-like chiaroscuro, Munich, 1934, there was one thing that struck me very forcibly and at once—that was the curious mixture of a somewhat simple patriotism with the "European" attitude. This seemed to be inherent in him, not acquired on some intellectual detour. This peculiar brand of *Europäertum* was quite characteristic of Bavaria. It was still manifest in peasants and the "simple folk," even in this century. No doubt it was a residuum of medieval cosmopolitanism. While the intellectuals of Europe were gradually getting rid of nationalism, the peasants of Southern Catholic Germany had not yet accepted it. With them there was a feeling of friendship for, or at least never any really hostile feeling toward, Latin peoples. This Latin and European affinity was, as everyone knows, the main reason why Bavaria originally did not display any enthusiasm for Bismarck's imperialism.

While reading little essays of Schmid's on Paris, Verona or Gmund, on Casals, Picasso or Slevogt, I had a familiar sensation which I could not identify at first. Ah, there it was—the same feeling one has when reading Mozart's letters from Paris, Rome, Dresden or Prague, or the diary of some medieval traveling craftsman. It is a European cosmopolitanism which has its roots in the soil of cultural tradition and is not acquired by philosophical speculation. Schmid said in one of his most beautiful essays ("The Catholic Element in Mozart") that Mozart's music is *naturaliter christiana;* just as one could say about people like Schmid, that they are Weltbürger by nature, sometimes in spite of narrow provincialism. As far as he was concerned, it was some sort of Latin patriotism which was obviously irrational, certainly not political, on the contrary, something of an "erotic" nature (in the sense that he himself occasionally used this word). Let us quote from an essay called "Parisian Impressions":

The general picture of the streets, the way the girls walk, the students argue with one another, the workmen have their meals, all this is somehow pervaded by a Latin atmosphere. I am resting in the shade of the plane-trees near the Quai on the Island of St. Louis and I am watching the fishermen. Their stoic calm is the same as in the days of Bouvard and Pecuchet, the same as depicted by Daumier who lived in that pretty little ancient house next to Baudelaire. Once more you hurry to see your Watteaus in the Louvre; once more you experience that feeling of happiness when facing the early Greek relief which a benevolent philologist has christened *l'exaltation de la fleur.* Strolling across the Place des Vosges you pass that grandiose Victor Hugo—Parisians celebrating enthusiastically the *centenaire du romantisme* do not distinguish very much between him and the really great Delacroix. Again you buy the same fresh wholesome fruit from the ladies of the Halles. Everything is as it used to be. You are again surprised and amused by the church of Sacré Cœur; its architecture is like majestically blaring brass music. However, while I gaze from the Eiffel Tower over Paris in the mild, veiling light of the setting sun I am reconciled with everything. I am greeting Les Invalides, the Seine and Notre Dame. There it is, Paris has caught me again.

There was nothing very original about all this and I had read similar things in other essays on Paris. And yet when one held these lines against the background of a certain petit bourgeois Upper Bavarian element in the book, they began to glow in an enchanting light. From there I penetrated a little further. The most remarkable feature of this man was something else—the perfectly homogeneous synthesis of artistic and spiritual or, better, of musical and religious values.

The word "synthesis" is not quite correct, for it implies that these elements once existed separately. In his case one could not conceive of them separately; this was a definite impression which the essays, in themselves not very significant, conveyed. Music was religion, allegiance to something; and religion, on the other hand was deeply interwoven with its modes of artistic expression. "*Musica sacra* penetrated and tempered *musica vulgaris,* the firstborn, with its creative breath," Schmid said. This profound organic relation was apparent everywhere, in his essays on Mozart and Bach as well as in that article on Paris. There he finished up in his own home, as it were, with the Benedictines of Solesmes and with the Gregorian chant, after having dealt with interesting technical details on Landowska and Casals, and on Cortot's interpretation of Couperin and Debussy.

I had the feeling of approaching more closely the tragic secret; the symbolic paradox of such a life and such a death. Nietzsche, not the neurotic of the "blond beast" and the "Antichrist," but the other Nietzsche, the prophetic historian, often proclaimed this as the specifically German tragedy, namely that political power and spiritual greatness exclude one another entirely. The Germany of Bismarck and that of Bach cannot live side by side; while one is in bloom the other must needs perish.

On a bright June morning in 1934 the storm-troopers entered

the house of a man with the common name of Willi Schmid. Did he protest? Did he swear to his innocence? This I do not know. He was taken into a police yard, put against the wall and shot. Immediately it was seen that there had been a mistake. A mistake? It did not matter whether there was really a mistake, or a "mistake" faked by a personal adversary. The latter possibility is excluded, according to people who knew the situation. It did not seem to me an accident at all, it was not "one" Willi Schmid who fell a victim. It almost appeared to me as if his common and typical German name, marking him for his fate, was no mere coincidence. No, he and his name symbolized that German element which was murdered "by mistake" in that most senseless of all revolutions.

After Nietzsche had become mentally deranged, there was found among his possessions a peculiar document—a warrant to arrest and shoot Bismarck. Bismarck was to Nietzsche the expression of a Germany he hated deeply, the Germany of military might. This silly, grotesque little incident sounds like the reversal of the tragedy of Willi Schmid. Here a personal individual event and the super-personal, symbolic destiny are but one. Here Thornton Wilder's Dominican would not find it difficult to decide between chance in its cold mathematical aspect and fate in its high significance.

They found among the numerous little notes and excerpts on Schmid's desk, a quotation from the letters of Saint Bernard to Pope Eugene the Third. *"Ordinatissimum est minus interdum ordinate fieri aliquid"*—"It is quite regular that sometimes something irregular should happen." This idea appeared quite frequently in Schmid's writings, the apparent irregularity of things which are regular in a higher sense, the perfection of things which are imperfect on a natural plane. For example, he says about Mozart: "The fact that the Requiem remained unfinished appears to have a mysterious significance, as it has in the case of unfinished Gothic cathedrals, of Bach's *Art of the Fugue,* and of

Saint Thomas's *Summa*." What a strange way of writing a motto about one's own life.

I came to believe that he was able to live through those last hours of cruel darkness with some inner light. In a beautiful essay on a Bavarian Franciscan, Sister Maria Fidelis, he had spoken several times of the vicarious suffering of unknown individuals. Curiously enough, he touched on this idea in connection with the history of post-war Germany:

Christ's sacrifice is of infinite value and lacks nothing. We, however, are often not worthy to partake of it. We can become worthy of it through our suffering and through the suffering of others. Oh, highest mystery. . . . Her life of sacrifice coincides with the storm which shook our country during the post-war years. We who hear about God's mysterious work in her soul feel as if we had been aided by a stream coming from this well.

After all, no one ever will know the secret of his last hours but again it seemed as if I could now apply the last sentences of that essay on Sister Maria Fidelis to the writer himself:

Such a hint . . . is not meant for the curious. Their desire to be thrilled by the miraculous is not fulfilled in this case. However, some others will be humbled by the ever-new miracle of Christ's working. They will be humble and grateful that our country was considered worthy of something sacred at a time when Antichrist seems to rule the world.

20. *Jonah*

EARLY in 1935 Professor Spielmeyer died. This happened only two months after my final return from the sanatorium. Then I knew that it was very dangerous to wait longer, and I looked for a position outside Germany. From the time before I left Munich for London, there was one scene which, for obvious reasons, has left an indelible trace on my memory.

It was in the assembly house of the Jewish Congregation of Munich. We were all gathered in the bare, office-like conference hall. There were representatives of all Jewish youth groups, and a few rugged individualists who were not affiliated with any particular group. Martin Buber had come to give us a brief course of instruction. The whole affair was planned to last twenty-four hours, and was intended as a model course. A new type of collective study of Scripture was to be demonstrated, and Buber had chosen the Book of Jonah as his subject.

Martin Buber, a man of middle height with a wavy black Assyrian beard and a big mane of hair, was seated at a desk surrounded by eager boys and girls. They were grouped like a parliament, although this had obviously not been intended. At Buber's right were the *werkleute*. This was a group of young German Jews who more than anyone else followed Buber's ideas, although one could not say that Buber had any real system which one could have followed. These *werkleute* were recruited from the liberal, "enlightened" Jewish middle class. They corresponded to an original group, the *kameraden*, which had undoubtedly been the most "German" one within the entire Jewish Youth Movement. Most of them were children of those well-to-do businessmen who used to wear silk hats when they visited the reformed synagogues once or twice a year, on the holiest of holidays.

Only a few years had passed since the *kameraden* had been sitting around campfires and reciting Goethe, Rilke or some obscure poet from the Northern German heath. During recent times, however, these young people tried to go back again to the source of Jewry, which the reformed synagogues could not give them. The world of traditional Orthodoxy was closed to them, strange and perhaps even repulsive. It is Martin Buber's indisputable merit to have offered a drink of the purest wine from the vineyard to those who had grown up in the world of Goethe and Rilke and who would never have found their way through the brushwood of Orthodox formalism. Although Buber had never intended to found a school, the *werkleute,* by accident, so to speak, had become his enthusiastic disciples. It is said that they built up fine co-operative farms in Palestine.

In that part of the hall which was facing the desk there were groups of *habonim,* formed out of the fusion of two groups, one of which had always been Zionist, and the other neutral but with Zionist sympathies. I had years ago belonged to one of these two groups. Now the *habonim* seemed to be interested in extricating as many young Jews as possible not only from Germany but also from the unhealthy atmosphere of commerce, intellectualism and assimilation. They had several camps in the country in which, during that phase by agreement with the Nazis, young Jews were still prepared for emigration. These people from the Jewish urban milieu were taught to till the soil, to make clothes and shoes and to live in the *kvutzoth,* the co-operative settlements of Palestine. Ludwig, then one of the leaders of the *habonim,* happened to be somewhere in Northern Germany at the time. The *habonim* assumed a rather non-committal position in Buber's course. These people, who had mostly grown up in a German cultural atmosphere, had an intensive program of Hebrew studies; nevertheless they were little interested in religious problems. Co-operative socialism, agriculture, and the Hebrew language were all that mattered, and this complexity of interests was loosely linked with some vague ideas on Hebrew tradition and culture. The majority of them were anti-orthodox.

Left of Buber were the *misrahi* and other Orthodox. There were some who looked pale and lean, with dark glowing eyes, bloodshot from waking, praying and studying. I knew them very well because I belonged to their synagogue, and took part in one of their study groups. They seemed to live in a world of their own. They wore black skullcaps and they hardly mixed with the others. During recess or in the evening they suddenly got up and, without the least embarrassment, said the Eighteen Prayers as if nobody else were around. To anyone who listened it sounded like a mechanical repetition of formulas, and this impression of ceremonial rigidity was emphasized by stereotyped movements, the bowing at certain words, the three paces back and forward at the beginning of the prayers. It was not quite clear why these people had come at all. Most of them seemed to know more about the etymology and the exegesis of the text than Buber himself. In spite of this, for some reason they rarely took part in the discussion.

Once only, towards the end, was there a quarrel. Even today the point under discussion seems important. For those who do not remember the Book of Jonah sufficiently, I should like to review it briefly: Jonah receives a special order from God to admonish the Gentile inhabitants of Nineveh who had succumbed to a life of sin. He wants, however, to evade his duty, and he flees (hence the adventure with the whale). But circumstances force him to land in Nineveh. There at last he carries out his divine mission: he predicts with prophetic certainty that Nineveh will perish within forty days. The Ninevites believe him, are converted, and change their mode of life for the better. Therefore God does not carry out the plan which Jonah had prophesied —He preserves Nineveh and its people. Jonah is extremely disappointed that his prophecy is not fulfilled. He settles outside the city and sulks about God and men, especially God.

The traditional interpretation of the Book of Jonah is as follows: Jonah, the only one among the Prophets who had to preach exclusively to Gentiles, was a proud Jew. To preach the word of the Lord to the enemies of the Jews, the inhabitants of Nineveh, hurt his feelings of national dignity. Therefore, he attempted to get out of his mission altogether, and later when the people of Nineveh were converted and saved, he stayed grudgingly and in isolation outside the walls of the city. This interpretation of the Book of Jonah has a meaning which I have already indicated.

Martin Buber, however, gave an entirely different interpretation: Jonah had received the order to predict the destruction of Nineveh. As a prophet, however, he knew beforehand that there would not be any destruction. In the eyes of the people of Nineveh he would appear as an impostor, because what he predicted with certainty would not occur. This was the reason why he tried first to dodge the issue altogether, and later, after he had played the rôle forced upon him, withdrew with a grudge.

All this was perhaps Buber's personal exegesis. At any rate, the way he proposed it sounded very modern and psychological. Now to an Orthodox Jew traditional exegesis is as ancient and as binding as Scripture itself. Therefore the *misrahi* presently began to open fire and a heated discussion developed in which the *habonim* and *werkleute* joined, although they knew nothing about it and did not care very much. The Orthodox insisted as if their life were at stake. I recall vividly how clusters of fanatically debating people remained after the *misrahi* and other Orthodox had already said their *maariv* (evening prayer).

The scene was outside time. Here were young Jews in the middle of Germany, an island engulfed by contempt, hostility and danger. If some SS leader had been in the mood for it, all of those who were there could have disappeared forever in a concentration camp, the same night. Nobody seemed to give it any thought. At that moment the only important thing was the significance of the written word.

How could I forget those two days? We hardly stopped to eat; everyone had the feeling of the keenest intensity and concentration. Everyone knew that "in the coming year" he would be "in Jerusalem" or in some strange land. Some, I fear, were deported to concentration camps and killed.

For me it was the last time that I was in close contact with the world from which I came.

"Should I ever forget thee, Jerusalem. . . ." Oh, how I should like to be able to see them all once more, my friends of those days, and tell them the story of a journey which seems to have taken me infinitely far away from them, but in reality has led me right into their midst.

IV
ENGLAND

WHEN I arrived at the pier in Harwich I had to queue with
a large number of people who were scrutinized by an immigration official. When my turn came, the man asked me whether I
was looking for work in England. I had been briefed and said:
"No, I am going to stay for a two weeks' vacation with friends."
He asked me to show a letter of invitation. I had been briefed
for this too. Triumphantly I reached into my pocket. But, alas, I
could not find the letter. Feverishly I reached into all my pockets.
The crowd behind me became impatient. The immigration official
finally decided to take the rest of the people while I looked for
my letter. When all the people had boarded the train, he took
me once more. "Don't you have any letter at all? Some letter, at
least, to show who you are." I felt reassured and pulled a letter
out. It was from Frau Spielmeyer and was addressed to a Neurology Professor in London. "The bearer of this letter was the last
assistant and favorite pupil of my late husband. He is looking for
a research job in England. . . ." The interpreter read this letter
to the immigration official. The official shook his head, and said:
"I am sorry, but you go back to Germany. . . ." The train had
been waiting for me, and now the engine whistled. The interpreter looked intently at my hat, took the immigration man aside
and whispered. Then they both looked at my hat. Finally the
immigration man said: "All right, go."

Now I was one of the Refugees. First we settled imperceptibly, like dust, in the huge cities of the Western world. Then there were corners in which the dust tended to collect, and in which it was easily seen. There were streets full of us: Greencroft Gardens, London, N.W.; Washington Heights, New York City. Many, however, settled like dispersed particles in Paddington, Ealing, or Hendon. Each one of us carried an invisible wall of strangeness around him because those summer evenings of our childhood in Königstein or in Starnberg were incommunicable.

There were times when you had to approach your neighbor. On a Sunday morning you needed small change in order to get the slot machine of your gas-heater going. The neighbor handed you the coins politely and to him you, in your dressing-gown with a towel around your shoulder, were the German-Jewish Refugee next door, part of that penetrating anonymity of the city, like the fog.

Parents arrived, and grandparents. Old men, patriarchs in their stores in Reutlingen or Chemnitz, or in their offices in Magdeburg or Ulm, whose lives had been part of the seasons and of the fragrance of Suabia or Saxony, turned into strange boarders and roomers. Their happiness was the joy of escape, something that evaporated unnoticeably and was absorbed by the city. They fell into the arms of Generosity but Generosity was no mother. It was a nurse with the odor of antisepsis.

All, even the oldest among us, learned the language. However, the city gave us only the hand-me-down, the second-rate words, instruments of practicality as useful and comfortable for the life of strangers as the underground, the bus, the park and the public bath. The infinite in language is something quite beyond public convenience. In our new land it had ripened underneath the gables in the Cotswolds, over brooks and heaths of Northern England, and over the wharfs of London for an eternity before we presented our passports at Harwich.

There was a new form of happiness and strength to be able to "get along" so soon in stores, on busses, in the laboratory, with patients. We used, with great dexterity and cunning, inexhaustible variations of nouns, adjectives, verbs, sentences, while all the time Language gazed upon us remotely. Our native language had become that of the Enemy. It was somehow associated with that thing behind us, that monstrous Anti-Mother, that dark and demoniac crater from which we had come. Hence, most of us tried frantically to hide everything that could ever remind us of it, even the

> *"Füllest wieder Busch und Tal*
> *Still mit Nebelglanz"*

which expressed the irretrievable melody.

When I arrived in London I obtained a research scholarship from the Medical Research Council at the most famous neurological center in the English-speaking world. A Jewish family which had founded that particular research scholarship had made a provision that a German-Jewish refugee was to have it. "Queen Square" was as much of a microcosmos of Britain as the Psychiatric Institute in Munich had been one of Germany. The consulting and teaching physicians exuded the atmosphere of Harley Street and of that mixture of sobriety, pragmatism, dryness and brilliant lucidity which is so characteristic of Anglo-Saxon science. There is no medium in which Neurology can thrive better, and therefore it was not surprising to see that the "Queen Square" people had brought that branch of medicine to its perfection, and maintained it on that level. The Homburg hat, the pin-striped trousers, the tightly rolled umbrella, and that doctor's leather case seemed to go well with a neat, intricate network of neurons which ran smoothly or fused and stalled somewhere outside the world of human suffering and passion.

In the bowels of the hospital were the ancient laboratories. The neuropathological laboratory was a huge room, the height of a church, with an entire wall consisting of an enormous window. The room resembled one of those old-fashioned woodcuts of laboratories one might see in an 1890 edition of the *London Illustrated News*. But even inside the building, one worked in the London air of mist and fog; our boxes for microscopic slides were always covered with a velvety layer of soot.

The technical staff seemed to mirror humorously the world of the "big shots," at least as I beheld them. There was the histological chief technician, a little man by the name of Anderson who had originally been a Yorkshire miner. He carried on his small body the head of a professor, different only by that imponderable something which attempts to devaluate, by some trace, the features of all intelligent people who are born in poverty. He had been working in the mines since the age of nine, and his fingers showed the characteristic "beatings." During the First World War the Dean of the Medical School and Chief Pathologist had discovered him in a base hospital, and since then Anderson's genius had been devoted to that delicate craft of microscopic staining. He had invented new staining methods, and had even published a successful small manual on the subject. Anderson worked at the head bench, and talked, sang and whistled incessantly.

Besides that England of recumbent reticence which is always represented in Continental magazines by a long-legged man with a shag pipe, there is an equally characteristic England which is unbelievably garrulous. The chief pathologist and his chief assistant were representatives of these two Englands.

The laboratory was a place in which philosophies clashed. I was bewildered to see that Anderson, with all his past and present, was a Conservative with just the trace of an inkling of Fascist sympathies. One of the lab boys belonged to the left-wing labor group, one boy was a staunch Catholic, the biochemist was a devout Baptist with the characteristic liberal tradition of English non-Conformism. The young research workers were physicians who came from Scotland, Ireland, Australia, the United States and Canada. While everybody was busily impregnating nerve cells with metal compounds or azo dyes, gently bathing microscopic sections in small glass vessels or titrating or centrifuging, there was a continuous repartee in what seemed to me many tongues. Incomprehensible remarks whirred past my head, released short salvoes of laughter or intricate chains of argument. At times the lab boys seemed to become exceedingly hot-headed. Conservatism appeared shamefully stripped of its glory by Socialism and Liberalism. Or the Catholic Church was squeezed mercilessly within a forceps of Nationalism and Marxism. Tempers flared and periods of silence followed. It only needed an interruption like the familiar call, "Tea is ready," and everybody sat down with an air of perfect amicability as football players do during half-time.

The relationship between the various levels of professional hierarchy was characteristically different from anything I had ever seen on the Continent. Between chiefs, assistants, technicians and charwomen there were walls which it took me a long time to notice. Yet the doors of the Dean's office were always open, towards the laboratory and towards the corridor. When the technician needed slides from that office he walked straight in, did not stop whistling, and the Chief did not lift his head from the microscope.

When I made my first appearance, there was no secretary to announce me. I had to place my hat—an impossible Continental affair with an umbrella-like brim—right on top of a celloidin microtome. I did not even find the time to take my greatcoat off; it was a huge gray Munich greatcoat, resembling an igloo. Everybody went on working, carefully giving the appearance that my presence was unnoticed. Yet I am certain to this day that my hat and greatcoat, and the fact that I attempted frantically to remain on the Chief's left side while walking, brought me the scholarship. Oddity was highly appreciated.

This, incidentally, I found confirmed throughout England. For instance, later when a lab boy had to be hired and there were many applicants, one pale dysplastic chap with a red frozen nose and bluish amphiboid extremities—one of those boys from London slums whose very appearance seems to call for more food and sunlight—got the job. His name was Bradshaw, and he had come by bicycle all the way from Clapham Junction to apply. The Chief christened him "foetus," not at all maliciously; it came as close to the true features as any designation could. Thus, Bradshaw was more or less permanently added to the collection. It was not so much the case of average people having the fun of selecting cranks; everybody, in order to be somebody, had to be a bit of a crank. This complicated system may well be the salvation of England within the type of world civilization which is about to develop.

All of us, even research workers with international reputation, had to do our own manual work, the cutting and imbedding of tissues, the handling of the ovens and microtomes, and the staining. Anderson, like many people from the north of England, had once sung in choirs and was expert on Handel oratorios. Thus, in order to enliven the tedious and monotonous work at the laboratory benches, when we were not engaged in arguments, we sang. Anderson conducted, and it happened not infrequently that a prominent neurologist from abroad who was being taken around in the hospital, found the entire laboratory, doctors and technicians, singing the "Hallelujah" chorus from *The Messiah*, while shaking tiny pieces of tissue suspended in various metallic solutions.

22. *Primrose Hill*

I DID not attempt to regard myself as one of them. The Jewish tragedy in Germany had made me conscious of false façades, and I sometimes saw camouflage even where there was none. Of course, there was the elderly German-Jewish refugee who spoke only English, even within his family, and wore plus fours and played golf. I did not want to be "one of them"; I had seen to what this led. However, Bradshaw and I were both accepted for the very reason that we were "different." Something else kept all us refugees psychologically corralled: our fearful gaze into the crater in which the others were still struggling. While to those around us Hitler was one other incident of European barbarism, an abstract political phenomenon, we knew that individual lives were gradually being extinguished. It was not the "Fascist problem," or the "Czech question," or "Chamberlain's moral victory" or "Chamberlain's moral abasement." These were abstractions, easy to cope with. But there was the hemiplegic old man in Eisenach from whom they took his housekeeper. There were my grandmother, uncle and aunt who were not allowed to leave the house before dusk, the same people with whom I had gone on gay hiking trips in the blue mountains of the Rhön. Letters increased which, under disguising words, showed that laughter and smiles had altogether disappeared, that Herr and Frau Masser were sitting with their eight-year-old boy in their attic, silent, wondering what I might be able to do. It was as if vises were closing imperceptibly around a hundred thousand necks. This kept us apart because it could not, in its concreteness, be re-experienced by "others."

Frau Masser's letter was written with the despair of the death-sentence. But letters have to be dealt with by committees. I am only Number 73 in the queue, it says so on my little card. The lady behind the desk tells me that I have to fill Form D but that I have to come again and queue in front of Room 6 where I shall get Forms A and B. If Frau Masser's wealthy uncle can bring proof within the next three days that he can guarantee her support in case of accident or illness, we might push her case through within the next three months. No, an uncle in the United States is of no use because his guarantee is of no avail to the British Home Office. In that case I have to fill Form C. The room where I obtain Form C is closed now but I can get there next Monday. Meanwhile the vise has closed by one thousandth of an inch. Where will it be when I return after three months?

Frau Masser has beautiful features and can play the Bach violin solo suites better than anyone I have ever heard. But this means nothing to the lady behind the desk and I do not blame her. The lady is kind, and it is only out of kindness that she sits there. She has dealt with the seventy-two people before me similarly, and there is nothing else she can do. In the files in front of her is compressed a multitude of lives full of love, pain, and happiness. Perhaps there are other Frau Massers who play Bach solo suites and have little boys, God only knows. But Form C must first be signed by that uncle and confirmed by the Home Office. The Home Office is overburdened with cases like this.

I am doing "research." I am interested in tumors of the thalamus, an area in the center of the brain. I am also interested in the Red Nucleus in Man. The Red Nucleus is a peculiar motor area in the human brain. Many people have wondered about its function and have made experimental studies on rabbits. However, the human Red Nucleus differs from that of lower forms, even from those of anthropoid apes. Perhaps its morphological change comes about parallel with the development of upright gait. I imbed brains in celloidin. It takes four weeks before I can make microscopic slices and stain them. Anderson and Doctor Cumings, who watch me sitting at the microtome, are obviously wondering about me. They know that my brother and my parents were left behind.

I go back to Room 6 at the Committee, with Form C filled out and signed. Meantime an entirely new regulation has come out. The Home Office has waived Form C altogether. Could we not try to get the Masser family into Australia?

If only I could get Frau Masser over here by magic into that large house near Hampstead Heath in which the people have so many rooms that are not being used. They could sit around the fireplace in the evening and listen to her playing the Bach solo suite or, if they do not like that, to Mendelssohn's violin concerto. They would listen to the beautiful music and watch her beautiful head. They would say, "We are glad to have this woman here, we are going to put her and her husband and her son up in that top-floor room. There is no difficulty for her, with her music, to find a way in the world."

Frau Masser remained unknown to those people. Meanwhile her letters became more imploring and more frequent. Perhaps it was really a question of Form C, the British Home Office, the Australian High Commissioner, the wealthy uncle's affidavit. Perhaps it was something else that kept her and her family back. After all, a great many people had found their way to Great Britain, more than to any other country in proportion to the population figures. But Herr and Frau Masser perished.

My little address-book had the names of all those whom I knew to have emigrated to London before me. One of the names was Liselotte's, who had left her bookbinder shop in Heidelberg. At the time when I came to London she was working as a bookbinder at the Warburg Institute.

I met her at the Cumberland Hotel for lunch. She looked me over, my umbrella-like hat and the igloo greatcoat, and asked me whether I was here on a special mission; in that case my disguise was very poor. I told her that nobody ever looked at me in the street. She said that in England nobody looks at conspicuous people in the streets; it was not done. She said that what had happened to Hitler regarding the Jews had happened to her with Germans; it was a horrible thing to say, but she could smell Germans. I said that I doubted that she could smell anything German in me because I was no German—I was a Jew.

I said that we were a segregated people, segregated by a mysterious fate, and that we ought to practice severe dietetic and other religious laws to keep a fence around us. This segregation had something to do with our mysterious *raison d'être*, and that a Jew must first go through persecution to be able to grasp this. I told her about the work my brother was doing with Jewish youth in Germany. She said that this was all wonderful, she had hardly ever met any Jews who were conscious of their Jewry. Most of the Jews whom she used to know, for instance among the university professors, tried to disguise their Judaism and be something they were not. At this I lowered my voice, glanced around the tables to see whether anyone was listening to us, and said that I wondered if Lewis' in Oxford Street was a Jewish store, because I had intended, from the time of my emigration, to buy only in Jewish stores. At this remark she became silent again and looked me over.

After a pause she said: "I don't know what's wrong with you boys who come out. You are all carrying something around you. I call it the cloud. There is a cloud around you. I had it too; only with me it was of a different sort. But we all leave that place over there with the cloud around us. It takes some time to get rid of it."

In order to reassure her I told her something else which was more comprehensible. I said that I seemed to be in a panicky fear of succeeding in the new country, or at least my wishes were two-pronged. It was the hesitancy of being born into a new world, the fear of birth. In the beginning I had discovered to my

dismay that with the wish of obtaining a job, I secretly harbored
the wish not to get it. There used to be a famous Munich come-
dian, Karl Valentin, a gawky and cadaverous man, who had
identified himself with an imbecile petit bourgeois to an extent
which was uncanny. He used to play the scene of a man in front
of a dentist's office, hesitating to push the bell and saying: "If I
knew for certain that he was not at home, I would ring." This is
often our attitude when we are confronted with new steps in life.
However, once emigrated, you had to ring the bell; there was no
going home.

With the mention of Karl Valentin a lost world was conjured
up; the world of the small people and their real life, the beer
halls, the market-women around St. Peter's, the infinitely funny
and likeable Bavaria which we had known when we were children. For a moment there was a rift in the cloud. We struck up
loud, thoroughly Continental laughter, and tears rolled down our
cheeks. Liselotte told me that in England one did not slap one's
knee, at least not in hotel dining-rooms.

She was living in a rooming-house adjoining Primrose Hill.
This is one of the places at which many planes of London seem
to intersect. One walks up there through Camden town, an area
in which working-class people live in narrow gray streets with
small shops. The grayness was disquieted and pitifully enlivened
by huge colorful walls of Oxo, Guiness, and Bovril, and by the
glistening canyon of the London, Midland and Scottish Railway.
You also can walk up to Primrose Hill from St. John's Wood, or
through Regent's Park, straight from the fashionable homes in
the neighborhood of Baker Street. All that is so close seems
worlds apart, but once one is up there, one is on a hill overlooking London, and the distance produces the peaceful illusion of
equality. Her room overlooked the trees on the hill.

She told me how she had come to emigrate. One morning her
father received a letter from the university authorities that he
was dismissed. They had discovered several Jews among his an-

cestors, so that he was exactly half-Jewish, all told. "According to this," she said, "I was only twenty-five per cent non-Aryan, you know." However, even her father with his Mosaic ancestors could have stayed, had it not been for his political convictions. So they used the Aryan legislation as a pretext to give him the sack. Liselotte herself received a letter from the Reich Commissar of Arts that she was permitted to continue her work. The house in Heidelberg was abandoned, terraces, garden, Neckar, Shakespeare plays and all. The Professor was betrayed and vanquished by the little wooden model of a stormtrooper which he had carved during those silent afternoons. He moved to an industrial city in the Rhineland and started a private practice. Spitefully he opened with it a little workshop in which he made braces and flatfoot supports with his own hands. Contrary to what the Reich Commissar for Art must have assumed, Liselotte did not make much of her seventy-five per cent. She left Germany.

In London she lived first as a guest of a leading British surgeon in Harley Street. There were seven domestic servants and in the morning, on waking up, she got her tea and *The Times.* There was dinner every night in evening dress. After three weeks, she moved out and took a small room near the Thames. There were days when she had no money left for the next meal. During the first two years, she had eighteen different jobs. She acted as a tourist guide for Germans (she showed me a linen cuff which said "Fremdenführer"). The pay was small and she had to live mainly on tips. The Germans all wanted to see historical spots, which she provided freely. At a certain place on the Isle of Wight, she never forgot to say that here a meeting between Napoleon and Lord Nelson had taken place.

At one time she posed for an advertisement of stockings, and after that she took part in an advertising film for the Savoy Hotel, "A Day at the Savoy." A stranger named Harkness and she had to play a couple living at the hotel, from breakfast to retiring. Harkness in his dressing-gown poured coffee and passed her toast with eggs and bacon, all in a room at the Savoy. After they had had breakfast the scene had to be shot again, and then they went off horseback riding in Hyde Park. After she had taught German at a girl's school, she found the position of bookbinder at the Warburg Institute.

We went to the house on Primrose Hill and I looked around the room. There was a beautifully lettered quotation from the German Romantic philosopher Schleiermacher, something about God in Nature. Hanging on the wall was a quaint Würzburg wine bottle and, on the same nail, a large rosary ("a farewell gift from Kati Huber," she told me). There were many hand-bound books, the collected works of Tolstoy, several volumes of Sigrid Undset, Goethe, Nietzsche, E. T. A. Hoffmann, Jean Paul, and a volume of essays by Bergson, beautifully bound. She showed me some of her lettering. She came from a German school of lettering which descended directly from Johnston, the man who had been the master of Eric Gill. She herself had never met Eric Gill.

I looked at the books and said: "Listen to me, I am serious. Don't think that this is going to be The Cloud or that I am crazy. . . ." And I began to tell her about my experiences with the Catholics in Munich and about the Yamagiwas; that I had discovered a new Judaism, and that it was Christianity; that I was in a great dilemma because here were my people and here was Jesus, the Christ who had come to us as well as to those who wanted to exterminate us. I had come to believe with Saint Paul that the true Jews of today were those Gentiles, like Frau Flamm and Doctor Yamagiwa, who followed Christ.

After I had finished she said: "Never mind, it *is* The Cloud and you *are* crazy. . . . Why are you not happy about your beautiful Hebrew tradition?" She said that she had never had any religious belief in a formal sense. However, in her darkest hours in London she had taken to reading the Psalms again and the Book of Job and they were a profound consolation. Compared with the power and grandeur of the Old Testament, the Gospel

was just sugary lemonade and the Saint Paul a traveling sales-
man.

All this sounded like a famous passage from Nietzsche. I found
out later that she had never read it. As a matter of fact,
Nietzsche had only expressed what a large number of Germans
with Christian background felt. This was probably a revolt
against the sweetened, unheroic, sofa-cushion variety of Christianity cultivated by the middle classes of the nineteenth century.

"Look here, you don't understand what I mean," said I, and I
started all over again. I said that her distinction between Judaism and Christianity was only a matter of public school terminology; that Christianity itself *was* Hebrew tradition, even Martin
Buber said so. That once you have understood the Messianic
spirit of Isaiah, there was an organic transition, a transition of
growth right into the Gospel.

But she remained adamant. She added that Luther was the
worst of all of them. "If I ever were a professing Christian, I
would be a Catholic." I answered that the Lutheran revolution,
if not Luther the man, was understandable when one considered
the externalized form of Christianity of his day. She would not
hear of it. Perhaps she was trying to appear clever.

There was something strange about all this. I, a Jew who had
discovered the Gospel, attempted to persuade a "Gentile" who
had discovered the Old Testament. The situation showed clearly
that thinking and talking meant little if unaccompanied by acting and living. Whatever our views may be, we had come
from roots far apart; she from an over-sophisticated academic
tradition, I from the merchant's house in the small town; she
from a liberal Lutheran, I from an "enlightened" Jewish background. We both had been instilled with Goethean humanism
but our revolts against the bourgeois tradition had taken entirely
different routes. We both had known the life of "freedom," the
perfect libertinism of European youth of the twenties, and the
hangover of nothingness and spiritual despair. No matter what

our views were, her indomitable courage and her straightness of action expressed reality much more clearly than all my talk.

We were both equally endowed with a sense of style. It should not be surprising that we first resolved to get married during a moonlit night in the churchyard in St. John's Wood. However, the so-called Nuremberg laws made our marriage dangerous for our relatives at home. We had to think very seriously of reprisals. This, on the other hand, made it more adventurous, and belonged somehow with the Full Moon and Churchyard.

I went to the town hall on Haverstock Hill. There were several floors with dismal corridors. On one door was written: "Deaths." The next one said "Marriages." At the desk I found a man of drooping appearance, with steel-rimmed glasses. I addressed him by stating that I was of German nationality and one hundred per cent non-Aryan, my future wife was twenty-five per cent non-Aryan on account of the fact that her father had two non-Aryan grandparents. Therefore our marriage, on the basis of the Nuremberg Laws, was criminal and punishable by at least twenty-five years of prison for the less-Aryan partner, that is to say myself. "Now I happen to know," I said, "that there exists a mutual agreement between Great Britain and Germany on marriage laws. That is to say a marriage which is illegal in one of the two countries is automatically illegal in the other."

The drooping man who had listened without interrupting said politely: "Would you mind repeating all this?" After I had explained in more detail, particularly about the percentages, he said: "My dear man, Great Britain is legally bound to such an agreement only as long as both countries' marriage customs are within the reasonable boundaries of morals. Sit down, young man. Let us suppose for a moment that Germany had introduced polygamy or a law according to which widows have to be burned. . . ." In the end he advised me, for the sake of our relatives in Germany, to keep our marriage secret and to live under separate addresses.

Once, when we walked down Oppidans Road, we saw a rotund pink-cheeked lady of about sixty standing in front of a house whose fence was newly painted in sky blue. "Here comes Destiny," said Liselotte. "Ask her whether you can have a room." The lady's name was Mrs. Silk. She said that she did let rooms, but only to special friends. However, after a little while she told me that there was one room free which I could have.

23. *On Hope*

THE NEW COUNTRY began gradually to engulf us. Everyone knows the atmosphere of the happy, wholesome family in Charles Dickens' novels, that family in which the young lad finds a haven of refuge after having been subjected to the cruelty of stepmothers, spinsters, headmasters and schoolmates. Precisely such a family were the Silks. Mrs. Silk had looked me over the same way as the Dean of the Medical School had done before. Then she had added us to her collection.

Oh, those bucolic breakfasts on Oppidans Road. Those merry nights with the logs singing in the fireplace, and Mr. Walters, a ginger-haired, long-legged young man, explaining everything about Chamberlain and Halifax. Evelyn Cooke, in between the incoming and outgoing boat (he was a ship's doctor), studied the Choral Preludes and the *Well-tempered Clavichord,* the latter with vocal accompaniment. Claude Silk, one of the sons, had been a medical missionary overseas. There he had lost his wife, who caught pneumonia while nursing a native. He returned with five children, and with five hundred dollars in his pocket. There seemed to be numerous other ladies and gentlemen, all with equally fascinating life histories. I never knew how many belonged to the family. Everybody seemed to be related to everybody, if not by blood, then at least by Mrs. Silk's maternal bonds.

She had that untiring, relaxed, effortless industriousness which appears to give the guest a moral right to sit longer than necessary at the breakfast table in order to thrash out some important point on the toasting of bread, the curing of bacon, and (alas) Chamberlain and Halifax. Her maternal rotundness protected us from demonic forces; even passionate and obscure quarrels among the boarders and the family seemed to lose their sting. That family was ill-defined in its frontiers; somehow we belonged to it and played our part.

Claude was a towering man with circular outlines, a huge peasant head, and big brown eyes. He wore a cassock with a leather belt and crossed himself when saying grace. He did not take any permanent job after coming back from overseas but deputized for other Anglican clergymen.

It was never quite clear how many of the people paid for their board; economics was subordinate to something else in the order of things. The crucifix was hanging there, the fireplace was burning, the framed cross-stitch patterns said something about Jesus and love and Jane Silk, 1883, as if all this were destined to be used by anyone who happened by. There was the spirit of ancient Catholicity, draped in a few pieces of national costume. I never knew what value that costume had in the eyes of those who wore it. When I spoke once to Claude about Roman Catholics he said: "Many of us admire them, some of us envy them."

However, the intrinsic suffering and passion of Europe were alien and remote. The sultriness and the neurosis and the animalism which contributed so much to the German revolution—all that could just as well have been part of Gehenna, for no inkling of it penetrated Mrs. Silk's house. I was obviously the victim of something which was not cricket; that was that. When Chamberlain saw Hitler, Mrs. Silk was satisfied. It was the decent thing to try anything to preserve peace.

Thus, in spite of Claude and Evelyn, and John, and good old

Mother Silk, and the biochemist and Anderson and Bradshaw and the Committee, we felt that between us and Germany had arisen a huge smooth wall of rock. When we listened carefully we could still hear those trapped ones inside—grandmothers, uncles, aunts, Herr and Frau Masser with their boy. We heard faint knocking here and some scratching there. There was nothing to be done. "Dear Sir, re: Mr. Ludwig Masser, File No. 723921 RS, In reply to your personal inquiry at the Committee on Feb. 19th, we advise you that the Cuban Government admits families with a temporary permit under the following conditions only. . . ."

The complexity and abstractness of human life in our time seemed to strangle the hearts of men. Mixed with the feeling of freedom and hospitality was the shuddering exposure to fear. This is the way a person must feel who, having escaped a shipwreck, spends the night alone in a lifeboat. What has become of those behind? Is this the same cold night through which all other ships are sailing while the passengers are snugly tucked into their beds? No wonder that, with all the warmth of Charity, we saw with heightened intensity the large City ground into a molecular mass of loneliness. All that I had once seen in Moabit, those lives spent by the poor in thousands of equal rooms, that infinite cacophony of voices, the posters for beer and those for life insurance, the implements without creation, the rapidity of communication without communion, all this blended into a piercing noise of negation.

It was in this mood that I came in contact with Saint Thomas for the first time. I read a book, *On Hope,* written by a German Catholic layman, Joseph Pieper. In this book the author expounded the teaching of the Angelic Doctor on the virtue of Hope. Until that time, Hope had been to me, as it is to most people, something purely natural and an everyday emotion. I remembered that in my childhood I used to see cheap symbolic oleographs representing Faith, Hope and Charity, and I used to wonder how Hope got into it. Hope seemed to be related to wish rather than virtue.

The book started off with the Christian concept of the *status viatoris*, Man in the state of a wayfarer. The opposite of the *viator* is the *comprehensor*. Man who has comprehended, who is in possession of the beatific vision, is no longer "on the way." As long as he is alive, however, he is in the state of a traveler. Human existence contains an element of "not yet," and this element has a dual significance; on one hand the absence of completion, and on the other hand a direction towards completion. This absence of completion contains a negation; it puts Man continuously into the dangerous proximity of nothingness. The dark abyss of freedom is the freedom to choose negation.

Willful choice of negation is possible. Since Man, says Saint Thomas, is a creature endowed with Reason, no natural means can prevent him from sinning, "because he originates from nothingness, and therefore he has the power to turn towards nothingness." Only when the *status viatoris* is abolished and the *status comprehensoris* is entered, is Man united with the Absolute Being and the freedom to choose nothingness is "tied." From this dynamic polarity between the *status viatoris* and the *status comprehensoris*, from this "direction towards" completion which is implied in the *status viatoris*, Saint Thomas, or rather Herr Pieper expounding Saint Thomas, evolved the theology of Hope.

To me it opened up, through a little gap, a gaze into a lofty Christian anthropology. The three streams of Hope, Faith and Charity were shown in their true perspective, not from below but from above. They assumed their full, wide, all-embracing significance which transcended whatever they "meant" emotionally on a natural plane. The dark antipodes of Hope were Despair and Presumption. Both destroyed the *status viatoris*, the "not yet" of human existence. Despair transformed it into naught, and Presumption faked comprehension. In both instances, the stream of becoming was arrested and transformed into petrifaction and death.

Hope as well as Despair, transcended their natural meaning and became infinitely deepened in Christ, the true image of Man. "Since our Redeemer," says Saint Thomas, "has created and perfected Faith, it was of equal salvation to us that He introduced us into Hope. This He did by teaching us prayer by which our Hope is directed towards God." Despair chooses Nothingness, Hope pierces Nothingness. "Even if He should kill me, I put my hope in Him," says Job. Since Hope has been heightened by the act of redemption, the potentiality of despair has been immensely deepened, too. If you want true Existential Philosophy, in the deepest sense of the word, there is Existential Philosophy for you.

These few sentences perhaps do not explain the shaking influence this book had on me at the time. Pieper not only supplemented Saint Thomas with the quotations from the early Fathers of the Church but with many references to modern philosophy, particularly that of the Existentialists. This resulted in an anatomy of despair and anxiety which surpassed anything I had come across in natural psychology. It was just as if a mathematician had tentatively introduced a factor, and saw that the formulas "worked." At times in Euclidian Geometry one makes a trial start with an arbitrary assumption, and comes to evidence. This was about the way I felt.

Someone once remarked that you should try experimentally to live for one day as if the Gospel were true, even if you do not believe it. In the same way I invite you to think of the nature of Man as if Christ had been God-Man and died for your and my salvation. The whole of anthropology as conceived by philosophers and psychologists is at once deepened in a very peculiar way. It is as if a great, but albeit two-dimensional, picture received a third dimension and came to life. If, as Auden once remarked, it is the function of the poet to introduce order into chaos, then God is our poet.

I used to sit on a bench on Primrose Hill and look over all the City of London. If it were true, I used to think, that God had become man, and that His life and death had a personal meaning to every single person among all those millions of existences spent in the stench of slums, in a horizonless world, in the suffocating anguish of enmities, sickness and dying—if that were true, it would be something tremendously worth living for. To think that Someone knocked at all those millions of dark doors, beckoning and promising to each in an altogether unique way. Christ challenged not only the apparent chaos of history but the meaninglessness of personal existence.

In the autumn of 1938 a Jewish boy shot a German Embassy official in Paris. This was followed by the first nationwide round-up of the Jews in Germany. For several days the newspaper vendors kept shouting something about murder. This time, I knew it was the real thing. Reha Freier arrived, I do not know how, and we sat waiting and talking, like the relatives of miners who are trapped in the pit. All she knew was that my brother had been arrested while coming to the rescue of a children's camp. He was taken to Buchenwald concentration camp.

We ran around in the streets, we sat in a little Lyons' tea shop, in the musty offices of the Jewish Agency, then inside some railway station, we went to the Committee, and to another Committee, again to the Agency. There was nothing practical we could do. Reha said the persecuted were stronger than the persecutors. They seemed to be full of triumphant joy, she said, and I should not worry. While they were being loaded into wagons, they sang the Psalms in ancient Hebrew melodies. As long as I was sitting with Reha Freier in those smoke-filled rooms, in front of teacups and cigarette butts, although we could do nothing, I had at least the feeling of being in contact with my brother because she was the last one to have seen him in freedom.

One evening, I began to talk to her about Christ, about the significance of His life and death, about Christians, about the

Yamagiwas and Frau Flamm, and about the Cardinal's sermon and Saint Paul. At this time I was already so certain that I must have sounded very convincing.

Like all of us, she had what you might call a cold admiration for the human person of Jesus.

"I do admit," she said, "that there is some strange mystery by which His suffering and death have drawn millions of people to Him for two thousand years."

I had kept all my thoughts back for a long time. Then it poured out of me under much pressure. The darkness, bewilderment and discord of the Christian epoch in Jewish history dissolved the moment you saw that one thing. The Christians who hit Jews were hitting Christ their brother. The Jews who rejected Christ rejected their own God, their own supernatural essence. As long as Christ crawled like a wounded man in the no-man's-land between those two fronts, no political measures would ever solve the "Jewish problem."

Reha became pensive and said: "All this sounds as if it must become very important to us Jews sometime."

She, a Zionist, a rather emotional Zionist at that, who spoke the beautiful Hebrew of Isaiah and of the Psalms, said that she could not believe in any Jewish concept of God as propounded in Scripture, and that Buddha and Confucius were just as much or as little relevant. Later in the evening she said: "It would all come so natural to us Jews, wouldn't it? There is something about that story of Mary the Virgin Mother as if it were especially written for us, and I could just see how we all would go for it."

In those days I went for the first time to a Catholic Church to pray, to the church of the Dominican Fathers in Hampstead near to our house. I went there every morning before work. I prayed at the altar on the right side. I had no idea what it was about, but somehow I believed in the power of prayer. I do not remember how I had come to believe in it but the efficacy of prayer had become something quite unshakeable to me. There was a peculiar intensity about it, because there was no immediate practical help which I could give to my father and my brother.

24. New Year, 1939

AFTER six weeks the first news trickled through: Ludwig was free again. Curiously he was one of the first seven people to be released. The Nazi authorities had asked for a panel of Jews who would be most important for a practical organization of a mass emigration of their people from Germany. Ludwig held a key position in the Zionist movement and in the organization of *hahsharah*, the type of farming settlement in which Jewish children were trained for Palestine. Therefore his person must have been important for the Nazis' aim, to get as many Jews as possible out of Germany in the shortest possible time. This was the reason for his liberation from the concentration camp among the first seven people out of the several hundred thousand who had been arrested in those autumn days.

After his release, it took quite some time before I could get direct news from him. His letters were short and cryptic but one thing was quite clear—he did not want to leave. With his twenty-three years, he was one of the few "senior" ones left with that multitude of Jewish children who waited to be admitted to Palestine. His presence was needed, and he had apparently the feeling of the captain on a sinking ship. I pleaded with him, I called him names, I implored him to think of his parents' peace of mind. Finally, towards the end of 1938 I had word that he was coming to London, albeit only on a visit.

My wife, our oldest boy, then a baby, and I were in Cambridge for a few days after Christmas. I had word that Ludwig was expected in London on New Year's Eve, so I left my wife and the child in Cambridge and hurried back to our flat.

It was the night of New Year's Eve and I was alone in the flat, when the bell rang and Ludwig came in. He looked thinner than ever. We embraced one another without a word. He grinned and kept his hat on. He sat down and said: "Play me some Schubert." While I played Schubert, he went into the kitchen and got a large box of cornflakes. He ate the entire content of the box and said: "Play me some *Well-tempered Clavichord*."

While I played, he got another box of cornflakes and ate them too. During the whole time we hardly spoke a word and he insisted on keeping his hat on. Finally he took it off. It was like a ceremony of unveiling. He was proud, and at the same time somewhat embarrassed, that his head had been shaved.

It was a strange way in which we greeted the year 1939 in that little flat on Oppidans Road. I still see him sitting there with his hollow cheeks and his shaved head, listening to Bach's preludes and fugues. After he was through with all our cornflakes, we sat and talked until dawn. From what he told me and what I heard later from others, I was able to piece his story together.

He happened to be in Berlin in the headquarters of the Zionist Youth Movement. Berlin was one of the few cities in which there was still a possibility of hiding oneself, probably only because it was so large. Ludwig had just decided to do that when a telegram arrived from some children's camp near Kassel indicating that the children there were in trouble. Though realizing the futility of it, he took the train. When he arrived late at night the Stormtroopers were already waiting for him at the station. The night before the S.A. had "stormed" the camp and beaten the children up. Ludwig and all the youngsters above a certain age were taken to Buchenwald.

Although the Nazis made even atrocities a streamlined, organized job, this time there was bitter chaos. The camp was in a horrible state because within two days thousands of Jews had been brought in from all over Central Germany. For several days they had no food at all. Many had already spent several days and nights standing up inside municipal halls, gymnasiums, fire-stations or warehouses in their towns and communities, before they had been transported to the camp.

In the camp there was *"Appell"* twice a day. This meant that people had to stand for several hours lined up in their yard. The old ones collapsed and were kicked to stand up again, or were carried away. After several days there were two meals consisting of potato soup and black stale bread. On account of the completely unsanitary conditions there was soon an epidemic of diarrhea. Ludwig wanted to spare me most of the details, but this one he told me. There was only one latrine which consisted of one huge cesspool; spanning this was one solid beam to sit on. The guards laughed at people thronging this place. Many of the old ones were too weak to keep their balance and fell down into the cesspool.

Everybody entering had his head shaved. There were a great number of upper respiratory infections leading to pneumonia, particularly in the aged. People were soon discouraged and demoralized. Ludwig saw this and organized among his own group little get-togethers with lectures on subjects of Jewish history and a course in Hebrew. There was such a general confusion and disorder that the guards did not notice such group formations or did not mind them. (Almost ten years later I experienced a most extraordinary coincidence. In an American psychological publication, *Journal for Social and Abnormal Psychology,* I came across an article written by a German-Jewish professor, dealing with observations on mass psychology of internes of concentration camps. The author himself had spent those days in Buchenwald. He spoke of the general demoralization and claimed that there was one group of young Jews who were a notable exception. This was a Zionist group who, under a leader, got together and formed something like a study circle. The point was that in situations of such extreme stress only those remain upright who have a goal strong enough to maintain their moral tension. In the description I recognized my brother.)

Ludwig told me that hunger bothered him more than anything else. As he grew weaker he developed delirious fantasies which had to do with cornflakes. There was a young Rabbi from Munich whom we thought funny because of the manner in which he used to give talks at ladies' tea parties about Jewish Ethics and such things. Ludwig used to imitate him, and succeeded in looking like him when he said: "Oh." This Rabbi was the one who shared his bread ration with Ludwig in the camp.

Uncle Julius was also taken to Buchenwald. The masses of people were so enormous that he heard of Ludwig's presence only when the loudspeaker gave the names of the first ones to be released. Ludwig got out just before his sickness became serious. He arrived one morning in Berlin, his head clean-shaven and without a hat. He had a little money in his pocket, and he told me that he was in a tortured state of indecision as to what he should first buy, a hat or cornflakes. He finally decided on cornflakes and walked home on foot because he was not allowed on streetcars.

In 1939 we finally succeeded in getting my parents out of Germany. Uncle Felix, far away in Chicago, had been able, with affidavits, money, and guarantees of one sort or another, to help us cut through the barbed wire. Later, I found out that he did similar things not only for his brother but for numerous people, among them people of whose existence he had never heard.

Our parents arrived one evening in May. Father looked tired and harassed but he was happy about the plane trip from Frankfurt to London which had been of utmost importance. Father and Mother topped off their last days in the old home by what they thought were luxuries. They had to spend all their money inside Germany, and they arrived with ten marks in their pockets.

Now they were sitting at the table in our small flat on Oppidans Road, their bags in the middle of the room. They kept reiterating, almost rhythmically, like panting animals, how lucky they were. Their new freedom was tainted with melancholy, but they talked well into the night. They told us about the goods they still had been able to buy and take with them—the silver, a few pieces of furniture, and particularly the linen. Father told me that he had learned English, and began to recite the story of a Herr Schmitt who visited Kew Gardens, and the conversation which Herr Schmitt had with Mister Brown, an Englishman who grew flowers.

Mother gave us all the details of what happened in those autumn days of 1938. A stormtrooper came and dragged Father into the middle of the street. He collected the children from the neighborhood, arranged them in a circle around Father, and said: "Now you all say with me in chorus—You dirty Jewish swine! One, two, three, you dirty Jewish swine." Most of the children failed to respond. All the Jewish men from our town were taken to Dachau, except Father, who was put into the town prison. We never found out why. Mother and the other women were put under house-arrest. Finally, after a week or so, they were freed again.

Three days after our parents' arrival, we learned that all their linen, the precious dowry of more than fifty years, and everything they had bought so lavishly in order to spend their last German money, was stolen in transit somewhere between Germany and England. Mother cried. Now, she said, they were stripped.

V
AMERICA

25. *Mount Royal*

At the beginning of 1939 I casually remarked to a Canadian neurophysiologist who was leaving for home: "If you ever should find a job for me in Canada, just send me a post-card." It was one of those things one does not really mean. Exactly three weeks later, however, a post-card arrived: "I have found your job."

Once in 1935 I had had the opportunity of obtaining a research scholarship at the brain research institute in Madrid, and a peculiar combination of circumstances resulted in my not accepting it, and obtaining a similar job in London. Half a year later the Spanish Civil War broke out. I have often asked myself what my future would have been had I accepted the first appointment. Shortly after I arrived in London, I got an offer to teach neuropathology at the Peiping Medical Union in China. We were very enthusiastic about going there, but when I learned that I could not have easily resumed my activities in London at an uncertain later date, the appointment in Peiping fell through. A few months later the Sino-Japanese war started. When I told Doctor Cumings that I was going to Canada, he said that this meant certain war. There is a beautiful story by James Thurber of a man who is fond of relating the most Providential hairbreadth escapes; in the end he is killed by a rock falling on him with astonishing accuracy under the most accidental circumstances.

My wife, our oldest boy (then one year old) and I arrived in Montreal on June 24, 1939. It was a Saturday afternoon. When the boat landed, all the bells of Montreal rang. We were told that this was the day of Saint Jean Baptiste, the patron of French Canada. In the streets we saw groups of marching men in very colorful uniforms, with music bands, who looked as if they were advertising department stores.

The manager of the Queen's Hotel was a jovial man with a cutaway. He spoke to us like a father, and as if he had expected our arrival personally for weeks beforehand. My wife was thrilled and asked: "How does he know?" I answered distrustfully, like someone who had made a serious study of life on the North American continent: "He doesn't. They learn this sort of thing in special courses." A room was reserved for us on the eighth floor. From there we looked over an endless forest of roofs, signboards and fire-escapes, with a thin rim of bluish haze which, we found out, was a faint indication of the St. Lawrence valley. The heat and moisture were such as we had never experienced before. It was as if the ceiling were closing imperceptibly down towards the floor, with us in between. The air in front of the window vibrated.

In the evening the telephone rang. It was a lady associated in some way with McGill University who had received one of the numerous letters of introduction sent ahead of us by an English neuropathologist. The lady called for us by car, showed us the campus, and took us to the top of the mountain. When we returned late in the evening, the telephone rang again.

"This is Mrs. Langdon speaking." She, too, had received one of those letters. "It must be ghastly in a hotel room, with a baby, on a day like this. Listen, my husband and I are leaving Montreal for a few days. Why don't you stay at our place? We are going to leave the key to the house under the doormat.

There is food in the Frigidaire." My wife told her that she was taking a great risk, since she had never seen us. Mrs. Langdon said she was prepared to risk it. The lady who had shown us around, took us to the Langdons' on the following day. For a few days we found ourselves the inhabitants of a beautiful house. There were wood-carvings on the walls, and pewter and silver in glass cupboards, old French-Canadian and English handicraft. Everything was laid out with taste. There was a cool lawn around the house. There was a hand-carved wooden crucifix, and in the bedroom we discovered an old yellowish photograph of a nun. There was a sentimental lure and temptation in all this; it was as if a corner of our childhood had extended that far. Such was our welcome on the New Continent.

I had obtained a working position at a mental hospital on the outskirts of the city. We took our apartment close to the hospital in an outlying suburban district. We got acquainted with a sector of life on the North American continent which is of greatest importance, and which will probably be of even greater importance in the future. This is the life of those people who are above the working-class, even above the white-collar proletariat in the European sense, and yet no longer bourgeois in the nineteenth-century sense.

Years ago we had acquired the Continental attitude of superiority towards all things American. At school some of our teachers made the cheap and arrogant distinction between "culture" and "civilization" which, I believe, goes back to H. S. Chamberlain, the son-in-law of Wagner. At that time we believed that America was Babbitt, Jazz and Hollywood. The first Americans and Canadians we met were the research fellows at the Psychiatric Institute in Munich, who had turned out to be people very sensitive to things of the intellect, and without our morbid tenseness. They were intelligent, open-minded, and lacked our heavy solemnity. Many of them had a surprising degree of natural charity and sense of community. Our inborn sense of the esthetic was alien to them, but they seemed to envy us for it with a humility which made us feel embarrassed.

Here, however, it was different. We found ourselves in a monotonous infinity of houses, ugliness insistent and threatening by the very fact of its seemingly limitless multiplication. The houses were jerry-built, rows after rows, creeping along like fungi mass-cultured by wealthy people who lived in cool stone buildings, far away from us. The houses were filled with settees; moonlit lake scenes with moose; mahogany radios; Jesus the Good Shepherd, souvenir de la Gaspésie; polished bedroom sets and so on. With insignificant variations the same uniformity prevailed on all sides. Thoughts were channeled into all this by radio and newspapers, as if an ocean were artificially aërated. It was as though the mystery of human existence itself were replaced by a Prefabricated Life.

In the middle of this, my wife settled with the determination of a brave soldier. We were poorer than those around us. We had to rely on my small salary, and almost half of it had to be sent to my parents in England. Before I was naturalized I could not think of being permitted to do some practice besides my other work. We had gone into debt to bring our old furniture with us. My wife built a small sheltered island out of our chests of drawers, the cupboard, the hope chest—most of it eighteenth-century handicraft from Franconia. All this, together with her works of lettering and binding, now seemed to have the function of watchful icons.

In spite of the fact that now we no longer wanted to be different, in spite of the fact that we made numerous friends, we felt segregated. Montreal shows, in a coarsened and seemingly static form, all the imprints and traces of the quarrels of the European family of peoples. At home in high school we used to have "living pictures," scenes in which an action was shown arrested .at a certain point, in a motionless pantomime. When you look down from the top of Mount Royal, you can almost directly perceive currents of European history of the last few centuries in a petrified form. There are French who seem to perpetuate the France of the time of Pascal, Monsieur Arnauld and the Port-Royal, a France which had dodged the impact of the Revolution. Here until a short time ago, political liberalism and the Catholic tradition were mutually exclusive. As in other Catholic countries, there is much voluntarily accepted poverty. In the province there is the genuine rural culture, with the family farm as a center. The clergy is suspicious of industrialism and of the city, and one has a feeling that most of the Frenchmen who live in the city rely on the soundness and indestructibility of the village. Calvinist prosperity, at one with the rest of the British Commonwealth, seems to look down upon all this with amused self-assurance. This, in turn, spurs the French into national resentment of an incredible tenacity. To many of them the Church itself becomes a vehicle of national exclusiveness, obviously the opposite of what she actually is meant to be. In between this are the Jews and the Irish, both of whom seem still to bear the resentment produced by the suffering in their European home countries. Thus, the city is parcellated, and everywhere there are frontiers of distrust.

We did not have any feeling of "belonging." We felt like rabbits who turn up accidentally in the middle of a fox-hunt. Even the Jews who were most charitable to us did not seem to grasp the true significance of what was going on in Europe. Most of them had the naive and understandable idea that if one only was able to beat Hitler "and his gang" everything was solved. The more sophisticated believed in a solution offered by dialectical materialism. Some Catholic people let us feel anti-semitism for the first time since leaving Germany. In Germany we had been subject to the cruel precision of a huge anonymous machine; here for the first time we experienced anti-semitism from person to person. At the beginning of the Hitler revolution I remember having overheard a Jew in a railway compartment remarking to another Jew: "You are lucky, living in a Catholic area!" But here the spirit of the Catholicity we knew in Europe seemed lost; it was as if these ethnic groups had brought along with them all their ancient animosities. There was no need to introduce any up-to-date form of racism, with all the ideologies of the twentieth century. It was all there in the form of preciously retained resentments of bygone times.

To the onlooker it appeared that the Church itself was incorporated into this maze of social and political petrifactions. Was it really true that we, Jews, Catholics and Protestants, had been huddling around our common God, in the darkness of persecution? The evenings at Frau Flamm's, the Cardinal's sermon, the brave Käsbohrer, Bruno Schulz and the "Living Corps," the old cook in Munich who informed me naively that "Our Lord Himself was a Jew"; all this seemed centuries ago. Gradually but surely it paled and faded away. I became almost convinced that I had been the victim of a wishful illusion. There was no drama of Golgotha. There was no cornerstone. Christianity was a haphazard temporal form of herding, there were tea socials, "charity drives," and the very Gospel itself had become part and instrument of political exigencies.

That Christ whom we had beheld! Had He detached Himself from all this, was He mercilessly removed from this place by the distance of time and space? Or was this His objectivation, an amorphous trace left behind by cosmic explosion? Those among us who, as Communists, had lived a life of sacrifice and danger out of "compassion with the multitude"—were they not infinitely closer to Him? Those who were among the rocks of Northern Palestine, renouncing the material benefits of the world of our childhood—were they not infinitely closer to Him?

During this time I got an occasional letter from Ludwig in which he described the life of his community. They were living in a poor co-operative without private property. In spite of the hardness provided every day by Nature, in spite of the threat

of Rommel's army, cowering just across the Egyptian border—
no, perhaps because of all this, there was a tone of joy and happiness in all his letters. They had removed another thirty acres
of rock; they had made an artificial fishpond in which they bred
European fresh-water fish; they had built a new community
house; he had introduced a choir and a small orchestra into the
school of which he was in charge. Compared with their way
of life our existence seemed to be the continuation of a lie which
we had wanted to flee. Their life seemed to be something real.
There is a round song, in Hebrew, of the psalm:

Behold how good and how pleasant it is for brethren to dwell together in unity;
Like the precious ointment on the head, that ran down upon the
beard of Aaron.
Which ran down to the skirt of his garment, as the dew of Hermon.
For there the Lord hath commanded blessing, and life for ever-
more.

"Brethren to dwell together in unity . . ." There it was again,
the lure of belonging. Providence had made me a Jew. There I
belonged with the fibers of my heart. There was the sheltering
warmth of blood. There, perhaps, was my task. How had I ever
come to doubt it?

And yet, far away at the back and just dimly perceived, was
another loyalty. Those Christians in Munich who had suffered
for us and with us during the night of annihilation, with whom
I had for the first time seen a super-national Israel—they seemed
to beckon me not to betray them. In that experience lay an obligation. I knew that there were ministers and priests in concentration camps. I knew that, with all the knavish brutality, there
were anonymous precious deeds of sacrifice in the name of
Jesus of Nazareth, the Anointed One in Israel, deeds of sacrifice
made by those who did not belong to us in the flesh.

There was no doubt about the natural place of my loyalty
and love during this most terrible moment in the history of the

Jews. I knew where I belonged by nature and by inclination. Here, in the New World, not broken by the apocalypse, everyone was still falling into his appointed place, within a frame of purely social and political categories. In fact nothing but that frame was visible. And yet, long ago, in those dark and dreadful days, for one moment the curtain of history had been torn open and we had seen the bleeding flesh of Christ.

For quite some time I thought that it was possible to remain a Jew and yet guard the secret of Jesus. I know that there are many who remain in this peculiar state. There are some very outstanding examples—Henri Bergson, Franz Werfel, Sholem Asch. It was impossible that, at this moment when our people was undergoing its agony, even Christ Himself would demand of one of us to become a deserter. Most of those Jews who remain with one foot at the threshold of the Church feel that, in such a moment of history, even Jesus would not have left the Jewish community of suffering. Yet there was something not quite clear in this thought. Because, during the Nazi persecution, for the first time in Jewish history since Christ, the Jews were not persecuted on account of their religion but only on account of their race. In fact, in Germany I had seen that Jewish Christians were frequently worse off than we who were also Jewish by religion. They were rejected by the "Christians" as Jews, and by the Jews as renegades. They shared the fate of Christ, of whom Pascal says that He is equally undesired by pagans and by Jews. Thus baptism as an escape from the fate of Jewry existed no longer. In this respect Hitler had, unwittingly, helped to clarify a spiritual issue.

During that time I spent many evenings in conversation with one of the Nuns of the Sacred Heart. I told her frankly that when I studied the New Testament, or Saint Thomas and Saint Augustine, or Pascal's *Pensées*, or Newman's writings, I saw a world which was entirely acceptable to me and to many Jews. Not only was it acceptable, but it represented in a pure light something which I perceived as our true home. However, this world, and the world of Christianity as it presented itself actually in front of our eyes, socially and politically objectivated, were two altogether different worlds. I did not even see any bridge. As long as this incongruity existed, it seemed almost to be the mysterious task of the Jews to keep out. I was approaching the paradox of which I spoke once before, the paradox of which, I believe, Werfel has been a victim.

At one time, I said, I had sworn that if I escaped from Germany I would do everything for the rest of my life to help the Jews. Now I had maneuvered myself into a corner of spiritual intricacies and paradoxes which appeared hopelessly insoluble. Moreover, I said, even if I embraced Christianity formally, there was still my wife and there were my children. To force my wife into anything which was alien to her would be atrocious. She was living a Christian life as it was, without ever calling it that.

The nun said that "helping the Jews" was not a problem to be solved on a purely natural plane. It would be very limited to think that I could help the Jews only by working on the land in Palestine, or by being a public promoter of racial justice, or by becoming a great Zionist leader. If I had really grasped the world of Saint Thomas and Saint Augustine, of Newman and of Pascal, I would have to admit one thing: that the pains and the blackout I was experiencing right now might be enough to "help the Jews," and might be infinitely more than what I could be doing in the practical order of things. If I did not understand this, I should leave Saint Thomas and Saint Augustine and Newman and Pascal alone.

The Catholic Church is a church of the multitude. Consequently the outsider, approaching her, faces a thick layer of mediocrity. We have associations of thought built chiefly on magazine articles, radio items and newspaper headlines. Whoever has experienced supernatural charity during the persecution on the Continent may stumble across a bigoted or anti-semitic priest—and with one such experience the vision of the Church seems forever gone. In Mozart's *The Magic Flute* the two people who are to be initiated in the Temple of Love and Wisdom are first repelled by rough guards; then they have to cross lakes of water and fire; and only after all this are they able to see the interior.

Thus, it took us some time before we saw the immense hidden treasure of anonymous sanctity in the Church; the spiritual power that flows to and from thousands of unknown souls every day. The stream of sacrifices made, for supernatural motives, by a multitude of working-class people, by religious in their communities, by priests and lay-people alike. In one superficial respect there is again a strange resemblance between the Jewish people and the Church: the misdeeds of one member are more broadcast than the sancity of a hundred others.

Gradually, we got to know many young priests with a profound and ardent social consciousness, with a sense of self-abnegation which I had seen before in some of the early social revolutionaries.

26. *Catechumen*

VICTORIN VOYER was the first French-Canadian whom I got to know more intimately. He was a post-graduate student who interned under me in a course of Psychiatry. For a long while we used to talk nothing but psychiatry. He accompanied me on ward rounds, and all I noticed for some time was his eagerness to learn, and our conversations remained confined to mere technicalities. However, he impressed me by his character; there was something wholesome, clean and straight about him. One day, after a ward visit to hundreds of chronic patients, he suddenly began to remark on the mystery of suffering. We climbed up on a high window-sill and crouched there, overlooking seemingly endless rows of beds. He sounded emotional, over-enthusiastic with the mere process of ideation (as one is at the age of twenty-six) and a little sentimental. However, he did say a few things which made me become attentive. I told him what I thought about this question, and he told me more about himself. He was obviously acquainted with contemporary Thomist philosophy and with the personalist movement, and when he discovered that we both shared the same interests he became so enthusiastic that he nearly fell off the window-sill.

During subsequent talks he told me about his childhood in a family of ten children on a Quebec farm; about their life of hard work and poverty; how his people got him through the University. His entire philosophy stemmed from that true simplicity of life. He gave me the story of his parents. It seemed like an endless story of small and bitter every-day sacrifices, willingly accepted, and strangely enough there was an atmosphere of hilarity and cheerfulness in all this. Worries either get you down or give you buoyancy. This was an immediate extension of the world of Frau Flamm and the old washerwoman, of the Kohen family—in short, of all those families in which I had seen religion form the organic basis of life.

All this determined his outlook to an astonishing degree. No matter what we discussed, whether labor or the Jews, nationalism or the war, there was the same warm spirit of charity and justice which enabled him to penetrate to the core of the question without any intellectual stunts. He explained to me, without condoning it, the social, economic and psychological background of French-Canadian chauvinism. He himself was anything but a Romantic or a Reactionary. Very quickly our friendship became solid. I, the German Jew who had been reared in a country thousands of miles away, who had participated in the mental Odyssey of the years after the first war, and he, the boy from the

French-Canadian village; we spoke the same language, we thought the same thoughts, and there obviously was something powerful enough to overcome all these forces of social, political and biological molding.

This experience was repeated, perhaps even more forcefully, when my wife and I made the acquaintance of two people who had a decisive influence on our further development, Jacques Maritain and Dorothy Day.

There again, looking at the surface of things, you could not think of two people more different. It seems, at first sight, that in order to understand Maritain fully you have to understand Europe, the Paris of the Schoolmen, and the Paris of Picasso, the *haute bourgeoisie* of the Republic and the Revolutionary intelligentsia from the East, the world of Virgil and the world of Jean Cocteau—in short the thousand ambiguities which seemed to characterize the human intellect in our century. And there is Dorothy Day, with her background of the non-conformist middle-class family of the American mid-west. Nothing could be more apart. Even in their conclusions there two people seem to be equally at variance. Yet it is not at all difficult to see why their influence on our lives should have been identical, so much so that when I think of them today I have the feeling of a unity of currents.

For a long time I had wanted to meet Maritain. In England I used to plan long letters to him which I never actually wrote. I thought that if there was one man in the Church who would have an answer to many of my questions, he was the man. Nobody in the Church seemed to have had a more profound understanding of the Jewish problem. He seemed, from his own experience, to understand the hundred twists of our intellect which were produced by our heritage of Marxism, Scientism, Freudism. In London I used to think that, if this man has come through the maze of all those experiences to accept Saint Thomas, there must be something to Saint Thomas. It was that certain feeling of assurance you have if you know that "somebody has been there before."

I was introduced to Maritain by chance. One day I mentioned casually to Mrs. Langdon, the lady who had given us our first refuge, that I was interested in the Catholic Church and in Thomism, and that I had been deeply influenced by Jacques Maritain. She told me that Maritain happened to be in America at the moment, and that he was going to be in Montreal in a week; she could see to it that I was introduced to him. One can imagine my feelings.

A week later I had to appear, at ten o'clock in the morning, in the house of a well-known French-Canadian family, to meet the famous man. Their home was furnished in the style of wealthy houses of the *fin du siècle:* there were huge rooms with recesses hung with heavy velvet draperies, richly framed oil paintings, alabaster sculptures. I was sitting in one of those grottos when a velvet curtain parted and Maritain came in, accompanied by the lady of the house who introduced us and left us alone. Since there were no doors, only draperies, I was childishly afraid that someone might be hearing what we said, although there was nothing secretive about it. I moved closely up to him and spoke in a low voice. It is peculiar that I do not remember our conversation with much detail.

Briefly I told him my story and he seemed to be deeply interested from the beginning. We spoke of reformed and orthodox Judaism, of Hassidism, of Dostoievsky's "Great Inquisitor" and the problem of iniquity in the visible Church. I told him about my spiritual experiences in London, and that I often believed that my conversion was nothing but a mirage produced by an unconscious desire to escape the destiny of a Jew. He implored me not to allow the precious fruit of my spiritual experiences to be corroded by psychological self-analysis, to believe in the genuineness of these insights which occur on a plane quite apart from that of primitive motivations. He spoke of the bleeding wounds on the visible body of the Church; of the divinity of Christ as a stumbling block for the Jews. He spoke in a peculiarly sketchy way, in hints rather than statements. Yet there was an impression of substance and clarity about everything he said. He held his hands compact and made movements with his fingers as if he were kneading material into thoughts. His head was attentively bent, his eyes had a remote gaze; although it was warm in the room he wore loosely around his shoulders a muffler which had no function as a piece of clothing.

Since I spoke almost in a whisper he had moved up closely and spoke also in a whisper. He asked me the most personal questions about my spiritual life but there was not for a moment the feeling of obtrusiveness or indiscretion. I had from the first moment the deep impression of a strange and pleasant form of personal directness which was the result of a great charity and humility. As we sat in the somber salon in the midst of velvet draperies and whispered about the *shehinah* and the divinity of Christ, I became aware of the uniqueness of the situation. We were stripped of accidentals of national and social origin, and circumstance found strange neighbors huddling. In moments of great intensity historical time ceases. I could just as well have been inside the catacombs, a helpless catechumen whispering to an apostle.

27. *Father Couturier*

Among all of us who were not allowed to participate in the war, and had to watch it from a safe corner, there arose a peculiar feeling composed of suspense and guilt. It was *our* war that was being fought. People who had grown up in the streets around us in a suburban part of Montreal were being seared to death by flames in mid-air and swallowed by tropical seas. They died for something which seemed only remotely associated with their lives in suburban homes, the assembly line of present-day existence. It was as if their deaths had already touched our hearts some years before, during the early agony of Europe and during those past days in Southern Germany. And we remained alive. To think that a man who lived on the floor above the drug-store at the corner of Wellington Street and Third Avenue was killed by a flame-thrower for something which seemed imme-diately related not to his own life but to that of Grandmother, Herr and Frau Masser, and Doctor Schulz.

Uncle Julius, the linguist and world-traveler, the international businessman, was now a worker in a valve factory in Stamford, Connecticut. He refused to make use of any of his business con-nections. He did hard manual labor for the first time in his life, and lived on the basis of an hourly wage, as his own factory-workers in Germany had done. I wrote to him and asked him why he did not, like other people, try to make a success in busi-ness; it would be so easy for him. He answered in a charming letter in which he described his daily life as a factory-worker, overalls, lunchbox and all. The letter was interspersed with quotations from Goethe, Schiller and Nietzsche. But he avoided my question. Uncle Felix wrote: "He reminds me of one of those penitent figures one finds in Russian stories."

I met a psychiatrist from California whom I had known in the Psychiatric Institute in Munich. "The first thing we ought to do after the war is over is to give people a rational outlook on life. The truth is that science is still being suppressed. People every-where in the world are laboring under a sense of irrational fear and guilt. Unless we remove all the out-dated morality and re-ligion of centuries, there will not be any peace on earth." This sounded familiar but I could not place it right away. "We gave the boys in the Navy personality tests, and I tell you that in my opinion over ninety per cent suffer from a guilt complex which is produced by our cultural religious pattern." I told him that the present world war was senseless unless seen in the light of the passion of Christ. He had encountered me only during my work on brain pathology, and looked at me with astonishment. "If you really have come to believe stuff like that, you must be schizophrenic." What he meant was that my ideas were crazy. They were apparently also dangerous to the form of post-war "cultural pattern" which he envisaged.

In the meantime, I went back to the nun at the Sacred Heart, and she encouraged me to go on praying. One evening I began again, after an interval of several years, to talk to my wife about my religious search. Again she said, as she had said years ago in London: "If I were a Christian at all, I'd be a Catholic."

"Look here," I said, "stop talking nonsense. If you want to be a Catholic it is not enough to have a sentimental attachment to Kati Huber, or to look at medieval paintings. I told you before that this means believing in the divinity of Christ, and in the Church."

I quoted previous conversations which she had long forgotten because at the time they had meant much less to her than to me. Once in the country, in Gloucestershire, she had said that Jesus had been such a perfect and ideal person that a legend had grown around him after his death, and people gradually came to regard him as a God. "I wish you would stop quoting me, I never remember from one day to the other what I say," she answered.

"All right," I said, "there is a Dominican priest here from France, Father Couturier, a priest-artist, and a friend of Matisse and Picasso. If you really are interested, I'll arrange for you to see him."

I had met Father Couturier through an introduction by Mr. Maritain. It was quite true that Couturier was an artist and a friend of Matisse and Picasso, but I was using this as a bait.

"How I hate to see people about something I know nothing about," she said. "But it sounds fascinating."

The following Saturday afternoon we had an appointment in the Dominican Monastery in Notre Dame de Grace. I left my wife with Father Couturier in a parlor. The parlor was glass-encased and looked like an oversized telephone booth. I could see the two through the pane. The priest was in a white gown. He was very tall and thin, with a small head, sunken cheeks and large, very lively gray-blue eyes. His short-cropped hair was gray. He had large expressive hands which he kept moving slowly, or hid in his large white sleeves. I could not hear what the two people were saying. He was leaning back with an amused and ironical air and she looked like an attentive schoolgirl, sitting straight at the edge of the chair. It so happened that I had a ski-suit and ski-boots on, and my steps were noisy on the stone-covered floor. I paced up and down, stopped to look at a map of the Archdiocese of Montreal, and at some rules and regulations printed in French. Then I went for a walk. When I returned, my wife emerged from the glass booth.

She looked excited and her face was slightly blushed. After we had said good-bye to Father Couturier, we walked a little in silence. I was very curious about her first reaction, but I did not want to ask. After a while she said: "I think I'd like to become a Catholic." That moment I had a very peculiar feeling which is hard to describe; I can come closest to it by saying, idiomatically, that I felt as if God had called my bluff.

How inadequately all this is told! Experiences which appear "emotional" and arbitrary are actually surface eruptions of developments which have been going on for a lifetime in the depth of a personality. It would be impossible to tell my wife's story. It is difficult to trace the sequence of one's own experiences. There is always a remainder one should leave untold. This is even truer when it comes to the lives of others, particularly those closest to us. But I have never seen anyone seized in the roots of his existence, as I saw it in my wife in those days. "Tell me," she asked me, "what did we talk and think about all the time before?" She pointed at the Gospel. "To think that this was the only thing that mattered, and I never realized it." On Whit Sunday, 1941, she and our two older children were received into the Church by Father Couturier.

Even then I doubted my moral right to leave the Jewish community by a visible sign. The issues of supernatural and natural charity, of natural and supernatural justice, of loyalty and of treason seemed so hopelessly entangled that I continued in a state of bewildered search.

28. Jerusalem in Every Man

WHEN we met Dorothy Day for the first time I had the same experience as with Jacques Maritain. We found everything again that had ever inspired us at any time of our lives. It was all there —the spirit of piety and peace I had encountered in orthodox Jewish families; Franz Burger's great heart and humanist generosity; the rebellious fervor of justice of some of the early revolutionaries; the sense of community, simplicity and self-abnegation of the Zionist Halutziuth; the sense of the beautiful which had enlivened those faraway days in Heidelberg and Munich; the lucid clarity, logic and common-sense which I had admired in my greatest academic teachers. Nothing was missing.

Something was added to all this, however, something of infinite importance. The limitations produced by the ethnic, social and temporal were removed, and there was something that transcended it all, something unifying which did away with immediate finality and promised further growth. Christianity never demands of you to deny anything positive you have ever loved. You find all of it again in Christ, but you find more. He does not want you to be nostalgic for the past, because the past is in Him. He asks you not to look back at the burning city lest you will turn into a pillar of salt. The Europe of our youth seemed centuries removed. Yet it was here, stripped of all that was arbitrary. What made it possible that this woman from the midwest and the boy from the Quebec farm, the philosophy professor from Paris and we ourselves, my wife and I, spoke the same language, and seemed to share the mysteries of our past, the suffering, the thousand eradications of a thousand bygone days, if it was not the One who united us with one simple gesture?

With Dorothy Day we had at once the feeling that we had always known her. If I could have, by some magic trick, taken her into my brother's *kvutzah* in Palestine, she would have understood right away (more deeply than in the common sense of the word) what they were doing. If I could have taken her into Haase's consulting-rooms in the slums of Moabit; if I could have taken her into Burger's classroom; or among the radical students in Frankfurt; or into the orthodox synagogue in Munich; or among the highbrows of Heidelberg, she would have *known* all this. But in addition she had something which they did not know; it was something like an other-worldly principle of purification and synthesis.

For those who do not know, I must explain that Miss Day is a onetime Communist. She is now the leader of the Catholic Worker movement. Among those in the present-day Church who have a vivid social consciousness, one can discern two different trends. There is one large group of people who feel that industrialization and Western urbanization in themselves are neither good nor bad, and that it is a duty of Christians to penetrate the city and the factory with the salt of the gospel. They are careful not to discard the impulse of justice immanent in Marxism and the Labor Movement. They feel that even our present-day technocracy can still be spiritualized. It took us some time to discover this sort of Catholic underground, a powerful movement among young people who are idealistic and ready for sacrifice.

On the other hand, there are those who feel that technocracy and industrialism have reached a stage at which they can no longer be reconciled with Christian principles. These are people who reject industrialization as such and attempt to by-pass it. The representatives of this group are the English Dominican Fathers, Eric Gill, Dorothy Day, the women of the Grail Movement, and Catherine de Hueck. They feel that the de-humanizing forces immanent in a technocratic society are too strong to be overcome in any way but by de-centralization or by the principle of voluntary poverty.

This perhaps sounds romantic and impractical. However, from knowing it, I should say that in a possible future society of pure pragmatism, both these approaches will be of equal importance. I have never tried to solve this problem. One cannot solve it by thinking. However, even if Dorothy Day and her followers were wrong in every single point, her merit will always remain the fact that she has transferred that peculiar immediate social consciousness of the early Communists right into the center of the Church, that is to say she has made innumerable Christians deeply aware of the social injustice right in our midst, Christians with the highest aim who otherwise would never have been aware of the urgency of the social question.

It is amazing to see how many young lay-people, priests and nuns, today have a spirit of identification with the underdog which is so familiar to me from intellectuals of bourgeois origin who, in the early twenties, gave away all their possessions and joined the Communist Movement. Many of those early Communists were Christian in their intentions, and would have done the same thing if, by some historical twist, the Marxist doctrine had not been associated with the elements of atheism and class-warfare. In fact, as various people have pointed out, the great socialist movements of the nineteenth century can be traced back to the Hebraeo-Christian tradition, but once this first impulse was spent, socialism merged into a de-humanizing managerial movement of which we may be entering only the first stage.

Now we see an amazing number of young Catholics who are taking up the social movement just at the stage where it was contaminated with nineteenth-century materialism, and they are baptizing it. One comes across these people in the most unlikely places. It is simply amazing to see in how many of them one can trace the influence of Dorothy Day or the European Dominican Fathers, even if the actual techniques vary as widely as the techniques employed by Mr. Nehru and Mr. Gandhi. Many profoundly religious people live an individualistic sort of Christian life, the life of "Christ and I closed up inside a bottle." They achieve a high degree of spirituality but the notion that the Negro problem, or the clearing of slums, or the problem of strikes in the coal-mining area has anything to do with religion, is quite alien to them. In the Middle Ages the visible Church was woven into the pattern of a society of castes. Consequently the great geniuses of Christian thought did not stress the problem of social justice in a way so that it can be transferred immediately to our time.

When the Reformation and the French Revolution overthrew that hierarchical society of castes, they identified the Church with that type of society and believed it not to be viable in any other social structure. It was just because the visible Church had been woven into that pattern that the principle of the brotherhood of man was taken up by the revolutionaries; it diffused, by a process of osmosis, from the Church into thousands of secular currents. This is the reason why the sense of social or racial justice is so natural to the convert who approaches the Church from outside, and he is bewildered to see that these ideas take such time and effort to become rooted in the consciousness of Catholic people. *His* great difficulty lies at the opposite pole. He cannot think of God in other but social terms, he cannot conceive of a Charity altogether detached from the social implications, a Charity which would still have to be lived if he were the only human being in the entire universe, if he were completely alone with God.

Now, however, we are at a turning-point of history. Things look as if the immanent moral *élan* of the great revolution had petered out, and that we shall have a scientific social apparatus in which the triad of Faith, Hope and Charity will be entirely replaced by a triad of Research, Insurance and Management. Whether the apparatus will be a Russian or American model does not concern us in this connection. It is no coincidence that precisely at this moment the Church reclaims all that has diffused into those secular currents; that she is re-assimilating the social elements of the gospel which had been disguised for instance in Marxism; that hundreds of young priests adopt the social teaching of the Church and become "radicals"; that the two poles of the gospel, the mystery of the personality and the mystery of the multitude, just begin to fuse again in the consciousness of the people.

Mr. Arnold Lunn once said that Protestant and Catholic piety approach the social problem in entirely different ways. The Protestant fights against unjust institutions—for example, slavery. The Catholic does not fight against the institution but identifies himself with the victim of injustice and lives with him, as Saint Peter Claver lived with Negro slaves. This statement is correct only as a historical observation, pertaining to a definite period. Right now we are witnessing a reintegration of those two currents in the Catholic Church.

The function of Jacques Maritain, Dorothy Day and others, has been to help in reclaiming land of Christianity flooded and carried away by secularism, drawing on the great principles in the social Encyclicals, and making many Catholics aware of crucial social issues. With us, however, their function was exactly the opposite. We had to be familiarized with other aspects of Christianity, those aspects which are alien to the outsider who brings natural social consciousness as his dowry into the Church.

I have said that in entering the Church one does not have to give up any single positive value one has ever believed in. You think of yourself as a traitor to your past. You think you have to leave Goethe behind, or Tolstoy, or Gandhi, or Judaism, or whatnot. But there is nothing which is good in all these things which you do not find again in the Church. Now it is ordered and synthetized. It is molten in Christ. Moreover, you do not have to accept anything which is repulsive to you in the Church, on a political or social plane. Nobody wants you to accept a totalitarian politician, or a priest who is obsessed by racial prejudice. All you have to accept is Christ and His Sacraments.

29. *The Print of the Nails*

I SURMISED from Dorothy Day, when I first met her, that she, too, must have had the "traitor complex" for a long time. However, from her and from other Catholics, lay-people, priests and nuns alike, I learned one thing: that you cannot come to grips with Christ as long as you think only in terms of social or political or ethnic references. You have to confront Him alone, divested of all this. Nor can you "figure it all out" intellectually. That comes afterwards. Faith, Hope and Charity are *acts*. They are by no means *non*-intellectual but they are much more than intellectual. They are not *non*-emotional but they are more than emotional. There is a German word, *durchleiden*, for which there is no good English translation. It means to experience and get to know something by suffering. To "suffer a thing through" with your entire being, rather than to "figure it out." This precisely is the lesson we received from people as highly advanced and widely different in their origin and in their avenues of approach as Jacques Maritain and Dorothy Day.

There comes then a moment when the question is no longer: "How can you enter the Church if you see how many of its members misuse it as a cloak for social injustice?" but rather, "How can you, if you have social consciousness and see the dynamite of social evolution stored in the Church, *not* enter it?"

The question is no longer: "How can you with your scientific training accept the doctrine of the Church?" The question is rather: "How can you who see how science is being used to construct a world which is no longer Christocentric, if you are deeply aware of the urgency to reintegrate the wealth produced by modern science into a Christocentric cosmology—how can you *not* become a Christian?"

There comes then a moment when the question is no longer: "How can you with your Jewish consciousness leave the Jewish community at the time of its most terrible persecution, and join a community in which there are many enemies of the Jewish people?" This question is, of all three questions, the most plausible one to ask. For this reason alone we may suspect that it contains a greater pitfall than the two others. To the outsider, on the plane of a low natural order, the Church itself is just another hostile camp. Indeed to some of its members it is an Irish institution (in the United States), a French institution (in Canada), and so forth. In the true mystical body there is no trace of an ethnic structure. However, my Jewish friends do not perceive that. Can you blame them? Their next-door Irish neighbors, or the priest around the corner, may be extreme nationalists. Now many of my friends have developed a Jewish national pride, since the time of the Nazi persecution. However, this is precisely the point at which the demands of Christ set it.

Rilke once wrote, around the year 1920, a remark which can be summarized as follows: "Supposing the Versailles Treaty were really an act of injustice against the German people, then we have two ways open. We can develop a spirit of more ardent nationalism and of revenge. Or we can do the opposite, we can discard all arms, even those of defense, abolish all remnants of an army, and try systematically to build up a pacifist state in the middle of Europe, a state that teaches a lesson in pacifism, no matter what the political constellations around us in the future may be. In the first case, Germany will most certainly be overtaken by a terrible fate. In the second case, she will experience a true re-birth."

To the Jew who lives in the post-gas chamber period of history, the alternative presents itself in a similar way. The Jew who has perceived Christ in the Church enters it not *in spite of* the fact that many of its members harbor an ignorant and prejudiced hatred against his people, but *because of* this fact. Here for the first time he is facing the demand of the Gospel in its terrible actuality.

In the late autumn of 1943, I went to see Father Ethelbert, an old Franciscan monk in Montreal, to ask him to receive me into the Catholic Church. I had spoken to Father Ethelbert on previous occasions. In fact I had had many talks with priests and nuns before, even in Munich and in London. People who roam around in the precincts of the Church for a long time become like bachelors who often get close to marrying but somehow do not find the turn. Tolstoy, speaking of bachelors, once said they become like beggars, meaning that they are like poor men who sit at the roadside while the stream of life passes by. I must have appeared like such a beggar to Father Ethelbert. At least I felt that I bewildered him. He understood many of my difficulties but much of it, many of the inner contortions of a European and a Jew and an intellectual, was alien to him. He reduced much of it to those simple principles of which he and I were both certain.

Father Ethelbert was a man of great simplicity. He, too, looked at me with that peculiar inward gaze I had seen so often in people who seem to look at something which is projected onto their retina from behind the eyes. He would say: "Look here, my good fellow . . ." then proceed to ask me a question and, without waiting for my answer, answer it himself. Then he would add, reassuringly: "That's right!" as if to confirm my reply, which I actually had not given. Perhaps he felt that my answers might be unnecessarily labored and complicated. It was a good thing for my vanity that he did not even seem to regard me as a rare specimen. He said that for instruction he would have to send me to Miss Sharp, a lady who lived at the Grey Nuns' convent. "Miss Sharp instructs our converts," he said. "She has a tremendous experience."

Miss Sharp was a blind and very old lady. She was a convert herself. "Now let's see . . ." said Miss Sharp, with that cheerfulness which dentists so often exhibit when they are laying their instruments out. She showed an utter disregard for the fact that I had acquainted myself with many of the intricacies of theology. I scarcely needed to mention to her that I firmly believed in the existence of God, when she set out to prove that existence to me. Her enthusiasm seemed to increase as she drove her points home. I do not think that it was so much the fact that her system was not adaptable to individual cases; I rather assume that the good Father had warned her of me as a dangerous freelancer. And this was a good thing.

One morning in December I said to Victorin Voyer, while we were in the ward: "Would you like to be my Godfather?" He jumped down from our usual window seat, slapped my back, pumped my arm, his jaw dropped and he began to burst forth with something which sounded like crying, laughing and talking all at once. The patients glanced at us in alarm.

There was a strange combination of Godfathers. My second Godfather was an old schoolmate of mine. I had met him in Munich only during our religious instructions which we received from the same teacher. He had been converted in Italy where he and his family had escaped from Hitler. I met him again, after twenty years, in Montreal and we discovered a strange parallel of destinies. Thus my spiritual protectors were a man from the French-Canadian village and a Jew from Munich. My wife and these two men accompanied me when I was received into the Church by Father Ethelbert on the Vigil of Saint Thomas the Apostle, December 21, 1943. It was only after my first Holy Communion, the next morning, that I looked at the missal to read the gospel of the day. It was the story of the man who insisted on seeing and touching the wounds of Christ so that he could believe in His divinity:

Now Thomas, one of the twelve who is called Didymus, was not with them when Jesus came. The other disciples therefore said to him: We have seen the Lord. But he said to them: Except I shall see in His hands the print of the nails, and put my finger into the place of the nails, and put my hand into His side, I will not believe. And after eight days, again, His disciples were within, and Thomas with them. Jesus cometh, the door being shut, and stood in the midst and said: Peace be to you. Then he saith to Thomas: Put in thy finger thither, and see my hands, and bring hither thy hand, and put it into my side; and be not faithless but believing. Thomas answered and saith to Him: My Lord and my God. Jesus saith to him: Because thou hast seen me, thou hast believed: Blessed are they that have not seen, and have believed.

VI

LETTER TO MY BROTHER

*Someone remarked that Shestov was a Jew. "Hardly," said
Leo Nikolaievitch, with doubt in his voice, "no, he is not like
a Jew. Name me one single unbelieving Jew. There is none,
not one."*
Maxim Gorki, Reminiscenses of Tolstoy.

*Some things lose their fragrance when exposed to the air; and
some thoughts, when translated into language, are thereby
robbed of their deep heavenly meaning.*

Saint Thérèse of Lisieux, Story of a Soul.

30. *Letter to My Brother*

YOU SUSPECTED for years that I would end up as a Christian. When you finally heard of the accomplished fact you showed neither astonishment nor disapproval. Nevertheless, you told me in your letters on several occasions that you would like to know what I really think and believe. I am going to try to tell you. Do not expect from me a systematic exposition of Christian doctrine. This has been done much better than I could ever attempt. It is expressed in the clearest and simplest form in the Creed, and there is nothing I could add to it. Instead I am going to give you a few thoughts in a personal and (you will be disappointed) unscientific way. After all, you know most of the preceding story anyway. It was written not only to explain how I became a Christian but equally to help Christians understand their brothers, the Jews.

In writing to you, I am not trying to argue you into anything. As Newman has said, nobody has ever been converted by an argument. Even if I attempted to do so I should have to know exactly where you stand, and I don't. I think that you believe in some form of Fabian Socialism. I could give you a list of names such as Sidney and Beatrice Webb, and a few others, and ask you to tick off the ones whose names correspond to your philosophy. It really does not matter. The thing that strikes me much more is the fact that you live in a community close to the soil; you own no private property; in the first years of your settlement (I do not know about now) you went through great hardships. I remember your writing to me some years ago from a holiday trip. You told me that you were sitting on the slope of Mount Carmel, and you were very proud to use a fountain-pen which your community granted to you in your capacity as a schoolteacher.

You, with your intelligence and your many other personal gifts, could have been very "successful" in the West. But you live a life of voluntary poverty, whether you call it that or not. Unlike you, I own a car and life insurance. Our life is probably much more comfortable than yours. It is the life of an average family in a North American city. You see the paradox. You live, apparently on the basis of an a-religious philosophy, a life which corresponds to what my religion teaches me. I, on the other hand, live in a setting which makes life in accordance with the precepts of Judaeo-Christian morality a questionable and problematic task.

This is one of the strange contradictions of our time. Even if I attempted to convince you, this paradox alone would seem to weaken my argument and strengthen it at the same time. It would weaken it: the fact that the majority of Christians did not behave in a Christian way has always weakened the Christian argument. But it would also strengthen it. Because, if I took the time, I am certain I could prove to you that, no matter what philosophy you talk, historically the impulse of your action is, in the end, derived from Holy Scripture. You may believe in some form of Western rationalism (shall I tick off the name of Bertrand Russell?), but you are living on an income derived from the immense treasure of the Jewish-Christian heritage. The fact remains that you live in a co-operative community not far from Lake Genezareth, and when you talk you do so in the language of Isaiah. I talk Isaiah, but in the language of Bertrand Russell, a language that did not exist in Isaiah's time, and in a place four thousand miles away from Lake Genezareth.

You and I are so much alike in our way of acting and thinking that people used to remark on it. Therefore, there ought to be a way of communicating. It is so long since we have met that it is very hard to know what questions you might ask me if we were sitting in the same room. Some time ago I sent you a reprint of an essay on a religious topic, and you told me that you liked it. You detached yourself from your own opinions and granted me my premises. This gives me hope that I may be able to make myself understood.

Inner Resistances

The inner resistances you might have are manifold. There is, of course, the point I mentioned above, the outward manifestation of Christianity in many of the people who profess it. I have no real answer for that one. I hide myself in shame. However, do not forget a lesson which we know so well from the history of Judaism, that is the fact that Evil has more publicity than Good.

Moreover, if you did believe in Revelation you would see that this belongs to the very essence of the spiritual dialectics of history; namely that the nucleus of Revelation in its purity is immediately surrounded by objective evil. We have only to study the Old Testament, particularly the Prophets, to see that. On the other hand, all those elements which appear good in the anti-Christian revolutions are derived and borrowed from Christianity. This could be the subject of a historical thesis.

Other resistances are of a more subtle psychological nature. When you hear words like "Fall," "Original Sin" and "Holy Ghost," thousands of childhood thoughts and sentiments and the very smell of Sunday-school come up. These words all belong in the category of the stork and the sort of thing you used to believe in before you were smart. "Original Sin and Science—what utter nonsense," you are inclined to say. It seems so much more clever to use terms such as Ether, Planck's Constant, or the Theory of Surplus Value.

Let me dwell on this for a moment. A good deal of the resistance of enlightened and modern people against theology is not at all directed against the teachings presented by that discipline. If the same ideas were presented in a more abstract terminology, nobody would see much discrepancy with Reason. Some of my agnostic friends are great students and admirers of Aristotle and Plato. Now the idea of Original Sin was anticipated by Aristotle, perhaps even more explicitly by his teacher Plato, and ideas strangely similar have been introduced by many non-Christian thinkers up to the present time. But those thinkers use abstract and involved terms. They spare you that smell of Sunday-school; they do not repel you. Philosophers and mathematicians feel at ease only in the abstract. It is only the poet who calls a spade a spade. We who are still hypnotized by the mathematical sciences revolt at an idea, even a possible truth, if it is presented in poetic form. (I am using the word poetic here in its larger, ancient meaning.)

Freud, a genius who has presented some of the most profound observations on the psychological nature of Man in what you might call mythological form, was curiously sensitive to this. In one of his anti-religious writings he discusses the triad of Science, Art and Religion. He remarks that, while Science represents truth, Art compared with Religion is "harmless" because it does not pretend to be anything but a figment. This statement is erroneous but it brings us close to the concept of Truth. Some of the news which you read in this morning's paper is true in the sense of ephemeral verifiable facts. Now what about Shakespeare's dramas, Tolstoy's novels, Michelangelo's paintings and Haydn's quartets? They are immortal precisely because they express eternal truths about Man and the World, truths much more profound than any item in the newspaper.

This does not mean that I think that Original Sin and the Holy Ghost belong to the realm of art. William Blake once said that Christ and His Apostles were artists. Actually they were neither artists nor scientists but something different. What Blake, an Englishman of the early industrialist period, meant to imply was that we cannot confine the concept of truth to the scientific order.

Therefore, I ask you to forget for the time being your Sunday-school complex. The terms used in Hegelian dialectics and those presently used by mathematical physicists only sound smarter than theological terms. That in itself does not mean that they come closer to the true nature of things.

Professor Heidegger and Babette Klebl

Before I go on expounding my belief to you I should like to interpolate a kind of historical note which may seem to be out of place and which anticipates some things I am going to say later. I do not know whether you remember Babette Klebl, the maid in the household of Herr and Frau Hirsch in Munich. She came from Neumarkt in the Oberpfalz, and her sister was a waitress in the Lowenbräu. Babette was a daily communicant. In fact, at times Frau Hirsch disapproved of her going to Mass at five every morning because she was afraid that the lack of sleep interfered with her efficiency and made her cranky. I remember that Babette's life was one of hard work and of what appeared to be incessant prayer. She had her shortcomings; at times she actually was cranky. Moreover, it did not take much to make her infuriated, but she always regretted it soon, and I must say that the most impressive note about her, apart from her piety, was her humor. Babette worked in the kitchen and lived in a small room decorated with cheap holy pictures. In times of stress, of sickness and of death in the Hirsch family, Babette suddenly seemed to be the solid center of the household. When Otto Hirsch, a noble and promising boy, died at the age of sixteen, the only person in the house who seemed to have a profound inner relation to Death was Babette. I rediscovered Babette's portrait later in Franz Werfel's novel *Embezzled Heaven*. Even the young man's death and the maid's attitude are described there. This seemed a strange coincidence until I discovered that there were many people who recognized their own Babettes in that story. Babette must be legion. The Kaspar Russes and the housemaids have played an important rôle in the history of conversions.

In my wife's case the situation was quite similar. Kati Huber, born in Hundsacker near Straubing in Lower Bavaria, exuded the odor of hard work, the righteousness of the Psalms and the peace of the Gospel. She too was a daily communicant. She lived this life apparently untouched by the vicissitudes of a sophisticated and overcomplex family. You would be quite wrong in thinking that this is sentimental glorification. Obviously the Babettes and Katis have their own shortcomings and their secret passions. But their approach towards life transcends ours. While we were engaged in a continuous flight from ultimate reality (our intellect lent itself so well for this purpose), there existed among us all the time people who lived unknown lives of humility and charity. And, believe me, they did it with mystical fervor.

I remember how I used to be somehow aware of Babette's superiority and maturity. One afternoon, while she was cleaning the table, I said to her: "Don't tell anybody but actually I too believe that Jesus Christ died for us on the cross." I cannot quite understand why I said this. I was in my teens then, and perhaps I wanted to let her feel that I knew what went on inside her. My remark caught her off guard. She blushed, and her goiter shook a little—a sign that she was moved.

Every one of us who has escaped the European catastrophe knows that those obscure lives were of great significance for us. A great number of intellectuals, Liberal, Catholic, Socialist and Fascist, betrayed us. Everything seemed so complex; there were so many questions of political expediency that the cleverest Professors were hopelessly entangled in an infinite labyrinth of dialectics. Some tried to build bridges of Fascism as others tried to build bridges toward Stalinism. I remember some of my Jewish friends who were enraged about cruelties committed in Fascist countries but felt indifferent about the same cruelties committed in Russia. The opposite was true of many Catholics. As the international scene shifted so did allegiances and loyalties. It was as if the devil had led us to one of those distorted mirrors one finds in amusement parks; only that there was nothing amusing about it.

The Kaspar Russes and the Babette Klebls did not become confused. As bats find their way in the dark by the reflection of supra-sonic waves which they radiate, these people sent out into a dark universe a continuous radiation of prayer and sacrifice, and from somewhere out there returned a continuous echo. Thus, they remained oriented. And in this way they were able to reduce the most bewildering situation to a simple formula. Their world was mapped out by the Gospel.

When the Hitler era broke loose, all things seemed to assume a nightmarish quality which is impossible to describe to anyone who has never lived under a totalitarian regime. Then it was interesting to watch the way in which the intellectuals tried to understand the situation. Our sociologists began to talk about the in-group and the out-group. The Marxist dialecticians became entangled in an acrobatic apparatus which just did not seem to fit. Professor Heidegger, that same Professor who had given beautiful seminars on Saint Augustine, tried to find his place in a Nazi world by elaborating some very involved ideas on Hegel and Existentialism. Not so Babette Klebl. She said: "What do they want to do against the Jews? It will end badly with these fellows because our Lord Himself was a Jew." This statement was simple and intelligent. Berdyaev and Maritain did not actually say more. Only they said it in a more diversified and interesting manner. Babette had a metaphysical concept of history.

Nothing has convinced me more of the divinity of the Church than this organic continuity between the Klebls on one hand and the Berdyaevs and Maritains on the other; that, without the Church, the Klebls would not be ennobled and wise creatures they are; that Intellect, without humility, is the most destructive force in the world.

The Betrayal

There is nothing original in what I have just been saying. When you read Tolstoy carefully, particularly his autobiographical notes, there is no doubt whatsoever that his greatest source of inspiration was the life of simple piety among the peasants and nursemaids of his childhood. The old Tolstoy who advocated an abstract Christian morality, deprived of all sacramental channels, refuted his own argument. For such a bone-dry ethical system would never have remained vital among the people from whom he drew his inspiration.

Goethe, that belated straggler of the Renaissance and perhaps its greatest son, worked his whole life writing a tragedy which has, when you come to think of it, a most extraordinary plot. It is the story of a man with an insatiable hunger for intellectual satisfaction and prestige, a man whose personality contains a self-perpetuating machine of expansion which can be stopped by nothing short of physical death. In the course of his career he cheats a simple pious young girl. But in the end he is saved by the contrition and prayer of that girl. This plot contains, if you allow me to use a big word, the immanent drama of the West since the Renaissance. At least we hope it does.

To make my point clearer, I should like to come back to the story by Franz Werfel. It does not belong to the same category as Goethe's story, but it may illustrate better what I want to say. The heroine of that novel is, as you know, a maidservant. She has a nephew for whom she saves every penny to enable him to study for the priesthood. She apparently succeeds. He writes to her every so often from the seminary and later from the various parishes in which he works. One day she wants to visit him but does not find him at the given address. After a long involved search she finds him in a suburb of Prague as a photographer, living a rather shady existence. He has never been a priest. Now during this scene the nephew makes his standpoint very clear and he is, for the first time, sincere. He says that he was unable to go through with the priesthood, it went against all reason, it seemed such an outrageous lie—the entire world of the Gospel and the Sacraments. Nobody with a modern scientific mind could possibly swallow this stuff.

That scene has highly symbolic qualities. The repulsive nephew represents, you might say, Hitler and Stalin. He presents, in a certain sense, also you and myself. We too have cheated the maid. The point is that the ever-increasing rift between intellect and faith does not occur as a pure accident, outside the moral order. The intellectuals have learned to say No so elaborately and in so many different ways that they can no longer say Yes.

Form a Sentence with "How Can You . . ."

Today I share Babette's faith. I presume it would be very difficult to reach her degree of perfection, or the degree of perfection of any one of those souls through whom I have come in contact with the spirit of Christ. But the very fact that I am able to share her faith is something which I regard as a great gift. In spite of the preceding chapters I cannot quite explain how it ever happened.

Now perhaps you will say: "How can you . . ." I do not know whether you personally would say this but many people do. They say: "How can you, as an educated person . . ." or "How can you, as a man with scientific training . . ." or "How can you, with knowledge of psychoanalysis . . ." There seems to be a great number of How Can You questions. In all sincerity I do not even understand why these questions are asked. This too I have in common with Babette. But there is a point in which she has an advantage over me; she is never asked, and therefore does not have to answer.

Let us first take the one on psychoanalysis. Several things may be meant by that question. What is most frequently implied is the idea that psychoanalysis has been able to reduce all matters of faith, in fact all transcendental matters, to natural motives. For example, one can take the life history of Saint Augustine, analyze it according to Freudian principles, and demonstrate the unconscious motives of his conversion. Then you have "explained" how he found Christ and the Church. (I believe that someone has actually done this.) But one can also take Nietzsche's life history, subject it to the same analysis, and demonstrate how he came to hate Christianity. I would not be a bit surprised if the basic psychological mechanisms were the same in the two cases. They frequently are. I could give you a very simple psychoanalytical commentary on the story which I have told in this book. If you are able to explain with the same method why one man becomes a Christian and the other one becomes an anti-Christian, there are only two possibilities. Either the psychological method is not valid to decide whether Christianity is true or not, or there are no truths which transcend the material plane of man's existence.

Looking at the history of the human spirit at long range, it is a tremendous thing that psychoanalysis has rediscovered the primary position of love in Man's world. This discovery was made from a materialist platform, as it were. What else could we expect from a genius who is a child of the nineteenth century? Lop a few of the accidental ornaments off and you have a psychology which reaffirms and enriches the Christian idea of Man. Psychoanalysis gives us an embryology of love. Christianity could make use of this very thing. Psychoanalysis shows us that the infant is more of a passive recipient of love than an active lover, and that it cannot bear hostility. As we become more mature, we are more able to love actively and we learn to be able to be rejected. Christianity teaches us that the climax of human perfection is to love infinitely to be able to be hated infinitely. This degree of human maturity has been reached perhaps only once in history, in the person of Jesus Christ. Psychoanalysis teaches us that *Amor* can be transformed into *Caritas*. So does Christianity. Later generations will see that in the rediscovery of the crude archaic traces of "love" in Man's physical nature, there occurs a decisive turning-away from that Manichaeism of which Western Man has been so dangerously ill. Moreover, psychoanalysis with its detailed care for the history of each individual and its emphasis on psychic injuries, reaffirms, more than any other discipline in psychiatry or psychology, the dignity of the human person. This is, in the end, one of the reasons why psychoanalysis has been rejected by Communists and Nazis alike. Freud's atheistic philosophy is a tragic historical accident, but it *is* an accident. His philosophical statements are amateurish and contradictory, and they can easily be separated from his psychology without doing harm to the latter. If you invert his materialist position you obtain an image of the psychological nature of man which is complementary to theology. However, the fact remains that psychoanalysis, like all great discoveries of the human intellect, can be used to make ammunition for nihilists or to provide balm for the wounds of mankind.

The question about science is even harder to understand. I have never experienced any conflict of that sort. Some time ago I read in a German history of philosophy that Pascal's early death was caused by the inner tortures he endured resulting from the conflict between Science and Religion. It is quite possible that Pascal suffered inner conflicts but there is no indication that this was one of them. I presume that de Broglie is a Christian and that Planck was a Christian. Pascal and Newton were Christians. It is possible that they were Christians *besides* being Scientists or *on account of* being Scientists, but why should they have been Christians *in spite of* being Scientists?

God

On the contrary, I should think that an atheistic Scientist would labor under conflicts. I was never interested in the usual proofs of the existence of God. This is the one point in which I approach Babette Klebl's simplicity rather closely. I often wonder how much good those proofs do, just as I wonder how much a man can become convinced by an argument that goes on in a class on art-appreciation. If I had to give a class on God-appreciation I should start off by talking about Science. People like Science perhaps because of the apparent principle of certainty. But I have often noticed that people love and admire the world of Science because of something which is beyond the material. An American psychiatrist remarked some time ago that at every moment of our existence there are going on in one single nerve cell processes of such infinite complexity that an assembly of all the Nobel prize winners in Chemistry could not imitate them. That remark was made in a connection entirely different from what we are discussing here. I do not even know what the speaker believes. But what he said is enough for Babette and me. We need no further evidence. Of course you must realize that one single brain cell is nothing. You have no idea what is necessary, in the way of chemical interaction, to enable you to think "There is no God." Those thirteen hundred grams of colloidal matter inside your skull represent a flawlessly integrated universe. Complexity in itself might not impress you. A chaos can also be complex. But a meaningful harmonious complexity, that is another matter. Some time ago a French biophysicist, in a popular book, calculated the time necessary for one protein molecule to occur as a chance combination of atoms (that is to say, by a process comparable to throwing dice) and he found that the theoretically assumed age of the earth would not be enough. Not your brain, just one molecule of protein. I do not know whether his argument is correct, but Babette and I are satisfied that the universe is no meaningless chance occurrence. To me the very fact that you read what I am writing here and understand it (never mind whether you agree with me or not) is proof of a First Cause. It is the proof that you who read it have been created by a Spirit. *Cogito ergo est:* I think, therefore He is.

There can be no incongruity between Science and Religion, at least not in the sense of belief in a First Cause, a Creator. As far as that first step is concerned, Newton and Pascal not only cannot have labored under any painful conflicts, but on the contrary—whatever great discoveries they made in the Natural Sciences must have confirmed the first basis of their belief. Their belief, in turn, helped them to integrate their discoveries. Those discoveries would have remained amorphous chunks if the scientists had not in the back of their minds continuously carried the idea of a meaningful Universe. No fragments of a jigsaw puzzle mean anything unless you are convinced that they are part of a whole which will finally turn out to be a picture. Every good scientist has a cosmology. He may be dimly aware of it and carry it with him as an ill-defined shadowy image, or it may be elaborate like that of the great Christian thinkers of the Middle Ages, or that of the evolutionists of the nineteenth century. It has in fact been shown that the evolutionist view of natural history, as well as the Marxist view of human history, are distorted derivatives of ancient religious concepts of the history of Universe and Man, and can even be traced back to them. There is no scientist who does not try to fit his findings, which are by their very nature fragmentary, into the jigsaw puzzle of some universal idea. For this reason I think that a perfectly atheistic scientist (if there is such a thing) would have to labor under serious inner conflicts. Reason must be perfected by faith.

Christ

Of course, most of those people who believe that Pascal-the-mathematical-physicist and Pascal-the-theologian kept a double ledger would still admit a First Cause. They have nothing against a God who represents a Euclidian entity. What they consider as incompatible with reason is the God of the devouring thornbush, the God who admonished and threatened a little desert tribe and finally sent His only Son as a Savior into the world.

Every human being experiences in his life a tragic dichotomy, a painful dualism. I believe that all children are somehow aware of it. When we behold the harmony of the heavens, when we see a landscape in sunset, when we hear a Mozart symphony, we experience something like perfection. We should like to eternalize the instant and address it with Faust: "Stay on, thou art so fair." And then we experience ugliness and decay, sickness and death, hatred and murder. That medium of absolute perfection seems to contain an element which makes for continuous deterioration. The Church has the only answer to this terrible paradox. It says that those moments of beauty and perfection *are* potential eternity. However, this perfection has been corrupted in time by an act of choice which was made possible by the creation of Freedom.

I pointed out to you that your own brain is a cosmic galaxy of electronic orbits, something which ought to fill you with wonderment and awe. But your thoughts are variable. You might plan a garden, or you might think of killing your friend in order to marry his wife. With this we introduce a possibility which is not implicitly contained in an infinitely complex and perfectly harmonious machine. That is the idea of Freedom. The same

Creator who made such a thinking-machine possible added Freedom.

Since there is a divine Creator and Spirit it would be extraordinary to assume that He led an existence completely independent from, and outside, the world He has made. It stands to reason that He could reveal Himself in History. Thus we find in History a strange exchange, a tug-of-war, a highly dramatic struggle between God and a small people which lived in an area that marked the crossroads of ancient cultures. Very early there was an inkling, and the indications became increasingly clearer as time went on, that this small people underwent all those earthly and spiritual meanderings not just for its own sake but to bring forth Someone whose life would be of infinite significance for everybody in the whole world.

If you were a believing Jew you would have no objections so far, because up to this point the Jewish and Christian teachings coincide. However, from now on you would raise objections and they would be twofold. You might say: "Are we living in a Messianic age? If so, count me out!" This is what I used to say for a long time. The story I have cited of the Rabbi who looks through the window at the announcement of the Messiah, and says, "I see no change," is the entire spiritual history of the Jews in the past two thousand years. It is that sense of disgust and impatience which marks all the early Jewish social revolutionaries who were sensitive to the lack of justice and charity in contemporary society. Today I disagree with that Rabbi but I have a deep sympathy for him and for the early social revolutionaries. Theirs is a holy discontent. In fact, I think that this discontent is one of the metaphysical forces of history. When Jews use as an argument against the Church the story of the Inquisition they do not quote it only because they got hurt in the process. There is again, deeply hidden, that disquieting sense of the paradox. Thus, their Messianic skepticism and their very existence are a continuous reproach and sting in the flesh of the Christians. When Saint Paul says that "blindness in part has happened in Israel until the full-ness of the Gentiles should come in," he is not only prophesying but he is exhorting the Gentiles. Fullness is not just something numerical, it has also a qualitative meaning. Unless the Gentiles come in in fullness, they cannot expect the Jews to see.

I do not agree with the Rabbi's remark. The prophecies have been fulfilled. The Christ has been on earth in the historical person of Jesus of Nazareth. However, with His appearance as such, society cannot be suddenly transfigured. That would presuppose a peculiarly mechanistic view of history. If the appearance of the Messiah just by its very happening converted the world into a world of peace and love, as the throwing of a switch lights a room, Freedom, which more than anything else made Man God-like, would be denied. We would be like those puppet figures in the ballet who dance automatically to the beat of the music and become lifeless the moment the music stops. The entire drama of Jewish history up to the appearance of such a Messiah (even if it happened only twenty thousand years from now) would be entirely meaningless. In fact, the only Christ who is compatible with a Judaic concept of history is the Christ who lived and was crucified, the incarnate God who was haunted and tracked down between party politicians and Roman imperialists, and igno-miniously executed. His Peace and His Justice did not mechani-cally transfigure the world independent of our will, but it did transfigure the secret depths of single souls. When Christ speaks of the effect of His first coming, He chooses metaphors such as "the leaven" or "the seed"; in other words He speaks of changes which are slow or hidden or scattered. This does not mean that we should not think of society and of politics in Christian terms, it means only that everyone has first to seek the kingdom of God (which is not of this world) and all those things will be added unto us.

The Church then offers a definite concept of the nature of Man and of the nature of history. It claims that the potential

Goodness, Truth and Beauty of this world were spoiled by the free act of Man, and that from then it was as if things contained something like a self-propagating element of negation, of nothingness. This can be best explained by an analogy which we find in the physical nature of the Universe. If you remember your physics you will remember that the second thermodynamic law modifies in a certain sense the law of the conservation of energy. It states that, although all energy is conserved, there is a higher probability of energy being converted into temperature than into any other form. This means that an increasing amount of energy will irreversibly remain temperature and that finally the cosmos as we know it is bound to die a "heat death." The tendency of energy to be converted into heat with a certain degree of irreversibility is called entropy.

In the world as we know it there exists, according to the Christian concept, something like a law of entropy. There is a negative process which we conceive as Evil, Sickness, Decay and Death which seems to have an intrinsic power over Beauty, Goodness, Truth, all those elements which imbue us with a sense of Eternity. The only means of reversing this process of "entropy" was the Incarnation. A second Eve appeared, the Blessed Virgin was immaculately conceived. Everyone was given a second chance. And God was incarnate. By His life and suffering and death, human history was inoculated with a new ferment, the only ferment which is capable of undoing that ever-expansive process towards nothingness.

If you were a believing Jew, you would have another objection. You would say that it is pagan to have any image of God whether in a human or in any other form. God did warn us frequently in the Old Testament not to make a graven image. But He did so precisely because He had already made an image of Himself, namely in Man.

People who do not believe in Revelation are irked by the idea of a God as represented in the Bible. They say that He is anthropomorphic. They want a philosophical God, if any. However, the specifically Jewish idea is not so much that God is anthropomorphic but that Man is theomorphic. There is an ancient discussion of the *Rabbonim,* I believe it is Talmudic, in which the question is under consideration: "Ma K'lal hatorah?" ("What is the fundamental principle of the law?") One Rabbi says: "Love thy neighbor as thyself," but another one counters: "There is a more fundamental one—He created Man in His image." This means that Man in the original idea of creation is God-like. If that is true there must be in God something to which the idea of Man is analogous. The Christian idea is a little more specific, and calls the something in God of which Man is, in a mysterious fashion, an image, the Second Person of the Holy Trinity. But she is only a little more specific about it than the Jews. Just meditate for a moment on that rabbinic discussion, and you come quite logically to that explicitly Christian notion of God. The idea of the Incarnation is nothing alien grafted upon the tree of Jewish tradition. The Jewish spirit is profoundly incarnational. In fact, that holy discontent which would like to see the whole of society transfigured, is psychologically part of that trend.

Four Possibilities

I have in my life experienced the most incomprehensible abyss of Evil, and of suffering, as far as it affected those closest to me. One of the sisters of our mother, her husband and their little son, and Grandmother lived together in an apartment in an industrial town in Western Germany. You remember Aunt Clara and Uncle Max and little Richard very well. We were often guests in their house and I used to go on hiking trips in the Thuringian mountains with them in the summer. They were simple, God-fearing people and they led good lives. Uncle Max was an ironmonger. He used to play the clown for us boys. On Friday night he used to bless bread and wine, and on Saturday he used to

take us to the Synagogue. Their lives were good in the sense
in which many people's lives are, and they might have died
the death of most good middle-class people. Death looks so uniform to us onlookers although it may well be the most individual
experience of each single person. At any rate, after a certain number of Friday nights, of hiking trips and of card games they might
have died. Their friends would have felt sorry and there would
have been obituary notices in the paper. They seemed to have
been destined to live the lives and die the deaths of millions of
those who now live around me. Of our grandmother, mother's
mother, I have similar memories, though in certain ways more
peculiar. She knew in her own way the quiet humility of sacrifice.
I do not want to go into her life any further than is necessary to
make her character understandable for those who did not know
her.

One morning, late in 1940, they were all awakened at five, and
told to be ready at five-thirty with as much as they could carry in
their hands. They were packed into an overcrowded train and
transported to the south of France into a concentration camp.
While they were kept there their relatives in the United States
tried to get them released. I wish I could write a separate book
to describe their agony of fear, hope, physical hardships, desola-
tion and inner darkness when, with the German occupation of
Southern France in 1942, all hope was gone. Grandmother
died in that camp. I still have some of her letters in which she
tried to make us feel better. Aunt Clara and Uncle Max and Richard were deported East. People were thrown into those trains
like potato bags, squeezing one another without adequate space
to sit or lie down. They were given no food or water, and they
had to evacuate as they were. Many of them did not arrive alive.
But those who lived saw scenes of which we could not dream in
our worst nightmares. Babies were killed by being smashed
against trees in front of their mothers. Finally the people were
shaven, stripped naked and killed.

I knew them. They were just as good as you and I, and in some respects they were better than many of us. Now here is something that might strike you as strange. The more I meditate on them, on those nightmarish last years, months and hours of their lives, the more I come to believe in Jesus Christ, the Son of the living God.

Let me make this clearer. Confronted with this horrifying picture of innocent suffering there remain only a few ways in which I can react. One is despair, moral nihilism and suicide. In fact, some of us who remained alive went this way. It does not take much to feel compassion for these suicides. For if the lives of those innocent victims ended with their death, I must deny God. If there were a God who allows this sort of thing, I should feel like Ivan Karamazov; I would not want to have anything to do with him. If my relatives who were tortured to death were annihilated at the moment of dying, if there is no meaning in their existence transcending the lives of their bodies then, obviously, God is worse than Moloch or Baal—or, much more simply expressed, there is no God.

There is a second possibility. I might have reacted, as I originally did, with an increased Jewish national fervor. Many Jews have done so and this reaction is even more understandable. I am not speaking of the settlement of the Jews in Israel, which was practically important, and may later from the viewpoint of the metaphysics of history, be very meaningful. I am talking only of inner data, of a nationalist ideology and of nationalist sentiments. I might feel quite gleeful at the suffering of the German people during the war. To some of them things happened which were similar to those which happened to the Jews before. For example, trainloads of thousands of Sudeten Germans were shipped from Czechoslovakia to Berlin. When the trains arrived it is said that only a minority of the passengers were still alive. One remembers how Nazified many Sudeten Germans had been in their attitude, and I must confess that there have been times in my life when I would have said: "Serves them right. Now they are getting a dose of their own medicine." I might not have put it so crudely, but that is what I would have felt. I might have said that the only way to get out of our misery was to become a powerful nation ourselves, no longer to be always at the receiving-end and to dish it out if necessary. Now it is obviously no solution to the problem if, instead of my innocent grandmother, the innocent grandmother of a Sudeten German is thrown into a train. But apart from this, I have indicated in several other places in this book that the meaning of Christ for the Jews, from the point of view of the philosophy of history, is precisely the fact that for us (and eventually for all peoples) there is no such thing as a *national solution.* Jewish-orthodox critics of the Gospel, no matter how objective and benevolent, never cease to discuss the famous quotation: "It is said unto you—love your neighbor *and hate your enemy!*" They point out that there is not a single passage in the Old Testament in which Man is commanded to hate his enemy. On the contrary there are several passages in which charity towards one's personal enemy is indicated. The Jewish scholars say that since all the other quotations from the Old Testament are correct and this one sounds like pure invention, it must have been interpolated at a later date. However, the meaning is clear if we consider the significance of "neighbor" as one belonging to the same people and "enemy" as a national foe. Because, though the Old Testament nowhere exhorts us to hate a personal enemy—when it comes to Moabites and Assyrians it is full of the spirit of "let them have it back, and plenty." We who have been, in a certain sense, the inventors of nationalist ideology (at a stage of our history when it was functional and spiritually justified) are asked to be the first ones to give it up. There have been individual Jews who, out of a spirit of charity, advocated and gave material help to the German people after the fall of Hitler. These persons have anticipated a profound metaphysical truth. If the Jews at the time of Christ, in view of the Roman occupation, had refused the "national solution" as He Himself did, they would have died as a nation but they would have died in Christ! They might have gone out into the world preaching the Gospel, or they might have lived a life of non-violence toward the Roman conqueror. In either case they would have lost their life as a nation in order to gain it. They would have transcended their racial destiny, and it is difficult to think what tremendous historical impulse would have come from a nation thus transfigured. Once when I was still in the throes of restlessness, before I entered the Church, I had a long conversation with a very learned, profoundly religious French-Canadian priest. This man shared the nationalist fervor which one finds among so many groups of racial minority anywhere in the world. In spite of his spirituality he was not free from that resentment which always seems to diminish the stature of a man. In the course of our conversation I pointed out to him how deep the traces of persecution and of anti-semitism are in every one of us, and that I could not believe that Christ would demand of me to join the ranks of those who, on the natural plane, are our persecutors. Everything in me, I said, revolted against the idea. He looked long and pensively at me, and finally he said: "Yes, if following Christ would require me to become British, I must say this would be a terrible demand." This sounds comical, and can be understood only on the basis of long-standing historical grudges, of subtle currents of hostility, irritation and spite, as they occur between racial groups. He continued to be silent for a while after his remark and I knew that he understood. Actually he brought forth no argument against mine. But curiously enough this little fragment of our conversation had a profound influence on my conversion. At that moment I knew in the depth of my being that we have to partake of the flesh and blood of Christ regardless of whether with persecutors or with friends. This and nothing else is the true and lasting remedy for hatred. It is a hard fact, but it is one of the many hard facts for which Jesus of Nazareth had to die on the cross.

I might have tried a third possibility. There were many years in my life when I would have looked through the eyes of dialectic materialism on the disaster which has overwhelmed us. I would have regarded this philosophy as the only true remedy. Now it has frequently been pointed out that there are actually two Karl Marxes. One of them was full of truly religious fury. He hurled curses at the capitalists of the nineteenth century and he uncovered the lack of justice and charity inherent in an industrialist civilization—very much in the manner of an Old Testament Prophet. His attempt to interpret history was in its motives much more spiritual than he realized. I suppose that an attempt to interpret history with the methods he used is better than no attempt at interpreting history at all. Many of the early Communists were followers of this Karl Marx, and their materialism was only a historical costume, the dress of the nineteenth century. Some of the Communists who were persecuted by the Czarist secret police are spiritually related to those Christians who today are persecuted by the Stalinist secret police. However, there is another Karl Marx, the streamlined Hegelian absolutist, the strategist of class-warfare. Unfortunately this is the Karl Marx who has been successful. And he has led to a world of horror equaled only by that other Hegelian grandchild, National Socialism. Yes, I remember very well when I used to talk of matters concerning human relationship and the future happiness of society in terms of production-level, the synthesis-coming-after-the-antithesis-to-capitalism, and lots of abstract things like that.

There is a fourth solution. This is a rationalist pragmatism which is becoming more and more prevalent in the Western countries. It is, you might say, a non-Marxist or "cold" form of materialism, a baby which seems to bear all the signs of a powerful future and of a good life-expectation. There was a short period in my life in which I would have adhered to this form of pragmatism. I might have said approximately as follows: "If we want to see in the future that no more innocent grandmothers, parents and children are tortured to death, there is only one way. Let us investigate objectively the roots of racial and of class hatred, with all the tools of present-day science, with methods of economic investigation, of sociology, of behaviorism, of psycho-analysis, in short with all the branches of science which occupy themselves with things human. Let us be as scientific and system-atic in the establishment of interhuman relationships as we have been in technology. Let us have some sort of international board of social psychologists to study and to control the relationships of groups of people. In order to be able to do this successfully we may find that we have to abolish metaphysical concepts of human existence because it is possible that those are the con-cepts contributing to tension. If we find this necessary let us be courageous and do it, let us sterilize the air and remove all germs of faith so that we may live more rationally and more peacefully in an aseptic scientific atmosphere. Human affairs have long enough been governed by Belief, let them be governed by Science and Usefulness. In the world of matter the road away from belief to science has led to the greatest technological prog-ress in history; why should we not make the same step in the world of human society? Once we freed ourselves from an an-cient cosmology the way was clear which led to Television and the Airplane. If we only freed ourselves from equally ancient concepts of the nature of Man we shall have a world in which human affairs, for the first time in history, will be governed by reason. In order to find out why man tortures man, and in order to avoid it once and for all, let us consult those who are objective about it—psychologists and social scientists." Thus I might have spoken for a short period in my life. In fact, if the signs of the times do not deceive us there is a great chance that, once Marx-ism is finished, we are in for a global experiment of this kind. To my mind there is only one form of society which is worse than the Marxist or the Fascist one—that is, precisely such a "scientific" society. Compared with it Germany and Russia would look like children's playgrounds. Man's life on this earth would come about as close to the idea of hell as anything on this earth may. Needless to say that there is nothing wrong with Economics or Political Science or Psychoanalysis or Social Science or any other similar subject. The great Russian thinkers of the nineteenth century, who were so distrustful of and hostile towards Science, mixed Science (which is precious) up with Scientism (which is destructive). It is this scientism as a norm of human life, without God as the center, which leads to a form of nihilism unequaled in history. Saint Augustine, himself an expert at decaying civilizations, once drew our attention to the meaning of the word "nothing" in Our Lord's terrible sentence: "Without me you can do nothing." This word is to be taken quite literally. Christ does not say: "Without me you cannot do very much," or "Without me you can do only a certain amount," or "Without me you can do only little." He says: "Without me you can do *nothing*." A Christ-less world, scientific or not, leads to utter negation, to nothingness. Germany and Russia have given pretty good examples of this. However, there are indications that secularism and pragmatism, which have by comparison led a rather amateurish existence outside Russia, may be shaped into some scientific-technocratic norm for human beings. This, not material destruction, would mean the end of Mankind.

The Solution

Thus we see four possible answers to the riddle of the abysmal suffering, which we have witnessed in our time. Not one of these answers is adequate. Each one of them misses the point. Despair is no solution; even if we wished to despair we cannot because we believe. Resentment is no solution; our dead ones themselves seem to warn us against such a spirit and it would so easily lead us to commit the same cruelties on others which were committed on us. Statism is no solution. Scientism is no solution.

There is only one way: Jesus Christ. If we are concerned with the suffering of those innocent ones, we have first to look at Him. If we are concerned with the Evil which has brought it about, we have first to look at ourselves. Everything else is deception. If I want to renew the world I have to begin right in the depth of my own soul. This is the only true and permanent revolution which I am able to achieve. Class warfare leads to another set of oppressors and oppressed; national revenge leads to another set of persecutors and persecuted; and the Board of Social Scientists for the Prevention of Intergroup Hostilities is the most dangerous mirage of them all because it makes us believe even more that the decisive battle is fought far away from us, outside ourselves; it turns Good and Evil into two pale abstracts; it seeks to de-humanize the issue.

There is something extraordinary in the suffering of Christ. It seems to include all human suffering, and yet it can be "completed" by the suffering of individual persons.

It includes all human suffering. In the famous opening passage of *Anna Karenina* we are told that "all happy families resemble one another, but every unhappy family is unhappy in its own individual way." The same could be said about single persons. No matter to what degree suffering individuals may resemble one another, there always remains, somewhere in the depth, a nucleus which is unique. In our work as physicians we listen to people's life histories every day. And although psychological science gives us insight into the intrinsic mechanisms of each one of these, although we are able to analyze, disentangle, classify, and name the things which hurt people, there remains in each case a secret element which cannot be reproduced nor re-experienced. It belongs entirely to that one soul. You would think that three mothers each of whom has lost an only child represented three stories of the same kind. They do only up to a certain point. When that certain point comes we encounter a strange uniqueness. It is the same with dozens of people innocently executed, or millions of Jews murdered, or so many people in forced labor camps, or so many millions with anxiety neuroses, and so on. I am not only talking about the subjective quality of experience which makes each individual a universe, I am speaking about something which, by its very nature, resists comparison. Suffering cannot be quantified.

There is only One Who unites all these secrets in His suffering, and that is Jesus Christ. The more you dwell on it, the more it becomes clear that in His agony He anticipated the hidden agonies of innumerable individuals. For centuries the Church has meditated on the Five Sorrowful Mysteries of the Rosary or on the Fourteen Stations of the Cross. And the more people did so, the more the Agony of Our Lord became revealed. It has innumerable facets. It anticipates, it contains your and my life in a singular way. Newman once expressed this idea of the Church in an unforgettable sermon on the Night of Gethsemani in which he unrolled before our eyes with poetic genius the universality and infinite multiplicity of the suffering of Our Lord. In our medical work we get to know this in its countless human mirrors. Everyone is familiar with that stage when the patient reaches something which is incommunicable, something which in this form does not seem to occur in anyone else's life. With this one aspect of his life he seems to be alone. But he is not.

We have all experienced scenes which seem to be fixed in our memory because of their stark terror. I remember how one night, eighteen years ago, as an interne, I had to inform a woman that her boy, an only child, had bled to death from a post-operative hemorrhage. It is an awful thing to say but in a hospital there is something "routine" about such an incident. Yet somehow, the scene in all its details is unforgettable, perhaps because of its simplicity; how the woman looked at the body of the boy for a while, and how she said to her husband: "This is our child." One of my relatives told me a story from Dachau. An old Jew who was rather sick used to walk around supported by his two sons. One day he collapsed and was soon dead. A stormtrooper kicked the body aside with his boot and said in front of the dead man's sons: "One Jew less—all the better."

In our work as physicians we see people with beads of the sweat of death on their foreheads; we see married couples in the struggle of mysterious enmities; we see drunkards threaten their children, and children in a despair of hatred against their parents. One of the first things we learn at Medical School about our own attitude is not to get emotional or sentimental about it; not to be too involved with our feelings. This is good advice. In fact, those physicians and nurses who are matter-of-fact are much more efficient and helpful than the ones who have their feelings involved all the time.

And yet, we must realize that it is Christ Himself who is present in all this suffering. It is He and His mother who were there, that night in the children's ward. It was He Whose body was kicked aside: "One Jew less—all the better." It was He who, with our father, was mocked by the stormtrooper. It is He who is present in the agony of millions of deaths and secret humiliation. This is neither sentiment nor melodrama—it is just a basic fact. I am almost tempted to use the word "scientific" in this connection, because it has nothing to do with emotions. It is an axiom. Our Lord Himself indicated it, and the Church has upheld it throughout the centuries. It is with this axiom in mind that Pascal said that Jesus is still suffering on the cross.

And, I said, if we are concerned with Evil we have first to look at ourselves. The Gospel teaches me that if I am concerned with making the world a less cruel place to live in I do not need that Board of Social Scientists. There is inside myself Evil to work on, enough to last me a lifetime. Dostoievsky's Father Sossima implores his monks that everyone should regard himself sincerely as worse than the one with whom he is dealing. There is not only a Communion of Saints but also a Communion of Sinners. Many present-day Christian thinkers have attacked modern psychology, especially psychoanalysis, because those who practice it frequently happen to profess an anti-Christian philosophy. These critics forget that psychoanalysis has reaffirmed that which the Church has taught all the time; namely, that potentially there is inside every man a den of murderers and thieves. Why these potentialities become manifest in your neighbor and remain latent in you, this is not for you to judge. The veil which separates the potential evil in you from the manifest evil of the man about whom you are going to read in tomorrow's headlines is thinner and more mysterious than you think—this is the catharsis which emanates from the great Russian writers of the nineteenth century and from psychoanalysis, this is the true purification of which modern man is so desperately in need. But it is only an elaboration of an old truth. Every act contains an element of timelessness, and every evil act contains an element by which I am endangered. For centuries every Catholic child, man and woman has prayed: "I have crucified my loving Savior Jesus Christ."

Now you will say: "First you discuss four possible solutions and you reject them. We must not despair. We must not get even. It is no good rebuilding society in any scientific way, Marxist or otherwise. And yet, supposing it is true that all innocent suffering is the suffering of Christ, supposing that everyone participates in the Evil to which the world is succumbing—what of it? Instead of a realistic plan you discuss a couple of lyricisms."

What you are tempted here to call lyricisms, the truths of the Gospel, are actually appallingly concrete. Consider for a moment all the theories regarding man to which we used to adhere. Society should be changed, world governments should be set up, people should be re-educated but we ourselves are actually not committed, or at least not necessarily so. It can all be done by others, by political actions, by committees, by bodies outside my individual life. When you come right down to it all this does not hurt us much, it can, if need be, go on outside the immediate orbit of our existence. If by lyricism you mean something pale and abstract, something that does not touch you really, this is lyricism.

But the Gospel demands our immediate action right now at this moment, and in the place in which we find ourselves. It says that our own soul, with the help of Grace, contains enough potential energy to change the world.

The Church

My dear fellow, I keep on referring to History and to Science and to Literature and whatnot. I do this because I want to remain, as much as possible, on a ground which you and I have in common. But I can refer to those things only as analogies and approximations. Divine Revelation and Faith are categories quite different from purely intellectual arguments. These categories are alien to you. Therefore, no matter what I say, this letter will leave a void between you and me. There is always something halfway about it, and we get stuck in those analogies.

The Incarnation was not only an event acted out in historical time. It left its indelible mark on the world. It was perpetuated in the life of men. I believe Bergson once said towards the end of his life that everything good that happened in the world since Christ has happened through Him. The Incarnation was perpetuated in a very specific way in the Holy Sacraments, particularly in the sacrament of the Holy Eucharist, in the Communion of Saints and in the visible physical unity of the Church. There are many saintly Christians in the world today who do not believe that faith in Christ necessitates faith in those other things. They believe that matter has been transformed once, as it were, at the actual time when God took human flesh, and that the subject was exhausted at that single historical event. That disbelief in the sacramental life of the Church has two roots. It is firstly based on an ancient and profound disrespect for

Matter, and secondly on the development of what the philosophers call Positivism which arose with modern science. It is possible that both these roots are two expressions of the same thing, and I believe that this disbelief corresponds only to an historical phase.

Non-Catholics think that revealed religion in general, and Catholic dogma in particular, are something which you get rammed down your throat. Again I am going to choose an analogy which does not quite explain what I mean. Let us suppose you said that a student of Music gets Harmony and Counterpoint rammed down his throat. You can try to compose without studying the laws which Bach and Mozart have expounded, just as you can believe in "some kind of higher being and the golden rule and all that stuff" without bothering about the statements made by Saint Augustine or Saint Thomas. There are people who have a wonderful natural musicality, and when they improvise music you find that, at their best, they rediscover spontaneously the theory of Harmony and of Counterpoint. However, you can always demonstrate that they would have done even better if they had studied those subjects. There are other people who know the entire theory of Harmony and of Counterpoint, but their own productions remain sterile. However, everybody, the most romantic composer and the most modern composer, keeps referring to Bach. It could not be otherwise. You can take a simple Euclidian axiom and develop all mathematics out of it. You can take a basic musical law and develop the *Art of the Fugue* out of it. Similarly you can take a phrase such as "God is Love" and develop Theology out of it. But you do not need to do it as a free-lancer; others have been there before. It has already been done by great mathematicians, by great musicians and by the Saints. Yet if the Church sees to it that Babette, in the way in which she lives her faith, is aided by the insights gained by Teresa of Avila, you feel a dark suspicion of some weird play for power. Non-Catholic Christians too live, to an extent of which they are usually not aware, on the wealth not only of the Gospel but also of the Doctors of the Church. The only really impoverished ones are our skeptic Western intellectuals. They refuse to practice the gift of Faith which would enable them to crown and perfect Reason. With Faith gone they are in the same position as that shipwrecked man stranded on an island with crates full of canned food but with no can-opener. He starved to death with all the cans in front of him. Likewise, the majority of our contemporaries are in possession of the heritage of Christianity and of all the immense treasures of Western spirituality—but they are unable to tap them.

In London I listened to non-Catholic preachers of various denominations. I was struck by several things. I never heard them say anything positive which was not compatible with Catholic doctrine. Every one of them, in his greatest fervor, seemed to emphasize and develop some special idea which I had also found inside the Catholic Church. The only points in which they were non-Catholic were points of denial. What originally had been impulses toward freedom seemed to have led to extraordinary subjectivism.

Although Catholic orthodoxy is the only form of Christianity acceptable to me, I do not like to talk about these things from the point of view of Catholic apologetics. During the persecution of Christianity we all experienced wonderful examples of heroism among Protestants and Catholics alike. I have myself experienced supernatural charity among non-Catholics. Moreover, our experiences have shown that the anti-Christian forces in history are so vehemently directed against anything which confirms and confesses Christ. At this moment a lot would be gained if people returned to Christianity, or in fact if they at least returned to the ethics of the Old Testament.

The Church is immutable in her teaching. There is only one supernatural truth, as there is only one scientific truth. What in the mastering of matter constitutes the law of Progress, in things of the spirit is the law of Preservation. I remember when I showed you the Papal Encyclical about the Nazis. You were quite impressed, and you said: "This sounds as if it had been written in the first century." That's just the point.

The Church mirrors the facets of History. The Gospel is always the same. But the life of the Gospel in the turmoil of the fourth century is seen in Saint Augustine. The life of the Gospel at the height of the Middle Ages (some people would say the early dawn of the Renaissance) is perceived in Saint Thomas. In the nineteenth century, the century in which the human mind began to rule systematically the material forces of the universe, the Church began to extol the Little Way, the mystic life in hidden "little people." This is the only logical answer to the threat of a coming managerial age. Christ always has the appropriate answer, and He gives it in His saints. I have mentioned how great intuitive geniuses, such as Goethe and Tolstoy, perceived the mystic significance of the "little people." The Church, quite independently, has emphasized that same point. But in doing so she only re-emphasized one aspect of her eternal doctrine. Every century the Church takes a red pencil and underlines certain words of the Gospel, words which happen to fit the occasion. "Many thoughts," says Father Sossima, "seem to lead us into a state of doubt. Particularly when we see the sins of men we ask ourselves: 'Shall we tackle all this by force or by humble charity?' Always decide in favor of humble charity. Once you have decided in favor of it you will conquer the whole world. Humble charity is a terrible force; it is the greatest force in the world; there is nothing like it . . ." Concerning the small inconspicuous acts of love he says: "Everything is like an ocean, everything is movement, and all things are actually in contact with one another. At one end of the world you cause a little motion, and from the other end of the world it re-echoes." This was written by a Russian of the nineteenth century, almost at the same time when Saint Thérèse of Lisieux lived that obscure life which represents the lesson for our present age. By that is not meant our practical philanthropy, the do-goodism of everyday life, which is important too but is only a beginner's exercise. The true thing is an intense, all-out transformation of our lives in the life and passion of Christ.

You remember that I remarked that I had a feeling of allegiance to the simple pious folk in Munich, and that this feeling of loyalty prevailed over my Jewish loyalty. I could not have gone back and said to them: "Look here, all this stuff about Jesus is nonsense. There is such a thing as Revelation but it is strictly a tribal affair. Forget about the Messiah . . ." And, as you remember, I felt I would side with our pagan torturers in speaking like this. But there was still something else to it. I knew that these people lived, or attempted to live, a life of heightened mystic intensity, the only life which offers salvation to man.

I shall never forget the morning of my first Holy Communion. Outwardly it was like any other morning in December. When I entered the church, the church of the Franciscan Fathers in Montreal, it was still dark outside. Inside there was that crowd of people you find in any Catholic Church in a downtown district of any large city. There were men and women from the small rooming-houses near the railway tracks, and from the areas around the shopping center. There were what seemed to be employees from a nearby hospital. Some of these were going to Mass after a night's work. Our lives—that of my wife, of my friends Albert and Victorin—had converged, and had converged with those unknown ones around us. And it was as if others were there: my parents, and Kaspar Russ, and the Kohen family, the Jews from the Canal Synagogue, and Jacques Maritain and Dorothy Day, and the pious old maids of our childhood homes. And there was no doubt about it—towards Him we had been running, or from Him we had been running away, but all the time He had been in the center of things.

O

P

Q

R

S